Cloak of Ashes

The Women of *Beowulf*
Book Three

Also by Donnita L. Rogers

The Women of *Beowulf*
Book 1 Faces in the Fire
Book 2 Fanning the Flames

Cloak of Ashes

The Women of *Beowulf*
Book Three

Donnita L. Rogers

Bagwyn Books

Tempe, Arizona
2015

Published by Bagwyn Books, an imprint of the Arizona Center for Medieval and Renaissance Studies (ACMRS), Tempe, Arizona.

© 2015 Donnita L. Rogers
All Rights Reserved.

For Don, always

Contents

Chapter 1	In Winter's Grip	1
Chapter 2	Escaping the Past	19
Chapter 3	Breccasberg	39
Chapter 4	Foreign Shores	55
Chapter 5	Planting	81
Chapter 6	Home in Heorot	95
Chapter 7	Warnings and Mysteries	113
Chapter 8	Gathering Clues	127
Chapter 9	Visiting the Dead	143
Chapter 10	Departures and Arrivals	157
Chapter 11	Decision Time	173
Chapter 12	Setting Sail	189
Chapter 13	Angle-land	205
Chapter 14	Wiswicca	225
Chapter 15	Roman Remains	241
Chapter 16	Calling the Goddess	261
Chapter 17	Sacrifice and Sorrow	273
Chapter 18	Starting Over	285
Chapter 19	Rendlesham	303
Chapter 20	Raido: Return	319
Chapter 21	Giving Birth	341
Chapter 22	Canterbury	369
Chapter 23	Bretwalda	393
Chapter 24	Yeavering	417
Chapter 25	Sutton Hoo	441
Epilogue		465
Author's Note		467

Acknowledgments

My ongoing appreciation to Marijane Osborn, at University of California Davis, for introducing me to *Hrolf Kraki's Saga* and for loaning me valuable source materials.

To Sam Newton, for breaking a path to the past that led me to Sutton Hoo in his two books: *The Origins of Beowulf and the Pre-Viking Kingdom of East Anglia* (Brewer, Cambridge, 1993) and *The Reckoning of King Raedwald* (Red Bud Press, Colchester, Essex, 2003)

To my travelling companion Suzanne Morris-Betchelder of Schulenburg, Texas, my thanks for her unfailing support and good humor.

My thanks to the staff at the Sutton Hoo Museum in Woodbridge, England, and to the National Trust of England for making the site and artifacts of this historic Viking ship burial available and accessible to the public.

To Tim Vick of Northfield, Minnesota, my gratitude for timely information and advice concerning nautical terms and procedures.

To Carol Horswill of Minneapolis, Minnesota, my thanks for sharing her library of Norse materials, especially Poul Anderson's masterful re-telling of the *Hrolf Kraki Saga* (Ballantine Books 1973).

My thanks to Barb Henwood of Northfield, Minnesota, for assistance in electronic transmissions.

My grateful thanks to Karen Anderson for her kind permission to quote from Poul Anderson's version of *Hrolf Kraki's Saga*.

Special thanks to old friends Heather and Terry Bogden and to new friend Debra Widgren for last-minute but crucial assistance during my sojourn at Lake of the Woods, Ontario, Canada.

As always, my deepest gratitude to my partner and sometimes co-author Don, whose aid and encouragement have kept me writing and whose editorial acumen has saved me from many a misstep.

For details from *The Saga of King Hrolf Kraki*, I used the Penguin Classics 1998 edition, translated by Jesse L. Byock.

Illustrations

Note: Illustrations are copies of pictures from ancient artifacts, drawn by the author

Ch. 1	Battle scene plaque from helmet at Sutton Hoo, England.
Ch. 2	Blacksmith with hammer and tongs; assistant with bellows. Carving on a stave church at Hyllestad, Setesdal, Norway.
Ch. 3	A pair of bronze scales from a Viking Age grave in Jåtten, Hetland, Rogaland, Norway, found with 8 lead weights in a small linen bag.
Ch. 4	Belt buckle in silver, gold and bronze with garnets and engraved figures. Aker in Vang, Norway.
Ch. 5	Funnel glass from a woman's grave at Birka, Sweden.
Ch. 6	Late 5th-6th century square-headed brooch from Nordheim, Hedrum, Vestfold, Norway.
Ch. 7	Bronze Odin, god of war, holding a sword and two spears, with his ravens, Huginn and Muninn. Uppland, Sweden.
Ch. 8	Bronze stallion found in Denmark c. AD 400-800. National Museum, Copenhagen.
Ch. 9	Funerary urn with runes from Sancton, Yorkshire. Urn with bossed and stamped decoration from Lackford, Suffolk.
Ch. 10	Amulet of Odin with his two ravens from Ribe, Denmark.
Ch. 11	Bronze cloak pin with gilt and silver decoration. Gotland, Sweden.
Ch. 12	A silver pendant, perhaps a charm to wear in battle, from Aska, Sweden.
Ch. 13	Kitchen utensils, implements and storage vessels from ship-burial at Oseberg, Norway.
Ch. 14	Combs carved from deer and elk antlers, held together by iron or bronze rivets, were prized possessions, often found in female graves.
Ch. 15	Gold buckle from ship burial at Sutton Hoo, England.
Ch. 16	Girdle hangers from Soham, Cambridgeshire; may have been worn by women as symbols of authority. British Museum.

Ch. 17 Memorial stone with runic inscription from Sjuota, Skokloster, Uppland, Sweden.
Ch. 18 Matronae with fruit; small clay sculpture from 1st or 2nd century CE. Bonn, Rheinisches, Landesmuseum.
Ch. 19 Glass claw beaker of Rheinish manufacture.
Ch. 20 Two warriors in boar helmets; a 7th century metal die for making helmet plates. Torslunda, Oland.
Ch. 21 Crystal ball from Chessel Down, Isle of Wight. Found in graves of upper class women in Kent. British Museum.
Ch. 22 Silver pendant from Foss, Iceland, representing Thor's hammer. The dragon head may represent the Midgard serpent. The maker or owner has cut a Christian cross into the middle. University Museum of National Antiquities, Oslo.
Ch. 23 Bronze stag from top of standard in ship-grave at Sutton Hoo, England.
Ch. 24 Game board found in Ballinderry, Ireland, and Viking Age dice found at Tåsen in Oslo, Norway.
Ch. 25 Gravestone cross of the 800's from Middleton, Yorkshire, showing a Viking warrior laid out in his grave with his weapons.
Epilogue: Bronze cloak pin with gilt and silver decorations, Gotland, Sweden
Author's Note: Silver hammer of Thor amulet, Skåne, Sweden

Map Captions:
Map 1: Northern Europe showing geographical relationship between Sutton Hoo and the principal Scandinavia sites.
Map 2: Seven kingdoms with principal site and towns of southern Britain c. 600AD.
Map 3: East Anglia: based on the Ordnance Survey map of England in the Dark Ages.

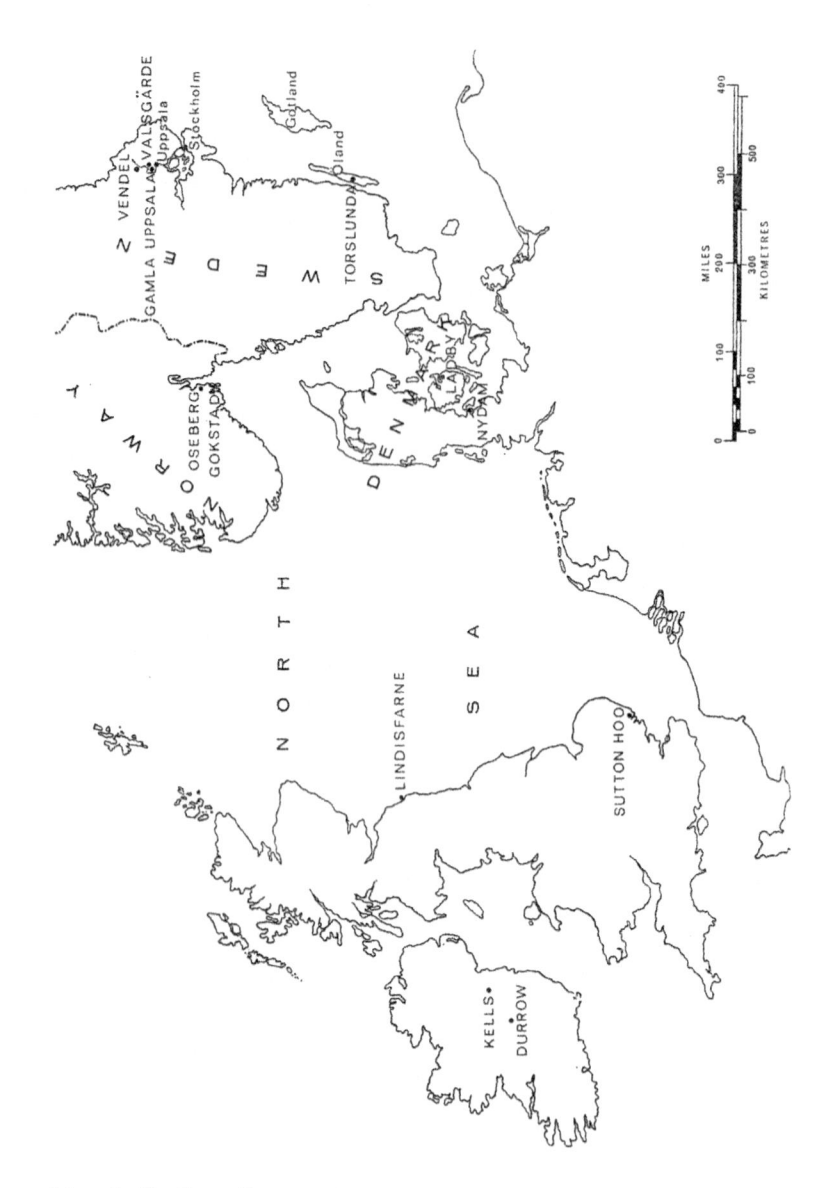

Map 1: Northern Europe showing geographical relationship between Sutton Hoo and the principal Scandinavia sites.

Map 2: Seven kingdoms with principal sites and towns of southern Britain c. 600AD.

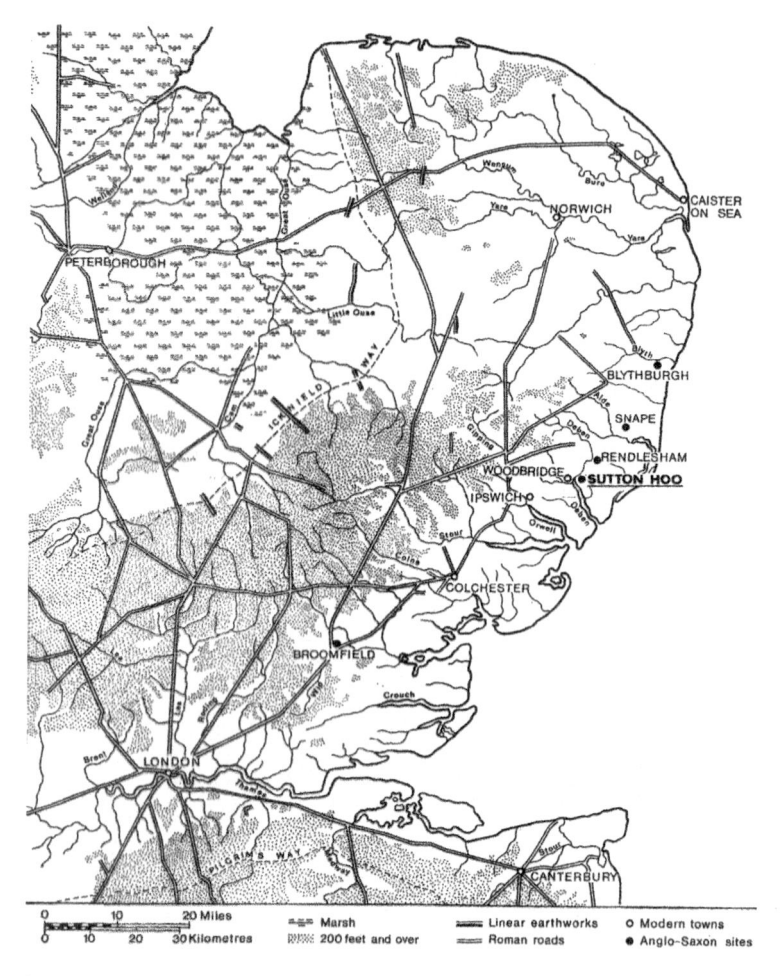

Map 3: East Anglia: based on the Ordnance Survey map of England in the Dark Ages.

Chapter One
In Winter's Grip

Battle scene plaque from helmet at Sutton Hoo, England.

"Lady Freawaru! Come quick! Blood has been spilt! A man may be dying!"

I raised my head, groggy with sleep. The rough voice had roused me from a doze beside the hearth, where I sat slumped on a bench, weary from another day without Beowulf.

"What? Who's there?"

Blinking I turned, searching for the speaker.

A tall figure with a wavering torch advanced from the doorway, swept in with a blast of cold air. I shivered, now wide awake.

"Redbeard? Is that you? What's happened?"

"A brawl in the young warrior's hall, my lady, a brawl that's turned deadly."

Redbeard's frowning face loomed above me. Rising hastily, I reached for my bag of herbs and potions, always ready on a shelf beside the fire, and called to my household.

"Ginnlaug, fetch wound bindings! Inga, bring my heavy cloak! Runa, you'd better come with me. I may need an assistant."

"Wrap warm; it's bitter outside," cautioned Redbeard. Indeed his beard and whiskers were white with hoar frost.

As soon as Runa and I were ready, Redbeard re-lighted his torch at our hearth and led us into the wintry night, using his bulky body to shield us from the worst gusts. As we leaned into the wind with heads bowed, I pondered the situation. Another brawl — the second one since Yule.

These dark days of winter are hard enough, but the bad blood between Beowulf's men is worse. Those young thanes branded as cowards for fleeing the dragon are in a difficult position. They cannot leave Eaglesgard in the dead of winter, so they have to endure the taunts of their fellows — or fight back.

"Who is it this time?" I called out.

"Grim again," answered Redbeard, turning back toward me. "And Tor. Tor got the worst of it this time. You'll see."

When we arrived at the longhouse where most of our young men were quartered, a somber scene met my eyes. Tor lay sprawled on a table, gasping, his face pale. Grim hovered over him, pressing a dirty cloth against a bleeding wound in Tor's side. Tears streamed down Grim's face as he stuttered in desperation.

"T-T-Tor, don't die! I d-d-didn't mean to do it!"

"Step aside, Grim," barked Redbeard. "Let Lady Freawaru tend to him."

I glanced around the room filled with silent men who stood as if frozen, their faces pale as Tor's. The place itself looked like a pig sty littered with the remains of many a meal: bones scattered on the floor, puddles of ale on every table, benches piled high with cloaks and sleeping robes. Immediately I took charge.

"Bring me clean water to bathe this wound!" I commanded sharply, pointing at the nearest man.

He jumped to life, directing Runa to the water barrel where she dipped a bucket and carried it to me.

"Runa, pull some mint leaves from my bag and boil water to make a broth," I instructed. "Tor has lost a lot of blood and will need nourishment."

While Runa did my bidding I examined Tor's wound. It was deep, but a clean cut — no doubt made by Grim's dagger. Tor stared up at me, blinking in recognition, but could not speak

"Listen to me, Tor. I am going to use special herbs to stop the bleeding. Then I will call upon the gods to help me ..."

Reaching into another pouch, I pulled out a handful of dried leaves and pressed them against Tor's wound. Then I leaned down close to his face and whispered softly so that only he could hear my words.

Sister Freyja, brother Freyr,
Thor and Odin come to Tor.
Take his pain and hurt away,
Heal to fight another day.

Three times I repeated the incantation. Gradually Tor's grimace relaxed and his eyes closed. Carefully I wound clean strips of cloth around his body, holding the herbs in place, then straightened, flexing my shoulders to relieve the tension they carried.

"Is he d-d-dead?" blurted Grim, reappearing at my side.

'No, he is sleeping," I said. "When he wakes you can feed him the broth Runa is preparing."

"Me? M-Me?" asked Grim, taking a step back.

"Yes, you. Are you not the cause of this wound — this quarrel?"

Grim hung his head, then looked up defiantly.

"Tor started it! He accused me of being the first to flee — said he would have stood his ground if I had not run like a rabbit when the dragon appeared!"

I stared at him coldly, envisioning the scene: Beowulf alone against the dragon while his "champions" fled to the woods.

"Well, were you? The first to flee?"

Grim gazed at me with anguish in his eyes.

"We all ran at once, my lady. I don't know who started it..."

"No," I corrected him, "not all of you ran. Wiglaf stayed to defend his lord!"

Suddenly my shoulders drooped and I shook my head bitterly.

"What's past cannot be changed. What matters now is how you respond to it. Fighting among your selves helps no one!"

I looked deliberately at each of the young men staring back at me.

"Beowulf saw some whit of courage and honor in each of you when he chose you as his companions. You have failed once, but you may be able to redeem yourselves . . ." I paused, lifting my head and shoulders. "Tell me, what strengths, what skills have you to offer, should I choose you to be *my* champions, *my* bodyguard?"

Heads came up and eyes widened at my words. Redbeard stepped forward and gave a slight cough.

"These are not bad lads, my lady. I trained most of them myself. Whatever else they lack, they do not lack for battle skills." He bowed and stepped back.

"Thank you, Redbeard, for your words. Now — "

"My lady?" interrupted Grim, his voice cracking, "beg pardon, but why would you need a bodyguard here in Eaglesgard?"

I gazed at him, taking him in: unruly red hair, scraggly beard, slight frame . . . Why, he couldn't be older than 15 winters, the same age as my brother Hrethric when he . . . Blinking back unexpected tears, I cleared my throat.

"I have a mind to travel, Grim, to other lands. I will need a band of brave young men to accompany me — to defend me if need be — to serve me as their lord!"

Even Redbeard gasped at this. Frowns appeared on several faces. I had not meant to say "lord," but now that the word was spoken, it felt right. I sought their allegiance in a bond of mutual trust and support. Grim broke the silence.

"I will serve you, my lady, if you will have me!"

Impulsively he knelt before me and bowed his head. Having nothing else at hand, I took a leaf from my bag and tucked it in his mop of red hair.

"I have heard it said that the Romans honor their champions with a wreath of bay laurel. Let this leaf signify that you are my man, Grim, bound to honor and serve me as long as you have life. Now rise!"

As he slowly got to his feet, I noticed a thin red line that licked around the side of his neck like a flame.

"What is this?" I gestured at his throat.

He flushed. "A mark obtained at birth, my lady. I do not know its meaning."

I studied him thoughtfully. "You are ever quick to act, Grim, sometimes before you've had time to think! Am I not right?"

He nodded, then cast down his eyes.

"Your quickness can be an asset, or a curse." I paused. "Your birthmark... hmm, your birthmark. Let me see it again."

Dutifully he lifted his chin.

"A tongue of fire," I mused. "There is fire inside you, Grim, a fire stronger than any dragon. You must claim it and learn how to use it when danger threatens."

Grim was gazing at me, awestruck. Behind him I saw other mouths agape, as if each man were hanging on my words. One strapping young fellow left the rest, stepping forward to address me. I recognized him as Eskil, like Grim a son of Eaglesgard.

"Lady Freawaru, if we pledge our service to you, what will you pledge in return?" he asked, looking me full in the face.

"A chance to regain your honor! Your good name!" I retorted. "Is that itself not worth more than gold? We will also find challenges and adventures! Eskil, I see that you have a bold heart. Boldness will be needed if we are to journey across the waters — as I intend to do!"

Eskil nodded in agreement, then asked another question, grinning as he did so.

"Shouldn't you make Grim swear an oath? An oath of loyalty?"

Before answering I let my eyes sweep across the room.

"Oaths can mean little. You all swore oaths to support Beowulf, but he died alone! I say that actions speak louder than any words. Who here wishes to redeem his reputation? Who is willing to join me?"

The grin faded from Eskil's face as his companions suddenly came alive, jostling their way forward to kneel before me.

"I'll be your man, my lady," shouted a stocky fellow dressed in animal skins. "My name is Gunnulf, son of Gunnar."

"Me too," exclaimed a man with lanky locks. "I am Alf, son of Alfred."

Now each man strove to outdo his neighbor in paying respect to me. I was heartened, even touched at this sudden display. Above their heads I saw Redbeard standing at the back, emphatically nodding approval. Runa's face was beaming too as she stirred the cauldron of broth at the hearth. The cauldron... Hmm. An idea came to me and I strode toward the fire, men parting before me.

"Comrades! Into this cauldron I will drop a rare, magical herb, one which steels the nerves and expands the heart, giving strength and courage when most they are needed."

Suiting deed to words, I carefully opened the deerskin pouch at my waist, drew forth a handful of fine red powder, and sprinkled it into the broth.

"A bitter brew, but bracing. A libation for heroes!" Seizing a mug from a nearby table, I dipped it into the cauldron and lifted the mug high.

"Comrades, let us drink to our new confederation!"

As if in a trance each man moved slowly, taking up a cup and dipping it in the cauldron. When I raised my mug to my lips, they all did the same. The fiery liquid that poured down each throat caused many to choke and gasp. I was barely able to swallow it myself. As it hit the stomach its warmth expanded, filling every vein with fire.

"By the gods, my lady, a potent brew!" sputtered Redbeard. His face streamed with tears as he drained his cup. "This should put backbone into any man!"

"Perhaps some ale now to wash it down?" I suggested demurely.

Redbeard nodded and called a thrall to bring in pitchers of barley beer.

That night I stayed long enough to talk with each man individually, learning his name and lineage and beginning to assess his capabilities. Grim duly ladled broth into Tor's mouth when the wounded man woke briefly, the same broth containing my secret ingredient.

Like Grim and Eskil, the other men who had grown up in Eaglesgard were comparatively young, most not yet able to grow a beard. Gunnulf was one of these, as were Sigrod and Anton. Gunnulf impressed me with his expressed devotion, which I suspected lay in the unhappy mischance of losing his mother at an early age.

Sigrod and Anton presented themselves as childhood friends who always strove to outdo each other. When Anton displayed a muscular arm for my inspection, Sigrod countered by stating that he could outrun Anton in any race. They were arguing over who could drink the most ale at one sitting when I turned my attention to the men who were not natives of Eaglesgard.

Alf told me of his homeland to the south, farther south even than my former home at Heorot. Wanderlust had led him to Beowulf's court. He reminded me of myself as a young girl, eager for new experiences. He claimed to be an expert navigator who had learned how to read the stars from his father, and was accustomed to being at sea.

Knud was a fellow Dane, though he knew of Heorot only from lays sung by the scops. His fine-textured hair was white as snow, but ruddy cheeks and sparkling blue eyes marked him as a young man of spirit. He declared himself to be a fine singer with a great stock of jokes and riddles.

"Songs and stories to lighten the heart may well be needed on our journey," I told him.

Bram was a slim, dark-eyed, dark-haired man who reminded me of the Baltic traders I'd once seen at my father's court. He spoke little and then in serious tones. He seemed the sort of steady fellow one could count on to stay calm in a crisis.

Vigo. Hmm, Vigo. He looked older than the others. His face revealed little of his inner feelings. I learned only that he and Tor had come to Eaglesgard from Brecca's court, from the land of the Brondings. When I told him of Beowulf's long-ago swimming match with Brecca, he smiled faintly.

"Brecca is old now. His sons Erik and Edvard rule jointly. Tor and I were not in their favor, so we came to Eaglesgard to serve Beowulf."

"When Tor recovers, do you think he will want to join our group?" I asked.

"I cannot speak for him," said Vigo soberly. "If he recovers you must ask him directly."

When Runa and I finally left the hall with Redbeard, many of the men had fallen asleep or passed out from drinking. The cold outside felt somehow less bitter with the fiery broth still lying in my belly. In our longhouse Inga and Ginnlaug were sleeping soundly. Before we went to our rest Runa asked me a question.

"What did you put in that broth, my lady? I took a taste but could not identify the final ingredient."

I chuckled. "A red powder I obtained in trade last summer from that merchant with the ginger tubers. Something called 'cayenne.' It burns the mouth at first, but dulls pain. It even aids digestion and cures winter coughs — but it must be used sparingly."

Runa chuckled too. "I wouldn't call a handful 'sparingly'."

I smiled. "It made an impression, didn't it?"

"It certainly did! All in all, a memorable night."

I yawned. "Now there is little left of it. I think we may allow ourselves to sleep late on the morrow."

Runa echoed my yawn, nodding. "Good night, my lady. May your dreams be fair."

They were, for I dreamed of Wealtheow, my mother.

The winter following Beowulf's death had been the coldest and darkest of my life. I ached for his solid presence, his voice, his touch, his arms around me. Nothing filled the void left by his passing. Even the Yule celebration had failed to lift my spirits. Only one tiny flicker of hope held any interest for me:, the possibility that my mother still lived, the possibility of finding Wealtheow.

She had come to me in dreams and visions, always just out of reach but always smiling as if to encourage me, her dark eyes filled with tenderness.

One gloomy afternoon, a few days after my visit to the young men's hall, I was sitting by the hearth in my own longhouse staring at the fire. Beowulf had built this home for me; every detail of my surroundings spoke of his love and care for me, down to the cloak pegs placed at exactly my height.

Over the years the oaken beams had blackened from hearth smoke, but the protective runes carved on them by Redbeard could still be made out by a careful observer: Algiz for protection, Eihwaz for defense, and Wunjo for joy and comfort. Redbeard was still with me, but Beowulf — gone.

I sighed and closed my eyes, letting his dear image take shape before me: Beowulf astride his great horse Frostmane, strong and glorious as any god; Beowulf in his high seat, lord of the assembly, lifting his goblet in a toast; Beowulf lying beside me, his face full of tenderness as he turned toward me...

Aagh! A stab of pain twisted in my heart. Never again would I gaze into those sea-blue eyes or taste the salty sweetness of his lips! Better to think of other things.

With an effort I exhaled and opened my eyes, returning to the present. From the weaving end of the longhouse I could hear the clack of beaters as Inga and Runa worked at the looms. Near my feet a log hissed and crackled as it crumbled into the fire. Its heat against my skin felt as welcome as a mother's touch. Ah, my mother. I closed my eyes again. Mother, Mother, where are you? I have so much to tell you. Beowulf is dead, killed by a dragon. Inga has grown to womanhood; she is ready to take a husband. I wonder... can I leave her... as you once left me? Oh, I mean no reproach, Mother. You stayed behind at Heorot to bury my brothers. Did you know then that I was ready to follow my own path ... without you? Now I find myself in just such a moment of decision.

"Mother? What are you doing?"

Inga's voice broke my reverie. I glanced down at the skeins of yarn in my lap, then turned to look at her face with its questioning eyes.

"Thinking — dreaming — remembering." I smiled up at her. "Dear Inga, you may have your father's chin and nose, but you have your grandmother's eyes — such beautiful brown eyes!"

Inga raised her eyebrows and reached cold fingers toward the fire.

"Grandmother? Weal... Wealtheow? Were you thinking of her just now?"

"Yes." I rose and stretched as the yarn tumbled to the floor. 'I think of her every day. Strange... I think she is calling me."

Inga's eyes narrowed. "Dark thoughts again? We need you here in Eaglesgard, Mother. I need you."

Taking my warm hands in her cold ones, she pressed them to her cheeks.

"You should be thinking about my marriage to Wiglaf," she chided, kissing my fingertips before letting them go.

"Nay, child, there is plenty of time to arrange that — oh, did I tell you that Olaf and Runa may be joined at the same time?"

Inga eyed me quizzically. "Then you've decided — "

"Yes, to give Runa her freedom. She has certainly earned it with her years of service." In a lower voice I added, "I will also provide the dowry so that she and Olaf can marry as equals."

Inga nodded. "Beowulf would have approved, as I do. In fact, Mother, I expected you to free Runa after Higd's death. Why have you waited so long?"

I considered, searching for the right words.

"I did not wish to lose her," I confessed, "but now that she and Olaf are to marry, they could come with me..."

"Mother!" Inga's voice grew sharp. "What is this talk of leaving? You have everything you need right here in Eaglesgard!"

"Almost," I said quietly, taking her hand. "Almost. Before I die I want to see Heorot once more, and I want to find... my mother."

Inga stared at me in disbelief, jerking away her hand.

"First of all, Mother, you are far too young to be dying. If anyone is dead it would be grandmother Wealtheow. Surely you don't believe she is still alive somewhere?"

"That's what I mean to find out," I said. "I will stay here long enough to see you married, but I will sail in the spring."

Inga shook her head vehemently.

"No! I don't want you to go!"

"My lady?" At Runa's voice we both turned. "My lady, I heard what you said. Is it true? Are you setting me free?"

Runa approached eagerly, the forgotten wooden beater still held in her hand. Framed by her still dark hair, Runa's face shone like the moon on a dark night.

"How much did you hear?" I asked in chagrin, hoping I had not given away Olaf's impending offer of marriage.

Runa flushed. "I heard only the words 'give Runa her freedom,' and instantly made a mistake in my weaving — but I've already repaired the damage," she reassured me. "Is it true — about my freedom?"

"Yes, Runa, it is true. I will make a formal announcement soon."

Runa's arms suddenly encircled me as she almost lifted me off the floor.

"Oh, my lady, thank you! Thank you!" Tears filled her eyes as she relinquished me.

"You should thank Olaf too," I said when I'd caught my breath.

"Olaf?" Runa's face reddened. "So you know he's been... talking to me?"

"Just talking?" I teased, then became serious. "Olaf is a good man, kind and dependable. Why, I'd trust my life to Olaf — as I may soon do," I muttered under my breath.

Runa looked past me at Inga, who was frowning. I sighed.

"Don't mind me, Runa. I find I'm talking to myself a lot lately. I must be getting old."

Runa laid her hand tentatively on my sleeve.

"My lady, your hair is no grayer than mine, and you have more years than me."

Inga laughed out loud at this.

"Mother is now the oldest woman in the settlement—and the most respected. You'd think she would be content with that!"

Runa looked slowly back and forth from me to Inga, and to me again.

"May I know what is happening here?" she asked quietly.

"You'll get an answer in good time, Runa." I straightened. "For now, the day is almost gone. It's time to give the stew pot another stir and have our evening meal."

Later that night I made a formal appearance in the new mead hall. Although it had been built on the same place where Beowulf's hall once stood, it still seemed alien to me—stiff and unyielding—almost menacing in its height and width. It loomed against the moonlit sky like a great beast, crouching to spring

Inside the hall the men of Eaglesgard were taking their ease, drinking, laughing or listening to a lay sung by the scop—something about Sigurd. I shuddered. Had Beowulf's death not killed their appetite for dragon stories? Wiglaf sat in Beowulf's former seat, taking no part in the festivities, his face set, his eyes gazing into space. He rose and called out to me when he saw me enter.

"Lady Freawaru! What brings you out on this cold night? And where is your attendant? Where is Runa?"

I advanced slowly, acknowledging with pleasure the greetings of thanes and athelings at each table I passed. Looking around the smoky interior, I searched discreetly for the ten young thanes in disgrace, but saw none of them. When I reached Wiglaf's high seat, I spoke directly to him.

"It is Runa I have come to speak about—to the whole assembly, Lord Wiglaf."

The word 'lord' did not roll easily off my tongue. It seemed only yesterday that this comparative stripling had sat among the young, untested warriors. Then the dragon had come . . . As Wiglaf raised his hand for silence, I cleared my throat and faced the assembly.

"Lord Wiglaf and men of Eaglesgard. I hereby make a formal announcement. Let it be known from this day forth that, in return for her many years of faithful service, I grant full freedom to my thrall, Runa the Finn. From this day forth she is to be accepted as a freeman, and treated as my kinswoman."

Olaf, sitting at a place of honor among the older athelings, looked up at me, his face beaming. He rose and lifted his mug of ale.

"Wes heil, I say, wes heil! Hail to Freawaru the fair, wise and generous! And hail to Runa, soon to be my bride!"

"Wes heil" echoed through the hall, mixed with some uncertain laughter. Marriage between a thrall and a freeman had never happened before at Eaglesgard — but of course Runa was no longer a slave.

"Lady Freawaru, may I escort you back to your longhouse?"

Olaf had come to my side, looking like a man about to burst with happiness.

"Of course, Olaf."

Smiling, I nodded a farewell to Wiglaf and left the hall with my old companion. We were barely outside before he spoke eagerly,

"May I ask Runa tonight, my lady?"

"Yes, I think that would be fitting, Olaf. Then her joy will be complete."

I held onto his arm as we crunched over frozen snow, guided by the full moon. The skies had cleared and the cold intensified, but I stopped for a moment to breathe in the frosty air.

"Olaf, do you remember winter nights at Heorot? Do you remember Hrothgar and... and Wealtheow?"

He glanced down at me in surprise.

"Of course, my lady. They were like father and mother to me. I can never forget them."

"Neither can I, Olaf, and I think... I think... Wealtheow is... calling me."

"Have you seen her ghost?" he asked soberly.

"Not her ghost, Olaf, Wealtheow herself. I think she is still alive — and she needs me to find her. Will you help me? Find her?"

Olaf took my mittened hands in his.

"My lady, if it is your wish. I will take you wherever you want to go."

"Good!" I smiled at his earnest face, no longer boyish, now a face seasoned by years of battle and hardship. "But first, let's find Runa!"

To my surprise Runa did not immediately accept Olaf's proposal of marriage. She revealed her concern to me the next day as we were clearing away the morning meal.

"Oh, my lady, I know that you have formally freed me, but everyone in Eaglesgard knows me only as a thrall. Would they not look down on Olaf for taking me to wife? I would not bring shame or dishonor to him — he is too dear to me!"

"Runa, be comforted," I answered. "Olaf has surely considered that before he asked you. Besides, we will not always live in Eaglesgard — not you, not Olaf, not me. I've been thinking..."

As we worked together I unfolded my plan: to depart in the spring — taking along the ten thanes accused of cowardice — to begin a search for my mother. Runa's eyes opened wide as she considered the possibilities.

"A new start — for all of us? Would you do that, my lady?" Hope filled her eyes.

"I would — and I will!" I said decisively. "You can help. We will need one or two young female thralls to come with us — girls with stout hearts and strong constitutions. You can help me select them."

Runa nodded. "I know just who I'd pick: those two girls brought in last fall from Finnmark. But, who else is to come with us? Any of the village women?"

"I think our Ginnlaug will want to join us. She's been desolate since losing her sister in the dragon raid. I'm also going to sound out Lise and Lempi."

"What about Dagmar? She never fully recovered from Higd's death. Perhaps she would welcome a new start as well?"

"Good thinking, Runa. I'll speak to her. Now, shouldn't you be speaking to Olaf? He must be eager for your answer..."

Runa wiped her hands on her apron and smiled a joyful smile.

"Yes, I will go to him... now!"

With a nod she snatched her cloak and headed for the door, but I heard her talking softly to herself: "Think of it. Marriage! To Olaf! As a free woman!"

Before I could leave Eaglesgard I had to consider the fate of those being left behind. After Beowulf's death many had wondered aloud if the Geats were not more vulnerable, more open to assault by our enemies:

the Frisians, the Franks, the Swedes. In the past Beowulf's reputation as a great warrior had kept us safe. Would his loss now expose us to attack?

The ashes of Beowulf's funeral pyre had barely cooled when Wiglaf had met in council with the elder athelings to consider our situation. I had not been invited to this meeting, but at its conclusion Wiglaf had sought me out, accompanied by my oldest friend at Eaglesgard, Redbeard.

Wiglaf was frowning as the two men entered my longhouse late that afternoon. He had wasted no time in stating the reason for their visit.

"Lady Freawaru, Ragnar Redbeard insists that the fate of our people — our future — may be revealed to you through your special skills... your sight."

"Aye, my lady," interjected Redbeard, not waiting for Wiglaf to continue, "I well remember our first meeting when you arrived on these shores. Although you were a stranger, you knew things about me that no one could have told you. And when young Herdred was lost on the downs, you told us where we could find him. Then there was your vision about the ice — the ice of Lake Vänern — that helped Beowulf plan his battle strategy. I'd say that any man not a fool would be wise to seek your advice!"

He concluded with a harrumph and a sidelong glance at Wiglaf.

"My lords," I said calmly, "please sit down and take refreshment before we talk. During the dead of winter we are surely in little danger. We have time to consider the path before us."

Redbeard smiled and settled himself at my table as I signaled for Runa to bring a pitcher of ale. Wiglaf stood, frowning, then slowly seated himself on the bench beside Redbeard.

"My lady, I do not understand this power of yours that others speak of." Wiglaf gazed at me earnestly. "What is this 'sight'?"

Once I would have hesitated to speak, but years of experience had given me confidence. Standing across from the two men, I leaned forward, hands on the table.

"It comes from the goddess," I asserted. "The goddess Freyja — she who marked me at birth with a touch of her falcon feather. When I enter a trance, when she lifts me from my body, I often see what others cannot — but I do not undertake such journeys lightly."

Inga had emerged from the weaving room as I was speaking and now came to me, her eyes glistening.

"So . . . you still wish to fly away, to leave us!"

Wiglaf turned to Inga in surprise.

"What do you mean? Leave who?"

"All of us!" cried Inga. "She means to leave Eaglesgard on some mad journey . . ." Inga choked up and could speak no further.

Wiglaf's eyes narrowed. "Do you foresee disaster for the Geats, Lady Freawaru?" His voice was harsh. "Do you seek to desert us?"

I shook my head vehemently.

"Nay, nay, all the omens have been good. When I consult the runes concerning the future of Eaglesgard I turn up Uruz, symbol of strength and achievement. I turn up Fehu, wealth, and Jera, good harvest and plenty. I do not fear for the Geats."

Redbeard's face brightened as he drained his cup and drew a hand across his dampened beard.

"See? What did I tell you?"

Reaching out to Inga, I drew her gently to my side before speaking again to the men.

"Do you think I would desert my own daughter if I saw danger in her future? On the contrary, but I do expect you, Wiglaf, to provide a safe home for her and your children — for there will be many! Fine sons and daughters!"

While I spoke Inga had remained silent, but found her voice as she turned to face me.

"Mother, won't you stay? Won't you wait with me to welcome those sons and daughters?"

I lifted my head, suddenly completely clear about the path before me.

"Nay, child, I am done with waiting! All my life I have waited: waited for winter to end, waited for men to return from war, waited for Beowulf to make me his wife. Nay. No more waiting. I am called and I must go. Soon. But I'm not going alone."

Wiglaf jerked to attention, but Redbeard gave me a knowing nod.

"I will leave in spring with a small band of men," I continued. "The same young men Beowulf asked to accompany him on his last battle. I have already sounded them out and they have pledged their fealty."

"Hmph!" snorted Wiglaf, rising to his feet. "Faithless pledges! Do you trust such men?"

For a moment there was silence. Then Redbeard too rose to speak.

"The way I see it, Lord Wiglaf, it would be a boon for us all if Lady Freawaru takes those outcasts with her. They are desperate to redeem themselves and she is giving them a chance."

Wiglaf frowned. "But where will you take them?" he exclaimed. "Who would welcome these exiles?"

Motioning both men to sit down again, I outlined my plan.

"Long winters past, Beowulf's father — himself an outcast — journeyed to the court of King Hrothgar seeking asylum. My father took him in and paid the price to reinstate him in his homeland. In payment for that favor Beowulf later journeyed to Heorot to free the Danes from the Grendel monster." I paused and took a deep breath. "We too will sail for Heorot, for Denmark. My father died long ago, but there is a chance my mother still lives — there, or elsewhere – and I have other friends as well, who will remember me."

Dear Goddess, may it be so!

Wiglaf gazed at me, considering my words. Finally he spoke.

"I see that you are determined and that your course is set. So be it. Eaglesgard will miss you: your commanding presence — and your — gifts May the gods go with you!" He rose. "Come, Ragnar Redbeard. Our business here is finished — almost."

Taking Inga's hand, Wiglaf turned aside with her, speaking in low tones — too low for the rest of us to hear. She smiled and nodded, then walked with him toward the door. Redbeard meanwhile drained his second cup of ale and rose, tossing a shaggy pelt over his shoulders.

"Farewell, Lady Freawaru. If I were younger I'd go with you," he said gruffly.

I took his gnarled hands in mine. "I know that, old friend. It will give me comfort to know that you are here in Eaglesgard where Inga can depend on you — as I have always done. For now, farewell."

Without more words, Wiglaf and Redbeard left the longhouse. I expected another argument from Inga, but she too seemed to have accepted my decision and made no further protest.

As winter slowly loosened its grip on Eaglesgard, I began to make preparations for departure, sorting through my possessions, deciding what to take and what to leave behind. To Inga I would give my mother's whalebone pressing board, for Inga, as queen of the Geats, would have more use for it than a wandering woman off at sea. I would also leave behind the looms and weaving tools, and a good supply of healing herbs.

One crisp afternoon I sent Runa to the drying shed to begin taking stock of our stores, intending to join her there as soon as I finished the last row of the tapestry on my loom — intended as a gift for Runa's marriage to Olaf, though I had not told her so. Humming to myself, I worked happily, tying the final knots to complete the piece before taking it off the frame.

When finished at the loom, I took up my cloak, wrapped it about me and stepped out into the late afternoon — into a beautiful scene of bright white snow and soft dark shadows. It always calmed me to visit the drying shed, a place fragrant with the mixed scents of many plants, and I hurried in anticipation.

As I drew near I thought I heard a muffled cry. Yes, it was a cry — then another cry sounded, louder — Runa's voice! A cry of terror and pain! Rushing to the door, I pushed it open and burst inside, light flooding in behind me. Sprawled on her back, her bloodied face turned up toward me, lay Runa. A man crouched over her, his hairy hand over her mouth.

Filled with rage, I instinctively seized the knife at my own waist and grabbed the man's hair. Jerking back his head, I slashed my blade across his throat, severing his jugular vein as decisively as I had once sacrificed an ox at the Great Blöt in Uppsala. As blood gushed forth, he collapsed face down on the floor.

Dropping the knife, I grasped his shoulders with both hands and rolled his great bulk to one side, exposing the face. It was a familiar face. Lars. It was Lars and in my fury I had killed him.

Runa lay unmoving on the floor, her tunic ripped open, her legs splayed apart. What Lars had done to her was all too clear. She stared up at me, round-eyed with shock, and moved her lips convulsively.

"Runa, don't try to talk. I'll get help."

Suddenly stricken myself, I sank to my knees beside Runa, my heart pounding. Lars was dead. I had killed a man.

Chapter Two
Escaping the Past

Blacksmith with hammer and tongs; assistant with bellows. Carving on a stave church at Hyllestad, Setesdal, Norway.

Pulling off my cloak, I laid it gently over Runa's trembling body. "Don't move. I'll get help."

Runa's lips formed a single word: "Olaf."

"Olaf? Nay, not yet. First we must get you back to the house and tend to your injuries. Time enough later to reveal what has happened — to Olaf and to the rest of the settlement."

Be wise, Freawaru, be strong. You must handle this situation carefully!

Inga and Ginnlaug helped me lift Runa and walk her slowly back to our longhouse. There we wrapped her in blankets and fed her hot broth to stop the shaking. Only then did we bathe Runa's bloodied face and sponge her body as I carefully examined her.

"No teeth missing, but your nose may be broken and you have bruises around your neck. Did he choke you?" I questioned, as calmly as I could.

Runa nodded, shedding fresh tears.

"The monster!" exclaimed Ginnlaug, staring at Runa's face in fascination. 'What could have provoked him?"

Runa winced as she opened split lips to speak.

"Lesson, he said, teach lesson — too proud — still thrall."

"Stop!" I commanded. "No more talking. You need to rest and recover from this shock."

"Olaf?" Runa's eyes were pleading. "Don't tell... Olaf."

I shook my head. "With Lars lying dead in the herb shed there is no way to keep this matter a secret — from anybody. I'll send for Olaf and Wiglaf right now, and we will discuss what needs to be done."

Once again the awful truth washed over me: Lars is dead and you are responsible. You have killed a man. Now I too began to shake.

"Mother, sit down!" Inga sprang to my side and gently guided me to a bench. "What happened, Mother?" she whispered, putting her hands on my shoulders. "What happened in the herb shed?"

I told her and Ginnlaug what I had heard, seen and done. "I killed him — I killed Lars. Now you'd best find Wiglaf — and Olaf — and bring them here. Lars' body will keep," I concluded bitterly.

Even in death Lars brings trouble upon us. He it was who beat his thrall so severely that the man ran away, stole a dragon's cup and brought the dragon's wrath upon us — which led to Beowulf's defense of Eaglesgard and his own death. Beowulf is dead. Now Lars is dead. I cannot be sorry for it.

When Inga returned with Olaf and Wiglaf, both men were visibly shaken. Wiglaf stalked straight to the hearth where Ginnlaug and I were preparing a mixture of hot ale and mallow to soothe Runa's throat.

"Is it true?" he barked. "Is Lars dead?"

I nodded, momentarily unable to speak.

Olaf rushed to my chamber, where he could see Runa propped up on my bed.

"Oh, my beloved," he cried, taking her in his arms, "Thank the gods you are alive! I could not bear to lose you!"

Despite her split lips Runa tried to smile and cleared her throat.

"Olaf," she croaked, "Olaf, I . . ."

"Wait!" I called. "The toddy is ready. It will help your voice."

Beckoning to Inga and Ginnlaug, I carried the mug into my chamber and put it in Runa's hands. Olaf got to his feet, but did not leave her side. Wiglaf planted himself beside the bed and stared at me with questioning eyes. I nodded.

"Runa," I said gently, "if you feel able to talk, we all need to hear what happened in the drying shed this afternoon."

Runa lifted her head and took a careful sip of the hot liquid.

"He — Lars that is — followed me into the shed," she began. "He said he was — curious — to see what — what magical potions we kept there. Soon as — door closed — he pushed me to the floor — and — and."

Her voice choked and she quivered as if reliving that moment. Olaf tenderly put an arm around her shoulders. After a moment she seemed to recover.

"He, he put one hand around my throat — pinned me down — tore open my tunic," Runa gulped. "He was talking the whole time, calling me 'whore' and 'bitch' — said I'd gotten above myself — would always be a slave in his eyes — now he'd make me serve him!"

Runa blinked back tears and her hands trembled as she raised the steaming mug to her lips and set it down. Olaf growled in anger and distress, his face grim. After clearing her throat, Runa leaned forward, staring straight ahead.

"When I tried to break free, he — he struck me — in the face — again — and again. I screamed — but no one heard me — until Lady Freawaru came. Thank the gods for you, my lady. His — attack — seemed to go on — and on — but it ended quickly — with one stroke of my lady's knife. Lars' blood fell hot on my face — almost choked me."

Suddenly Runa's face grew fierce, her eyes glowing like live coals and her voice gained strength as she spat out the next words.

"I'm glad I tasted it — tasted Lars' blood! I'm glad he is dead!"

I was relieved to see Runa's spirit returning, glad that Lars had not crushed the spark that was Runa. Wiglaf had listened to her recital with a set face, betraying no emotion, but now he frowned and turned toward me.

"Lars could be a brute, but he was a respected member of the court, one of the athelings on the council. His death will not be taken lightly. Lady Freawaru, as his killer you must prepare to defend yourself."

"What? Killer?" Inga was on her feet immediately. "Mother was defending Runa from her attacker! There is no crime in that!"

Wiglaf looked calmly at his bride-to-be. "What Lars did was wrong, but was it necessary to kill him? Was there no other way to stop him?"

"Lord Wiglaf." Olaf rose, eyes flashing, after giving Runa's hand a firm squeeze. "Had I been there I would have killed Lars with my own hands—for attacking and dishonoring the woman I'm taking to wife! Would you not have done the same in defense of Inga?"

Now all eyes were fixed on Wiglaf. He sighed.

"Yes, of course, but . . . to be killed by a woman . . . ?"

My own eyes narrowed and I rose to face him, hands on hips.

"So, is that the problem? You think it unnatural for a woman to play a man's role? Better for everyone, then, that I leave this kingdom as soon as possible!"

As Wiglaf looked at me, momentarily disconcerted, another idea struck me.

"If it's a matter of wergild, I have treasure enough to pay his man-price, if there is any family to demand it."

Wiglaf and Olaf looked at each other in doubt.

"Family? I know of none," said Wiglaf, "but some of the older athelings—Ragnar Redbeard, perhaps—may be able to tell us. For now, we should move Lars' body and prepare a funeral pyre."

"What?" I flared up again. "An honorable burial? After what he's done?"

Now Olaf was frowning.

"Forgive me, Lady Freawaru, but Wiglaf is right in this matter. A public funeral for Lars will show the settlement that his death was . . . an accident, that your deed was a spontaneous reaction to a shocking discovery, not willful murder."

I stared at him, then bowed my head. "So be it. I will cast Runa's bloody cloak on the flames as an offering!"

After the others had left the room, Runa beckoned me to her side to impart one more whispered detail.

"My lady, when I was struggling to prevent Lars from... forcing himself on me... he laughed and said I was no better than the queen... said that she had welcomed his advances."

I listened in shock and growing awareness. Hygd? Hygd! Her... pregnancy. Of course! Beowulf was not the father... Beowulf had been true to me!

"Mother? What is it now?" Inga's face in the doorway pulled me back to the present.

"Nothing. Nothing. Let's let Runa rest now; she's been through so much."

In the days that followed, news of Lars' death created shock and consternation, but no one seemed to blame me. To my surprise a few blamed Runa! Surely, it was muttered, she must have invited his attentions? Heartsick at this interpretation of events, I pressed forward with preparations for our departure.

Others, all women, hailed my act as a justifiable defense. Lempi and Lise were among this group. The sisters expressed their support in the form of gifts: a cauldron of soup one day, a packet of dried cod on another. During their visits I talked to them about my plans to leave Eaglesgard and invited them to join me. Both expressed interest, especially when they learned that Grim and Eskil were to be members of my bodyguard.

"Grim is a good man," observed Lempi shyly. "We once talked of marriage—before that awful encounter with the dragon—Oh!" she flushed. "Beg pardon, my lady. Still, I wonder... perhaps in another time and place...?"

"Yes," added Lise, nodding emphatically, "and in different circumstances Eskil might actually take notice of me. Our families grew up together and he sees me only as a former playmate, not as a grown woman!"

I had to laugh at the direction this conversation was taking.

"There will be hardships to endure on this journey, ladies. It won't exactly be a haven for lovers!"

"Still...," countered Lempi, smiling, "anything can happen!"

I smiled back, ruefully. "Yes, I have certainly learned that lesson!"

Privately I often pondered Wiglaf's question about Lars: "Was there no other way to stop him?"

Re-living the moment, I once again saw Runa's stricken face and the great bulk of the beast hunched over her. Ahhh, yes, the beast, the beast. I had slit Lars' throat just as I'd sacrificed the ox at Uppsala — a sacrifice to appease the gods. I had sacrificed Lars to save Runa.

Shortly before the burning of Lars' body, Redbeard came to my door holding in both hands a long object wrapped in sealskin.

"My lady?" he began, looking around the longhouse, "Are you alone this morning? I have something for your eyes only."

"Yes, come in. My women have errands." I glanced at the package he carried. "Come over to the hearth light and show me what you've brought."

Redbeard strode toward the fire, holding the package before him like an offering, then laid it respectfully on the table. As he pulled back the wrappings I came to his side, curious to see what would be revealed.

A blade — or part of one — a broken sword blade, scorched and stained, lay before me.

Puzzled, I scanned its surface, marveling at the workmanship: inlaid with twining beasts and runic inscriptions, familiar inscriptions, Wait! Could it be . . . ? A long-locked vault in my heart suddenly sprang open and I caught my breath, shuddering.

"Redbeard! Is it Beowulf's blade?"

He nodded solemnly. "It's Nagling. Beowulf's sword."

"But I thought it was destroyed!" I cried, "In the dragon battle!" I paused to recollect. "Wiglaf once showed me the hilt end, which he'd kept as a kinsman's inheritance, but he told me that the rest of the sword could not be found!"

Redbeard slowly shook his head.

"There can be no mistake. I know this blade."

"How did it come into your hands?" I asked in perplexity.

Redbeard scowled darkly. "I found it hidden at the bottom of Lars' sea chest."

"Lars? So, he'd kept it for himself!"

Redbeard shrugged.

"Now the question is: what should be done with it? It's too late to add it to Beowulf's mound, and certainly not fitting to bury it with Lars. No one else yet knows of its existence. I thought it right that you see it first, my lady. I thought perhaps you should have it."

Cloak of Ashes

I stared at him. "Let me think."

Shocked by the sudden and unexpected appearance of Beowulf's sword — as if from beyond the grave — I could not answer immediately. Finally, however, I found my voice.

"Wiglaf has the hilt end and you — we — have the rest. Could the two be joined? Could the sword be made whole again? This could become a great treasure for Eaglesgard, an heirloom for all the Geats."

Redbeard nodded, smiling.

"My lady, you speak wisely. If it is in the power of our smith to accomplish the deed, this sword shall be made whole. I will take it to Oskar today — after I get the hilt end from Wiglaf."

Redbeard rewrapped the blade carefully, turned and bowed.

"Good day, Lady Freawaru. You are a treasure which Eaglesgard — and I — will miss."

After Redbeard's departure I sat by the fire. Hot tears rolled down my cheeks as scenes from earlier days came to mind. In one, young Herdred placed his father Hygelac's damaged sword in the hands of old Oskar. Could Beowulf's blade be re-forged as well? The answer would not come for many days. In the meantime there were other matters which required my attention.

Runa asked that her marriage to Olaf be delayed until after we left Eaglesgard. Both Olaf and I agreed that this would be wise. Runa was greatly relieved that Olaf still wanted to marry her and touched by his declaration that the new slant of her nose only added to her beauty. For my part, I was relieved that Olaf was still willing to captain our ship.

Inga's wedding was another matter. Both she and I wanted to see her securely joined to Lord Wiglaf and acknowledged as queen of the Geats. Even before Lars' funeral pyre had burned to ashes, our personal preparations for the wedding were underway.

New clothes, fresh bedding, woven wall hangings — all that Inga would need to set up her own household — were ready for use, temporarily stowed in our storage chests. I was also leaving her everything of value in my own longhouse. She would be well equipped to start her new life with Wiglaf.

A spring wedding would put a strain on our food stores, especially providing enough drink to meet the expectations of a nine-day celebration. Fortunately our friends at Hrethelskeep came to our aid, supplying fresh meat and dried mushrooms to add variety to our feasts, and even a supply of honey for fermenting into mead.

Few made the journey to attend in person, but Ragnhild and Thorkel came, as did Thora and Rolf, travelling on horseback over muddy paths and through melting snows. Inga greeted with delight these friends of her childhood, and I was glad to get news of my former home.

"Ana survived the winter, but she is very frail," confided Thora after we had embraced. "Brita takes good care of her. Ingeborg is far pregnant with her second child, else she would have attempted the journey."

"And what of Wulfgar?" I asked, remembering the tall, stalwart leader of our group from Heorot. His union with Ingeborg had gladdened my heart.

"He dotes on his little boy, and keeps the rest of the young men in fighting trim. He misses you," added Thora, "as we all do. And now I hear that you are leaving again? Leaving Eaglesgard?"

"Yes, I must go."

Thora laid her work-worn hands gently on my own.

"Is it this — this Lars business?"

"No — and yes. I have other reasons, but I am sure that both Runa and I will be glad to leave this place!"

I did not tell Thora that 'this Lars business' had entered my dreams, that Lars' sullen visage reared up before me night after night, causing me to cry out and awake dripping with sweat, that neither Runa nor I spoke his name aloud. Both of us were ready to leave painful events behind us — if we could.

During the wedding ceremony, conducted in the mead hall, tears came to my eyes when Wiglaf laid the hammer of Thor in Inga's lap, sealing their union. Now her position in Eaglesgard was secure. Now I could safely leave.

On the ninth and final day of the celebration a final shock was visited upon us. In the midst of a friendly wrestling match with his mates, Tor suddenly collapsed. Once again it was Redbeard who called me to the young men's quarters, but this time there was no life to save.

Tor lay in a twisted heap on the longhouse floor, soiled with his own vomit. According to the other men Tor had been sick for days, complaining of a pain in his belly, but no one had told me, busy as I was overseeing the wedding celebrations. Now, as I knelt beside the still body, I could find no heartbeat.

"This morning he felt w-w-worse, Lady Freawaru," stuttered Grim, kneeling beside me, "but he tried not to show it. I saw him gasp after downing a cup of ale, and there were beads of sweat on his forehead as he watched us wrestle. Suddenly he spewed out the ale and dropped to the floor clutching at his side."

Grim's face was pale as he gave me these details.

"Is it my fault, my lady? That's the same side where I . . . I knifed him in that brawl . . . but his wound had healed—I'd seen it with my own eyes—it had healed!"

"Calm yourself, Grim. I don't know the answer to your question. Perhaps I myself am at fault. Perhaps there was infection that I overlooked. Perhaps . . ."

"Lady Freawaru," interrupted Redbeard, "I have seen others die in this manner before. Tor's death may have nothing to do with either you or Grim."

Grim and I gazed up at Redbeard blankly.

"Perhaps," I asserted. "But wergild will be expected. Perhaps Grim and I should share the burden of payment?"

Redbeard stroked his beard gravely.

"As you see fit, my lady. I know that Tor came from a noble family of the Bronding tribe and they will expect a suitable man-price for the loss of their son."

I mused. "Hmmm, the Brondings . . . I think our plans must be altered; we must first sail to Tor's homeland before heading to Heorot. We will convey the wergild to Tor's family in person."

Redbeard nodded approvingly.

"That would be wise, my lady. The Brondings have always been our friends and allies. With Beowulf gone, we will need their continued support."

Wiglaf too approved my new plan and even contributed weapons to make up the total deemed appropriate for Tor's wergild. Tor's body was burned in a quiet ceremony attended by his nine former companions, but I saved out a medallion he'd worn on his chest: an image of Sleipner, Odin's eight-legged horse—to give to his family.

As soon as the ice began to break up along the shoreline, Olaf and our nine young men set to work refurbishing the cargo ship we would use for our journey. First they spread tar along seams that gapped with age. Tears in the sail were mended; rough oars were made smooth and new ones fashioned to replace those battered by rocky landings. As a finishing touch, the hull was repainted a bright blue and Redbeard himself added a pair of glaring eyes to the prow.

"That should scare old Jormungard himself, should he chance to cross your path on the seas," joked Redbeard.

"Jormungard?" echoed Knud. 'Isn't that the world serpent Thor caught on a fishing expedition?"

"The very one!" crowed Redbeard. "Thor finally had to let him go, but Thor put his feet through the bottom of the boat in the struggle."

I shuddered at the story, remembering the many tales of sea monsters I'd heard over the years.

"May the gods protect us," I muttered to myself.

My women and I collected supplies and packed storage chests. Lempi and Lise had decided to join me, after convincing their mother of the advantages.

"We told her we'd have a better chance of finding husbands," giggled Lise.

I had noticed that opinion varied widely at Eaglesgard regarding the status of the young men who had failed Beowulf. Except for Redbeard, most men were adamant in their condemnation, while many women took a softer view.

Concerning Lars' death at my hands, no one spoke critically to my face, but there were whispers behind my back and I met with hard looks from some in the settlement. Reflecting, I realized that many of my party were leaving Eaglesgard to escape past losses. I had lost Beowulf. The nine young men had lost their reputations as warriors. Runa had lost her virginity in the rape. But we have all survived, I told myself, and we will make new lives for ourselves — in other lands. There is also the possibility of finding Mother. Mother, I am coming!

The two thralls Runa picked to accompany us were young girls acquired in trade the previous fall from somewhere in Finnmark. Runa brought them to my longhouse one morning for my evaluation. I was seated at the table sorting herbs for our trip — a task normally conducted in the drying shed, but both Runa and I had avoided that place since Lars' attack. Runa had told me earlier that the two were sisters who'd been working for Old Greta, but Greta was willing to trade them both for the new calf produced by Krona, saying the girls ate too much.

The two seemed very shy and awkward when they straggled in, but Runa encouraged them to give me their names and ages.

"Mari," mumbled the taller, skinnier one. "I have ten winters."

"Berit," said the shorter one. "Nine winters."

I looked askance at the scrawny figures, wondering why Runa had chosen them, but she spoke for them immediately.

"Don't worry, my lady. I've had my eye on these girls all winter. They are hard workers and quick to follow orders. You'll see."

"I hope," I muttered, then cleared my throat to address the pair.

"Girls, you are here to serve me and my women. You will be treated — and fed — well."

At this their faces brightened.

"Berit, you will help Runa prepare the stew for our evening meal. Mari, you may start by carefully packing these bags of herbs into this chest."

Mari reached out a tentative hand, picked up the bag nearest her and brought it to her nose.

"Chamomile?" She raised her eyes to my face.

"Why, yes — so you know herbs?" I asked in surprise.

"A few," she acknowledged. "My mother used to . . ." Her eyes suddenly clouded with tears and she dropped her head hastily.

"Your mother? I see. It's alright, child. Losing one's mother is hard. I know. Now get on with your work."

After a full day carrying cargo down to the harbor, our ship was fully loaded and ready for the journey. I spent the last night before departure with Inga and Wiglaf in what was now their longhouse. It was to be a night for the giving and receiving of gifts.

After a simple meal served on their finest tableware, I presented my gift to Inga. Some weeks before, I had asked Redbeard to carve a single falcon feather, a long, pointed wing feather, of birch wood, replicating the mark of Freyja I bore on my shoulder. (He had assured me, with some discomfort, that he did not need to see the birthmark itself.)

The result pleased me: a piece that lay on the hand light and smooth as an actual feather. On one side he had carved runes of protection and fertility: Algiz, Inguz and Berkana. This would be my parting gift to Inga, a talisman to keep beside her in my absence. Inga received it tearfully, holding me long in a tender embrace.

"I will treasure this always," she whispered.

Then, to my surprise, Wiglaf announced that he had a gift for me! While Inga reseated me at the head of their table, Wiglaf disappeared momentarily into their bedchamber. He emerged clutching a long object that extended from his chest to the floor. As he passed the hearth I caught the flash of bright metal, and my heart turned over. Could it be...? It was.

"Beowulf's sword," declared Wiglaf proudly.

He placed it on the table before me.

"After many trials, Oskar finally succeeded in re-forging the blade," he said. 'Now, Lady Freawaru, it is yours." He paused. "We have not always been friends, my lady, but tonight — on the eve of your leave-taking — I wish to show my respect and gratitude for all you have done, with this parting gift."

I placed my fingertips on the ancient blade. For a time I was silent, contemplating the sword — Beowulf's sword — through misty eyes. Finally I looked up to see Inga regarding me with a look of distress.

"Have we done wrong, Mother? Does the sword bring you pain?"

I nodded and smiled as I wiped my eyes.

"Yes, yes it does, but greater than pain is the joy I find in your wish to please me. Thank you, my daughter. Thank you, Wiglaf — my son — for the honor you do me. I deeply appreciate your kindness, your thoughtfulness, the love you show me. I am not ungrateful, but Beowulf's sword belongs here in Eaglesgard. Perhaps it could be hung in the mead hall, near the throne where Wiglaf sits as leader of the Geats. Beowulf's sword would be a continuing reminder of past glories and an affirmation of Wiglaf's right to rule."

During this speech Wiglaf had stood stiffly, as if he'd taken offense, but now his features relaxed in a slight smile.

"Lady Freawaru, I should never underestimate your generosity and your wisdom. Whatever you command shall be done!"

He bowed low, then rose with a broad smile on his face.

"Let us celebrate the return of Beowulf's sword and drink to the future!"

The evening concluded with golden mead drunk from silver goblets.

Next morning I rose before dawn, bidding goodbye to the dear house that had been my home. Other goodbyes had already been said. Now it was time to leave Eaglesgard for the adventure before us. My heart was light as I made my way toward the cliff edge, joining the dream-like shapes of my women and our crew of young men in the early light. A fresh breeze blew from the south-east, a good omen for the start of our journey to the land of the Brondings.

"Good morrow, Olaf. Good morrow, Runa."

I greeted these dear friends warmly as I tightened my cloak about me. Together we made our way carefully down the cliff path to the harbor, to our waiting ship, to our new lives.

It had been many winters since I'd been onboard a ship and I found my body reluctant to adapt to its unaccustomed motion. Despite Olaf and Alf's expert guidance, I felt uneasy as we picked our way through the daunting maze of rocks and skerries that bordered the Wedermark. This time I was not carrying a baby. My baby had grown up; my baby was now queen of the Geats.

My thoughts flew back to my first landing on these shores — before Beowulf's death, before Hygd's death, even before Hygelac's death...now Lars was dead, and Tor...

No, Freawaru, no. Do not think of death. Think of life and all that it may hold. Think of Runa, soon to be wed to Olaf. Or...think of those two little girls you bought for the price of a spring calf!

"My lady?"

Runa's smiling face appeared at my side, her eyes bright with excitement.

"Can you believe it?" she breathed. "Thank the gods we are on our way at last!"

"Yes, thank the gods. Olaf says we are only two day's sail from the land of the Brondings — if this breeze holds. We may have to spend only one night ashore."

Rising to stand beside her, I turned my face to the wind.

Unfortunately the breeze did not hold and soon all of our men were seated at the oars — all our men and one of our women, for Ginnlaug had volunteered to try her hand at rowing, taking the place left vacant by Tor's death. I smiled to see her awkward but earnest efforts, remembering my long-ago trip to Moon Cliff when Brita and I had shared this chore. By the end of the day Ginnlaug's face dripped with sweat, but she gamely kept to her task, becoming quite proficient as she was cheered on by shouts of encouragement from our young oarsmen.

Lempi and Lise helped Runa and me hand out food at intervals and when we beached our craft on a rocky shoreline they assisted in setting up camp for the night.

"This place looks much like Eaglesgard," said Lise, glancing up at the cliffs above us. 'Is the world the same everywhere?"

A chuckle from Knud made her flush.

"You haven't seen much of the world, have you? These cliffs are nothing compared to what lies ahead: magnificent mountains, filled with trolls and giants! Why, the land we're going to is even called Jotunheim, 'giant home'."

"Hmpf!" sniffed Lempi, "I don't believe in giants—but are there—dragons?"

Knud's grin instantly faded and he turned away without answering. Vigo stepped forward to address her soberly.

"Don't believe everything Knud says. I grew up in Breccasberg and neither I nor anyone I know has ever seen a dragon."

"Breccasberg? Is that the seat of the Brondings?" I asked, leaning forward to stretch my back.

"Yes, my lady, and a beautiful place it is!" A light grew in Vigo's eyes as he continued. "Mountains, waterfalls, forests—and a good harbor at the mouth of the fjord."

This was the longest speech I'd ever heard from Vigo. Apparently his homeland was as dear to him as Heorot was to me.

Runa put Mari and Berit to work setting up two cooking tripods while Olaf directed the men in erecting tents for our overnight stay. It was hard to find a level surface on the rocky beach, but after a day at sea I did not worry about a wakeful night. Soon the aroma of fish stew bubbling in a cauldron roused the appetite I thought I'd lost.

After all had eaten, Sigrod and Anton built up the fire and we gathered around it to relax and review the day—except for the two thralls, whom I sent down to the shore to wash our bowls and pots.

"Look at my blisters!" exclaimed Ginnlaug, holding up both hands proudly.

Cloak of Ashes

"You did well," said Olaf, "but you'll need a day off to let them heal. Does anyone else want to help tomorrow—in case we need rowers again?" He looked around the circle at the women. Lise, who had been staring fixedly at the fire, raised her hand.

"I'm just as strong as Ginnlaug. I'll try!"

"Very good," said Olaf. "Once we turn our ship to the west we should get some help from the wind, although Vigo tells me it can be variable in these parts."

All eyes turned toward Vigo, who nodded.

"Yes, as a boy I fished this coastline with my uncle. We made some great catches off this very shore. That cod we ate tonight was good, but wait until you taste our herring! Nothing better than winter herring, fat and firm!"

"But it is already spring," objected Lise, yawning.

"Not where the herring live," declared Vigo. "The colder the water the firmer the flesh. Late in the season herring get skinny and soft."

"Ugh!" frowned Lise, then changed the subject. "Does anyone know a story to tell?"

"I do!" announced Knud. "I heard a good one from Tor, who said he had learned it from his grandfather."

For a moment we were silent, thinking of the reason for Tor's absence from our circle. Then I prodded Knud to begin.

"Well, we're waiting. Go ahead!"

As we settled ourselves to listen, Knud rose and took a few steps back and forth as if to gather his thoughts.

"Once upon a winter," he began, "a hunter up in Finnmark caught a big white bear. 'What a prize!' he thought. 'I will tame this bear and take it with me on my travels. Then no one can refuse me anything!' So he did just that.

One night when it was almost Yule, very cold, with snow deep on the ground, he came to an old farmhouse nestled in a mountain valley. He knocked at the door and asked for shelter for himself and his bear. A farmer lived there, whose name was Hodge. He cried out 'Alas! I would gladly offer beds to both you and your bear, but a pack of trolls will soon be arriving, as they do every Yule. My family and I were just preparing to leave, for the trolls sleep in all the beds and eat everything in the house!'

'Hmm,' said the hunter. 'Perhaps I can help. Let me and my bear sleep under the benches and we will see what we will see.' Farmer Hodge gladly agreed to this. Before he and his family left, they prepared huge pots of porridge and heaps of sausages for the hungry trolls, then scurried from the house. The hunter and his bear lay down under the benches to take their rest.

Soon the trolls arrived: some big and some little, some with two tails, some with none, some with noses like pokers and ears furled and curled. They set to work with gusto, guzzling the porridge and stuffing their mouths with sausage. One little troll saw the bear's nose sticking out from under a bench. Taking a sausage, he poked it at the bear, saying 'Furry cat, furry cat, will you eat a bite?'

'GRRR!' growled the bear, which sent the sausage flying. 'GRRR!' he growled again, and the little troll went flying. 'GRRR!' he growled a third time, emerging from under the bench, which sent the whole pack of trolls flying. They ran for their lives, out the door and down the valley, finally disappearing into the mountains.

The next winter farmer Hodge was outdoors seeking a Yule log for his hearth, when he heard a voice bawling from the forest.

'Hodge! Hodge!'

'What do you want?' cried Hodge.

'Does that big cat still live with you?'

'Yes indeed,' shouted Hodge, 'and she now has nine kittens, all bigger and fiercer than herself.'

'Thank you,' bawled the troll in the wood. 'That is all we wanted to know.'

From that day to this the trolls have never again visited farmer Hodge at Yule — or any other time.

Snip, snap, snout. My tale's told out."

Knud's story was met with giggles from just beyond the circle of firelight. I made out Mari and Berit standing together, holding hands. Runa rose and addressed them severely.

"Have you two finished the washing up?"

They bobbed their heads and faded into the darkness. I rose too and arched my back, yawning and working out the stiffness.

"Bedtime for us women," I announced. "We may reach Breccasberg tomorrow, and we'll want to be at our best."

Obediently the other women got to their feet and headed for the tents. On the way Lempi took me aside to whisper. "Are there trolls at Breccasberg, Lady Freawaru? My mother often talked of trolls."

"I don't know, Lempi. Probably not. We'll soon find out."

The next morning Olaf wakened me early, stopping at my tent to rap on the frame.

"The wind is up, my lady. We need to take advantage of it. No time for eating now—that can wait."

"Very good, Olaf." Inside the tent I yawned and nodded, reluctant to shake off the dream I'd been having, a dream of flying—flying with my swans back in Heorot. "We'll be ready."

Yawning again I struggled out of my sealskin bag and called to the thralls huddled together under a robe, for I had chosen to shelter them in my tent.

"Girls! Get up! Wake the others and start packing. We need to leave immediately!"

Obediently the two rose, stretching and shaking themselves like little dogs.

"No food this morning, lady?" asked Mari timidly.

"That's right. We'll eat later on the ship."

As they tumbled out of my tent I chuckled to myself. Always hungry, those two. Old Greta must not have fed them much! My mother had always treated her thralls well. My mother...

"Lady Freawaru? May we take down your tent?"

Gunnulf's ruddy face appeared at the opening.

"Yes, I'm ready."

Hastily gathering the few bundles I'd brought ashore, I emerged into the bright light of a clear, crisp day. A breeze from the east carried hints of sun-warmed pine needles and new vegetation. I breathed it in, filling my lungs with the promise of spring.

That morning after the sail was hoisted and we were well at sea, I picked my way over bags and around sea chests to find Vigo standing at the bow, gazing out to the north. After he acknowledged my presence with a slight bow, I began to question him.

"This Brecca of Breccasberg. What is he like?"

"A good king, my lady, but worn with the cares of many winters. Once an able fighter and always generous to his men—not like his sons," Vigo concluded with a growl.

"His sons? I met them once in Hrethelskeep: big, brawny, red-haired men. Why do you dislike them?" I asked, eager to learn what we might be facing upon our arrival at Breccasberg.

Vigo shrugged. "Like — dislike — not important. Fairness is important. They treated me unfairly — one reason I left to join Beowulf's men." Vigo turned away from me and fell silent.

"What happened?" I prodded.

Scowling, he turned back to face me.

"They took the land that was rightfully mine after my father died!" he declared.

'Vigo," I said sternly, placing my hand on his shoulder. "Remember that you have sworn to serve me as your leader on this voyage. Now is not the time to settle old scores. We — that is, the Geats — want to retain the Brondings as our allies."

At that moment I wished that Redbeard were standing beside me. He knew how to control such young men without even raising his voice. As I looked into Vigo's eyes I saw resentment still simmering there, but at least he accepted my admonition with a show of respect.

"Whatever you say, my lady."

As we made our way north and west along the coast line, we encountered floating ice slabs, some half the size of our ship. They ground against the hull when we could not avoid them.

"Spring is slow in reaching this country," I observed to Olaf. He stood at the tiller, while Alf acted as lookout at the bow. "Are we in any danger?"

"Don't worry, my lady. Our ship may be old, but it is still seaworthy. Aeschere used the best materials in the building of it."

"Aeschere." I turned the word over on my tongue. "I have not heard or said that name for many a winter. Aeschere — killed by the Grendel monster's dam. Aeschere — my father's boon companion. Olaf..." I broke off momentarily, gripped by a wave of emotion. "Olaf, what do you think we will find at Heorot?"

"Heorot? We're headed for Breccasberg, my lady."

"Yes, I know, but Heorot is our final destination."

Olaf raised his eyebrows.

"Only the gods can tell, my lady — unless you have seen something?" He looked at me quizzically.

"Only vague images, Olaf, nothing clearly."

I settled myself on a nearby chest and sank into silence, allowing those vague images to rise again before me: images of fire and slaughter, images of a sleeping warrior and a great bear wreaking havoc. What could they mean?

Berit approached cautiously and waited for me to acknowledge her.

"Yes?"

"Is it time to hand out food, lady?"

"Yes, little one, it is. Ask Runa to direct you."

Rising I shook off the troubling vision and followed Berit to join my women.

At midday the breeze slowed, then stopped altogether, so Lise got her chance to row.

"Ugh!" she cried to Ginnlaug. "How did you do this? It's such hard work!"

"Indeed it is!" agreed Ginnlaug sympathetically.

Listening to them talk I was reminded of my long-ago rowing lesson from Unferth, my old rune master. Would he still be alive? Would I see him at Heorot?

"Lady Freawaru?"

It was Runa, smiling broadly as she knelt beside me.

"Olaf says we won't make Breccasberg today, now that the wind has fallen, so there will be one more night ashore."

"Thank you, Runa. I had guessed as much—but you look very happy!"

"Do I?" She laughed. "Making this trip as a free woman, with Olaf, makes all the difference!"

"Perhaps we can arrange for you and Olaf to wed while we're in Breccasberg," I said, "although we won't be there long."

"How long, my lady?"

"Only long enough to pay our respects to King Brecca and deliver the wergild to Tor's family. I'd say less than a moon."

How wrong I was in that prediction!

Chapter Three
Breccasberg

A pair of bronze scales from a Viking Age grave in Jåtten, Hetland, Rogaland, Norway, found with eight lead weights in a small linen bag.

Vigo had told us that Breccasberg was located on the western side of a great fjord. To get there we would first pass rocky islands too numerous to count, then cliffs with high, narrow waterfalls. The truth of his account was soon revealed.

"Indeed, this must be a land of giants!" breathed Lise. She stood at the starboard gunnel, leaning out over the water as she gazed up in awe.

"Careful, sister. I don't want to lose you," cautioned Lempi, coming up behind her. Lise's blonde locks flew into Lempi's face as she hugged her sister tightly.

The wind had come up again, this time from the south — just in time to push us toward our destination. I thrilled to the rushing movement of the ship, recalling my long-ago realization that sailing felt like flying with the swans. For a moment I lifted my arms to the sky and closed my eyes, my hair streaming behind me. Since Beowulf's death I seldom wore the white kerchief that kept it bound, signifying marriage.

Slowly I opened my eyes and made my way across the deck. We had seen few signs of human habitation up to this point. Earlier in the morning we had passed a fishing boat, but the men aboard were busy with their nets and only acknowledged our hail with a nod.

As we flew northward the land beside us grew more distinct. Walls of rock rose from the sea, backed by distant mountains capped with snow. The air had an icy tinge, and I shivered despite the warm cloak I'd wrapped about my shoulders.

"My lady, do you need your fur robe?"

It was Runa, solicitous as always for my wellbeing.

"Thank you, Runa, but no." I paused, turning to face her. "When we get to Breccasberg we must both remember that you are no longer a thrall, but a free woman. You no longer have to wait upon me!"

She smiled. "Yes, my lady, I will be sure to remember that! But . . . I'm wondering what sort of impression you wish to make on the court at Breccasberg. Your fur robe is a fine one, and you may wish to unpack some of your adornments."

Her words were both a question and suggestion.

"There are other matters to consider first. Since we come unexpectedly, we must proceed with caution. Our ship is clearly a cargo vessel, not a warship, and we have Vigo to speak for us to the coast guard. Still . . . once we have arrived we can assess the situation more fully."

"Yes, my lady. You speak wisely."

"Runa, I've been thinking. While we're in Breccasberg I'd like you to take charge of our two young thralls. Keep them busy and out of trouble."

"Yes, my lady." Runa paused. "Have you any further tasks for me?"

"Only one." I smiled, taking her hand. "Always be my friend and companion."

"Yes, my lady."

We laughed, turning our faces toward Breccasberg.

Late in the morning we made our way into a wide fjord that disappeared into the distance. We sailed for quite some time before Vigo cried out. "Breccasberg! Ahead to port!"

Long before the settlement came into view, we were hailed by a lone guard standing on a cliff. Through cupped hands he demanded our

Cloak of Ashes 41

identities and our business. Immediately Olaf and Vigo stepped to the bow of our ship. At Olaf's nudge, Vigo spoke first.

"I am Vigo, son of Tovar. You know me well, Halvor, though I have been absent for many winters. Olaf and I bring a company of Geats, and a Danish princess, to visit Breccasberg."

"And I am Olaf, son of Ole, come from the court of Eaglesgard to see King Brecca and to deliver wergild to the family of Tor, son of Torfinn," shouted Olaf.

After taking all this in, the coast guard signaled to an unseen companion, who shortly appeared at the base of the cliff on horseback.

"Proceed, strangers," he called. "I will ride ahead to alert the court of your arrival. Vigo can help you steer safely up the channel. Fare you well."

"A promising start," muttered Vigo, waving a response to the sentinel. "I hope we get as kind a welcome from Brecca's sons!"

At a signal from Olaf the sail was dropped and our men moved to take their places at the oars. Neither Ginnlaug nor Lise were called upon to row this time. Vigo stood in the bow, peering at landmarks as we made our way up the increasingly narrow, twisting channel, guiding us to avoid submerged rocks.

In places a dark forest of pines and firs came right down to the shore; in others great expanses of rock lined the waterway. Here and there tiny flowers and stunted shrubs peered out from crevices.

It was midday by the time we reached the settlement itself, perched on an incline above the harbor, a patchwork of light gray rock and dark longhouses backed by low hills. Clearly it was a market day, for longboats and cargo ships filled the harbor, ranged below rows of huts and tents that lined the shore.

A market? Immediately my spirits rose. Market days at Heorot had always been my favorite as a girl! We were arriving at an opportune time! My women apparently shared my anticipation, for they hurried to the bow, chattering excitedly.

"I wonder if they'll have any pretty glass beads?" squealed Lise.

"But what would you have to trade for them?" asked Lempi, laying a hand on her sister's shoulder. "This looks like a rougher sort of market to me."

Indeed, as we drew closer on the port side I could make out heaps of animal skins, stacked antlers, whalebone, furs, what looked like lumps of soapstone, and — at the far end of the row — a small group of figures tied together with ropes around their necks — clearly the slave market.

"We're not here for trading," called Olaf from the tiller. "Our business is with Brecca . . . but," he added, seeing the dejected looks on the faces of Lise and Ginnlaug, who had turned to look at him, "there may be time later to visit the stalls."

Carefully maneuvering our craft, Olaf and Alf found a suitable place to slip in between two longboats and we plowed up onto the stony beach. Breccasberg. Now what?

The man on horseback who had instructed us earlier reappeared. He looked to be close in age to the men in our crew; his hair was plaited all over and a wisp of beard graced his chin.

"King Brecca will receive you — just your leaders, not the whole crew," he added, sizing up our group.

After a brief consultation, Olaf, Vigo, Runa and I went ashore to follow our guide through the crowded market, leaving our companions on board with Alf in charge.

"I wonder if Lise will somehow manage to visit the market while we're gone," murmured Runa in my ear.

"I hope Lempi keeps her under control," I answered, frowning. "We don't know these people. It is best to be on our guard."

Despite my words I felt no fear as we made our way through the noisy throng of traders. My senses were assailed with shouts and cries in many languages, strange costumes worn by even stranger men, and smells — what smells! The reek of freshly tanned hides almost overpowered me. I held my nose to keep out the stench and blinked my watering eyes.

Scattered among the men, clusters of women stood talking, perhaps exchanging gossip, perhaps discussing the quality of the goods displayed. Through the crowd ran several children, giggling as they chased one another. One little girl with rumpled russet hair brushed past me, laughing. I smiled, seeing myself in her at that age.

As she ran on, another figure caught my eye: a giant of a fellow dressed in bearskins. Something about him seemed familiar, but menacing. I looked away quickly and tightened my grip on Olaf's arm. Olaf smiled at me and looked back to check on Runa, who accompanied Vigo. Soon the big man was lost from view as we pressed through the crowd.

Our guide, who told us his name was Elling, led us up a series of rock ledges that had me panting before we reached the top. At the summit stood the mead hall, an imposing structure overlooking the harbor.

Brecca's mead hall reminded me of Heorot as my father had originally planned it: tall, massive, with heavy oak planks set upright forming the walls and gabled ends that reached toward the sky. I saw no gold on the exterior here, but the central doors were heavily carved with intricate figures of men and beasts. An impressive introduction to the home of the Brondings.

Elling repeated our names to the hall guard, who nodded and slowly opened the heavy oak doors. A wave of warm air greeted us and drew us inside. As my eyes adjusted to the interior light, I noticed that every wall was hung with rich tapestries. Ah, the Bronding women are skillful weavers! We may find kindred spirits here! But first, the king.

The throne stood near the hearth, at the far end of the almost empty hall. The bent old man seated on it gave me a start. Knowing that Brecca and Beowulf had been boyhood friends, I'd expected to see someone of Beowulf's age, but the man before me looked more like . . . my father. The throne on which he sat was elaborately carved, with arm rests that ended in the heads of gaping beasts.

I blinked and let the man's features come into focus: long gray hair with a beard braided in three parts, dark, deep-set eyes and hollow cheeks, a pinched nose but a generous mouth. Was this . . . ?

"King Brecca welcomes you to Breccasberg," announced a smooth voice at the king's elbow. A figure I had not noticed rose and gave a slight bow.

"I am Ulrik, son of Unger. I am the king's advisor. What is your business with the king?"

"We are here as emisaries from the court of Eaglesgard," I said with authority.

Kneeling respectfully before the king, I took his frail, dry hands in mine, noting the stiff fingers crooked toward his palms. Impulsively I kissed them, then raised my eyes to his face.

"King Brecca, I am Freawaru, daughter of King Hrothgar of the Danes. I have come from the land of the Geats to bring you news of their king, your old friend Beowulf."

At the word 'Beowulf' a light flickered in Brecca's eyes and he motioned for me to rise.

"What . . . what news?" he asked, in a voice that sounded dry from disuse.

"Sad news, my lord," I said gently. "King Beowulf is dead, killed by a dragon. Beowulf now sleeps in Valhalla."

For a time Brecca was silent, staring at the floor as if searching his memory.

"I won, I won the swimming match . . . didn't I?" he said, looking up at me with watery eyes. Then he slowly shook his head. "In Valhalla, eh? Beowulf has beat me again."

A wistful grin revealed several teeth missing from his lower jaw.

"A straw death," he muttered. "That's all that's left for me — a straw death!" He shook his head again, then fixed me with a steady gaze.

"We must talk. You stay. Ulrik!" he shouted, making us all jump. "See that our guests are given refreshment and treated well. This lady . . . stays with me."

"Thank you, my lord," I said quickly, "but more of our party are waiting aboard ship. We are seventeen in all: seven women and ten men."

Brecca grunted and gestured toward Ulrik.

"This man will see to their needs. Bring your people — all of them — to the mead hall tonight. You must meet my sons, busy at present with the traders. Now, my lady, you must be thirsty after your long journey . . ."

The longer he spoke the stronger Brecca seemed to become, growing larger before our very eyes. Even Ulrik seemed taken aback.

"Careful, my lord. Do not excite yourself!"

"Excite myself?" roared Brecca, rising to his feet somewhat painfully. "By the gods, here is a woman to excite any man!" He took a tentative step toward me. "What did you say your name was, my dear?"

"Freawaru, my lord, daughter of King Hrothgar of the Danes, former wife of Ingeld of the Heathobards, and most recently . . . friend and advisor to King Beowulf."

"Friend? Advisor?" Brecca reached for the arm rests and sat down heavily. "If I had been Beowulf, I'd have made you my wife!"

I gulped. "That was his intention, my lord, but the dragon . . . intervened." Suddenly tears filled my eyes and I bowed my head.

"Forgive me, Lady . . . Freawaru." He reached a gnarled hand toward me. "It has been long since anyone, man or woman, has roused me as you have done."

He glanced at the rest of my group, standing quietly behind me. "Who are these people, my dear? I have not met your companions." Olaf stepped forward and bowed low before speaking. "Olaf, son of Ole. I served both King Hrothgar and King Beowulf in their times and now I captain Lady Freawaru's ship. This," he said, pulling Runa gently forward, "is Runa, my bride-to-be."

"Welcome to you both," said Brecca. Then he squinted at the fourth member of our party. "Your face is familiar. Vigo, my boy, is that you? I thought you'd left us long ago."

Vigo dropped to one knee, then rose to face Brecca squarely.

"Yes, my lord, I did leave the court, but I now follow this lady and it was her wish to visit the Brondings. We come with wergild for Tor, who lost his life in Geatland."

"So." Brecca surveyed us with raised eyebrows. "I see there are many stories here to be told –but that can wait for tonight. Ulrik, see that our guests are escorted to suitable quarters. Send in ale –nay, wine — for the lady and me. And ask Old Elsa to attend me here — at once!"

"Yes, my lord. At once!" echoed Ulrik, nodding and backing away. "Come with me, the rest of you."

Olaf and I exchanged quizzical looks. Vigo looked wary, but Runa was smiling. "All will be well," she mouthed to me before turning to follow Ulrik and the others out of the mead hall.

As soon as they were gone, Brecca struggled to his feet again and drew himself to full height.

"Lady . . . Freawaru, you make me feel my manhood again!" he declared.

I smiled. "You do me honor, my lord."

Inwardly I wondered: is this a good moment to offer my gifts as a healer? There are herbal remedies that might relieve the pain in those crippled hands of his. Hmmm. No, do not focus now on the man's infirmities. Wait for a better time.

Aloud I said, "Lord Beowulf often told me of your prowess as a young man, King Brecca, and he valued your aid in times of war."

Brecca nodded. "If Beowulf is gone, who now rules the Geats?"

"His kinsman, Wiglaf, who is married to my daughter, Inga."

"Why have I not heard of this before?" he growled, looking about the empty hall. "Where are my sons? Where are my advisors?"

"You mentioned their business with the traders," I offered, "and Beowulf's death happened last autumn, shortly before the onset of winter. No boats could leave the harbor after the ice formed."

A muscle twitched in Brecca's face and he put out a hand as if feeling in the dark.

"Beowulf's death? You say he's dead?"

My heart sank at these unexpected words. I feared that Brecca's body might have outlived his wits. That would explain why his sons were ruling in his place.

"Yes, my lord, Beowulf is dead. But I am here in his place, to comfort you if I may."

A skinny young servant girl entered shyly with wine and two glass beakers, which she set carefully on the table before us. She glanced at Brecca with fear in her eyes, and I wondered if the old king sometimes became violent. What would I do if he turned on me?

As if in response to my thoughts, Brecca began to shout.

"Edvard! Erik! Where are my sons? Attend me, someone!"

Heavy footsteps interrupted his tirade as a red-faced old woman, wider than she was tall, waddled into the hall, mumbling to herself.

"Old fools, young fools, they're all alike, then. Can't let a body have any peace!"

She planted herself in front of the throne, ignoring my presence.

"What is it this time, King Brecca?"

"Elsa? Where is Brigitta? Where are my boys?" queried Brecca in a peevish tone.

"Brigitta is dead, my lord, long dead. Your sons are down at the harbor collecting tribute and fees from the traders." She cocked her head at me. "Who is this woman, then?"

Brecca reguarded me carefully.

"I don't know... wait! She comes from Beowulf... and... she's going to stay with me!"

"Huh!"

Dismissing the servant with a curt nod, Old Elsa, as I understood her to be, picked up the wine pitcher, poured two glasses, handed one beaker to the king and the other to me. While Brecca noisily quaffed his wine, Elsa turned to me and spoke quietly.

"Beg pardon, my lady. I don't know why Ulrik left you alone with the king. As you may have seen, he is not always... himself."

"Yes, I noticed," I acknowledged. "I am Lady Freawaru from Geatland. I bring news to Brecca and wergild to the family of Tor."

Elsa eyed me gravely, hands on hips. I noticed that she wore heavy gold arm bands, and her apron was trimmed with fine embroidery. She heaved a sigh.

"So Tor's dead, is he? Well, well. That will come as a heavy blow to Torfinn and Erna. He was their youngest and their last, you know. How did he... but that can wait. We'll need to get you properly settled, then. No doubt that's why the king sent for me. I have space for guests in my longhouse and I..."

"Elsa!" interrupted Brecca. "Don't drown the lady in words! Let her drink her wine!"

Elsa grinned and bobbed a bow.

"Whatever you say, King. When she's finished I'll take her to my quarters — Oh, my lady," she said, turning back to me, "how many attendants came with you?"

"Four women and two young female thralls," I answered, lifting my glass.

"I can easily house you and your women, then, and the slaves can sleep in my cattle byre."

I nodded, finishing my wine.

"Some of my party left earlier with Ulrik, but the rest are still on board ship. Should we...?"

"Don't worry, Lady, what was it? Freawaru? Yes, Freawaru. Old Elsa will take care of everything, then. But, we can't leave the king alone..." She paused to take a breath. "We'll have to wait until Ulrik returns."

Fortunately we did not have long to wait. Ulrik returned with Olaf and all of our men, two of them carrying the chest containing Tor's wergild.

"Set it behind the throne," instructed Ulrik. "Tonight here in the mead hall you can make a formal presentation to Tor's parents and explain the circumstances of his death."

Grim glanced at me nervously, but I gave him a quick smile. King Brecca looked on, his face blank, making no comments and asking no questions, as each man was presented to him. Finally he spoke.

"My sons. Tonight you will meet my sons."

Nodding and bowing we made our exit behind Old Elsa, leaving King Brecca and Ulrik alone in the hall.

"Where is Runa?" I whispered to Olaf, taking his arm.

"Herding your women through the market," he grinned. "They insisted on having a look — but they should be finished by now."

I chuckled. "So Lise got her way!"

That night in the mead hall Brecca's sons sat on either side of him, presiding as equals with their father. They welcomed our party graciously, offering us a table near the throne. After a bountiful feast of cod, venison and that winter herring Vigo had bragged about, all washed down with liberal quantities of ale and mead, the formal business of the evening began.

Speaking for the Geats, Olaf solemnly announced the death of Beowulf, but gave few details. After he sat down, no one spoke. Finally Edvard and Erik rose to speak words of praise for Beowulf, recalling their part in his campaign against the Swedes.

When they had finished, another warrior rose to speak: the giant I'd seen in the market. Now I recognized the man. Of course! Bodvar Bjarki! I'd met him before — in Uppsala — in company with Unferth.

"My lords," he was saying, "no better king ever lived — so brave in battle, so kind to his people. Beowulf's fame will never die, but live on in the hearts of all who knew him."

Amazed at such eloquence from this brutish-looking man, I shed a tear of gratitude for his words. Others spoke later, but I did not heed them, lost in my own memories.

At length Brecca nodded to me and called for Tor's parents to come forward. As they made their way, I rose, asked Anton and Sigrod to put two benches together, then directed Grim and Gunnulf to bring out the heavy chest from behind the throne and place it on the benches. I stood beside the chest as the parents approached, both lean and tall, walking with great dignity.

When they stood before me, I spoke. "Torfinn and Erna, I greet you with sadness. We Geats have brought the wergild for your son Tor."

Dry-eyed, they listened as I recounted the series of events that had led to Tor's death: the initial stabbing in a brawl among hall-mates, my attempts to heal the wound, then — weeks later — Tor's sudden collapse. I carefully omitted the reason for the brawl and any mention of Tor's lack of bravery in the dragon episode.

"His comrades and I have provided Tor's man-price," I concluded, "to honor a warrior of great promise, struck down too soon."

Torfinn reached into the chest and, with trembling hand, drew out a helmet. He gazed at it a moment, then let it fall with a clatter back into the chest.

"Alas," he cried, "I have no more sons to wear such gear. Yet, I thank you for your courtesy in bringing it."

We exchanged bows and I started to back away, relieved that my explanation of Tor's death had been accepted. Then I remembered the token I'd saved from the funeral pyre.

"Wait — there is something else I can give you — this."

Pulling the drawstring on the pouch at my waist, I withdrew the horse medallion on its silver chain and held it out to Erna.

"Odin's Sleipner. Tor wore it always."

She frowned, then snatched it from my hand and hurried away without a word. Torfinn bowed and quickly followed. Behind me I heard muttering from the throne. "An Odinist? Odin-lovers?" It sounded like Edvard. Mystified, I turned to search his face, but once again Bodvar Bjarki had risen, requesting permission to address the assembly. When it was given, I returned to my seat at our table.

"Lords and ladies . . ." he began, giving a slight nod in my direction, "I have a tale to tell that all of you must hear, for you may someday face a similar challenge. It concerns the Swedes — in particular, King Eadgils, and the Danes — in particular King Hrolf. It is a tale of treachery and deceit!"

At that he had the attention of everyone in the mead hall. Bodvar took a long draught of mead and looked around the hall, then set down his mug and wiped droplets from his beard.

"Our King Hrolf has amassed such a company of champions and berserkers that his fame is great," he declared. "Yet one thing diminished his greatness: the fact that he had never recovered his father Halga's inheritance, wrongfully held by King Eadgils of Uppsala. One day I reminded him of this failing and swore that all his men would back him if he wished to challenge the Swedish king. As some of you may know, King Eadgils has become a powerful sorcerer, cruel-hearted and bold. He slew Hrolf's father by treachery and won his mother's love by magic."

I turned to my companions in astonishment and whispered.

"Is this true? Do any of you know this history?"

All shook their heads, and Runa put a finger to her lips as Bodvar resumed his tale.

"I will not now tell you of all our adventures on the journey to Uppsala, but when we arrived we were twelve champions riding behind King Hrolf. When we entered Eadgils' hall — a place beset with snares and pitfalls — we deemed it wise not to betray which man of us was the king.

Eadgils, greeted us with taunts and insults. Then from behind the wall hangings a host of armed men sprang forth to attack us!

I led the defense with Hjalti beside me wielding his sword Goldhilt and King Hrolf the blade Skofnung. As the battle neared his throne, Eadgils feigned outrage, calling for peace in the hall so that he might properly greet his kinsman, Hrolf."

All this time I had been following Bodvar's account with amazement, as had my companions. Not a sound could be heard in the hall except for Bodvar's booming voice.

"When the hall was cleared of corpses," he continued, "Eadgils bid fires be lighted the length of the hall, with he and his men seated on one side, our party on the other. As the fires blazed, Eadgils called out, 'I do not see my kinsman clearly yet. Build the fires higher!'

Hotter and hotter, red-hot as wolf tongues the flames licked at us, singeing our hair and scorching our clothes, and still Eadgils bid the fires be built higher. Something had to be done! Svipdag and I leapt to our feet, each grabbing one of the men piling logs on the fire, and flung them howling into the blaze.

Then King Hrolf roared, 'He flees no fire who leaps it' and flung his shield on the flames. We all followed him, leaping through the flame-wall to catch Eadgils and slay him. But he ran to a hollow tree that stood in the hall and used his magic and sorcery to escape."

Bodvar paused to refresh himself from another mug of mead. All around him folk were murmuring and shaking their heads in wonder.

"Trial by fire?"

"Sorcery and magic!"

"Bodvar!" someone shouted, "What happened next?"

Bodvar cleared his throat and continued his story.

"King Hrolf's mother, Queen Yrsa, arrived privately to meet her son and provide us safe quarters for the night, but our trials were not over. That very night Eadgils sent a giant boar to slay us, but King Hrolf's great

Cloak of Ashes

hound Gram attacked the boar without hesitation, tearing off its ears and ripping flesh from its cheeks, until the beast was forced to withdraw.

Still we were not safe, for Eadgils' men now set fire to the house where we were lodged. We had to hurl ourselves against the wall planks to burst through. Outside we faced a brutal battle against men in mail shirts. We soon thinned their ranks, but once again Eadgils disappeared.

Returning to Eadgils' hall, King Hrolf boldly took the high seat himself, and there received his mother. Queen Yrsa gave him a silver horn filled with jewels and gold rings, more than enough treasure to equal his father's inheritance. She also gave us fresh horses, for our own had been shamefully abused and mutilated in the stables — on Eadgils' orders.

Soon we were on our way, riding out of Uppsala without opposition. When we reached the Plain of Fyrisvoll, King Hrolf saw a gold ring glowing on the road in front of him. Sliding off one of his own arm rings, he tossed it onto the road, saying 'I will not stoop for gold, even if it is lying on the road — and let none of you pick it up either!'

That sounds like cousin Hrolf I thought to myself — ever the proud one! Yet I must admit that his courage in the face of such enemies does impress me!

"As we rode on," continued Bodvar, "war trumpets sounded from every side. 'It is as I thought,' said the king. 'That ring was set out as a trick to delay us.' Then he reached into the horn, which Beygad carried, and tossed handfuls of gold and jewels onto the road, strewing riches the length of the plain.

Immediately our pursuers halted, jumping off their horses to grab and brawl, vying to see who could pick up the most treasure. Soon King Eadgils himself appeared, raging at his men for the delay. He raced ahead to catch us, but King Hrolf drew out Sviagris, Eadgils' favorite ring, and threw it down on the road.

Seeing this treasure, Eadgils reached out with the shaft of his spear to retrieve it, bending low over his horse. King Hrolf then galloped back, crying 'I have made the greatest of the Swedes stoop like a swine!' Coming up behind Eadgils, Hrolf sliced both cheeks off the Swede's rump!"

I gasped, and roars of laughter shook the hall.

"Did you hear that? Sliced off his buttocks!"

"Hard to sit your throne after that, I'd wager!"

When the laughter subsided, Bodvar continued.

"Eadgils, faint from loss of blood, was forced to withdraw. King Hrolf recovered the ring Sviagris, shouting 'Now you know that I am King Hrolf, the one you have sought for so long!' For good measure, I myself, Bodvar Bjarki, gave Eadgils' horse a mighty slap to send it galloping home. We killed the rest of Eadgils' men and so were finally free to go our way."

Bodvar nodded his head in grim satisfaction.

"Yes, King Hrolf regained what was rightfully his: his inheritance — and he avenged his father's death better than if he had slain the murderer!"

Shouts of approval echoed through the hall. Inwardly, I too rejoiced. Surely this means that the Geats need not fear the Swedes for some time to come! One less enemy to threaten my Inga! Suddenly a man whose back had been turned to me, rose to his feet and cried out.

"Wes heil to King Hrolf! Hrolf Kraki, King of the Danes!"

Kraki? Why, that is the name I once gave to my cousin Hrothulf years ago! How comes it that he is called 'Kraki' before all this folk?

In amazement I squinted to make out the features of the man waving his goblet.

Ah, I might have known. Wherever Bjarki goes, there also goes Hjalti! But this Hjalti is far different from the stripling I met at Uppsala. Broad-shouldered, with muscles bulging in his forearms, and a wide smile on his weathered face... he looks every inch the confident warrior!

Hjalti must have felt my eyes upon him, for during the ensuing hubbub he strode to my table and bowed low.

"Lady Freawaru, well met. What brings you to Breccasberg?"

"I'll ask you the same question," I answered evenly. "After your apparent defeat of King Eadgils, I would have thought you'd return immediately to Heorot."

He shrugged. "We've already been back. Bjarki and I had in mind a side trip to visit Brecca's market — to get trinkets for the ladies, you know," he added with a grin.

My eyes widened in amusement.

"With all your soldierly duties, you still have time for women?"

"Of course!" laughed Hjalti. "I myself have several sweethearts, and Bjarki is betrothed to one of King Hrolf's daughters."

Now my amusement turned to sudden surprise — and something like anger.

"So, Hrolf took himself a wife! Who is this new queen at Heorot?" Hjalti shook his head vigorously.

"Nay, nay, King Hrolf has never married—but he has two daughters from liaisons with freemen's daughters. They are named Drifa and Skur." Reaching up, I took his hand.

"Sit with us, Hjalti, and tell me about King Hrolf's court. After our stay in Breccasberg we plan to visit Heorot, and I would learn more of conditions there."

"Gladly, my lady, but first let me fetch Vögg. I fear he may be hiding away from this great assembly, unsure of his place in it."

"Vögg? Who is Vögg?"

"You'll soon see. Excuse me."

Hjalti bowed again, then hurried off to make his way through the hall. I turned to my companions at the table.

"Wonder of wonders! King Eadgils is laid low, and Bodvar Bjarki takes a wife!"

"Why do you wonder at that, my lady?" murmured Runa beside me. "Surely every man deserves some happiness."

I stared at her, taken aback, but before I could form an answer Hjalti had returned, hauling a small, skinny young man with a beak of a nose below pale blue eyes, and not much of a chin. He was shabbily dressed, but below his sleeve a glint of gold gleamed in the rush lights.

"Pardon, ladies." The lad hesitated as Hjalti drew him down to a place beside us. "Pardon."

"This is Vögg," said Hjalti matter-of-factly. "He did us much service at the court of King Eadgils, and now he serves King Hrolf Kraki."

I lifted my hand as we moved down to make room for the newcomers. "Hjalti, I want to ask you about that name. How did Hrolf come to be called 'Kraki'?"

"Oh, I can tell you about that, my lady," beamed Vögg, "for I myself gave him the name. I told him that he was almost as bony as me—a real kraki—tall and thin as a tree ladder. Then all of his men laughed and hailed him as King Hrolf Kraki. He rewarded me with these gold rings! See?"

Proudly he lifted his arms to display two coils of gold.

"A most generous reward for a simple jest!" I remarked.

Vögg's face fell.

"Oh, no, my lady! I vowed on the spot that if ever King Hrolf is overcome by his enemies, and I alive, I will avenge him!"

Stifled laughter greeted Vögg's declaration, but he was so boyish and so earnest it was impossible not to like him.

"So, Vögg, what is your future now?" I asked lightly.

"Oh, my lady, to serve King Hrolf and his men, as long and as bravely as I can!"

"Well said, Vögg." Hjalti clapped the youngster on the back. "The lady beside you is King Hrolf's cousin, Lady Freawaru. She is coming soon to Heorot to revisit her homeland. Mayhap you will serve her too."

Vögg's eyes grew wide and he nodded his head.

"Gladly, my lady, gladly. Vögg is at your service."

Chapter Four
Foreign Shores

Belt buckle in silver, gold, and bronze with garnets and engraved figures. Aker in Vang, Norway.

During their brief stay at Breccasberg, I arranged to hold several conversations with Bjarki and Hualti. From Hjalti I learned further details about their journey to Uppsala, details not disclosed by Bjarki in his public account, details which filled me with some foreboding.

Hjalti and I had found a suitable place on a rocky ledge overlooking the harbor. We were sitting there comfortably, letting the spring sunshine warm our backs as we dangled our feet. Over our heads gulls cried as they swooped and soared. Hjalti was eager to speak, delighted to tell me more.

"King Hrolf started out with his twelve champions, plus twelve berserkers and a hundred warriors. Along the way, however, the king sent the berserkers and all of the warriors back to Heorot, so when we finally arrived at Eadgils' court we were a small band."

"What? Why did he send back so many men?" I asked in astonishment.

Hjalti's eyes narrowed.

"On the road, in the midst of the wilderness, we met a tall old man wearing a broad-brimmed hat and a blue cloak that seemed to wrap him in shadow, leaning on a spear. He called himself 'Hrani' and offered us hospitality for the night — all of us! He provided it too: fine food and good cheer. But during the night it grew so cold that many sprang up to fetch more clothes and blankets. In the morning Hrani advised King Hrolf to send back half his troop — the fifty warriors who had shivered the most — saying they would face worse challenges at Eadgils' court. The king did so."

"What?" I exclaimed again. "Why would the king take such advice from a stranger?"

Hjalti shook his head.

"We all knew there was something uncanny about this Hrani. King Holf even muttered, 'You are no common man,' when he agreed to accept his advice."

"Hmmm. I see. Go on."

Hjalti took a deep breath.

"On our second night, though we had travelled far over hills and through wildwoods, to our surprise and wonderment we met the same old man. Again he offered us hospitality for the night and again the king accepted. Hrani's hospitality was good, except that a great thirst overtook us in the night, and everyone save the king and us champions drank deeply from the mead barrel at the end of the room. Hrani observed this and told King Hrolf that worse troubles than thirst awaited us at Eadgils' court."

Hjalti paused, as if remembering that night, then resumed his story.

"The next morning a blizzard kept us indoors, and that night the fires were stoked so high that sweat rolled off us in waves. Many men shifted back from the heat, but the king never moved an inch, and we champions sat our places beside him. Again, Hrani gave advice: 'King Hrolf, send home all those men who moved back from the fire.' In the end, the king sent back his remaining fifty men as well as the berserkers. That left us twelve: Bjarki, myself, Svipdag, Hvitserk, Beigadh, Hromund, Hrolf the namesake, Haaklang, Hrefill, Haaki, Hvatt and Starulf."

Slowly I repeated the names to myself, then startled as an image suddenly came to me.

"Tell me, Hjalti, since your name means 'hilt,' are you not the hilt to Bjarki's blade? And is not Svipdag the shield? Are you three the heart of King Hrolf's defenses?"

Hjalti nodded in satisfaction.

"You speak true, my lady, but there is more to my story."

He cleared his throat and his voice dropped lower as he leaned in toward me.

"On our return from Uppsala we encountered Hrani a third time. Again he invited us inside his hall, a room of fire and shadows. This time on a table lay a sword, a shield and a byrnie. Hrani offered these as gifts to King Hrolf, but the king frowned, for in truth the weapons were black and ugly and strangely made. When King Hrolf seemed to treat the gifts as unworthy, possibly accursed, Hrani flew into a rage, declaring that great woe would befall us for refusing him. As a result, we mounted hastily and rode off, although night was almost upon us."

I had listened with growing dismay to Hjalti's story, and could contain myself no longer.

"Hjalti! Surely that was Odin the Wanderer in the guise of a mortal! You had his favor in the battles against Eadgils, but now...?"

Hjalti nodded ruefully.

"Yes, my lady, but now... We all came to the same conclusion, for when we reconsidered and rode back to make peace with Hrani, both man and hall had disappeared. Only then did King Hrolf recall that Hrani had only one eye."

A shiver went through me. Odin the One-Eyed, Father of Victories. To lose his favor is to face certain death in battle. I shivered again. Despite our differences in the past, I do not wish to see Hrolf—or Heorot—destroyed.

It was of Heorot that I spoke with Bodvar Bjarki. King Brecca was keeping me close to entertain him with tales of Beowulf's deeds, but I managed to slip away one afternoon when the king drifted off to sleep, joining Bodvar for a stroll through the market. Bodvar was seeking a gift for his bride-to-be; I was seeking information.

In the area nearest the settlement we saw local goods laid out for inspection: tools, soapstone molds, whetstones and bars of iron. Nearby, baskets of down and feathers invited us to touch, as did the furs of bear, marten, otter and beaver. Walrus teeth glistened in the afternoon sun, and antlers caught at the edge of my gown as we made our way toward the foreign traders, offering such goods as grain, honey, salt, wine, glass — and thralls.

Near the slave market I noticed a flash of color. Oh, yes, that little russet-haired girl again. I saw her run quickly up to a chained woman, press a hunk of bread into her hand, then dart off again. How remarkable! But I had business of my own to attend to.

"Tell me of King Hrolf," I began, taking Bodvar's arm. "How has he fared since becoming king, since the death of my father?"

"That was before my time at Heorot, as you know, my lady, but I've heard that at first King Hrolf was too lax with his companions, letting them riot at will. At the same time he was over generous, freely giving out treasure. It was said abroad that no king's men were better housed, clothed, feasted, armed and ring-bedecked than his men. That is one reason I decided to join him."

"I see," I said, nodding in understanding. "Oh, look, Bodvar, an amber merchant! You may find something at his stand for your Drifa."

Stepping around a stack of ship's rope piled high as my waist, we made our way forward.

"What is her coloring, your Drifa?"

Bodvar paused and stared as if seeing his woman before him.

"Fair, but with a glint of red in her hair — much like yours, my lady."

"Then amber would be perfect for her! Let's see what's on offer."

After Bodvar settled on a necklace of amber beads interspersed with gold roundels, we headed back toward Brecca's hall. On the return walk I heard more of my cousin Hrolf's doings, for with his trading behind him, Bodvar was ready to talk.

"King Hrolf established a new settlement after the mead hall at Heorot accidentally burned. He named it 'Hroar's Spring,' in honor of your father, and there houses hundreds of warriors and berserkers. With these warriors he has brought all the islands around Zealand under his control, as well as the province of Scania. His strength and his right to rule are unquestioned. It is an honor to serve him."

"The king is lucky to have such men as you, Bodvar," I said quietly. "And I did not know of this new settlement you spoke of. I am glad my father is remembered in the naming. Perhaps . . . perhaps Hrolf and I could be friends, after all. Perhaps."

I frowned, then brightened.

"How fares my old friend Unferth? Is he well?"

Bodvar turned to me and paused, as if considering.

"I cannot say, my lady. Unferth keeps to himself and is seldom seen. When he does come to the mead hall, he sits with the berserkers."

"Berserkers? Aye, he has some experience with such men."

I remembered the story of Unferth's own blind rage long ago and the unintentional killing of his two brothers.

"My lady, may I ask a question of my own?" Bodvar's voice interrupted my reverie.

"Why, of course, Bodvar. What is it?"

By now we had reached the mead hall and paused before the doorway. Bodvar turned and faced me squarely.

"My lady, Vögg reports that some of the young men in your bodyguard are openly boasting about you. They say the Lady Freawaru is a woman to be feared. They say she killed a man back in Geatland . . . What say you?"

I swallowed hard and drew back, then lifted my head to meet his gaze.

"It is true, Bodvar, though the act was not intentional — that is, not entirely."

Looking about to see if anyone were near, I drew Bodvar into the entry hall and there quietly described the events which had led to the death of Lars, ending with "In that moment, I was beyond the self I had known before."

Bodvar was silent for a moment, then spoke soberly.

"The fierce blood of the Skjoldungs courses in your veins, my lady. None of us can escape our Wryd. My two brothers are proof of that truth, as may I be one day," he concluded, eyes downcast.

"What do you mean, Bodvar? What truth?"

He raised his chin.

"The blood of beasts flows in my family line — a legacy of my bear-bewitched father. My older brother is a man from head to navel, but has an elk's body below. My second brother has the feet of a dog. I myself feel the pull of some terrible power within me that seeks to burst forth. Indeed, you saw it in Uppsala, Lady Freawaru, when you named me 'shape-changer.' I know not when the beast within me will come out, but I know it will come."

I took Bodvar's huge hands in mine and pressed them gently.

"Do not fear your own strength, my friend. You would not use it to do evil — only to protect those you love. I swear by the goddess that this is true."

He stared at me, then withdrew his hands. Reaching into the pouch at his waist he drew out the string of amber beads and held it aloft.

"So... my Drifa is safe... from me?" he choked.

"Yes, my lord, yes. Your Drifa is safe."

Suddenly Bodvar's other arm swept me into a bear hug that lasted only a moment. He released me, smiling.

"Thank you, Lady Freawaru. You have greatly eased my mind."

Into the silence that enfolded us broke the voice of Old Elsa.

"Lady Freawaru, is that you? King Brecca is calling for you!"

My women and I were by now quite comfortably settled in Old Elsa's house, where she lived with her daughters, Sonja and Liv, and their servant Josefa. Sonja and Liv were tall, big-boned women who had long slender fingers that flew over the loom like birds. They, I discovered, were responsible for the fine tapestries hanging in Brecca's mead hall. I spoke admiringly of their work, and our friendship was sealed when I shared with them gold threads from my sea chest.

Josefa, a lively girl barely older than Berit and Mari, immediately took charge of my thralls, putting them to work scrubbing pots, hauling firewood, and cleaning out the cattle byre. As the time was near for taking the cows up to higher pasture, Josefa also offered to take one or the other thrall with her for assistance and company. Neither was eager to go, for they had heard stories of trolls in the mountains. Josefa laughed at their fears, claiming that trolls were dumb-witted and slow — too slow to catch quick-witted girls. One night after the evening meal she told this story.

"I once heard that a troll on the east side of the valley shouted out, 'I hear a cow bellowing.' Five years later the troll on the west side of the valley answered, 'it could be a bull as well as a cow.' After another five years, the troll on the east side cried out, 'If you can't keep quiet and stop all this chatter, I'll have to move!'"

Mari and Berit did not join in the laughter that followed, and looked more worried than before. Josefa's tale set off a round of reminiscences among the womenfolk.

"I've always heard that if cows are tired in the morning, huffing and puffing, it means that trolls have ridden them," said Sonja, nodding wisely.

"Not all trolls are stupid," said Liv. "Why, I've heard that a troll once saw an old farmer bury his money under a storehouse, securing it with a magic spell so that no one except the farmer himself could dig it up. Later, when the old man died, the troll carried the body to the storehouse and used the dead man's hand to dig up the treasure."

A collective shiver followed this story, and for a while we sat in silence, staring into the fire. Then Old Elsa spoke.

"All this talk puts me in mind of a tale my grandmother used to tell me at bedtime, then. It goes like this: Once upon a summer there were three billy-goats on their way up the mountains to get fat on the rich green grass. They had to cross a rock bridge over a waterfall, and under that bridge lived an ugly old troll. It had squinty eyes, ears as big as platters, and a long nose that ended in a snout.

First came the youngest billy: trip, trip, trip, trip.

'Who's that tripping over my bridge?' growled the troll.

'I'm the littlest billy and I'm on my way to the mountains to get fat on the grass,' said the goat in a teeny, tiny voice.

'I'm coming up to eat you!' roared the troll.

'Oh, no, don't eat me! Wait for my brother. He's much bigger than me!'

'Oh, very well,' grumbled the troll.

Soon along came the second billy: trot, trot, trot, trot.

'Who's that trotting over my bridge?' growled the troll.

'I'm the second billy goat, on my way up the mountain to get fat on the grass,' said the goat.

'I'm coming up to eat you!' roared the troll.

'Oh no, don't eat me! Wait for my brother. He's much, much bigger than me!'

'Very well then,' grumbled the troll.

Finally, along came the biggest billy goat: tramp, tramp, tramp, tramp. He was so heavy the bridge creaked and groaned under him.

'Who's that tramping over my bridge?' growled the troll.

'I am the *big* billy-goat!' said the goat in a big, deep voice.

'Now I'm coming up to eat you!' roared the troll.

'Come right ahead!' roared back the goat.

When the troll appeared on the bridge, the big billy charged it, poked out its eyes with his horns, and butted it over the edge into the waterfall below. Then he went up the mountain, where he and his brothers ate lots of green grass and got very, very fat. As for the troll, you can see it to this day: a big lump of rock at the bottom of the falls. Snip, snap, snout, my tale's told out."

A murmur of approval rippled around the circle of listeners, but I noticed doubtful expressions on the faces of Mari and Berit.

"Of course," remarked Josefa after a moment, "What you really have to worry about up in the mountains are not trolls, but wolves — and bears. Of course if you have your lur pipe with you, you'll be in no trouble."

"Lur pipe? What... what's a lur pipe?" asked Mari through chattering teeth.

"I'd show you," said Josefa, yawning, "but mine is up at the hut — too heavy to carry back and forth. It's a long, wooden pipe that you blow into, hard. It makes an awful noise and scares off the wild beasts."

Sonja looked up with a smile. "I remember as a young girl making lurs out of birch bark. We'd cut a spiral in a tree, peel it off and wind it into a long cone shape. We used them just for fun, though, and by the end of one day it would be worn out."

Wide-eyed, Mari looked from Sonja to Josefa.

"Don't worry, little one,' said Runa dryly, reaching out to pat Mari's hand. "They just want to scare you. If you have no fear, a troll can have no power over you."

Josefa grinned. "The mountains do hold dangers, but they also hold delights — like blueberry bushes and cloudberries and wild flowers among the heather."

Berit's eyes lighted up at the mention of food, but Mari still frowned.

"Time for bed, then, everyone," declared Old Elsa, rising. "And Josefa, if those girls wake up screaming in the night, you're the one will have to quiet them!"

Long after Josefa and two little thralls had retired to their loft above the cattle, I could hear Lempi and Lise whispering from their benches.

"See? I told you mother was right. There *are* trolls in these mountains!"

Cloak of Ashes

Ever since our arrival at Breccasberg, I had wanted to thank the goddess for our safe journey, so one morning I asked Old Elsa where the women here made their offerings.

"Oh, you mean to the nisse? We generally leave a bowl of porridge in one of the outbuildings at nightfall, then."

"Nisse? Is that a local goddess? I don't know that name."

Old Elsa regarded me with amusement, hands on her broad hips.

"Why, nisse are the spirits who guard our houses and farms! Some calls them 'tomte' or 'tusse,' but anyway it's bad luck not to feed them. Now I don't hold with giving offerings to nix and the like, water spirits, you know, but we've always honored our nisse. Don't the Geats do the same?"

"Nooo," I said slowly," that is a custom unknown in Geatland. By offerings, I meant to the goddess Freyja and Nerthus, Earth Mother. Are they not honored in this country?"

Old Elsa frowned. "Thor is the god we honor — though some do worship Odin, then. Mostly it's the men who tend to such matters."

I was shocked to hear this. How could the Brondings ensure the fertility of their fields, their animals, their people, without the blessings of the goddess? I tried not to show my dismay, however, and tried again.

"Do you have any sacred places where offerings are made?"

Old Elsa screwed up her nose and blinked.

"Well, there are holy springs nearby, and rock carvings in the mountains — but then they're a ways off."

"Rock carvings?"

Instantly my thoughts flew to the place where Beowulf and I had first become one. I smiled at the memory, then realized Old Elsa was speaking again.

"If you want to see them, ask Vigo to take you. He knows the area."

"Thank you, I may do that. But it concerns me that no tribute is being paid to the female gods here. Were there ever — in the old days — sacred rituals conducted?"

Old Elsa frowned. "Queen Brigitta used to lead the women in some such, but she died long ago . . . I don't really remember."

"Do you think the women of Breccasberg would be interested . . . in renewing such rituals?" I asked tentatively.

"Can't say."

Old Elsa drew herself up somewhat stiffly and blew out a breath.

"Plenty to do here already. Spring planting and all... If you're staying a while, you could help, you and your women, then," she said pointedly, waving toward the benches where we had slept.

"Of course we'll help," I said quickly. "We'll be happy to. I am especially interested in herbs: the kinds you grow here and how you use them."

Her gaze softened.

"Well now, that's something I *do* know about! The herb shed has been my care for many a moon. Come with me, then. I'll show you!"

The rest of that morning was spent in a large, airy drying shed, hung with row after row of herbs. Most of them I already knew, but a few were new to me.

"'Yarrow' you call it? And what is its use?" I asked, sniffing the pale, dried flowers Elsa placed in my hand.

"To stop the flow of blood and ease pain from wounds," she said matter-of-factly.

"A most valuable herb!" I exclaimed. "I wish I'd known of it when treating Tor's wound! And what is this plant with the large, coarse leaves?"

"Dock. Good for skin rashes, then. All parts of the plant can be used — roots, seeds and leaves — boiled and mixed with animal fat."

"Again, most useful. Now here's another plant not familiar to me." I held up a long, dry root.

"That's kvann. It doesn't grow here, so we get it from traders. Some place the root directly on wounds to help with healing, but I use yarrow for that. I make a tea from the leaf and fruit of kvann for stomach problems –and sometimes give it to the younger women when they have cramps with their moon blood."

That morning Old Elsa also taught me the use of tepperot, for stopping diarrhea, and juniper for relieving pain in the joints.

"Elsa, you have been most generous in sharing your knowledge with me," I said warmly. "How can I thank you?"

After a moment she pulled down a handful of leafy stalks and held it out to me.

"If you can get kvann to grow here, we'd all thank you! I've had no success, though I've tried many times."

"Perhaps..." I began, an idea forming in my mind. With the help of the goddess, perhaps Earth Mother herself... Aloud I said, "I'll be glad to try."

As we left the herb shed, I thought I saw a small figure darting around the corner.

"Who's there?" I called.

In response I heard only a giggle and the sound of bare feet padding away over the dirt path. When I turned to Elsa, she simply shrugged.

"Probably little Gerda. That girl has free run of the settlement since her parents died. Her remaining kin don't look after her properly." Elsa shook her head.

"Gerda, you say? What does she look like?"

"A scrawny imp with wild red hair. Now, about the kvann..."

When I spoke to my women later in the day, they responded eagerly to the idea of working in the gardens.

"Beg pardon, Lady Freawaru, but I do sometimes feel, well, useless here," said Lempi as she sat by her sea chest rearranging its contents. "It would be good to get my hands in the dirt again."

Beside her, Lise nodded agreement. Runa was even more blunt.

"What are we doing here, my lady? You've given the wergild to Tor's parents, but have made no move toward departure. Olaf tells me that our young men are getting restless too, not content with joining the occasional hunt."

I stared at her in surprise.

"Why, King Brecca bids me stay," I began, "and I had thought to help the women here reconnect with the goddess. They seem to have forgotten her."

Ginnlaug now surprised us all. She'd been stirring a pot of fish stew at the hearth, but suddenly turned to face us.

"Oh, don't go yet, Lady Freawaru! There's a man here who... likes me," she concluded shyly.

"What?" exclaimed Lise. "We've only been here a few days! Who is this man? How did you meet him?"

Ginnlaug reddened and put down the ladle.

"His name is Roald. He caught my eye at the market when our group was walking there, and later he spoke to me in the mead hall."

Ginnlaug's plain face shone with a light I had not seen there since before her sister's death.

"He's not handsome," she continued, looking down, "but then neither am I."

"Oh, Ginnlaug!"

Suddenly both Lise and Lempi sprang up and flung their arms around their companion.

"You're too good for any of these Brondings!" declared Lempi, tears in her eyes.

"For once I agree with my sister!" cried Lise, hugging Ginnlaug tightly.

"Stop! Stop! I can't breathe!" laughed Ginnlaug, shaking them off gently. She turned to me.

"I would not have spoken, my lady, but I have a strong feeling that... something may come of it."

Her last words were almost a whisper. All eyes now turned to me. What should I say? My own mind was not settled, yet...

"I have already promised our help with the spring planting," I said. "Beyond that — we'll see."

Ginnlaug beamed as Lempi and Lise embraced her again.

Just then Sonja and Liv came in from the dairy where they had been churning butter.

"What's happening?" asked Liv, wiping her hands on her apron.

"Ginnlaug has an admirer!" blurted Lise.

"One of the Brondings!" added Lempi.

"Oh? Who might that be?" asked Sonja, looking askance at Ginnlaug.

"His name is Roald," she said, flushing proudly. "He's tall and thin, with a scar on one cheek."

Sonja and Liv looked at each other with raised eyebrows.

"We know what he looks like," said Sonja slowly.

"We also know that he has a sweetheart on a nearby farm!" added Liv. "You'll be in big trouble if Hildeburh hears that Roald is courting you!"

"What?" cried Ginnlaug. "He told me he had no other woman!"

Liv smirked. "That's just man talk. They all say that. You can do as you like, but I'd warn you to steer clear of Hildeburh!"

Ginnlaug looked bewildered. "But I don't even know her!"

"You soon will," said Sonja, "unless you put Roald in his place and have nothing more to do with him!"

Now Ginnlaug looked totally miserable. Running to the door, she seized a cloak and fled from the longhouse. For a moment there was stunned silence as we looked at each other. When Lempi and Lise moved as if to follow Ginnlaug, I held up my hand.

"Leave her alone for now. She will have to work this out for herself. In the meantime, let's have no more talk on the subject."

Quietly, each woman returned to her work.

That night Olaf arrived at our door unexpectedly. He appeared to be in a very good mood as he entered Old Elsa's house, despite having to duck under the low door frame. He carried a very large bundle loosely wrapped in birch bark that left a trail behind him. Old Elsa bustled forward immediately.

"Here now — what's this, then? Are you dripping blood on my floor? Give that to me!"

Olaf handed over the heavy package, grinning.

"It's elk!" he announced. "A big kill! The lads and I brought it down this morning, but it took us the rest of the day to butcher it and pack it back to the settlement. Vigo took us far into the forest to hunt, for we wanted to contribute to the food supply — and I'd say we've done it!"

Runa embraced him, smiling, as the rest of the women crowded around the table where Elsa was unwrapping the meat.

"Ooh, we haven't had elk all winter!" squealed Liv.

"I like deer well enough, but elk is my favorite," declared Sonja.

"Me too," added Lise.

"There's enough here for a really big stew, then," declared Elsa. "Why, this could feed half of Breccasberg!"

"Let's do that — let's feed *all* of Breccasberg!" I cried, approaching the table where Elsa had already begun cutting the red mass into smaller chunks. "We could use the whole carcass. We could give a feast in the mead hall — to thank our hosts for their hospitality. What do you think?" I directed my question at Olaf, who nodded, and Elsa. She nodded also.

"If King Brecca approves. He is still the king. You'd better ask him, then."

"I'll do that! First thing in the morning!"

Olaf now turned toward me. "My lady, may I have a word with you?"

"Of course. Come this way."

We withdrew to the far end of the longhouse, away from the chatter of the group around the table, now all busily chopping and cutting. Before Olaf could speak, I had a few words to say.

"I congratulate you on a most successful hunt! And I'm glad to hear that Vigo has put his knowledge of local conditions to good use. Overall, how are they faring, our young men?"

Olaf rubbed his chin.

"They need to be kept busy, my lady. After the hunt today they're in high spirits, but they'll fall to quarreling soon enough. You made them your men, my lady. What would you have them do?"

He looked at me expectantly.

"Until we can leave for Heorot — soon, I hope — I have in mind a short side trip to see the rock carvings in the mountains nearby — after spring planting is done. Can you keep the men under control for a few more days?"

Olaf grinned. "I'll try. Now, my lady, I came here to bring up another matter: Runa and me. You once said we might be married here in Breccasberg. Do you still think that could happen? Soon?"

"Hmmm, yes, your wedding. I wonder... but there's so little time..."

"What are you thinking, my lady?" Olaf interrupted, looking at me with pleading eyes.

"The mead hall feast. Perhaps... we could announce your betrothal there?"

"Yes! Oh yes!" exclaimed Olaf, seizing my hands.

Amidst the group at the table I saw Runa's head lift and turn toward us.

"One problem, Olaf, is that this would delay our departure for Heorot. We'd need to make wedding preparations, and then there are the nine days of celebration for the wedding itself. Why, we might be here until mid-summer! I had hoped to be on our way long before that!"

Olaf sobered and dropped my hands.

"My lady, I know that Heorot is our destination, but we'll still have good sailing weather for many moons. A little delay here won't make that much difference, will it? Runa and I have waited so long!"

Again, his eyes pleaded with me. I nodded sympathetically.

"You are quite right, Olaf. So... to save time and to spare you further waiting, we could turn the mead hall feast into... your wedding feast. You and Runa could be joined in marriage then. What do you think?"

"I just heard my name," said Runa, appearing at Olaf's elbow. "What are you two talking about?"

"Our wedding, my dear!" announced Olaf, reaching out to enfold Runa in one arm. "Our wedding, here in Breccasberg!"

Runa frowned and eyed me with something like irritation.

"Am I always the last to be told about important decisions?"

"Calm yourself, Runa." I smiled. "Olaf brought it up and convinced me that the time is right for your union. Be grateful to him, not angry at me!"

"Beg pardon, my lady, I am grateful—to both of you!" Impulsively she embraced us both. "How soon?"

Extricating myself from her grasp, I laughed. "As soon as arrangements can be made—perhaps very soon. I will speak to King Brecca in the morning."

After some confusion about who was to marry whom, King Brecca gave his permission for both the feast in the mead hall and the marriage of Olaf and Runa.

"Are you sure, my dear, that you don't want to marry Edvard—or Erik?" He peered up at me from his customary place in the throne chair. "Fine lads, but backward with the women..." he drifted..."not like me ... I married Brigitta when she was just a girl... never thought I'd outlive her..."

Tears welled up in his eyes and he reached up to wipe them.

"So you'll be staying here for now? Good! I like that!"

Rousing himself, he bellowed an order. "Ulrik! Where are you? See that this lady is provided with whatever she needs!"

If Ulrik was surprised to learn that a wedding would take place two days hence, he did not show it.

"I will send messengers throughout the settlement to announce your intentions, and yes, we have a Hammer of Thor for the hallowing—a fine one made of bronze. Old Elsa can help you with the female side of things."

Old Elsa was indeed a great help, though she rolled her eyes when I first told her what we planned to do.

"So soon, then? Why does it have to be so soon?" she asked. "Is your Runa with child?"

"No, no," I replied. "It's not that, though we would be happy if she were. No, it's my own need to hurry to Heorot that pushes us."

I did not tell Elsa, or any of my women, that almost nightly my mother was appearing to me in dreams. At some times she seemed calm and serene; at other times she seemed to reach out as if from a dark pit, beseeching me to come to her, to save her from being swallowed up in darkness. Such dreams shook me, but in daylight faded into nothingness.

"Of course you know that the bride must wear red," said Elsa.

"No, I didn't know that. Why red?" I asked in surprise.

"To honor Thor, of course!" She shook her head. "I see that you're going to need a lot of help with this ceremony, then!

"We'll be very grateful for... your advice," I said meekly.

Finding something red was more of a problem than I'd anticipated. I never wore that color myself, feeling it did not accord with my auburn hair. Runa owned nothing red. We had begun to despair, when Ginnlaug provided the answer. She had watched as Lempi and Lise searched through their chests for any object of the desired color, without results. Slowly she opened her own chest, drew out a small bundle wrapped in linen and brought it to Runa.

"Here, Runa," she said quietly. "My mother made this long ago. I was saving it for my own wedding day—someday—but now I think that day will never come. Take it and wear it to join your Olaf."

We all crowded around Runa as she opened the bundle. Inside lay a long length of pattern braid woven in threads of grey and red with red rosettes worked on the surface.

"It's beautiful!" gasped Runa, tears coming to her eyes. "But, oh, Ginnlaug, I can't take this. You'll find your Olaf one day!"

"No, take it," said Ginnlaug, closing Runa's fingers around the braid. "There should be just enough to edge the top of your kirtle, and it will set off your dark hair. I want you to take it—please."

Runa gulped and embraced Ginnlaug fiercely.

"Thank you, thank you," she breathed into Ginnlaug's hair.

Cloak of Ashes

The wedding of Runa and Olaf was a relatively quiet ceremony — at the start. Runa looked like a queen, resplendent in her braid-trimmed kirtle and a circlet of gold I had placed in her hair. Olaf wore his best blue cloak, which brought out the deep-sea blue of his eyes. As they sat side by side in the throne chairs, their smiles lit up the hall.

King Brecca had delegated the blessing of Thor to his sons. Edvard proudly carried the great bronze hammer into the hall, and Erik used it to make the sign of Thor over the couple before placing it in Runa's lap. The bridal cup was drunk, and the feast began — such a feast!

As if released from a spell, everyone in the hall suddenly burst into exclamations as the elk's head was brought in first, carried by two servants, mindful of its spreading antlers. They set the head at the feet of Olaf and Runa. Next came bowls of steaming hot elk stew, followed by trays of freshly baked bread and pots of freshly churned butter. My women and I had labored late into the night to help produce these basics, and the results were greeted with enthusiasm by those assembled — a small group, to be sure, but this was spring planting season and most men were out in the fields supervising their thralls.

Foaming cups of ale were poured and toasts drunk: to Thor, to Freyr, to Niörd, to Tyr, to Bragi, and finally, to Odin. When I proposed a toast to Freyja, there was polite compliance, then everyone resumed eating.

"Who is Bragi?" whispered Ginnlaug at my side. She had been worried about seeing Roald in the mead hall, but did not want to miss Runa's special day. So far her would-be lover had not made an appearance.

"Bragi is the god of speech," I explained. "He gives men inspiration and he frees their tongues to compose verses."

"I wonder if Roald drinks to Bragi," muttered Ginnlaug. "His tongue knows how to fashion fair words."

I gave her a silent glance of sympathy — and saw, over her shoulder, a man enter the hall who must surely be Roald: tall, thin, with a prominent scar across one cheek.

"Don't turn your head, but I think Roald has just come in."

Her eyes widened in consternation.

"What should I do?"

"Stay seated and stay calm. If he speaks to us, I will answer him."

Ginnlaug shrank down on the bench, but I shook my head and pulled her upright.

"You have nothing to be ashamed of. He is the one who deserves blame!"

Like a bear drawn to honey, Roald made a bee-line for our table. There he stopped and bobbed an awkward bow.

"Lady Freawaru, is it?"

"And who might you be?" I answered coolly.'

"Roald is my name, Roald son of Radegar."

The women at my table exchanged meaningful glances. Liv tittered and put her hand to her mouth.

"What is your business with me?" I asked, keeping my face composed.

Roald cleared his throat and began, hesitantly.

"Ginnlaug... uh, the lady beside you... that is, she told me she is... under your protection. So... I was hoping... that I might have your permission... to court her!" he concluded in a rush.

"Should you not be asking that question of Hildeburh, your intended? She would surely have an opinion!" I said sharply.

Roald's mouth fell open and his face reddened. For a moment he gaped like a fish gasping for air. Then he turned — and ran straight into Vigo.

"Is this fellow bothering you, my lady?" glowered Vigo.

"Not any more — are you, Roald?"

The man shook his head dumbly, and backed away. Beside me I could hear soft sobs from Ginnlaug. Vigo remained standing beside our table, looking at the departing Roald.

"That fellow is a strange one. He seldom speaks to women. I'm surprised that he approached you!"

"What?" I cried. "We'd heard that he already has a sweetheart on a nearby farm, a girl named Hildeburh!"

Vigo frowned, looking puzzled. "That can't be true. Where did you hear that?"

Now all eyes turned to Liv, who squirmed in her seat, then spoke defiantly.

"Hildeburh herself told me! She said she was going to marry Roald one day! And when Hildeburh says a thing, she means it!"

Vigo laughed. "I wonder if Roald knows of her plan? I'd wager he doesn't!"

Beside me Ginnlaug was making choking sounds and I turned to pound her on the back.

"Are you alright?"

"Yes," she gasped, tears in her eyes. "Perhaps . . . perhaps Roald is innocent — and you drove him away!"

I sighed. "We will sort this out, I promise. But today is Runa and Olaf's day. Let us be joyful and help them celebrate appropriately."

"That means more ale!" grinned Vigo. "But I came to ask you a question, Lady Freawaru. I'd heard that you are interested in seeing the rock carvings in the mountains. Perhaps during the days of celebration we could make a brief trip to the site?"

"Thank you, Vigo, I'd like that very much. Perhaps . . . two days hence?"

"Agreed!" he nodded. "I'll go tell the lads."

'Oh, can we go too?" begged Lise. "Lempi and I have never seen these rock carvings."

I sighed again. "Yes, of course. We can all go — except for Olaf and Runa, who may have other plans . . ."

Our shared laughter seemed to restore good humor to the table.

I was glad to see the residents of Breccasberg enthusiastically taking part in the activities that followed the wedding: storytelling, wrestling, horse fights, riddle contests, tests of strength — and of course lots of drinking. Two of our lads, Sigrod and Anton, defeated all wrestling challengers and were finally forced to face each other. Anton came out on top — literally — and Sigrod ended up with a twisted ankle. Elsa, who had been among the onlookers at this contest, immediately hauled Sigrod off to her longhouse for repairs. Curious to observe her methods, I followed.

"Since you're here," she said, looking at me with resignation, "you can prepare a poultice to wrap around his ankle. Use some of that clabbered milk left from yesterday and mix it with barley flour. Spread it on a clean cloth."

She turned to Sigrod, who had limped in beside her.

"Here, you, stretch out on this table so I can feel for any broken bones, then."

Wincing and grinning, Sigrod obeyed. Elsa took off his leather boot, turned her back to me and bent low. To my surprise, I heard her spit, then begin mumbling what sounded like an incantation. Wanting to hear what she said, I worked as quietly as I could. Fortunately she

repeated the spitting and the mumbling twice more, and I was finally able to catch the words:
"Thor rode over a stony plain
One goat stumbled, its leg did sprain
Thor dismounted to cure the pain
He made the injury good again."
She jerked her head up. "Is that poultice ready, then?"
"Yes, here it is."
I hastened to bring the cloth and hand it to her. She inspected it carefully, grunted, then bound it around Sigrod's ankle.
"There. That should do it, then. No bones broken, but no wrestling for awhile."
Sigrod sat up. "My thanks to you — and to you, Lady Freawaru."
Grinning gamely, he slid off the table and limped out of the longhouse.
"Always a few injuries during a wedding celebration," observed Elsa, shaking her head sagely.
"Are you the healer for all of Breccasberg?" I inquired.
"I'm the one they come to first," she declared with a touch of pride in her voice.
"My mother, Queen Wealtheow, was the healer at Heorot and I learned much from her, but I'm learning more here. Milk, for example. I did not know it had healing powers."
Else regarded me with a mixture of surprise and pity.
"I've also used milk to soothe wounds and treat infections. Some say it can even ward off the evil eye, but I'm not sure about that."

The next day I saw another instance of the part Elsa played in the settlement, when she was called to attend a neighbor woman in labor. Elsa's daughters and my women had gone to watch the horse fighting. Since I had no desire to watch two beautiful stallions pitted against each other, I had stayed behind in the longhouse with Elsa.
"Come with me, then. You may be useful," she had barked, gathering up supplies.
"It's her third," puffed Elsa as we made our way to Gunnvor's door, "so this should be an easy birth, but you never know."
Behind us trailed Berit and Mari, their arms full of juniper branches, for Elsa had declared that burning juniper would keep away evil spirits.

As we entered, Gunnvor cried out, and my mind flew back to the awful night when Hygd had died in childbirth.

"May the goddess be with you!" I called out, my eyes fixed on the pale, sweaty woman writhing on her bench.

"Goddess?" she gasped. "I need... Old Elsa!"

"I'm here, then," announced Elsa flatly. She turned to the thrall who had fetched us. "Has her water burst? And where are Gunnvor's women?"

"I don't... I don't know," faltered the young girl. "Gone to watch the horses, I think."

"Huh!" grunted Elsa. "A fine time to leave alone a woman about to deliver! You two!" she shouted at my thralls, "put those branches on the fire, then leave us — all of you."

As the thralls scurried out, she turned to me.

"Lady Freawaru, if you'd like to help, check Gunnvor's opening, then; see how wide it is."

Mutely I advanced, pulled up Gunnvor's soaking wet gown and gently spread her legs.

"Her water bag has broken and I'd say... two fingers."

"Good, good! Gunnvor, relax until the next wave comes. It won't be long now."

But it soon became apparent that Gunnvor was in difficulty — and I saw the reason why.

"The head is not showing . . . there looks to be a foot presenting instead. The baby is turned wrong!"

Elsa's face fell; she muttered under her breath and began massaging Gunnvor's swollen belly, but nothing helped. Gunnvor's screams rent my heart. The situation was becoming desperate.

"Elsa, if we can get her down on her hands and knees, the baby might turn. That's worked before in Geatland."

Elsa turned on me fiercely, paused, then nodded. Together we eased Gunnvor off the bench and onto the wood floor, with me supporting most of the woman's weight.

"Come child, come child, let me see your face," crooned Elsa. "Come child, come child, come into this place."

I held my breath as Gunnvor moaned. For a time nothing happened. Then a crown of dark reddish hair appeared in the opening. Still crooning, Elsa eased out the head — and finally the body — of a large baby boy. Holding it up by the ankles she gave it a smack on the bottom and the infant wailed. Gunnvor collapsed, face down on the floor, weeping tears of relief and joy. I helped her turn over to receive the child on her breast.

"My baby... my boy... you saved him" she gasped.

As Elsa cut the cord that bound baby to mother, I asked about the afterbirth.

"Where do we save it? No doubt Gunnvor will want to bury it — and the cord — to protect her son from any evil use of it."

Elsa stared at me. "What a strange idea, then! You Geats are very superstitious!"

I would have protested, but I was fascinated by what I saw Gunnvor doing to her new son: she'd raised up on one shoulder and was squirting breast milk in the baby's eyes.

"Why is she doing that?" I asked, gesturing.

Elsa snorted. "To protect the baby against blindness, of course! Now, Gunnvor, where are your swaddling cloths?"

"On that shelf — to your right," said the weary mother, "and the insect dust is next to them in that small wooden pail."

Insect dust? What possible use can there be for insect dust? This time I kept quiet and simply watched as Elsa bathed the still-squalling infant in warm water that had been prepared earlier by the thrall. Next she sprinkled a yellow dust on a length of cloth and wrapped the baby tightly inside it. Instantly the child grew quiet.

Elsa now directed me to prepare a small pouch of chamomile flowers soaked in warm milk to soothe Gunnvor's sore birth canal.

"If we'd been called earlier, we could have given her a chamomile potion to relieve the labor pains," clucked Elsa. "No better herb for every stage of childbirth, then," she added. 'It can even help relieve the darkness of mind that sometimes follows the birth."

I nodded. "I've used it in other situations too: it can stop excessive bleeding and reduce swelling and inflammation. Yes, an excellent herb," I agreed.

I had noted the word 'we' in Elsa's earlier statement, and was pleased to be included

By now I had finished washing Gunnvor, and we helped her back up onto her sleeping bench. Elsa laid the baby in its mother's arms and sighed deeply.

"Our work here is finished, then," she breathed. "Now if her women would just return..."

Even as she spoke, the door flew open and a group of women and children burst into the house. The children ran to Gunnvor's bench. "Meet your new brother," she said weakly, managing a smile.

That night I joined the on-going wedding celebration in the mead hall, ready for songs and stories and riddles after the stress of my day. Runa and Olaf presided, as was the custom, but this time not in the throne chairs—where Brecca and his sons had resumed their usual places. I slipped onto the bench beside Ginnlaug at our table and whispered, "What have I missed?"

"Their Bragi-man, as they call him—their scop, their singer—has just finished reciting a long lay about Sigmund the dragon-slayer; earlier someone told a story about Thor dressing as a woman to get his hammer back from the giants."

I chuckled. "A favorite bedtime story when my brothers were little."

Glancing up, I saw Olaf rise, goblet in hand, and look about the hall. "Who has a riddle for us? Or who is ready to give us a verse?"

Slowly a burly man sitting near the front got to his feet and faced the assembly.

"Here is my riddle:"
Often I wrestle with wind and waves,
I dive to seek the depths in strange places.
I am strong in the struggle if I grow still.
If I fail in that, their force outweighs mine.
Wrenching me, they rout me instantly,
Fetch off what I must fasten.
I can resist if my root holds,
And stones stoutly keep me firm
Against their force. What is my name?

Murmurs filled the hall as Ginnlaug turned to me. "Do you know the answer, my lady?"

"Perhaps, but..."

Just then a tall young man leapt to his feet and shouted, "An anchor! It's an anchor!"

"Right you are," grunted the riddler, sitting down heavily.

The young man spread his arms wide and called out, "I too have a riddle, though it may embarrass the ladies present! Here it is:

"A man came walking where he knew

She stood in a corner, stepped forward,
The bold fellow, plucked up his own
Skirt by hand, stuck something stiff
Beneath her belt as she stood,
And worked his will as they both wiggled.
The man hurried; his trusty helper
Plied a handy task, but tired at length,
Less strong than she, weary of work.
Thick beneath her belt swelled the thing
All good men praise. What am I?"

I heard titters across the hall, but noted that Lise's face held a knowing smile. She rose from her seat and held her hand high for silence.

"I have had some experience with this thing of which you speak," she began.

Explosive laughter erupted across the hall.

"... but as all women know, this thing is the servant of women," she continued. More laughter. "It is bound to do her bidding, for this thing ... is ... a churn!"

Lise sat down amid hoots of approval. Now Vigo rose from our table and walked to the front of the hall.

"Here is a short one:
Who are the two who ride on the wind?
Three eyes have they, ten feet, one tail.
Hunting the living, claiming the dead,
Warning of pestilence, sickness and war."

A hush fell over the hall. Finally Edvard himself, the king's son, rose to his feet.

"Vigo, your riddle is ill-chosen for a wedding celebration, but I will answer you. You speak of Odin the One-eyed on his eight-legged horse, Sleipner. We do not honor Odin in this place, for he is not a god to be trusted. We honor Thor, honest like other men."

"Thor, Thor, Thor," chanted several young men nearby, pounding the table and raising their glasses.

Edvard held up his hand and the chanting ceased.

"I will close this night with a riddle of my own." He cleared his throat.
"I saw a traveler with neither eyes nor hands,
Shoulders nor arms. On one foot must it
Furrow its fields on mighty journeys. It has

Many ribs, a mouth in its middle.
It ferries goods to king and folk, brings
Yearly tribute in its belly. Tell me now,
Man wise in words, what this thing is."

His final words were directed squarely at Vigo, who had not wavered from his position.

"My lord," he said quietly, "you speak of a ship — and so we are equal."

Vigo left the front and returned to our table, his face stormy.

"What is it?" whispered Ginnlaug beside me. "What's wrong?"

"I don't know," I whispered back, "but I intend to find out."

Chapter Five
Planting

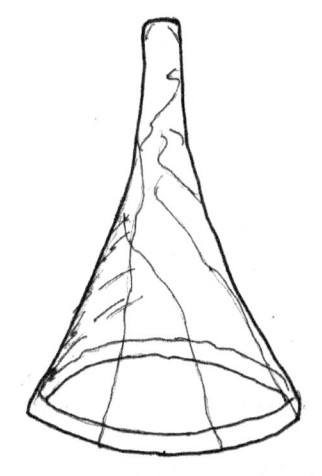

Funnel glass from a woman's grave at Birka, Sweden.

After we left the mead hall that night, I took Vigo aside to learn more about his previous history with Edvard. As we walked together in the full light of early summer, I asked him quietly, "What is the source of the ill will between you two?"

Vigo scowled.

"Edvard listens only to Edvard, since he knows he is always right. You heard him belittle Odin: that's how he also treats Odin's followers, which included Tor and me — one reason I left Breccasberg."

I pondered this.

"Does his brother Erik share his views? I've seldom heard Erik speak."

Vigo gave a snort.

"Erik blows with the wind, depending on which side can give him an advantage. He is quiet, but crafty."

"Hmm. Vigo, you once told me there was also a problem getting your rightful inheritance. Has that issue been settled?"

Vigo scowled again.

"Not to my satisfaction. When my father died, Edvard claimed the land, rightfully my land, as unpaid tribute—which Tovar did not owe in the first place! Having no relatives to support me, I could not defeat Edvard's claim."

"That's not right!" I exclaimed. "Did you take your case to King Brecca?"

Vigo laughed a hollow laugh.

"Brecca assured me the land was mine, but his word no longer counts. His sons control everything!"

Vigo's face looked grim.

"I see why you were so reluctant to come here—and I have put you in an awkward position," I said regretfully.

A faint smile crossed Vigo's face. "Revenge may yet be mine."

"What? Revenge? Be careful, Vigo—and remember that you have sworn an oath to serve me."

"My lady?"

Ginnlaug had caught up with us and was touching my elbow timidly.

"Someone is following me—and she looks very angry."

All three of us turned to look back. Ginnlaug was right. A beefy, red-faced woman was storming full tilt in our direction.

"It's Hildeburh," announced Vigo, chuckling. "Be prepared for a fight!"

As we stood, transfixed, the woman halted in front of us, eyes glittering, hands waving wildly.

"So you're the hussy who's trying to steal my Roald!" she bellowed.

To my surprise, Ginnlaug stood her ground.

"Has Roald told you that?" she asked coolly. "Or does Roald even talk to you?"

Hildeburh's mouth fell open and she charged at Ginnlaug, hands outstretched to grab her hair.

As Ginnlaug sprang back, Vigo thrust out an arm to stop the panting Hildeburh. All this commotion had attracted attention, and we quickly found ourselves surrounded by curious folk. I saw Liv's face in the crowd, looking gleeful but anxious.

"Let's get to the bottom of this," I declared, stepping between the two women. "Hildeburh, are you betrothed to Roald?"

"N-no," she stuttered, "but..."

"Hildeburh, were you ever promised to Roald by your parents?"

"No," she said again, turning even redder, "but..."

"Then what claim do you have on Roald?" I concluded.

Suddenly Hildeburh burst into angry tears.

"B-but, we grew up to—together," she hiccupped, "and he was always... nice to me... and I always thought we'd..."

Her outburst ended in a fit of coughing.

With the prospect of a female fight diminishing, most of the onlookers faded away, until only Liv remained. She put out a hand to comfort her sobbing friend.

"I tried to warn you, Hildeburh, I tried."

Hildeburh swatted away Liv's hand.

"Now I'll never get married! Roald was my last chance!" she wailed.

Then Hildeburh sniffed, drew herself up to her full height and spat at Ginnlaug, hissing, "Curse you! Curse you! I wish Roald had never laid eyes on you!"

Ginnlaug avoided Hildeburh's spittle, but blanched at her words, and Hildeburh followed up on her advantage.

"Yes, you'll be cursed if you marry Roald! You'll bear him no children! You'll... you'll..."

Suddenly Hildeburh turned and ran, still raging and sputtering. Ginnlaug, Vigo and I stood looking after the wretched woman. When I looked back at Ginnlaug, a faint smile played on her face.

"I never wanted children," she said quietly, "but I do want Roald."

When Ginnlaug and I finally reached Elsa's longhouse, I was exhausted. There are still three days left of the wedding celebrations, I thought to myself; what else can possibly happen? I soon found out.

On the day chosen for our trip to the rock carvings, an unexpected knock on the door brought an invitation—or was it a summons?—to join Lord Edvard on a tour of the area, by ship.

"You can't refuse him" advised Elsa. "You are guests in this country, only here with his permission."

Annoyed and perplexed, I turned to the messenger waiting at the door — a young lad with big eyes and bushy yellow hair.

"Please tell Lord Edvard that I will be happy to join him — if I may bring my women with me. Go now, and bring back his answer."

The lad nodded and ran off. He soon returned with Edvard's answer: bring your women. Lempi and Lise squealed with delight, but Ginnlaug was less enthusiastic.

"I was hoping," she said, "that after what happened with Hildeburh, Roald might try to seek me out again."

"Today is only one day," I said to console her. "I think Roald may speak to you — soon."

Somewhat mollified, Ginnlaug joined her companions in preparation for the outing.

Admittedly it was a fine day to be onboard ship: fair and mild with sunlight sparkling on the water. Edvard was clearly trying to be a gracious host, and his ship was a fine one. Instead of the wide-beamed cargo ship we'd grown accustomed to, Edvard's long, elegant craft flew through the water, propelled by sixteen oarsmen when wind did not suffice. Although its gracefully curved prow did not end in a figurehead, I noticed a finely carved animal head on the tiller, manned by Edvard himself.

His ship took us deep into the fjord. To the north and west we saw huge tree-covered mountains separated by deep valleys, and occasionally caught glimpses of snow-covered plateaus. Sheer cliffs lined most of the winding fjord. To the east we saw broad sloping valleys that opened onto comparatively flat areas. Here we saw an occasional farmer's house among the gently rolling land, backed by endless dark forests. A few fishing boats bobbed along the shoreline.

"It's so warm here," I observed to Edvard, removing the heavy cloak I normally used on shipboard.

He smiled, showing a full set of evenly spaced teeth below his bristling red mustache. He handed the tiller to one of his men and came to stand beside me at the ship's rail.

"It's due to the westerlies," he explained, "the prevailing winds that bring in moist air. This fjord never freezes, so we can use it all year. Even as far north as Finnmark the fjords rarely freeze over."

"Finnmark? Two of my thralls came from Finnmark," I murmured. "Do you often travel that far?"

"Indeed yes. As you may have noticed, Breccasberg is rich in trade goods — including thralls."

"So, your wealth is based on trading . . . not raiding?" I commented lightly.

Edvard frowned, then laughed.

"Trade and tribute are certainly the main sources of wealth here. The Lapps and Finns, for example, pay a yearly tribute in walrus skins, whalebone, oil, robes, feathers and the like. Why, one high-ranking chief recently sent fifteen marten skins, five reindeer robes, one bearskin, ten baskets of feathers, a mantle of otter skin and sixty lengths of sealskin ship rope!"

He smiled broadly, clearly very pleased with himself.

"Is it not the same in Geatland?" he asked.

"Not exactly," I said. "Beowulf never required . . . tribute . . . from his neighbors."

Then, remembering that a disagreement over tribute lay at the heart of the contention between Edvard and Vigo, I changed the subject.

"I did see wonderful baskets of down and feathers displayed in the market. Which birds provided those?"

Edvard shrugged. "Probably eider ducks from along the north coast — and sea eagles. We also have ptarmigan in the mountains and many kinds of wild fowl in the forests." He looked at me shrewdly. "Do you fancy a feather cloak — like Freyja's?"

His question caught me off guard.

"Why, no . . . that is . . . I do not wish to rival a goddess." I looked at him directly. "I am surprised, Lord Edvard, to hear you speak of the goddess Freyja. The women of Breccasberg seem to have little interest in such matters."

Edvard looked away.

"My own mother once worshipped the goddess," he murmured, "but it did not save her." He turned back to face me. "It is best not to put your trust in things unseen."

With an apparent effort his face brightened. "Now, my lady, we have almost reached the place you've been wanting to see: a legacy from the ancients, carved in rock."

Taking the tiller again, he steered toward a sheer rock face coming up on the port side. As we drew closer, he called out "Hold your oars!"

As we glided to a stop, my women rushed to the gunnel and we craned our necks to look up. Above our heads but clearly visible loomed a profusion of colorful lines incised in the rock: circles, human figures, ships, animals, more ships with men in them... we gazed in awe at these images from the ancient past.

Unlike the straight lines used in rune-carving, I saw that these images included circles within circles, and elegant curved lines depicting horses drawing carts, farmers plowing, warriors with weapons...

"Look, Lady Freawaru!" Lise was pointing up to the right. "Are those oxen? They look so big!"

"Those may be the aurochs I've heard about," I reflected. 'See the size of their horns?"

Ginnlaug was counting aloud the oarsmen placed inside the longest ship: "... ten... twenty... why, there are thirty men in that one ship!"

"Yes, they must have had to row," I added, "for I see no mast or sail."

"How old are these pictures?" asked Lempi.

Edvard answered for me. "I know not, but they were here in my grandfather's grandfather's time."

Beside me Lempi shivered. "This place makes me feel... uneasy. Do you feel it, my lady?"

"Yes, I do." I put an arm around Lempi's shoulder. "I hear the voices of the dead, speaking to us through pictures."

Now Edvard raised his voice to be heard above the rising wind.

"I've also seen stone circles and burial mounds further inland. They may be connected to these carvings."

I nodded and shivered myself, gazing at the images in reverent silence. My thoughts flew back to Geatland, where Beowulf and I had once stood hand in hand, gazing down at similar images from the past, trying to puzzle out their meaning.

"Have you seen enough?" called Edvard from the tiller.

"A moment more," I called out, looking for something that resembled a woman, or — as I had seen on the rock carvings in Geatland — a man and a woman coupling. Nothing of the sort met my gaze.

"Yes, thank you, that's enough," I shouted back to Edvard. "Thank you for showing us this — this great treasure."

As we pulled away from the site, Lempi leaned toward me.

Cloak of Ashes

"Why would the ancient ones leave such pictures here?" she asked.

"They were probably marking a sacred place nearby — as Edvard suggested — where fertility rituals might have been performed," I said.

"Fertility rituals?" Lempi gazed at me. "Do you mean for...?"

I nodded, smiling. "For success in hunting perhaps, for fertility in fields, animals and humans. For the same reason we sacrifice to the goddess."

On the return trip at dusk we sailed past numerous islands hunched like great beasts ready for sleep. Above us pink clouds were lit by a huge red sun that dropped suddenly behind the western cliffs.

"You will dine with me tonight," shouted Edvard. "We will... review the day."

"As you wish, my lord," I answered, but felt no great joy at the prospect. "I'm sure your father will want to hear of our... adventure," I added.

He frowned, but nodded.

As my women and I trailed up to Elsa's longhouse that night, tired after an exhilarating day, the little girl with russet hair was waiting outside — for me.

"Here, lady." She held out a long white feather, a swan's feather.

"For me? Why, thank you... are you Gerda?"

She nodded shyly and was about to dart away, but I caught her hand — briefly.

"Please wait, Gerda. Why are you giving me this?"

"I like you," she said, flashing a smile, and was off.

"What a strange child," commented Lise, looking after the slight figure already almost out of sight.

"Strange because she likes me?" I teased.

"No, strange because she moves like... a wild thing, like a little bird. Her feet barely touch the ground!"

"She's so thin she probably weighs less than a bird," commented Ginnlaug. "If she comes around again, we should invite her inside for a good meal!"

I nodded agreement.

"Speaking of meals, I must get ready to go to the mead hall and share a meal with Lord Edvard."

"Perhaps Lord Edvard likes you too!" said Lise mischievously. "Perhaps he'll give you a white feather!"

"If he does, you'll be told," I said dryly. "Now let's see if Elsa needs our help with supper."

That night at the mead hall I was directed to a side chamber, where I found that I was to dine alone with Lord Edvard. At Elsa's insistence I had added some jewelry to my costume, and Edvard nodded admiringly when I entered.

"I like to see a woman adorned with gold," he declared. "It becomes you. Sit down!"

Biting my lip at being commanded like a servant, I nevertheless smiled graciously and took a place across the table from him.

"Where is King Brecca tonight?" I asked coolly. "I did not see him in the mead hall."

"His joints are bothering him again. He's getting old."

Edvard shrugged and poured wine for the two of us.

"He should see Old Elsa for a remedy — perhaps a dose of juniper," I offered. Evard made no response.

Picking up my wine, I took a sip and let its sweetness soothe my irritation. Edvard leaned forward, breathing heavily. I could tell he had already consumed a quantity of ale.

"Shall we drink a toast to Freyja?" he murmured.

"That would be fitting, as we are still celebrating the marriage of Runa and Olaf for one more night. Hail to the goddess of love!" I lifted my cup.

"Hail," echoed Edvard, draining his cup and setting it down with a bang.

"It is of marriage that I would speak ... Lady Freawaru."

He fixed his large round eyes upon me — and belched.

"Has Brecca been pressuring you again?" I asked lightly. "I have told the king repeatedly that I will never marry. I serve only the goddess."

Edvard regarded me dolefully and belched again.

"He told me you would say that, but women often change their minds. What can I do to please you?" he asked earnestly.

"You could give back to Vigo the land that is rightfully his!" I blurted.

Edvard's face darkened and he rose, scowling.

"That is no business of yours, lady. I keep what is mine, and that land is mine! Say no more about it!"

He sat down again, but spoke little during the meal that followed, and swore at the servant who was slow to refill his cup.

Freawaru, I told myself you have been a peace-weaver in the past. Call upon those skills now. Say what you know to be true—but say it carefully.

"Lord Edvard," I said finally, "I thank you for the great hospitality you have shown me and my people. The bond between the Geats and Brondings is a tie of long standing that should remain unbroken. I leave soon for Heorot. Let us part as friends."

Edvard hiccupped and wiped his mouth with a sleeve before responding.

"Lady... Lady Freawaru. I thank you... for your gracious... words. Friends... we shall be—but I'm not saying I'll give anything to Vigo!" he finished in a rush.

"As you wish, my lord," I said calmly. "You are a generous man. I'm sure you will deal fairly with Vigo."

Edvard stared at me thoughtfully and nodded, imperceptibly.

When we left the side chamber, a tall fellow standing in the shadows stepped forward. It was Roald. He addressed Edvard respectfully.

"Lord, may I have leave to address this lady?"

Edvard looked in surprise from Roald, to me, to Roald.

"It's alright, Lord Edvard," I said, placing a hand on his arm. "Roald is courting one of my women. Isn't that right, Roald?"

A smile spread slowly across the man's homely, honest face.

"Yes, my lady, that's right."

All the women in Elsa's house were still up when I returned. Liv and Sonja stood working next to their mother at the three looms. Lise and Lempi sat together winding yarn onto shuttles. Ginnlaug was standing at the worn wooden table, chopping vegetables for tomorrow's stew. Lise raised her head upon my entrance.

"Well, my lady, were you offered a white feather?" she smirked.

"Yes, but I did not accept it. Ginnlaug, however, can expect a visitor soon!"

A shriek drew all eyes toward Ginnlaug. Gasping, she held up a finger dripping with blood. Elsa turned, assessed the situation and shouted an order:

"Liv! Quick! Fetch the nest!"

Liv dropped her shuttle and hurried to a dark corner of the longhouse. Reaching up, she extracted a long stick from a crack in the wall and brought it to the table. On one end hung an empty wasp's nest.

"Give me your hand," commanded Elsa, waddling over.

Mutely Ginnlaug lifted her left hand, now covered with blood. Elsa tore off sections of the papery nest and pressed them against the wound. Sonja brought her a strip of linen to bind it off.

"There, then. That will absorb the blood and help it clot," declared Elsa. "If infection sets in, we'll soak it in fresh, hot cow manure!"

Ginnlaug's face wavered between tears and laughter. Finally she smiled, weakly.

"Thank you, Elsa. I'm not usually so clumsy!"

Contrite at having startled Ginnlaug with a knife in her hand, I patted her shoulder gently.

"Forgive me, Ginnlaug, for the surprise, but you will be seeing Roald in the morning."

The next night was the final feast in the nine days of celebration for Runa and Olaf's wedding. I had barely seen Runa in all that time, except for her nightly hosting of festivities. She and Olaf spent most of their time in a longhouse they were sharing with the family of one of Elsa's brothers.

The elk meat had long since been consumed, but the silver in my chest purchased quantities of dried cod and fresh herring to extend the feasting. Brecca himself had insisted upon supplying ale for all the participants, in honor of his old friend Beowulf, he said.

On that final night I looked about me with satisfaction. King Brecca, Edvard and Erik sat in their proper places in the throne chairs; just below them Runa and Olaf presided over the feast. Despite the onset of summer and the heat from the hearth, Runa was wearing a dazzling white fur collar — Olaf's morning-gift, she'd told us, a fur he'd found in the market, something called 'ermine.' It set off her dark hair and eyes beautifully. Seated across from me at our table were Ginnlaug and Roald, who only had eyes for each other. Ginnlaug's plain face was radiant as she basked in Roald's attention.

The longer days of summer seemed to encourage merry-making, and the number of celebrants had grown each night. Tonight the mead hall was nearly full: thanes and athelings dressed in fine tunics and cloaks, farmers and their wives in working clothes, our group of Geats

Cloak of Ashes

with hair freshly washed and braided, even a few foreign traders, all eating and drinking, carousing together. A positive conclusion to our stay in Breccasberg.

I had not found time to re-introduce goddess worship to the women of Breccasberg, but I had helped plant the herb gardens—including a small plot devoted to kvann. We'll be leaving before it can sprout—if it ever does—but I did sacrifice to Earth Mother when I planted the seed. In time kvann may grow and flourish here. I smiled, recalling that morning.

I had chosen a private moment, rising early and slipping out to the herb gardens before Elsa's household was awake. As I knelt in the freshly turned earth, I prayed to Nerthus, asking her blessing on the seeds we had planted. Then taking the knife that hung at my waist, I pricked a finger and let drops of blood fall onto the soil. When I looked up, a small face met mine.

"What are you doing?" asked Gerda, crouched at the edge of the plot.

"Making a sacrifice," I answered calmly. "Sometimes we must give up something precious to bring about good."

"May I help?" she asked.

"Yes, but not with your blood," I said. "After I am gone, you could water and tend to the seedlings."

"You're going away?" Her face filled with dismay and she sprang to her feet. "Don't go!"

"I must—my mother is calling me."

Now why did I say that? The child has lost her own mother . . . how foolish of me!

Gerda stared at me for a moment, then turned and fled.

"Lady Freawaru? Would you like more ale?" Lempi's voice brought me back to the present.

The next morning Olaf, Vigo and I went down to the harbor to examine our ship, to assure ourselves that all was fit for our voyage to Heorot. While Olaf was inspecting the hull, Vigo took me aside, an uncharacteristic smile playing over his face.

"Lady Freawaru, Lord Edvard has made me an offer. He still wants to keep my father's land, as it lies next to his own holdings, but he has offered other land in exchange—on the strandflat—or, he will give me the equivalent value in livestock. What would you advise?"

My eyes widened in surprise and pleasure.

"So . . . Edvard has made you an offer! Well, well — but what is this 'strandflat' you speak of? I do not know of it."

"The strandflats are narrow strips of flat land along the coastline, suitable for habitation," he explained.

"Hmmm. Do you wish to remain here, Vigo — to settle on your . . . strandflat?"

He took time to answer.

"No, not really, but what would I do with livestock? I am no farmer!"

I smiled at his lack of vision.

"Trade them to me — or Olaf — or Roald — to set up households wherever we settle! There is room on our ship for more cargo — but how many animals would there be?"

Vigo reflected, counting on his fingers.

"Two cows, five pigs, and ten sheep," he said finally.

"We once carried horses on this ship," I announced. "Your few animals should be no problem — but the choice must be yours."

Vigo nodded. "Then livestock it is! I'll tell Lord Edvard of my decision."

He bowed and hurried off, whistling. I had never heard Vigo whistle before.

It took an extra day to bring the livestock to the harbor and get it all on board — including two roosters. Apparently Vigo liked roosters. Then Roald showed up with his dog, a handsome elkhound with a tail that curved like a ship's prow.

"His name is Blæki. I can't leave him behind — he's always been with me," declared Roald, as the dog wagged its tail at me.

Despite the brevity of their relationship, Roald was clear that he wanted to join Ginnlaug on the voyage to Heorot — especially when he learned that he could take her place at rowing.

" . . . but have you no family who will miss . . . the dog?" I inquired delicately.

"No, none. I had a bench in my grandfather's house, but he died last winter and his brother wants the house — so, you see, my lady, I am free to follow Ginnlaug — that is, to join your company, if you will have me — and Blæki."

"You are most welcome — both of you," I said, for I had already decided to accept him.

"So…" I said to Runa later that day, "With Roald added to our group, we are a band of eighteen — a goodly number! And so, on to Heorot — at last!"

I could not know how that number would change.

Chapter Six
Home in Heorot

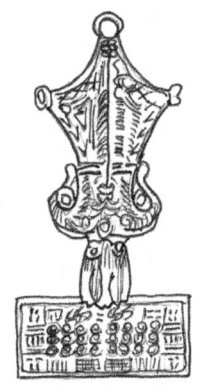

Late 5th-6th century square-headed brooch from Nordheim, Hedrum, Vestfold, Norway.

It was early morning when we left Breccasberg. We had already said our goodbyes—to Elsa and her household, with fond embraces and a few tears—to King Brecca and his sons in a formal leave-taking the night before.

Edvard had given us advice on the fastest route to Heorot. Instead of following the coastline back the way we had come, he said it would be only a two-day sail from the mouth of their fjord to the northern tip of Danish land—if the winds were favorable. According to Edvard several small islands just south of the fjord provided places where we could lie up and wait, if necessary. All of this was confirmed by Vigo, so this became our plan.

Sharing the cargo space with Vigo's animals created some problems, but we adapted. Makeshift pens amidships held each group of animals, although the two roosters could not be contained, and had the run of the ship. Mari and Berit were charged with feeding the animals and cleaning up after them. Even if the thralls were diligent in their duties, it would be a noisy, smelly journey for everyone! Olaf had immediately offered to buy the animals from Vigo when he and Runa found a place to settle — presumably at Heorot — and the rest of the crew accepted the temporary inconvenience with good humor.

"Cow dung is one thing," declared Lise, wrinkling her nose, "but those pigs ... whooeee!"

"Stay upwind of them and it won't be so bad," I counseled, as each of us found a place to settle. We seem to have acquired more goods during our stay in Breccasberg, I thought as I cast my eyes over the crowded deck. I didn't remember having so many sacks of grain. No matter. We were all aboard now and ready to leave for Heorot.

Olaf stood at the tiller. Our ten men, now including Roald, manned the oars on each side. My women and I had arranged ourselves on our sea chests back near the stern. Most of the non-animal cargo was stored up front in the bow, where Mari and Berit had also found places.

As we made our way south down the winding fjord and out to the open sea, I looked back at the magnificent terrain, breathing in its beauty. Towering cliffs and wooded mountain sides, steep waterfalls coursing down bare rock, dark headlands and green islands — all were vividly defined in the clear light of summer.

"Look at that rock pile," called Lise, pointing to the base of a cliff. "I wonder if that was once a troll?"

Lempi laughed. "I'm glad we've seen no trolls — or giants!"

"My lady," began Ginnlaug, lifting her hair to feel the breeze, "How long will we be at sea?"

I stood up, adjusted the robe folded under me, and sat back down.

"If the wind holds, two days until we reach the mainland. Then we'll follow the coastline down to Heorot — for several more days."

"But ... won't that put us at sea overnight?" asked Ginnlaug, her eyes growing wide.

"Yes, it will, but with the summer light there will be little darkness. Olaf, Vigo and Alf will take turns at the tiller so each man can get some sleep. Don't worry. All will be well."

Cloak of Ashes

When we reached the islands mentioned by Edvard, we did pause for a time, but not to wait for a favorable wind. Roald's dog Blæki, previously content to lie tied beside its master as he rowed, now rose and stretched, shaking itself. Pulling free of the rope, it trotted to the bow and began nosing about. Soon it began to bark furiously — at one of the grain sacks.

"What's the matter with that dog?" cried Lise.

"Maybe there's a mouse in the grain — or a rat!" suggested Ginnlaug, coming to the dog's defense. "Should I go forward and take a look, my lady?"

"Ooh," squealed Lise. "Don't let it out if there is one!"

"Maybe it will calm the dog if you open the sack," I agreed, curious myself to see what was agitating the animal. "Oh, wait, Ginnlaug, I'll do it. You must keep your bandaged hand clean."

I rose and made my way forward.

"What's the matter, Blæki? What is it, boy?" I murmured as the dog began to paw and sniff at the grain sack. "Do we have a stowaway aboard?"

The sack was strangely misshapen and someone had been careless in tying the top shut, for it gapped open on one side. Then I heard it: a sneeze — and the sack shook.

"Who's in there?" I demanded, jerking back in surprise

Through the gradually opening top emerged a head of russet hair.

"Gerda? Gerda! Get out of that sack!"

As the bag tipped over, Gerda crawled out, sneezing and shaking off barley grains. I pulled her to her feet and stared at her dusty face.

"You could have suffocated in that grain, child!"

With both hands I began brushing barley grains from her hair, her neck, her bare arms, her thin tunic. "By the goddess, what are you doing here?"

"I want . . . I want . . . to be with you, lady," she said meekly, and sneezed again.

"Olaf!" I shouted, looking back over my shoulder. "We must stop! We have a serious problem!"

Without hesitation Olaf gave the order: "Back oars!"

Seizing Gerda by the wrist, I hauled her, sniffling and wailing, back to the stern, where my women stood gaping.

"Don't take me back! Let me stay with you!" sobbed Gerda.

"Of course we must take you back — but it means losing a day's sail to do so!" I fumed, vexed at this unexpected delay.

"Wait, Lady Freawaru, wait." Runa was advancing with arms outstretched. "I know something of this girl's situation. Let me have a word with you."

First she knelt and embraced the sobbing Gerda.

"Why don't you go and make friends with Blæki — the dog who found you — while we women talk."

Gerda gulped and nodded and turned to Blæki, who had followed us to the stern, tail wagging vigorously. She knelt and hugged the dog's neck, letting it lick her dusty, tear-stained face.

Lise, Lempi and Ginnlaug crowdeded around Runa and me, eager to hear what Runa had to say, but I spoke first.

"We can't just keep her," I protested. "She'll be missed in Breccasberg by her family, she'll . . ."

"By your leave, my lady," interrupted Runa, "the child's only family is an uncle — who treats her none too well, from what I was told in Breccasberg. He may have even . . . abused the girl," concluded Runa solemnly.

I stared at Runa, my vexation draining away. "Still . . ." I wavered.

A small hand reached up and touched my elbow. Gerda looked up with pleading eyes.

"Please, lady. No one will miss me. My uncle doesn't want me. He often said so. He left this morning to fish. He'll be gone for days. Please let me stay with you, please!"

So naked was the plea, so desperate, I was deeply touched. Yet what would be the repercussions if we kept Gerda? Her sudden absence, coinciding with our departure, might well be taken as a deliberate abduction.

"Olaf," I asked, turning to my captain, "What is your opinion on this matter?"

Olaf shook his head.

"It is, of course, for you to decide, my lady, but children do disappear from time to time. Gerda could have been seized by raiders. Who is to say?" He shrugged.

"My lady, I can look after her,' offered Runa. "I may be too old now to have children, and I would welcome a little girl in my life."

But Gerda had ideas of her own. Seizing my waist, she cried, "You, lady. I want to stay with you!"

"Hush, child." I stroked her touseled hair and plucked a grain of barley caught in the tangles, then put my arm around her trembling shoulders. I turned to Runa.

"A kind offer, Runa. Thank you. If Gerda stays she will be my charge, but we could both look after her."

Taking Gerda's face in both hands, I addressed her most tenderly.

"We are all one family here: Runa and Olaf, Ginnlaug and me, Lempi and Lise. You'll be joining our family if—if we sail on for Heorot."

I took a deep breath and lifted my head.

"Olaf? Is there wind enough now for our departure?"

"Yes, my lady, there is!"

"Then hoist sail for Heorot!"

A cheer went up from the men at the oars and the women gathered around Gerda and me. Gerda snatched my hand, kissed it hard, and began jumping up and down. So it was that we added another member to our band.

My women immediately began fussing over our new companion.

"You must be hungry!" said Ginnlaug, pulling out bread and cheese from our travel stores. "How long were you hiding on the ship?"

"All night," replied Gerda, reaching for a crust. Then she stopped. "Those girls are hungry too," she said, pointing to the bow. "I heard them say so."

"Girls? What girls?" We all looked toward the bow, where Mari and Berit peered at us above the rows of grain sacks. "Oh, you mean those big girls. Well, yes, I suppose they are."

Ginnlaug turned to me with questioning eyes. "Lady Freawaru?"

"Go ahead. We'll feed everyone before getting underway again, but that will mean less food later today. We can have only cold food at sea."

Gerda ate ravenously, as if she'd taken no food for days. She was so small... I wondered.

"How old are you, child? Five? Six years?"

"I have eight winters," said Gerda through a mouthful of bread.

Lempi found a comb and coaxed Gerda into letting her untangle the girl's hair, while Runa sponged the girl's face and arms with fresh water. Lise had been rummaging in her sea chest and now held up a plain woolen tunic.

"Here, this should almost fit you if we belt it around the waist. You'd be cold at night in that thin shift of yours!"

Gerda let herself be dressed and we all laughed as she danced about in her new clothes. Making my face as serious as possible, I said dryly, "There is also work to be done on this ship. What can you do to help, Gerda?"

"I can milk a cow!" she declared, pausing in her dance. "I can milk, and I can feed the chickens!" She smiled triumphantly and spun into a small bow.

I sighed. This girl is going to be a handful!

Our night at sea passed uneventfully. The men took turns sleeping in their places, while we women slept on deck bundled in our robes. Once I awoke to find Gerda missing from my sleeping robe, and raised up on one elbow to find her sitting beside me, gazing at the stars.

"Some stars make pictures," she said, pointing at the lights barely visible in the summer sky.

"Yes, and I know a few of their names," I said, sitting up. "That is the Great Wain, and over there — Freyja's Spindle. Now come back under the robe. I need your warmth," I lied.

Gerda grinned and wiggled down beside me. Soon I heard her even breathing, punctuated with little snores that sounded almost like sobs.

Ginnlaug had been sick during the night, and both Lise and Lempi looked pale in the morning light.

"It's not so much the sea — it's those pigs!" complained Lise. "I can't get that smell out of my nose!"

"A rooster kept me awake," declared Lempi, yawning.

Only Runa, as usual, made no complaint. She was her usual quiet, capable self, up early to help Gerda with the milking and to help our thralls dispose of the nightly wastes.

"We're one day out," called Olaf cheerfully from the helm.

"How can you be sure?" I called back.

"Knud's begun to recognize signs: the currents, the birds... he grew up along this northern coast."

"It can't be too soon for me," grumbled Lise.

By the time we reached the Danish mainland, everyone was ready to get off the ship. Our young men had had to row most of the afternoon,

Cloak of Ashes

and with little wind everyone was sweating under the burning sun. Gerda seemed apprehensive as we approached.

"Is this a... friendly land?" she asked.

"This is a safe, new country, my homeland," I assured her, "where you will be welcome."

Will she? Will I? Will any of us? Doubts troubled me as we neared Danish soil. We're closer to Heorot, but also closer to Hrothulf, my old enemy. How will I be received, the daughter of the former king?

"Just ahead!" shouted Olaf. "That sheltered bay to starboard—we'll camp there tonight."

"Thank the goddess," I breathed. "Almost home."

It took us five more days to work our way down to Heorot. Overnight camps were sometimes extended to allow our men to hunt for fresh game. Every night my women and I kept the cooking pots boiling. Being on the water whetted everyone's appetite; some even looked hungrily at Vigo's roosters!

As we neared the maze of islands and channels that contained my homeland, Olaf needed all his skills of navigation—and his memory—to pick the right passage. I did not know the waters immediately north of Heorot, nor did Knud, so it took some time before once familiar landmarks began to appear: a jutting promontory, a headland shaped like a helmet, a shingle beach. When we began to see swans gliding over the dark water, I knew we must be near.

Mid-day on the fifth day, we finally located the mouth of the fjord leading into Heorot. Now Olaf and I could relax—that is, until we saw smoke on the skyline! Fear clutched at my heart as I recalled that long-ago day when I'd returned to Heorot to find my father's mead hall in flames.

"What is it, lady? What's wrong?"

Gerda had come up beside me and now peered at my face.

"I don't know yet—but that smoke ahead does not bode well!"

Now all my women were on their feet, eyes fixed on the rising smoke.

"Wait, my lady." Runa turned toward me. "I may have lost track of the days, but haven't we reached the solstice? That smoke could be coming from..."

"Balefires! Of course! It is midsummer! That must be it!"

Still, I kept an anxious watch as we sailed on. At the mouth of the harbor Olaf spotted the first of several coastguards and raised his hand in greeting. The man returned his hail and disappeared, presumably to report our arrival.

The old landing was still in place, but we passed it by, for Bodvar had told me to look for a new pier further up the fjord, closer to Hrothulf's new hall. Where my father's hall had once stood proudly atop the long hill above the harbor, I now saw a low cluster of longhouses, probably built to accommodate Hrothulf's many warriors. On we sailed, accompanied by several swans trailing in our wake.

Do you remember me, my swans? Freawaru is coming home!

"Look, lady. What's that?"

Gerda was pointing straight ahead, directing my attention away from the smoke that spiraled off to starboard. Following her finger, I saw a great structure looming through the trees, its roofline tall as the tallest branches. This had to be the hall of my cousin Hrothulf, now King Hrolf Kraki.

"It's so green here!" observed Lempi from the other side of the deck.

"And flat...," added Lise, beside her.

"Green? Flat?" I looked about me. "Yes, compared to the countries we've come from, it certainly is. It just looks like home to me."

Now I also became aware of our sunburned faces and overall windblown condition. What a ragtag crew we must look.

"Quick!" I said to my women. "Let's freshen up before we get to the landing, We want to make a good first impression."

Each woman hastened to make adjustments, straightening her clothes and patting down her hair. Even Gerda tightened her belt to pull up the hemline that would otherwise pool around her feet. I tucked a stray wisp of hair under my head cloth, which I'd decided to wear at Heorot to emphasize my status as a once married woman.

As we drew closer to the landing, I saw three figures standing on the dock. One towered above the others. Beside him, for the tall figure was surely a man, stood a woman, to judge from her dress. The third figure might be a young man. Was this a welcoming party sent by the king? Or just local folk who were simply curious to see strangers?

By now we had dropped sail and were rowing ever closer to the waiting trio. The tall figure raised one arm in greeting.

"Hail to the Lady Freawaru! Welcome to Heorot!" he bellowed.

"That's Bodvar Bjarki's voice!" I cried in relief. "These are friends waiting to receive us!"
Indeed it was Bodvar, with his wife Drifa and . . . Vögg, the young fellow from the Swedish court. They were waiting to welcome us and escort us up to the new settlement, which lay at some distance from the harbor, perched on a series of low hills. After making introductions, which included Blæki, Roald's dog, we left our gear behind on the ship and started up the path with our hosts, looking about to take in these new surroundings.

Drifa took my right arm, while Gerda clung to my left. Bodvar walked with Olaf and Runa, followed by the rest of our band, Vögg bringing up the rear. Drifa was a tall, handsome woman with wide cheekbones and large eyes as brown as the hair that peeked out from under her head cloth. She wore a bright blue kirtle edged with embroidery and around her neck hung the amber beads I'd helped Bodvar select back in Breccasberg. I liked her immediately. As we walked, I looked for familiar buildings.

"There's the eld-hus where we did most of our cooking — when I was a girl," I said, pointing out to Gerda a long, worn structure.

"Oh, that's just a storehouse now, my lady," offered Vögg, who'd come up behind me. "There's a new cookhouse in the settlement proper. King Hrolf has planned everything perfectly!"

"Indeed?!" I smiled, aware of the fact that one of King Hrolf's daughters was walking beside me.

She nodded. "Father likes order in all things — but I expect you know that, since you grew up together." She glanced sideways for my reaction.

"People can change over the years," I murmured. "Tell me, Drifa. When were you and Bodvar married?"

"We've just finished our honey moon," she said, blushing slightly, "in time for the summer solstice celebration. You arrive at a good time!"

"We saw the smoke," I acknowledged. "I loved the balefires as a girl." As did my brothers — now dead, perhaps at Hrothulf's hand!

"What's wrong, lady?" Gerda's keen eyes looked up as she tugged at my hand.

"Nothing, child, nothing really . . ."

Drifa seemed not to have noticed my momentary discomfort.

"You will stay with Bodvar and me in our longhouse, you and your women. It's new and quite large. Vögg will find places for your men. How long might you be staying?"

Now I was truly at a loss, but gradually found my voice.

"That depends... on many things. One of them is the sort of reception we receive from your father."

Drifa stopped and looked at me in surprise.

"Father has always spoken well of you — and he prides himself on his hospitality!"

By now we had reached the settlement, a maze of longhouses, workshops, sheds, storerooms and other outbuildings, all clustered around the imposing mead hall — which we paused to admire.

"A grand hall!" I exclaimed, "but I see no antlers hung above the door as they once were at Hrothgar's Heorot." My throat suddenly constricted.

"No, father thought it might bring bad luck, since the former hall burned twice," said Drifa brightly, "and we don't call it 'Heorot' anymore."

"Oh, yes, I remember: 'Roskilde,' 'Hroar's Spring,' in honor of my father. I must thank Hrothulf for that — I mean, King Hrolf. Is he inside?"

Drifa laughed. "No, like almost everyone else today he has gone to the hilltop where the balefires burn. But come inside. I'd like to show you the hall."

With Olaf's help she pulled open the heavy carved oak doors and we followed her through a spacious fore room into the dim interior.

There were two floors in the main hall. A gallery running around the upper level, open to the central space, was supported by a double row of great wooden pillars, carved and painted. The ground floor of hard-packed earth was strewn with rushes and juniper boughs. Down the middle ran two long fire trenches, with wood stacked at the far end.

The usual benches were ranged against the outside walls, with tables in front. The king's high seat and a companion seat, framed by two smaller posts, were placed against the north wall. In the flickering light of the wall-mounted torches I could make out tapestries, animal skins, horns and other carvings decorating the interior.

"The rooms above contain enclosed sleeping spaces for father and his chief guests, but I thought you might prefer the relative quiet of our house," said Drifa. "Father's warriors can be very boisterous at night, especially the berserkers."

"Berserkers? Ah, yes. That reminds me: do you know where I can find the man named 'Unferth'?"

Drifa wrinkled her brow. "I've heard the name, but... no. You'd better ask Bodvar."

By now Gerda had seen enough of the mead hall.

"Lady, can we see the fires now?"

Apparently my women—and men—had the same question, for they suddenly clustered around me like chicks around a mother hen. I looked at their expectant faces and turned to Drifa, who laughed.

"Of course you may! Everyone is welcome. Come! Bodvar and I will lead the way."

Happily we trooped out of the mead hall. In the open air I heard laughter and singing, coming from the direction of the smoke. I had thought to send Mari and Berit back to the ship with two of our men to begin unloading supplies, but decided that this could wait for later. On the way up the hill, Drifa pointed out a house with fresh sod on the roof.

"That's our longhouse, Bodvar's and mine. We only have two servants, so there is plenty of room for your party—including Olaf and Runa."

"How thoughtful of you," I said, grateful that Drifa recognized their need to be together.

Ahead of us the sounds of merry making grew louder. Shouts and bursts of nervous laughter drew our attention to a clearing just below the crest of the hill. There a handsome young man stripped to the waist stood poised at one end of the space, facing a band of attackers—for the young men facing him held long, thin splinters of wood. One by one, each man advanced and launched his spear at the human target. Each time the intended victim dodged the lance and the onlookers cheered.

"What's going on?" whispered Gerda at my elbow.

"I'm not sure, let's wait to see what happens next," I whispered back.

Just then a young boy totally naked except for a blindfold over his eyes, was led forward and a stick put into his hand.

"Go! Now! Hit him!" shouted the young men.

A hush fell over the bystanders as the lad stumbled forward, stick extended like a small spear. When he met his quarry, he jabbed blindly. The victim instantly dropped to the ground and lay as if dead. Immediately shrieks and wails went up all around us, and I realized what was happening.

"It's Balder — Balder is dead — that is, his death has been re-enacted here. Don't worry, little one, the man on the ground is still alive — I hope!"

Gerda stood in shocked silence, then turned and buried her face in my gown. "That's a bad game, a horrid game," she muttered.

I was shocked myself, never having witnessed such a scene.

"Is this ... mock killing ... a usual part of your midsummer celebration?" I asked Drifa, who was staring at the body on the ground as if willing it to rise.

"What? Oh yes, that is ... no. We only began it last summer. It was Skuld's idea, and the king always listens to Skuld." She spoke as if in a trance.

"Skuld? Who is Skuld?"

"Father's sister — well, half-sister. I'll tell you about her later."

Drifa looked distressed, so I let the matter drop. By now the young men had lifted their fallen comrade to carry him off the field. To my relief he winked at us as he passed by. A wave of relief rippled through the crowd as well, which now made its way toward tables heaped with food and drink. The naked young boy was scooped up into the arms of a tall young woman — presumably his mother — and carried off.

"Now there will be toasts — to Balder and to Odin," explained Drifa, in something more like her normal voice. She knelt to speak to Gerda.

"The children will be up by the bonfire. Perhaps you'd like to join them — if your mother approves?"

Gerda lifted her face to mine. We smiled.

"Though I gladly claim Gerda as my charge," I said, "I am not her mother — another story to be told later. Yes, child, run and play."

Gerda hesitated for a moment, then yanked the belt from her waist, shucked off her woolen tunic and darted up the hill in her shift, bare legs flashing in the sunlight. Behind me I heard Vögg chuckle.

"That one flits like a sparrow — yes, a sparrow. That's what I'm going to call her from now on: 'sparrow'. It fits her." He smiled broadly at having bestowed another name.

"If it sticks, you'll be receiving another naming gift, Vögg," I said.

"Oh, no need, my lady. All I ask is the chance to serve you."

Now Bodvar took the lead.

"Come, Lady Freawaru. King Hrolf is prepared to receive you."

I took a deep breath. So, after all these years, I must face my cousin again. The last time I'd seen him, I was fleeing for my life! You are a king's daughter, Freawaru, a queen's daughter. Be not afraid. Be strong.

As we approached a table set apart from the rest, a man seated at the far end rose to greet us. He was tall and slender, with dark eyes and dark hair tending toward gray. I recognized the nose, straight and thin, and the jaw—the Skjoldung jaw, so like... my father's. I gulped. Hrolf's mouth was fuller than I'd remembered it and when his lips parted, his voice was low and steady.

"So, cousin, we meet again." He held out both arms, then let them fall as I bobbed a quick bow.

"King Hrolf."

Our eyes met. To my surprise I saw no rancor there, only a mild curiosity. Where was the Hrothulf of our past? Could he have changed so much?

"Please join us. You and your companions will need refreshment after your long journey."

He waved a hand and servants scurried to bring mugs and ale.

"Thank you. We accept with pleasure your generous hospitality," I mouthed as we were seated around the long table and I continued to survey the man before me.

I had to admit he made a regal figure with his tall stature and rich dress, for he was attired in exceedingly fine clothes: a white linen shirt with embroidery on the sleeves, a tunic of black with gold threads worked into it, worn over red breeches secured with a tooled leather belt and silver buckle. The red cloak thrown over the back of his chair was edged with marten fur. A simple band of gold encircled his head, and a magnificent length of twisted gold wound up his arm. I mentally berated myself for not dressing to match such magnificence—but Hrolf had begun to speak.

"... and Olaf tells me you have come bringing these young champions who wish to join our court. Is that your wish also, Lady Freawaru?"

I had not expected a direct question so soon. I paused.

"That will be as the goddess directs, Lord Hrolf. I wish first, if I may, to reacquaint myself with my former home, and any old friends who have not forgotten me."

"Ah, perhaps you speak of Unferth," said Hrolf. "I'm afraid you will find him much diminished. But for now let us feast and enjoy the day at this, the year's turning. You are most welcome to everything Roskilde has to offer."

He signaled again and platters of food and trenchers were set before us. Suddenly we all realized how hungry we were.

We sat with Hrolf and his court late into the evening, watching the sun as it briefly vanished and rose again. Above us the balefire roared and crackled, its heat radiating in waves. I now recognized the ridge as the same one used in my childhood for midsummer celebrations, chosen because it stood closest to the life-giving sun.

Memories flooded over me: chasing and being chased by my brothers as we ran screaming and shouting round the blazing pile; watching as farmers drove their cattle through the smoke to rid them of disease... Gerda appeared from time to time to cram in a mouthful of food, then run whooping back to join the other children.

At our table I saw Bodvar leaning down to hear something Drifa was saying. Olaf had his hand over Runa's hand as they sat side by side. Roald and Ginnlaug sat gazing at each other across the table as if they were entirely alone. Lise and Lempi were laughing at something Vögg was telling them. Our young men were busy eating venison and drinking the excellent wine provided by King Hrolf.

Here in the twilight, outdoors on the hillside, free from the usual protocols of life in the mead hall, everyone seemed at ease. I looked around me at the faces: my people, Hrolf's people — faces which could all belong to the same family. Am I foolish to think I might find my place here... in Heorot? Hrothulf seems changed... and for the better. But this is Heorot no longer; it is Roskilde now.

When I looked into the depth of the blazing fire, I seemed to see other faces: Mother, Father, Aeschere, Ana... and finally... Beowulf. I closed my eyes, letting the balefire's warmth penetrate the coldness that lay about my heart. A little spark that was Gerda jumped out and danced beside the fire. When I opened my eyes the image of Mother's face rose again before me. Mother, yes. You still call me? What am I to do? There was no answer.

The bonfire, so huge when we first arrived that it had seemed to rival the sun, was finally reduced to a sprawling bed of glowing embers. By the time we left the hillside, our clothes and hair smelled of smoke, and Gerda's face was smudged with soot. I felt strangely happy, as if I had somehow been blessed by taking part in this sacred ritual.

Alf and Knud had been sent back to the ship earlier to help Mari and Berit bring up our sea chests, so fresh night clothes were waiting for us when we reached Bodvar and Drifa's longhouse. Bodvar carried the drowsy Gerda on his back, her arms flung round his neck. In his strength and his kindness he reminded me of . . . Beowulf. Again I felt a sudden moment of grief.

The next day Gerda and some of my women accompanied me as I sought out what was left in Heorot that might match my memories. I led them to the edge of the settlement, near the river that flowed into the fjord.

"Beside this old oak I used to sit and practice rune-carving," I told them, stroking the rough bark of the tree. "And my brothers and I learned to swim in this very stream." The river still looked inviting in the heat of midsummer.

"Oh, lady, may I jump in? I know how to swim!"

"Yes, Gerda, but first, off with your shift! Ginnlaug is sewing a new tunic for you, but it won't be ready for a few days."

I had hardly finished speaking before Gerda had stripped and jumped into the water.

"Ooh, it's cold . . . I like it!" she squealed, splashing and laughing in the waist-deep stream.

Lempi, Lise, Ginnlaug and I sat down on the edge of the bank, took off our shoes, and dipped our toes in the cool water.

"Runa will wish she'd come with us when she hears about this!" crowed Lise.

"I miss Runa," said Lempi simply.

"I do too," I said, "but she is part of Olaf's life now. We can't expect to have her company all the time."

"I wish I could spend more time with Roald," said Ginnlaug wistfully.

"You'll see him tonight in the mead hall," soothed Lempi.

We sat silently for a time, thinking our separate thoughts. Then I called to Gerda.

"Come out now, child. I want to show you a special pool of water, the place where my mother and I offered sacrifices."

Gerda climbed nimbly up the mossy bank and shook herself like a little dog before donning her shift. Taking the end of my apron, I toweled her wet curls.

"My hair was this color when I was your age," I observed.

She grinned up at me. "I'm glad."

The pool, when we finally found it, was more of a marsh, swampy and full of rushes. The hut where Mother used to keep her ritual things had collapsed, and it was evident from the overgrown path that no one any longer came here to make sacrifices.

"What did you do here?" asked Lise, wrinkling her nose at the smell of stagnant water.

"We offered locks of our hair to the Earth Mother," I said, remembering clearly that chilly morning, standing naked before my mother's knife.

I was a mere child then, awed by the sight of Mother as priestess, leading her women to the sacred pool, offering their locks –and mine—to the goddess, imploring her aid against our terrible enemy. Mother, Mother, where are you now?

"Why?" asked Lempi, swatting at insects, "Why did you sacrifice your hair?"

"Why?" With difficulty I pulled myself back to the present. "We wanted her protection from the Grendel—a monster who invaded our mead hall and devoured thirty men in a single night!"

"Did it stop the monster?" asked Gerda, all eyes and attention.

"No, nothing stopped it, although Unferth came close. Nothing stopped it... until Beowulf came. He killed the Grendel monster... with his bare hands."

All of them stared at me in amazement.

"I've heard stories about that, but I thought they were just... stories," said Ginnlaug, shaking her head.

"It's a true story," I assured her. "There are people still alive in this settlement who can confirm the story. King Hrolf is one. Unferth is another. You have met the king and I'm hoping soon to talk with Unferth."

Later that day I had my wish fulfilled. Bodvar told me where Unferth was to be found, but cautioned that he might not welcome visitors.

"I'm not a visitor," I protested. "I'm Freawaru. Unferth has known me since I was a child."

"May I go with you?" asked Gerda.

I hesitated, then decided to bring her along—after giving some instructions.

"He's a very old man and he can be... crochety," I warned, "so don't speak unless he addresses you first."

"I'll be quiet," she grinned. "Besides, I like old people."

Bodvar offered his servant to direct us, a skinny young lad named Eyvind, who trotted briskly ahead as he led us past most of the houses to the edge of the settlement.

"Watch out for his ravens," said Eyvind. "They'll bite if you get too close!"

"Ooh, ravens. I like ravens!" declared Gerda, hurrying to keep up.

"You won't like these!" predicted Eyvind, who stopped suddenly before what looked like a hut for grain storage. "Here it is. Shall I wait for you?"

"No need. We can find our way back. Thank you for your help."

As the lad trotted off, whistling, I looked askance at the scarred wooden door and rotted timbers. Could Unferth really be living in such a place? Unferth, once a respected member of King Hrothgar's court?

I rapped firmly on the door. No answer. I rapped again.

"Unferth, are you there? It is Freawaru, King Hrothgar's daughter. You were once my rune-master. I've come to see you, to talk with you. Please open the door."

Silence. Then a rustling sound and the shuffle of feet. I heard the bar being drawn back and the door slowly creaked open. A tall, disheveled man with gaunt face and sunken eyes appeared in the doorway. For a moment he stood blinking in the bright sunlight, then reached out a trembling hand.

"Freawaru, ah, ... I've been expecting you. Beowulf said you would come."

Chapter Seven
Warnings and Mysteries

Bronze Odin, god of war, holding a sword and two spears, with his ravens, Huginn and Muninn. Uppland, Sweden.

"Beowulf? Perhaps... perhaps you have not heard? Beowulf is dead, my lord, killed by a dragon."

My voice faltered as I spoke the fateful words.

Unferth fixed me with a piercing gaze and scowled. "Beowulf is alive. I spoke to him this morning. But who...?" his eyes shifted to the girl beside me, "who is this? Are there two Freawarus?"

Gerda grinned and bobbed a slight bow. "May I see your birds?"

Unferth stared at her for a moment, then turned wordlessly and disappeared inside the hut. We heard him cackling and cooing. He re-emerged with two ravens, one on each shoulder, their talons gripping his cloak.

"Hold out your arms," he commanded, pointing at Gerda.

Without hesitation she put out her bare, bony little arms.

"Wait!" I cried, attempting to step in front of Gerda, but Unferth shouldered me aside with surprising strength.

"Call them!" he commanded again, his eyes on Gerda.

Confidently Gerda opened her mouth and called: "Auk Crauk, Auk Crauk."

One raven flew down to her arm, settling on her wrist, where she stroked its shaggy throat with her free hand. Then the second raven flew down, landing on her right shoulder. Gerda stood grinning, but my heart was beating fast with alarm and anger.

"Call them back, Unferth!" I stormed. "How could you endanger this child? Those birds might have attacked her, bitten her! Please, call them back now!"

Unferth shrugged and gave a long, shrill whistle. Immediately the ravens returned to his shoulders.

"I'm not hurt, lady. They like me!" declared Gerda. She turned to Unferth. "What are their names?"

Ignoring my anger, Unferth knelt stiffly, bringing the ravens to Gerda's level.

"The one on my right is Huginn. The one on the left is Muninn — and they do like you."

Rising slowly he turned to me. "There is more than one way to recognize those marked by the gods, my lady. You bear a feather mark from Freyja on your shoulder. This girl — like me — can talk to birds."

He smiled. For a moment he had sounded like my old rune-master, calmly teaching me the meanings hidden in symbols. But . . . his earlier reference to Beowulf . . . ?

"Unferth, I should not have doubted you," I said carefully, at the same time putting my hands on Gerda's shoulders. "This is Gerda — or 'Sparrow' as Vögg calls her. She is . . . under my care."

"'Sparrow,' repeated. Unferth. "Hmm, yes, that suits her: 'Sparrow'."

"I . . . we would talk with you, Unferth. Where would you suggest?"

He regarded us thoughtfully, then turned and disappeared into the hut again. When he reappeared, the ravens were gone.

"The oak — by the river?" he said.

I smiled for the first time. "Yes. Most suitable."

Cloak of Ashes

It took us some time to reach the river, for Unferth walked very slowly. On the way I spoke of the major events in my life since our last meeting at the Great Blöt in Uppsala: my move to Eaglesgard, the death of Hygd, and finally, the death of Beowulf. Unferth listened without comment, while Gerda danced along, sometimes running ahead, then returning to walk sedately beside me.

When we had settled ourselves down against the old oak, Unferth spoke at last. Despite his age, his voice was still deep and strong.

"Why have you come to Heorot?" he asked. "My birds have not told me."

I took a deep breath. "Wealtheow calls to me. I seek news of my mother."

"Wealtheow?" His eyes clouded over. "It has been long since I have thought of that fine, brave woman."

I leaned forward and took one of his dry, gnarled hands in mine.

"Unferth, can you remember the morning when I fled from Heorot with my companions? Mother was to come with me, but at the last moment she stayed behind—to properly bury her sons, according to Ana. You were there. What happened... after I left? Where did Mother go?"

Unferth shook his head slowly.

"I cannot tell you. I gave my word."

"Your word? To whom?"

"To Wealtheow. I took an oath never to reveal where she was going ...even to you."

I stared at him in desperation.

"Can you tell me if she is still alive—somewhere?"

Unferth shook his head again.

"I do not know. No word has come from them."

"'Them'?" I seized on the word. "Can you tell me who was with her?"

Now Unferth refused to speak further, staring into the distance as I put more questions to him. Finally, using the trunk of the oak to assist him, he rose and headed back toward the settlement. I got up and followed him.

"Unferth," I pleaded, "I'm sorry to have been so insistent, but Mother is calling me and I don't know where to find her!"

Gerda, who had been sailing oak leaves on the stream while Unferth and I talked, ran to catch up with us. Confidently she took Unferth's hand.

"May I visit your birds again?" she asked, looking up.

He nodded twice, but said nothing. In silence we walked back to his hut, but I had to make one more attempt to reach him.

"Unferth, would you join me in the mead hall one night? No more questions, just... well... perhaps you could tell me... about your talks with Beowulf? I miss him so much!"

Tears flooded my eyes as I blurted out this admission. Unferth paused at his door and looked at me.

"Beowulf, yes. I will speak of Beowulf."

Then he entered the hut and closed the door. I heard the bar being slid into place.

That night after the evening meal, I asked my hosts about one person I'd not yet seen in Roskilde: Hjalti.

"Bodvar, I don't think I've ever seen you before without your friend Hjalti by your side," I said to him as we lingered at the table.

He gave Drifa an affectionate glance.

"Drifa has had something to do with that," he declared, smiling, "but right now Hjalti and Svipdag are gone on a mission for King Hrolf: collecting tribute from the under-kings of the other islands. They should be back any day."

"Collecting tribute? I've heard of that practice. Is that how King Hrolf can afford to... dress so well?" I said lightly.

Drifa laughed. "Father has always been particular in that respect. He likes to make a good appearance. He also has a craving for cleanliness," she added. "He even built his own sauna so that he can steam and scrub daily, as he pleases. Was he like that as a boy?"

I had to pause to avoid nearly choking on my ale.

"We did not spend much time together," I murmured. "Hrothulf, that is, King Hrolf, was always off with my father and the other men, learning battle skills."

I clearly remembered his practicing those battle skills on me: "Freawaru, you be a Frank and I'll be a Dane. Now fight!" but I did not think it appropriate to share this memory.

Cloak of Ashes

Just then a double knock at the door followed by a triple knock drew our attention.

"Why that could be . . ." said Bodvar, rising from his bench, "the very man we spoke of earlier!"

He strode to the door and pulled it open. There indeed stood . . . Hjalti. He grinned and bobbed a greeting.

"Good evening, Drifa, Bodvar. I see you have company, so I won't stay long."

He stepped over the threshold.

"Why, it's Lady Freawaru! A most pleasant surprise!"

I rose. "It's good to see you again, Hjalti."

"How long is Roskilde to have your company?" he asked, lifting my hand to his lips.

Why do people keep asking me that?

"I cannot yet say, Hjalti."

Bodvar embraced his old friend and drew him over to the table for a mug of ale. When Hjalti had taken a drink, he began to recount details of his mission.

"Möns, Langeland, Turö, the southern half of Fyn . . . Svipdag has gone to make a full report to King Hrolf, but I can tell you that every under-king paid his dues—including Hjörvardh of Odense!"

He nodded in satisfaction and took another drink.

"Well done!" exclaimed Bodvar. "Hjörvardh! King Hrolf was wise to bring Hjörvardh under his control—even if it took trickery to do so."

"Trickery? What trickery?" I asked, suddenly attentive.

Trickery and slyness were hallmarks of the Hrothulf I once knew!

Hjalti and Bodvar looked at each other uneasily.

"We heard the tale from Svipdag," began Hjalti slowly, "for he was out hunting with King Hrolf that day on the island of Fyn, with King Hjörvardh, who rules the northern half of that island. After a successful boar kill, King Hrolf unbuckled his sword belt and asked Hjörvardh to hold it while Hrolf made water. Hjörvardh did so, pulling Scofnung from its sheath to brandish the sword and test its handling."

Here Hjalti and Bodvar grinned at each other, clearly relishing what was to come next.

"When King Hrolf took back his sword and sheath, he declared in a loud voice, 'This we both know, that whosoever holds the sword of a man while that man takes the belt off his breeches, he shall be the underling ever afterward. And now you shall be my under-king, and do my bidding as others do.'"

Hjalti suddenly slapped his knee and bent over, gasping with laughter.

"Poor... poor Hjörvardh! Despite his sputtering and the later days of haggling, in the end he had to give his oath to Hrolf and become his man. He had to humble himself!"

Now Drifa leaned forward. "You left out one important part," she declared. "King Hrolf gave his sister Skuld to Hjörvardh in marriage!"

This comment sobered both men.

"Ah, yes... Skuld," muttered Bodvar. "Hjörvardh could save his pride by saying he was tricked, but he did want to marry Skuld — though only the gods know why."

"As for Skuld, she wanted to be a queen," said Drifa quietly, "but she does not seem to relish her husband as an under-king."

Skuld again? I studied the three faces, suddenly so serious.

"It's late," said Hjalti, rising. "I bid you all good night."

The next day I was introduced to Skur, Drifa's sister, who arrived early in the morning. Where Drifa was soft and womanly, Skur was stiff and straight, with dark hair and eyes — clearly a child of Hrolf Kraki. Nevertheless, her smile was friendly and her greeting seemed genuine.

"Lady Freawaru, welcome to Roskilde," she said, embracing me warmly. "I hope my sister is providing well for you?"

She shot Drifa a challenging glance, and I sensed a playful rivalry between the two.

"Indeed, I could not ask for better hospitality," I replied emphatically.

Skur turned to take the hand of the silent man who had arrived with her: a tall, rawboned, wide-shouldered man with a long yellow beard and an eye-patch on the left side of a scarred and craggy face.

"This is Svipdag," beamed Skur. "We are betrothed!"

"Svipdag!" It is an honor to meet you! I have heard much of your bravery and sacrifice at the court of King Edgils," I declared warmly.

"My lady. I thank you for your kind and understanding words."

He nodded, then turned to Drifa. "I would speak with Bodvar."

"He and Hjalti have gone down to the harbor with Olaf, one of Lady Freawaru's men. You can find him there."

Svipdag nodded again. "Beg pardon, ladies, but I must now see Bodvar."

He departed, leaving Skur, Drifa and me alone in the longhouse, for Gerda and my women had gone out to explore with Blæki, and the thralls were working outdoors. This was my chance to ask about Skuld, but first I wished to respond to Skur's announcement.

"Congratulations on your betrothal," I said, as we three sat down together. "Your Svipdag is a famous warrior — but not overly talkative, I notice."

Skur smiled. "He speaks when necessary, and always to the point."

"When will you be married?" I asked politely.

"In the autumn, between first frost and Yule." She eyed me appraisingly. "How long will you be staying?"

That question again!

"I can't say yet. I have not yet received... direction from the goddess."

Drifa and Skur exchanged glances.

"Lady Freawaru," began Drifa. "We have heard from Father that you possess... special powers."

"Yes," I nodded, "a gift from the goddess."

"With respect," continued Drifa, "we are wondering what these powers are and how you use them?"

Her voice ended on a rising note.

"Fear not — I am no witch!" I laughed, but stopped short at the stricken look on their faces.

"Do you... conduct... secret rites?" whispered Skur, her eyes big.

I considered. "If you think consulting the runes is a secret rite, then yes I do. But I also lead women in worshipping Nerthus, Earth Mother, and Freyja, goddess of love and fertility. We owe our very existence to such great beings!"

While I was speaking I saw the faces of Drifa and Skur gradually relax.

"When she was alive, our mother led such celebrations," confessed Skur, "but she has been gone for many winters." She reached out to her sister and squeezed her hand.

"My own mother is gone — but may yet live. Finding her is the main reason I've come to Heorot," I suddenly revealed.

Both women looked surprised.

"But we were told you could see into the future!" burst out Skur.

I smiled ruefully. "Yes, but not everything is revealed to me in my visions, including my mother's whereabouts."

Drifa nodded sympathetically. "How can we help you?" she asked.

"I do not know if that is possible. My mother, Wealtheow, left Heorot long before you were born. Of those yet living here, only your father and Unferth would remember her . . ." I drifted into silence. "But tell me, please, about your father's sister — the woman called Skuld. I never heard her mentioned when I was growing up in Heorot — but there were many secrets kept from me as a child."

Once again troubled looks were exchanged between the sisters. Finally Drifa spoke.

"It is no secret to tell you what every Dane knows," she began. "Our father's father Halga — or 'Helgi' as some called him — once slept with an elven woman of the ocean deep. From this union came Skuld, King Hrolf's half-sister. She is married to King Hjörvardh, as you heard last night. They live at Odin's lake, where thralls are drowned to honor the One-Eyed."

She gave a shiver of distaste and Skur now picked up the story.

"Many say that Skuld is a witch-queen, ready to do evil to those who would stand in her way."

I stared at the two women in astonishment.

"What does she look like, this witch-queen?"

"Some men call her beautiful," said Skur, "with her clear, white skin and storm-green eyes."

"Her hair is black as a raven's wing," added Drifa, "and she seems to move without sound, like a wave on the water."

Now Skur continued. "Skuld is smooth-tongued, skilled in getting her way, but I've heard she is given to shrieking fits when crossed, and gives nothing she is not forced to give!"

Both sisters lapsed into silence, frowning.

"It seems you have no great love for your aunt Skuld," I observed.

"She's a dangerous woman!" blurted Skur, "but Father refuses to see that!"

"Dangerous? How so?" I asked.

Skur lowered her voice. "Skuld is said to be deeply steeped in witchcraft. It is reported that she consorts with Finnish wizards and practices secret rites in the forest. Who knows what she is about?" She grimaced.

"Father invites her to every Yule feast. He'll probably invite her to my wedding!"

Then she brightened. "Lady Freawaru, you can see into the future — at least partially. Would you use your powers to see . . . to see what Skuld is plotting?"

"Your suspicions may be misplaced," I answered slowly, "but I will . . . do what I can." I considered. "Do you have anything in your possession once worn by Skuld?"

The sisters looked at each other.

"There's that head cloth you gave Skuld at her wedding feast," said Skur to Drifa. "Remember? Skuld tried it on, then gave it back to you, deeming it not fine enough for her new status as a queen!"

Drifa nodded, her eyes narrowing. "I meant to burn it, but kept it for a cleaning rag. It should be here somewhere . . ."

She rose and went to the shelf where cooking pots and serving platters were kept. "Here it is."

She returned with a gray, stained square of cloth and held it out to me. "Will this do?"

"Yes, thank you," I said, taking the cloth and tucking it into the bag at my waist. "Please understand. I do not undertake lightly the summoning of a vision, for it requires entering a trance state. A first step would be to consult the runes." I smiled. "I was taught long ago by an excellent rune-master: Unferth."

Skur suddenly grew excited. "Perhaps you could read the runes on the cross guard of Father's sword, Scofnung. No one has yet been able to decipher them!"

"Perhaps, but one mystery at a time," I replied. "For now, I will retire to the oak tree and see what the runes may reveal."

"May we go with you?" asked Skur eagerly.

"Not this time. I need solitude to interpret the runes correctly. But," I added, seeing their disappointed faces, "there is something else you could do. See that Unferth has food; I fear he has not been eating."

"Of course! We can do that now," promised Drifa.

Alone with my rune bag beneath the great oak, I knelt down and spread a white cloth on the ground before me, then settled myself to receive what the gods might offer. Placing my hands on my lap, palms up, I closed my eyes and began my invocation.

"Odin, All-Father, giver of runes, I call upon you now. Open my inner eye, reveal to me what Skuld intends toward the king and his court."

Quietly I waited, taking several slow, deep breaths, opening myself to the world beyond myself. When at last I felt ready, I reached for the bag on the ground beside me. Putting my hand into the bag, I let the runes seek my fingers. This one? No, nor that one . . . Finally my fingers closed around a single rune. I drew it forth and laid it on the white cloth before me. Only then did I open my eyes.

Hagalaz: rune of disruption! Like hail, a natural force, an elemental power beyond one's control, Hagalaz forecast great damage, a radical break with all that has gone before. Shaken, I quickly reached for a second rune — and drew out Nauthiz, rune of constraint, adversity, misery and pain.

A great dread spread through me as I sat, now unable to move.

Who and what is this Skuld? What powers does she possess that could evoke such dire warnings? I do need to know more . . . Yes, yes, much more. A trance may be necessary after all.

When I got back to Drifa's longhouse, late that afternoon, Gerda and my women had just returned. Rushing to me, Gerda seized my hand the moment I entered.

"Lady! We saw the mounds where dead people live!" she exclaimed. "Maybe I'll see my mother and father there one day!"

Frowning, I looked around for Runa.

"What have you been telling this child?" I demanded sharply.

"Beg pardon, my lady, but she knew what sort of place it was without our telling her," said Runa quietly, coming forward.

"How did you happen to stray so far from the settlement?" I grumbled. "I used to ride there with my father on his horse, but it's a long way to walk — and you were unaccompanied!"

"Blæki ran off," volunteered Gerda eagerly, "and I ran after him!"

"That's right," added Ginnlaug, "we all followed Gerda and ended up in that . . . frightful place!" She concluded with a shudder.

"Frightful? Even as a child I found the burial mounds . . . comforting," I said, remembering those long-ago visits.

"We weren't alone, Lady Freawaru," confided Lempi. "Roald and Grim and Eskil came with us. Roald's dog wouldn't leave without him, and the other two men . . . just came along." She blushed.

I nodded, understanding why these men in particular might want to join them.

"Can we go back, Lady?" begged Gerda. "Can we?"

"Yes, we may, another time, but Gerda, your parents' remains must be buried back in Breccasberg. Those who lie in the mounds here are the ancestors of my family—the Skjoldung line—and others who once lived in Heorot."

"Oh." For a moment Gerda seemed to shrink into herself; then she lifted her chin. "Do your mother and father sleep in those mounds?"

"No, child, no." I sat down and lifted her, all arms and legs, onto my lap. "My father's burial ship was burned and sank at sea. My mother... is still alive," I said emphatically, nuzzling my chin in her sweaty hair. "Now..." I stood up and she slid off my lap. "Let's see how we can help Drifa with the evening meal. You may start by setting out bowls on the table."

As Gerda obediently commenced her task, Runa came close to my side.

"Something else has happened," she murmured. "What is it, my lady? I see... disquiet in your eyes."

Turning to her, I spoke in low tones.

"Oh, Runa, my runes have revealed a great danger, an awful fate, hanging over Heorot! I will tell you more after dinner."

Later that night, after Gerda had fallen asleep and the younger women were preparing for bed, I asked Bodvar, Drifa, Olaf and Runa to join me for a walk outside, ostensibly to enjoy the summer twilight. There had been no suitable opportunity to report my rune findings during the evening meal, nor did I want to unduly alarm the entire household before seeking further information.

When we had walked a short distance from the longhouse, Drifa exclaimed, "Tell us! What did the runes say? I've already told Bodvar about our concern."

"Runes?" repeated Olaf. "Why did you consult runes, my lady? What is amiss?"

All three stopped and looked at me expectantly.

"At issue, as Bodvar and Drifa know, is the possible power of Skuld to bring harm to King Hrolf and his people," I said carefully.

"Skuld? Isn't that the king's own sister?" queried Olaf.

"His half-sister," corrected Drifa, "but please, Lady Freawaru, tell us what the runes revealed to you!"

"The worst possible news,' I said gravely. "At the least, they predict a time of trouble and misery. At the worst, they reveal a powerful force, an elemental power beyond our control, aimed at the destruction of Heorot!"

All were silent, absorbing this dire news. Finally Bodvar spoke, measuring his words.

"Lady Freawaru, I do not doubt your divination, but intent and ability are not the same. It is known that Skuld bears some . . . ill will . . . to her brother's court, but has she the means to cause real damage? I do not think so."

"But Bodvar, don't you think Father should be told of this — this rune-reading?" asked Drifa, turning to her husband.

"Wait, Drifa, wait." I help up my hand. "Before we present this matter to the king, I will take the next step: entering a trance state. I will visit Skuld on her own ground."

"No!" burst out Runa. "No, my lady, that is too dangerous! Every time you return from such a journey, you are exhausted; you have lost a part of yourself. You never fully recovered from your last such 'visit' — to the dragon."

"Dragon?!" exclaimed Drifa, her eyes wide with wonder.

"Skuld too may be a dragon," I admitted, "but I must seek her in her lair if I am to learn her plans. Tomorrow I will prepare myself for the necessary ritual. I'll need your flute, Runa, and someone to beat the drum."

Drifa and Bodvar looked at me in doubt, but Runa nodded reluctantly.

"As you wish, my lady. You know I am always ready to serve you."

As it turned out, Gerda beat the drum. She had watched as Lise, Lempi, then Ginnlaug tried unsuccessfully to beat a steady rhythm following my example.

"Let me try!" she begged. "I can do it!"

Indeed she could, her strong little hands pounding out a rhythm steady as a heartbeat.

"That's exactly what I need! Thank you, child!"

I had not thought to involve Gerda in the ritual, so I now sought to prepare her for what might happen — as well as the younger women, who had never witnessed such a rite.

"When I enter the trance, I will leave my body behind—in spirit—and fly to far places. When I return, I may collapse and seem to be dead or dying... but I will revive, I will come back to you!"

"Promise?" whispered Gerda hoarsely.

"I promise," I said fervently.

"If I were truly a sparrow, I'd fly away with you!"she declared, shaking off sudden tears.

"Thank you, little sparrow." Encircling Gerda's thin shoulders, I embraced her tenderly.

For the vision ritual I chose a location near the marshy pool, far enough from the settlement not be to heard or disturbed. Only Gerda and my four women came with me.

I had noticed the discomfort displayed by both Drifa and Skur concerning anything that might seem to resemble witchcraft, and told them they could best help me by preparing a rich broth to replenish my energies after the 'visit.' Drifa had immediately selected her fattest hen and wrung its neck; she and Skur were plucking its feathers when I and my group left for the pool that morning. Gerda carried my drum, Runa her flute.

In a small clearing I used the staff I'd brought to draw a circle in the dirt, a small circle.

"I will stand inside the circle, holding a cloth once touched by Skuld," I said, pulling the object from my bag. "When I give a signal, Gerda will begin the drumbeat and Runa will add the flute as I begin to turn. Ginnlaug, Lise and Lempi—you will sit outside the circle and be prepared to catch me if I should fall. Now. Is everyone ready?"

All nodded solemnly. Taking a deep breath, I stepped inside the circle. Clutching Skuld's head cloth, I raised it to the sky, invoking the goddess.

"Freyja, great goddess, hear me! Come to your Freawaru, blessed with your mark. Lift me on your falcon wings, enfold me in your feather cloak. Carry me to the heart of Skuld's domain, into her secret heart, that I may see what is hidden there. Lift me, great goddess. Carry me afar and bring me back safely to my body."

At my nod, Gerda began a steady beat on the drum. Runa added a high, floating melody on her flute. I began to turn inside the circle, slowly at first, then faster, rotating ever faster. As the figures around me blurred, I closed my eyes and gave myself up to the drumbeat and the melody. Soon I lost all sense of my body.

Am I floating? Flying? Yes ... I feel wind on my face and my wings beating the air!

For a time I coasted on the currents, then dipped and soared in a soundless world. Gradually the air grew colder and I sensed a distant storm approaching, a looming mass of darkness ... Suddenly I was pulled into the darkness, plunged headlong into its icy heart. All motion ceased. Gasping for breath, I hovered above a high headland.

Below me I beheld a skeletal figure, a woman, her long, black hair streaming in the wind. She carried a long pole to which was affixed the skull of a horse. The woman turned, seeming to sense an intruder. She lifted the pole, pointing the skull directly at me. A shaft of hatred blazed from its empty eye-sockets, blinding me, scalding me. With a shriek I fell, plummeting to earth.

"Lady, Lady, come back!"

Hot tears were falling on my face. I struggled to lift my lids and managed to open one eye. Above me knelt Gerda, sobbing bitterly.

Chapter Eight
Gathering Clues

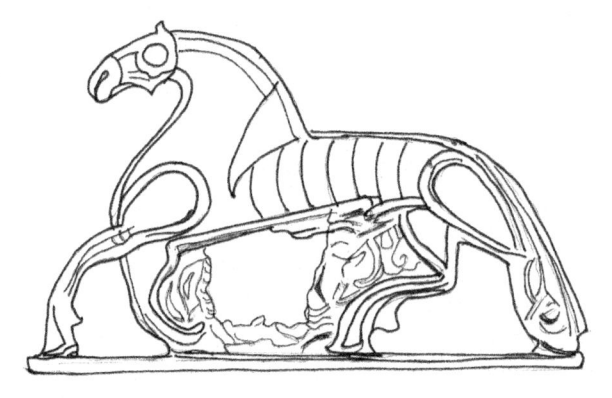

Bronze stallion found in Denmark c. AD 400-800. National Museum, Copenhagen.

Lempi and Lise held me; Ginnlaug was bathing my face. I struggled to rise, but Runa placed a hand on my shoulder.

"Wait, my lady. Too soon. Give yourself more time to recover. You've had a great shock." She was staring at my face with a look of wonder and dismay.

Gerda put it into words. "Lady! Your eye hairs! They're gone! But you're alive!"

"Yes, thank the goddess, I'm alive," I said slowly, reaching up one hand to touch my eyebrows. They felt... scorched.

With the help of my women and my staff I was able to walk back to Drifa's longhouse. She was stirring a pot of chicken stew when we entered, Skur beside her tasting it with a long ladle. Skur dropped the ladle when she saw my face.

"You've been hurt! What happened?" She rushed to my side.

"Sit here," directed Drifa, indicating a bench near the hearth, "where we can see you better."

"I'm alright," I protested. "I'm just... drained... from the encounter."

"With Skuld?" asked Drifa sharply.

"Yes, with Skuld. You and Skur were right. Skuld's power is greater than I imagined — and more malevolent!"

The two sisters were now intently studying my face.

"What happened?" asked Skur again.

I recounted what I could remember of the vision; when I described the horse's skull with its empty sockets, Drifa shuddered.

"An evil eye! She sent an evil eye to blast you — curse you — possibly even kill you!"

Skur hurried to the hearth, dipped up a bowl of stew and brought it to me, carefully.

"Here. You need this after what you've been through!"

"I'm hungry too!" piped up Gerda, sitting at my feet.

Our laughter released some of the tension that lay heavy in the air.

"Yes, let's all have a bowl," said Drifa, "and I have a salve for those eyebrows of yours, Lady Freawaru."

All that afternoon the women kept me inside, resting in Drifa's own bedchamber. Gerda stayed beside me, cross-legged on the floor, occasionally reaching up to touch my hand as if to assure herself that I was still alive. At times I fell into a light sleep and dreamed; at one point I felt the distant pull of darkness, a darkness that sought to suck me into its gaping maw. When I woke with a start, sweating and crying out, Gerda was there to comfort me.

Drifa's salve, a mixture of dockweed and animal fat, soothed my burning brow but did not take away all the pain, so I directed Runa in preparing a tea of kvann and yarrow. By evening I had begun to feel much more like myself, though it would take some time for my eyebrows to grow back.

That night Drifa asked me to tell Bodvar what I had experienced. He listened in silence, then shook his head.

"It may be that we have underestimated Skuld's... powers. The king should hear of this. In the morning I will take you to him for a private hearing."

The morning was fresh and fair as Bodvar and I left the longhouse. After the trauma of the day before I felt glad to be alive. I smiled, breathing in the warm, pine-scented air, though I wore my head cloth low over my brows to shield them from the sun. Somewhere nearby—perhaps from a hidden nest—trilled the sweet voice of a lark, sweeter even than Runa's flute.

Bodvar led me to Hrolf's private chamber on the upper level of the mead hall. From the gallery I could overlook the hall itself, and through a series of openings cut just below the roofline, the courtyard beyond. From this height I could see past houses, fields and pastures all the way to the fjord. Near the harbor loomed the burial mounds of my ancestors. Did my brothers now lie there?

King Hrolf received me graciously, wine in actual glasses already set out on a small, polished wood table. I glanced about the paneled chamber, expecting rich hangings, but it was sparsely decorated with only a few fine robes and furs to indicate royal status.

Hrolf himself was another matter; once again he was dressed in clothes of the finest fabrics and workmanship: a finely woven white linen shirt under a short tunic of light blue wool, the sleeves edged with bands of gold thread. Gold also gleamed on his arms and fingers, but he wore no circlet on his head this morning.

"Good morrow, Lady Freawaru—or may I call you 'cousin'?" he began, seating me at his table as Bodvar left the room.

"'Lady Freawaru' will do," I replied with a token smile, "though we are cousins."

He sat down across from me, graceful as a cat.

"Bodvar tells me that you have a matter of great import to bring before me, but first—please try the wine. I have it brought in from Francia."

He must think to impress me. Beowulf often served such wine!

A shadow must have passed over my face, for Hrolf leaned forward.

"Never fear. I won't try to seduce you." He smiled, glancing at the shut-bed built into one corner.

"If you did try, I still carry my knife — and it is always sharp," I replied evenly.

His smile disappeared, to be replaced by a frown.

"I do remember a long-ago encounter with that knife," he reflected, "but those days are long past. Let us get to the business you have brought. What do you have to tell me?"

What else do you remember, cousin? Do you remember my brothers, and my mother?

I pushed aside my own thoughts to answer him.

"It concerns your half-sister, Skuld. I have seen her in a vision directing curses at your court. She means to do you great harm, in any way she can."

Hrolf raised an eyebrow. "Skuld? Harm? Why, what could she do? Burn down my mead hall? Blast our fields? Attack with an army? Surely, cousin, you have been carried away with your own supposed powers of sight! Skuld is no danger to me or my court . . . Perhaps you are the danger, spreading lies and rumors about my sister!"

He had risen during this speech and stood glaring down at me. I too rose and faced him.

"Tell me, King Hrolf, did I not have eyebrows when we met at midsummer?" I removed my head cloth so he could better see my face. Taken aback, he stared at me.

"By the gods! I thought you looked . . . different. They are gone! What happened?"

"In my vision Skuld blasted me — with the anger she feels toward you! She did this to me and she has the power to do much, much more — to you." I drew myself up to full height. "King Hrolf, I only became involved in this matter at the request of your own daughters. They fear Skuld and fear the damage she may do to your kingdom!"

Slowly we both resumed our seats.

"So . . ." muttered Hrolf, almost to himself, "some of the reports I've been hearing may contain a grain of truth . . . yet my daughters have always been jealous of Skuld . . . this may be merely women's talk . . ."

"King Hrolf," I interjected, "I have told you what I came to say. It is for you to decide how to respond to the information." I began to rise.

"Nay, cousin, stay. I would have more talk with you — and you have not yet tasted your wine."

"Very well," I said, sitting down. "In fact, I will propose a toast: to the memory of King Hrothgar and Queen Wealtheow!" I lifted my glass.

Hrolf did not hesitate, raising his glass as well.

"To Hrothgar and Wealtheow. They were father and mother to me!"

We drank and set down our glasses.

"Cousin Freawaru, let us begin again," said Hrolf, wiping his lips with a fine white cloth he drew from his tunic. "I know that in the past we were not always...friends...but we were children then."

"Not always," I countered. "We were adults when I left Heorot — after the deaths of my two brothers!"

"Ah, now it comes out. You blame me still for their deaths," exclaimed Hrolf. "I swear to you by all the gods, I had no hand in their...demise."

"Snake!" I hissed, glaring into his dark eyes, "How can I believe you?"

I jumped up, knocking over the table and sending our glasses crashing to the floor.

"How can I believe you — you, who taunted and tormented me from your first day at Heorot! You — who forced yourself upon me! You — who usurped my brother's place on the throne! You — you — would you had never been born!"

Shocked by my own outburst, at the pent-up rage built up over so many years, I stood aghast. What had I done? So distraught was I that it took me a moment to realize: Hrolf had not moved, but sat staring at me as if frozen.

Slowly he rose, righting the table. He brushed aside the broken glass with his elegant boot and gestured for me to resume my seat. Shaken, I did so, moving as if in a dream.

"Freawaru," he said, staring through me, "you are not the first to wish I had never been born. My own...mother...said that. Her departure from my life was the reason I came to live at Heorot!"

"I did not know that," I whispered, suddenly spent.

"To my mother's horror," continued Hrolf, his eyes glazed, "she had just discovered that she was married to . . . her own father. So, she fled — from him — from me — from the Danemark — to escape the gods' punishment, but, of course, there is no escape..."

So, those whispered rumors I'd heard as a child in the women's hall, those abruptly silenced conversations...this had been their topic: Hrolf, the bastard child of incest.

I stared at my cousin in astonishment. Hrolf's eyes fixed on mine.

"You once told me, cousin, that one day I would be a great king; do you remember that? Your prophecy has come true, has it not? Look around you at all I have: this settlement, the warriors who serve me ... I lack only one thing: a woman who would love and understand me. I thought, after Hrothgar died, perhaps ... Wealtheow ... but she also spurned me."

"What! You wanted to marry my mother?" I was on my feet again. "No wonder she fled from Heorot! You drove her away!"

Hrolf looked stricken. "No — no — I swear to you! I never touched her, I didn't hurt her," he pleaded. "I was as surprised as Unferth when she disappeared!"

"You are lying! You know something you're not telling me — just like Unferth!' I cried, clenching my fists.

Hrolf rose, pain still showing on his face.

"Cousin, cousin, calm yourself!"

Heading for the door, I paused.

"Yes, there is more between us that must be settled," I said firmly.

As I stood there momentarily, Hrolf advanced and gestured toward my face.

"Cousin, thank you for your warning about Skuld. I am truly sorry that, in attempting to help me, you have met with injury. But your hair ..." reaching out slender fingers, he touched a lock that curled about my shoulders ..." is still a wonder."

Before I left Hrolf's chamber we agreed to meet again on the morrow, and he asked that I be his honored guest in the mead hall that night. By the time I returned to Bodvar and Drifa's house I was again exhausted, but also elated: I had stood my ground with the king.

"Well?" Both Drifa and Skur were waiting when I entered.

"What did Father say?" asked Skur.

"Did you convince him that Skuld is a danger?" asked Drifa.

Runa took one look at my drooping shoulders and led me to a bench.

"I've made a start," I said, sitting and removing my head cloth, which I had donned immediately after leaving Hrolf's chamber. "Now it is up to the king — and the rest of you — to deal with Skuld. I'll take no further part in the matter."

Drifa and Skur looked at each other uncertainly.

"But, you won't ... abandon us, will you?" pressed Skur.

"No," I sighed, "but I must be about the business that brought me to Heorot in the first place; I must unearth the clues that will lead me to my mother."

Drifa and Skur still looked uncertain.

"Right now," I declared, "I must rest and recover, for I am to be introduced in the mead hall tonight, and I want to look my best."

"We can help with that!" said Drifa, her brow clearing. 'Outside, everyone, so Lady Freawaru can get some rest!"

That night I was accompanied by both Bodvar and Hjalti as I entered the mead hall. I had dressed with care, wearing my finest kirtle and shift, trimmed with gold braid. On my head cloth I had placed the coronet of jewels given to me by Ingeld, my long-ago husband: in their filigreed setting nestled a lustrous pearl, a blood-red ruby, and a stone as blue as the bluest sea.

Earlier that evening Gerda had declared, "You look beautiful!" as she kissed me good night, something new she had added to our bedtime ritual.

"Thank you, my sparrow. Perhaps tomorrow we will visit the mounds again. The king has promised me a horse to use during our ... visit. Have you ever ridden a horse?"

She shook her head. "No, but I'd like to — could we go fast?"

I had laughed and assured her that we would ride like the wind.

Inside the smoky hall, Bodvar and Hjalti led me straight to the throne chair next to King Hrolf, who was already seated.

"But that is the consort's chair," I objected, stopping short.

King Hrolf rose and made a low bow before me, in the presence of the whole assembly, then took my hand. "Tonight you are the queen of Roskilde," he murmured.

What is he doing? Is this one of his tricks?

Facing the assembly he said loudly, "Tonight we are honored by the presence of Hrothgar's daughter, the Lady Freawaru. All hail, Freawaru!"

"All hail, Freawaru!" came the response.

As he seated me, Hrolf murmured again. "Don't look so surprised! You certainly don't want to sit near my berserkers! You'll be much more comfortable by my side."

Berserkers? I settled myself and looked at the row of tables nearest the throne. Indeed, the men who sat there looked a fierce lot: ugly, unkempt, shaggy giants, men of the roughest sort. They were belching and guffawing, throwing bones at a poor serving lad they had tripped up in passing.

"Here, enough of that!" roared Bodvar Bjarki, hauling the lad to his feet. To my surprise the berserkers instantly subsided, growling and grumbling.

Beside me, the king nodded with satisfaction. "They respect Bjarki," he said, leaning toward me, "with good reason. Bjarki is more feared than any other warrior—except for Svipdag. Svipdag once killed three berserkers in a row in a holmgang."

"Holmgang? What is that?" I asked, mystified.

"Actually a holmgang is a small island," explained Hrolf. "Warriors go there to settle scores, man to man. Either a cloak is set down or four willow wands are used to mark off the field, and blows go by turns. The man who is driven beyond the cloak—or wands—is deemed the loser, though sometimes the contest goes on until first blood, or yielding, or... death." Hrolf smiled grimly.

I looked at him in horror. "Do you sanction such brutal activities?"

Hrolf shrugged. "I strive to rule as Hrothgar did, by peaceful means, but there is often need for strength—and sometimes, intimidation. My berserkers serve a useful purpose."

I could barely hear his words above the rising clamor in the hall: cheers and laughter, the clatter of serving bowls, dogs barking, people singing...

"You entertain a large host!" I almost shouted to be heard.

"Yes," Hrolf shouted back. "And this is not all of my force. With my berserkers, and champions such as Bjarki and Svipdag, we are proof against any threat!" he concluded emphatically.

Is he thinking of Skuld? A physical threat may not be all that he should fear.

As the evening wore on, I was able to move freely about the hall, accompanied this time by Vögg. He assured me that Unferth was not present, but I still glanced at the doorway whenever a new person entered. Thus it was that I met Borghild.

A tall woman with gray hair and brawny build, she was ushering in two thralls carrying a heavy cauldron, which she helped them attach to a chain over the hearth. Something about her face and the decisive way she moved seemed familiar... I searched my memory.

"Excuse me, Vögg. I would speak with that woman." I nodded toward the figure bending over the hearth.

"Our cook? Is there something wrong with the food, Lady Freawaru?" Vögg looked at me anxiously.

"No, no," I assured him. "The food is... excellent. Go on ahead, please, and tell Olaf that I would speak with our young men. I'll only be a moment."

"As you wish, my lady." Vögg left to do my bidding.

The woman was already heading for the door when I caught up with her and laid a hand on the back of her shoulder.

"Beg pardon, but are you... Torgun, the blacksmith's wife?"

The woman turned and eyed me suspiciously. After taking in my dress and jewels, her face went blank and she made a slight bow.

"Torgun was my mother's name, my lady. Why do you speak of her?"

"Torgun was my mother's friend," I replied, "and you must be the daughter who looked after my two brothers during our women's rituals."

The woman squinted and peered at me through the haze of wood smoke.

"My mother was your mother's friend?" She stood, puzzling. "Do you speak of Queen Wealtheow?"

"Yes," I smiled, delighted to hear that name on the lips of someone from Heorot.

"Then you must be Wealtheow's daughter! You look just like her!" Her face crinkled in a broad smile.

"Indeed I am. I am Freawaru. What is your name? I would have more talk with you."

"Borghild, my lady, Borghild. We are very busy in the eld-hus at present, but you can find me there any time of the day."

"I understand. Please go on with your work. Oh, and Borghild—the food is excellent."

She beamed, bowed again, and hurried out of the hall.

I found Olaf, Vögg and our crew of young men seated in a dim corner, taking their ease. All rose when I approached their table.

"Lady Freawaru, if you've made friends with the cook," teased Grim, "ask her to serve more of this eel stew. I've never tasted better!"

Enthusiastic nods from the others backed up his statement.

"I'll be sure to tell her," I smiled. "Please, everyone, be seated."

As they resumed their places, I raised a hand to touch my eyebrows. "Before anyone asks, I'll explain my strange appearance," I said matter-of-factly. "In a recent vision I had an encounter with a suspected sorceress, who blasted me with her wrath." I paused. "The eyebrows will grow back."

Shocked, the men exchanged glances of awe and wonder.

"Now," I went on, "tell me what you men have been doing since our arrival? I've not seen you for many days."

Slowly, as if shaking off a bad dream, Sigrod and Anton turned to each other.

"We've been helping Hjalti exercise and break horses," volunteered Anton.

"Good. I hope you can recommend a horse gentle enough for Gerda," I responded, "and one for me."

"Lady Freawaru, I know just the animal for Sparrow," declared Sigrod. " . . . a little fjord horse, very tame. As for you, my lady, I'd suggest Sunbeorht — a spirited mare, but tractable."

Now Grim spoke up. "Eskil, Gunnulf and I have been learning how to feed and care for the hawks — under Vögg's supervision."

"Oh, I'd love to see them!" I exclaimed and turned to Vögg. "Where do you keep them?"

Vögg swelled with importance. "In a loft near the edge of Roskilde. Yes, the king's champions have entrusted me, Vögg, with the care of their valuable birds — a weighty responsibility!" he declared. "I don't let any of the thralls touch them — no indeed! Only those who have a gift for hawking — as these three seem to have — can approach them."

I thought of Gerda calling the ravens, and suggested, "Perhaps they would allow me . . . ?"

Vögg looked dubious.

"Perhaps. They can be vicious killers . . . why, when we were in Uppsala, King Hrolf's hawk, Highbreeks, wiped out every hawk in King Eadgil's mews — ripped them apart with his beak and claws! Served Eadgils right, too, for maiming our horses!"

After a moment's silence while we envisioned that scene, Alf cleared his throat.

"Knud and I have spent most of our time at the forge, helping Jörgen make chain mail—a slow, and very hot process."

"That is good to know!" I exclaimed. "I did not know you two possessed such skills!"

Knud laughed. "I can do more than tell stories, my lady."

"That leaves you three," I said, nodding at Vigo, Bram and Roald, who were sitting together on one side of the table.

"Yesterday's venison came from our hands," said Vigo quietly. "Roald's dog has been keen to hunt, though we've not yet found elk on this island."

"Nor will you," I said, "but red deer are plentiful here. A great rack of one's antlers once hung over the entrance to... my father's mead hall."

As I said these words my voice broke, and several men glanced up in curiosity. Olaf now put a question to me.

"With respect, my lady, the men have been wondering if you intend to settle here, or continue your search for Wealtheow... elsewhere."

I swallowed. "Soon, I'll be able to answer that question, Olaf, soon." I rose. "Now I must say good night to King Hrolf before leaving the hall."

All rose and bowed respectfully as I left the table, again with Vögg at my side.

The next day dawned mild and breezy—a perfect day for a ride, as Gerda reminded me.

"We'll go, I promise," I told her, "but first I must speak with the cook—that is, with Borghild. She remembers my mother."

"Can I go with you?" asked Gerda, as usual.

"Yes, you may. My visit with Borghild should not take long. Then we'll walk to the meadows where the horses graze. Sigrod said he'd help us pick a mount."

"Ooh!" squealed Gerda. "A fast horse!"

"Well, maybe not at first... we'll see."

Despite having eaten a large bowl of porridge to start the day, the smells coming from the cookhouse made my mouth water. Smoke spiraled from the roof vent, and we could feel heat radiating from the open door as we approached. Inside I could see what looked like a small army of thralls at work.

At one hearth young boys turned spits over the fire, threaded with chickens, ducks, even whole piglets. A second hearth held two bubbling cauldrons hung on tripods, ready to receive the offerings of the thralls scurrying from table to hearth. At a row of tables along either side stood young girls chopping vegetables: cabbages, carrots, onions. Others were gutting fish or cutting chunks of meat into smaller pieces for stew.

In addition to the smoke hole in the roof, I noticed that small openings had been cut in the gable ends and lined with some sort of transparent membrane to admit more light. When she saw us in the doorway, Borghild barked an order over her shoulder. Wiping her hands on her apron, she came toward us, blowing a wisp of hair out of her eyes.

"A busy morning — but it's always like this," she said as we stepped outside. She gestured toward a pair of benches beneath a tall ash tree. "We can sit and talk a bit out here, if you like."

I nodded and followed her into the shade. She sat down with a sigh as I seated myself across from her. Gerda slowly circled the tree, inspecting its climbing possibilities. Borghild looked at me expectantly.

"I have not seen my mother since I was a young bride," I began, "but I do believe she is still alive, for I feel her calling me." I paused. "Borghild, can you remember the last time you saw Wealtheow?"

Borghild nodded decisively. "I do. Your naming of her and Torgun last night brought back old memories." She paused, shaking her head and staring at the ground. "That was a dark time for Heorot, it was. King Hrothgar had died and no one knew who would take his place. Then Wealtheow's sons both died — but of course you know all that, my lady — you were there!" She raised her head to look at me quizzically.

"Yes, for a brief time," I acknowledged. "I came back from the country of the Heathobards after my husband's death. Then, after my brothers ... died, I left Heorot and my mother was supposed to come with me, but she stayed behind. Later I heard that she had indeed left Heorot, but no one could tell me where she'd gone. I'm hoping you can help me."

Borghild pursed her lips. "The queen sometimes confided in my mother, but as far as I know, she did not tell Torgun where she was going."

"Did you ever hear them talk about my mother's homeland?" I asked. "Mother never told me much about her family or where she'd come from ... A country, perhaps, or a name?"

Borghild considered. "Yes, I do remember one name, because I thought it an odd name for a family; something like Wylfing ... or ... Wulfing ... or ... Wuffing?" She shrugged. "It's been a long time."

"Yes, and I'm grateful for your willingness to help. Now, you said you remembered when you'd last seen Wealtheow?"

Borghild nodded. "Yes. It was late one night, it was. She'd come to our longhouse — I remember how surprised I was to find the queen at our door, but Mother seemed to be expecting her. They went off together and were gone a long time."

"What was she wearing — Wealtheow, I mean. Was she dressed for a voyage?"

Borghild frowned. "I don't remember — but I do remember that she seemed light-hearted, somewhat excited — which seemed strange to me, considering she'd just buried her sons!"

Light-hearted? Excited? What could have happened?

"Did your mother say anything to you when she came back home that night?"

"Yes," nodded Borghild, "she did. She said it very solemn-like, almost to herself; a kind of prophecy, it was. She said, 'they will not return while Hrothulf lives.'"

"'They'? Who did she mean by 'they'?"

Borghild shrugged. "I don't know. She didn't say."

My mind had just begun to whirl with possibilities when a shriek above us made us both jump up. Gerda came crashing down through the branches... into Borghild's strong, outstretched arms.

"Good thing you're light as a feather, my girl!" laughed Borghild as she set Gerda gently on her feet.

Gerda gasped, catching her breath, then squeaked, "I'm a sparrow!"

"Are you hurt? Let me have a look at you, child!" I reached out both hands in alarm.

Gerda shook her arms and wiggled her legs. "I'm alright," she announced, cheerfully.

And so she seemed to be.

"Can we go ride the horses now?"

When we reached the meadow where the horses usually grazed, Sigrod was waiting, but with only one horse. He had tied a rope around the neck of a shaggy little fjord horse and now handed the other end to Gerda. Apologetically he explained to me that Sunbeorht and the other mounts were being used for hunting.

"Ooh! What's its name?" Gerda exclaimed, taking the rope and reaching up to pat the creature's nose.

"He doesn't have one — so you can call him whatever you like," said Sigrod.

Gerda eyed the small animal. "He'll tell me his name," she said seriously. "Can I ride him now?"

Sigrod bent down to pick up a sleeping robe, folded it and positioned it on the little horse's back.

"This will be your saddle for now. You'll sit here and hold on to the rope around his neck." Glancing at me first for permission, he asked Gerda, "Are you ready to try him?"

Gerda nodded an enthusiastic yes.

"Then up you go!"

Sigrod swung Gerda up onto the make-shift saddle and settled her on the horse, her skinny legs splayed out on either side of the animal's broad back. It gave only a brief shiver and cropped a mouthful of grass. Taking the lead rope, Sigrod gave it a sharp tug and the horse began to move, plodding slowly forward.

"Look, Lady, I'm riding!" shouted Gerda. "But Sigrod, how do I make it go faster?"

"That's fast enough for now," I called. "Let the horse get used to you first!"

Instinctively Gerda banged her heels on the horse's side and it picked up speed. Sigrod began running alongside to keep up.

"Slow down, Gerda!" I shouted. "Sigrod — make her slow down!"

Grinning, Sigrod used the rope to turn the horse in a wide circle as Gerda bounced gleefully on its back. As she circled, I was transported back to my own childhood and the feel of the horse under me as I galloped across the meadows or trotted out to the burial mounds. Hmmm ... perhaps tomorrow I would visit those mounds ... alone. Round and round went Gerda and Sigrod. Finally I called to her.

"Have you had enough riding for today?"

"No, but ... Strongfellow says I can ride him again whenever I want."

"Strongfellow? Is that his name?"

"Yes," said Gerda confidently. "That's his name."

That night Gerda woke me with cries of terror. Hurrying to her bench, I shook her gently.

"Child, child, wake up! You're dreaming! It's Freawaru. You're safe!"

Shuddering, she blinked and gaped up at me.

"Is it gone?" she whispered. "Did you make it go away?"

"What? What did you see?" I gathered her in my arms and held her close.

"The monster, the monster that comes at night," she whispered, still shuddering against me.

"It is gone," I assured her. "You're safe. You were dreaming — a nightmare."

With a shuddering sigh she closed her eyes and I eased her back onto her bench.

"There were monsters when I was a girl," I murmured, "but they are all gone now. Beowulf killed them."

The next morning King Hrolf sent Hjalti to me with an apology for not providing the promised horse. To make amends, the king himself would take me riding. I had mixed feelings about this offer — or was it more of an order? Did he intend to control my movements while I stayed in Heorot? Was he afraid I might learn something he preferred to keep hidden?

"Thank you, Hjalti. Please tell the king I will be ... honored to have his company."

To Gerda I said, "No, child, this time you can't come with me. The king and I have ... private matters to discuss."

That afternoon when Hjalti led Sunbeorht directly to the door of Drifa's longhouse, I was prepared for riding, dressed in a light kirtle and barley-colored tunic open at the sides — an adjustment Runa had made for me. Hjalti cupped his hands to help me mount, and I slid easily up onto the fine-grained leather saddle. The bridle was likewise a fine one, decorated with fittings of bronze.

The name 'Sunbeorht' befitted the horse: a dainty cream-colored mare with a white mane and tail, radiant in the sunlight. Gerda looked up at me enviously.

"Will you ride like the wind today, Lady?"

"Perhaps," I laughed, looking forward to that very possibility.

When King Hrolf arrived on Deofol, I was taken aback, for the contrast could not have been more marked. His powerful stallion was black as the night sea, a blackness set off by the silver and gilt mounts that decorated bridle and reins.

"Is he really a demon?" I asked, referring to the horse's name. "If so, I may not be able to keep up with you."

"Never fear," replied Hrolf, flashing his full set of white teeth, "I have no intention of losing you!"

Once again he was carefully dressed, this time wearing finely-fitted leather leggings and boots below a blue cloak that floated about his shoulders.

"Where shall we ride, cousin?"

"To the burial mounds?" I suggested. "I would see the place where my brothers lie."

"To the mounds, then," said Hrolf. He wheeled his mount and we set off, riding side by side at a leisurely pace through the settlement.

Chapter Nine
Visiting the Dead

Funerary urn with runes from Sancton, Yorkshire. Urn with bossed and stamped decoration from Lackford, Suffolk.

It had been many moons since I'd been on horseback, but Sunbeorht soon put me at ease, responding to the slightest pressure on flank or bit. Hrolf's mount was clearly a warhorse, well-muscled and a full head taller than Sunbeorht, which meant that Hrolf had to lean over to talk to me. I sat straight and tall in the saddle, looking demurely ahead, my head cloth tied on tightly.

"Hjalti and Sigrod — picked a good horse for me," I said as we ambled slowly past rows of longhouses.

Hrolf nodded. "Hjalti is a good man. I call him 'Hjalti the Highminded'!"

"Why is that?" I asked, puzzled.

"Hjalti was once the butt of ridicule in the mead hall — before Bjarki took him in hand," explained Hrolf. "Now he is respected and treated with deference. He could have retaliated, but he has taken no revenge on those who once scorned him." Hrolf looked thoughtful. "One can learn much from such a man."

I turned to look up at my cousin, somewhat amazed. He sounded sincere, even humble.

"Are all your champions so . . . high-minded?" I asked lightly.

Hrolf nodded emphatically.

"Yes — in different ways. I am most fortunate in my followers. But, tell me of your own life — in Geatland. Did you come to know Beowulf?"

Jerking my head, I stared up at Hrolf. How could he ask such a question? Yet . . . how could he know?

"Beowulf and I were to become husband and wife," I said quietly. "I lost him . . . to the dragon."

Hrolf reined in Deofol and reached out a hand. I too reined in my steed.

"I am sorry. I did not know of your . . . connection. Forgive me," he said, his dark eyes filled with emotion. "I know what it is to lose one's beloved. My Solveig . . . is gone."

Hrolf speaking of love and loss? I did not expect this!

"Your Solveig? Please tell me of her," I urged, curious to learn what sort of woman could love and be loved by Hrolf.

"Solveig: her name suited her well, for she brought sunshine into my life," declared Hrolf, "at a dark time when I was seeking to find my way. It was after Hrothgar died, after you, then Wealtheow, left Heorot."

Ah, I must ask him today what he remembers of that leave-taking.

"She was walking in this very meadow — the one we're riding through now — gathering wildflowers, when I first saw her." Hrolf's face brightened at the memory. "Golden hair flowed down about her hips when she rose to face me. I remember her face was sunburned and sprinkled with freckles . . . Even on tiptoe she barely reached up to my chin . . ."

His voice choked and he fell silent. We sat motionless on our horses in the middle of the meadow dotted with cornflowers, dandelions and clover, the mid-day sun warming our shoulders.

"She wanted to marry, but I would not take a commoner's daughter to be my queen." Hrolf shook his head as if to rid it of a persistent regret. "She gave me two beautiful daughters . . . before she died."

"Ah," I said softly, "Drifa and Skur. Wonderful women. Your Solveig—did she die in childbirth?"

Hrolf stared at me wordlessly.

"I killed her!" he said finally.

"What? What do you mean?" I exclaimed in horror.

"I as good as killed her," Hrolf said bitterly. "It was my fault she died. I left her sick and alone while I made war on neighboring tribes—to expand my kingdom! I wanted to live up to your prophecy! I wanted to be a great king!"

His eyes had taken on an unsettling glitter.

"King Hrolf," I said quickly, "Wyrd has its way in this world. There are times when we are powerless to prevent the loss of what we hold dear. Let go of guilt. Holding on to blame steals one's courage!"

Hrolf stared at me a moment longer, nodded slowly, then picked up the reins.

"Let us ride on—to the mounds."

The burial mounds were much as I remembered them: green-clad hillocks spaced irregularly on a headland above the harbor. I had loved coming here as a child with my parents, loved to hear that I came from a long line of mighty rulers. To me it was a place of peace. Hrolf and I dismounted near the first mound, slightly smaller than the others.

"I do not recognize this one," I said. "Whose ashes does it hold?"

Hrolf opened and closed his mouth, then opened it again.

"Your brothers. I thought that's what you wanted to see—the place where your brothers lie," he said simply.

Now it was my turn to stare at him.

"Yes..." I said slowly. "My brothers: Hrethric and Hrothmund."

Silently handing the reins of my mount to Hrolf, I turned away from him and began to circle the mound, keening softly.

"Brothers, dear brothers, I am here. It is Freawaru who calls you, who mourns for you, who grieves for your loss—noble sons of a noble king."

I stopped and bowed my head, arms outstretched, palms open to the sky.

"Do you rest easy in your bed of earth, my brothers? Or do you thirst for justice, for revenge against those who cut short your lives? Oh, speak to me, my brothers! Speak to sister Freawaru!"

Hrolf's hand on my shoulder stopped my supplication.

"What are you doing, cousin? Do you truly seek to wake the dead?!" Hrolf gazed at me in alarm. I shook off his restraining hand, fiercely.

"Do you fear them, Hrothulf? Do you fear what they might tell me?"

He drew back, but shook his head.

"Your brothers were honored with all due ceremony—Wealtheow saw to that. Their funeral pyre was richly decked with weapons; horses were sacrificed. Neither they—nor you—have reason to reproach me. Why... I myself will lie here one day, one of the Skjoldung line. I would not wish for... unquiet neighbors," he said with a faint smile.

"You would jest about my brothers' deaths?" I blazed at him. "You, who fed them the poisonous mushrooms?"

Once again Hrolf shook his head and sighed.

"What can I say, cousin, what can I do to convince you of my innocence? I would take an oath on Hrothgar's grave, were he buried here. My own father..." he looked unseeing into the distance,"... lies somewhere in Sweden, in a mound erected by my mother... his own daughter."

He shook himself and held out his hand.

"Come, cousin, be at peace. Let us walk quietly among the graves of your—of our—ancestors."

Almost involuntarily I took his hand, a slender hand but strong. As he gripped my own, I felt something hard inside me shift and let go, leaving a space... perhaps for reconciliation.

As we walked, our horses trailed behind us, now and again cropping the rich green grass. I named the occupants of mounds I could identify.

"...and that's grandfather Halfdan's. He used to come out and wave at me from atop his war horse," I said, only half teasing.

Hrolf gave me a sidelong glance but said nothing.

"Cousin," I said, adopting his chosen form of address, "where lies Aelric, father's old harper? Was he buried with Hrethric and Hrothmund? That would have been fitting, since they died together."

"Aelric? I do not remember that name," declared Hrolf, passing a hand over his eyes. "I do remember that only two remains were buried in that mound, for I myself saw them interred there."

He looked at me apologetically. "I must confess, cousin, that I do not recall many of the events surrounding your brothers' deaths. Mostly I remember what Unferth told me... afterward."

I looked at him curiously.

"Do you remember the morning I left Heorot?"

Hrolf regarded me uncertainly.

"Partly. I remember being angry that you were leaving and wanting to stop you. I remember holding someone — Brita, was it? — and charging into the cookhouse where bodies lay stretched out on tables... After that I don't remember... anything."

"You mentioned Unferth. What did he tell you of that morning?"

Hrolf squinted, as if trying to peer into the past.

"Unferth told me that he'd had to resort to physical measures to protect you — hence the lump on my head — but that all would be well."

Hrolf reached up to rub the back of his head and smiled ruefully.

"Sometimes it takes a heavy blow to bring a man to his senses!"

His eyes were gentle, free of rancor or bitterness.

"Cousin Freawaru, we have little family left to us, you and me. Let us cherish what we have."

"Yes... cousin, but families may also nurture the seeds of their own destruction! Have you given further thought to... Skuld?"

Hrolf grimaced and sighed.

"Indeed, I have thought long and deeply about my sister." He fixed me with a penetrating gaze. "You yourself, Freawaru, understand the strength of the bond between brother and sister. I heard it in your words at the mound back there. It is not easy to break the bonds of blood!"

"Still," I persisted, "you have the safety of others to consider as well as your own. And Skuld may not experience the blood bond as you do, being only... partly human."

Hrolf bowed his head, then lifted it.

"Freawaru, there is something I must show you — back in my quarters. It may help explain the... special relationship... I have with my sister."

My eyes widened, but I nodded my head.

"Very well. I will be glad to see it. Now I would speak of another relationship: mother to child."

Hrolf winced, but managed to clear his features. By now we had reached the edge of the headland. Far below us lay the harbor with long ships and cargo vessels drawn up to its piers and landings. Hrolf removed his elegant cloak and spread it on the grassy knoll.

"Please, sit. Here we can be lord and lady of all we survey!"

I settled myself on a corner of the cloak, feet folded under me, as Hrolf sat down gracefully across from me. The fabric of the cloak felt soft against my bare legs, and the sun warmed my shoulders.

"Hrolf," I began, "I have heard from Bodvar and Hjalti that your mother welcomed you warmly at the court in Uppsala and helped you regain your rightful inheritance."

A smile spread slowly across Hrolf's face.

"Yes. Yrsa—my lady mother—was most gracious to me and my men. Also," he added proudly, "she risked her own life to help us."

"Cousin, if I may ask, did her loving reception there heal—at least partly—the wound inflicted when she... abandoned you as a child?"

Had I gone too far? Probed too deeply? Hrolf's face darkened and he scowled mightily. I hastened to make my point clear.

"I only ask, cousin, because I too was abandoned—by Wealtheow—when she stayed behind in Heorot and let me sail off into the unknown. I need to find her once more, and I believe she wants me to find her, for her spirit seeks me from afar. Cousin, King Hrolf, I need your help to find her!"

Hrolf looked up at me, his face full of sorrow.

"What do you wish to know?"

"Whatever you may have heard: family names, countries, scraps of history—anything that might connect Wealtheow to another place—a place to which she might have fled upon leaving Heorot."

Slowly Hrolf nodded.

"I will need to ponder your request, to search my memory. I will need some time, cousin. For now, let us take our ease and enjoy the fine day!"

He waved an arm toward the fjord, where sunlight sparkled on the surface and bits of white bobbed on the water. I smiled and pointed.

"My swans. They have carried me on many a journey!"

Hrolf looked at me curiously.

"You can fly, cousin?"

I nodded. "When the goddess lifts me and gives me wings."

"A great gift, cousin. I envy you," said Hrolf.

"But you are the king!" I retorted. "Many must envy you your position."

A soft nose nuzzled the back of my neck and I fell forward, laughing.

"Sunbeorht! Where are your manners?"

I got to my feet. Hrolf also rose and looked about for his mount.

"Perhaps it is time to return to the settlement. There I can show you ... Skofnung."

"As you wish, King Hrolf." I smiled. "I'm beginning to understand why people speak of you as a great king."

A true smile spread across Hrolf's face. "You honor me, Lady Freawaru."

He helped me mount Sunbeorht, then vaulted lightly into the saddle on Deofol. On an impulse I urged Sunbeorht into a gallop. Caught by surprise, Hrolf too set his steed galloping and soon we were racing neck to neck, past the mounds and into the open meadow. My head cloth blew off and I let it go, shaking out my hair to let it stream in the wind.

By the time we reached the settlement I felt exhilarated and triumphant. Gradually we slowed the horses to a walk and finally reined them in outside the mead hall. Leaning forward over Sunbeorht's neck, I whispered, "Well done, girl!"

Inside Hrolf's chamber he opened a dark, ornately carved oak chest that stood at the foot of his shut-bed. Lifting out a long object wrapped in fine linen, he laid it reverently on the table where we had shared wine.

"Behold," he announced, folding back the wrapping, "Skofnung!"

It was a broad sword, with a blade that shimmered and changed color like water in the sea. The hilt was dark wood inlaid with gold wires, topped by a clear stone that gave off shafts of light.

"It never rusts," he declared, "and it always hits its mark."

"How did you come to have such a marvelous weapon?" I asked, gazing at it in wonder.

"Ah, that is the story I brought you here to tell," said Hrolf, smiling. "Please be seated, cousin, and I'll send for wine. Oh, and I've already sent a servant to retrieve your kerchief."

"Thank you," I murmured, seating myself. I reached out to touch the cross guard, where I saw faint lines inscribed in the metal. They felt like ... runes, but seemed to shift under my fingertips. Hrolf nodded ruefully.

"I see you have already found them. Even Unferth has not been able to decipher their meaning! But now I must tell you how I acquired this sword, for it concerns my sister Skuld."

He sat down across from me and lightly stroked the shining blade that lay like a boundary between us.

"Several years ago when Skuld was budding into womanhood, her guardians sought me out with their concerns. They spoke of dark practices, midnight wanderings and other behaviors unbecoming to a young woman. They begged me to follow her one night to see what she did in the wild woods — and I agreed."

Hrolf paused to admit a servant with a pitcher and glasses. Hrolf himself poured the wine and handed me a glass before filling his own. After we had each taken a sip, Hrolf resumed his story.

"I did follow her — in the dead of night — as she slipped soundlessly through brush and forest, never looking back. Of a sudden I stumbled into a clearing where a tall stone, frosty in the moonlight, reared up before me. Beside it stood a woman — a beautiful woman — wreathed in shadow, wreathed in hair blacker than Skuld's, and in her hands, palms up, she bore this sword."

Hrolf paused, a look of wonder and longing lighting his face.

"She spoke to me, called me 'son of Helgi,' and warned me not to seek my sister further. I remember her very words: 'Grief soon enough is given to men; never foreknow your Wyrd . . . let the girl go and live out your lifespan . . . dreading no dark to come. At last may you stand and laugh at the Norns, so winning the war you lost'."

Hrolf's voice trailed off as he stared straight ahead. Then he shook himself and laid both hands on the blade before us.

"She gave me this sword, named 'Skofnung,' made by the dwarves, she said, and bade me use it ever against evil. Then she disappeared . . . and I sought Skuld no more. Since that night my sister and I have each followed our own path."

As I listened to Hrolf's story, I'd been running my fingers lightly across the faintly incised runes on the hilt. They seemed to repeat in sets of three, but I could not be sure of their individual identities.

"So . . ." I said, "you accepted the bargain offered by Skuld's mother, but you took the sword at a price: remaining ignorant of Skuld's true nature!"

Hrolf nodded reluctantly.

"You put it bluntly, cousin, but, yes, I did make a bargain, and I intend to keep it. So the subject of Skuld's possible treachery is . . . closed."

"I see. Of course, that is entirely your affair, King Hrolf." I stood up and smiled. "Thank you for showing me this treasure and telling me its story. I am honored by your confidence." I took up my glass for a last sip. "Now I should return to my women and Gerda, but first I must ask a favor."

"Anything within my power," said Hrolf smoothly, draining his own glass as he rose to join me.

"Please invite Unferth to the mead hall tonight and seat us together. He has promised to speak of... Beowulf."

"With pleasure." Hrolf walked with me to the door, opened it, then looked me full in the face. "I am glad we have had this time together, cousin Freawaru. Let us be enemies no more."

I nodded and left him standing in the doorway, a tall, graceful figure who held himself like a king.

Gerda and my women were eager to hear of my morning's adventures with the king, but I gave them only the barest sketch of our conversation.

"Did you see dead people?" asked Gerda hopefully, coming up behind me.

"No, no, not really," I laughed, turning. "I was too busy talking to the living." I looked around the longhouse. "Where is Drifa?"

"Gone to her sister's, I believe," said Lempi. "We told her we'd take care of the baking today."

"So that's why Gerda looks like a ghost — she's covered with flour!"

Gerda laughed and sneezed a great sneeze.

"I've been helping!"

Several piles of bread dough lay mounded on one flour-covered table; at another Mari and Berit labored, grinding more grain on Drifa's two heavy querns. Idly my fingers scribbled a few lines in the flour dust, lines which caught Runa's eye.

"Drawing runes, my lady?"

"Runes? Am I?" I looked down at my handiwork.

"Yes," said Runa. "There is Thurisaz... and Wunjo... and Pertho... a strange combination, especially starting with a troll rune!"

I stared at the lines I'd drawn in sudden recognition.

"The runes on Hrolf's sword hilt: I touched them but didn't understand them! Runa, please help me interpret this. The marks repeat three times in the same order. And you're right: they do seem to have little in common. Thurisaz — gateway to other worlds, Wunjo — bringer of light and joy, Pertho — secret female powers."

"Oh, my lady," breathed Runa, her eyes growing wide, "long ago my grandmother told me that a troll rune at the start of a sequence reverses the meaning of what follows ... which would mean ..."

"... that Wunjo becomes darkness, madness and frenzy ... Pertho becomes perverted lust ... and the repetition would increase the power of both!" I concluded, almost breathless with discovery.

"Oh my lady," whispered Runa again, "these are ill omens indeed!"

By now Lempi, Lise, Ginnlaug and Gerda had surrounded the table, alarmed by the dismay in our voices.

"What's wrong, lady, what does it mean?" cried Gerda, pulling at my gown with flour-covered fingers.

"It means I must once again be the bearer of fateful news to King Hrolf," I replied grimly, then looked around me at the circle of anxious faces. "This is a very serious matter. This is a confidential matter, not to be spoken of outside this longhouse! Swear by the goddess, all of you!"

"We swear ... by the goddess!" they echoed.

From outside the open door a sudden "Auk Auk" caught our attention.

"A raven!" cried Gerda. "That's Huginn!"

She dashed out the door, followed by Runa and me. The bird flew down from a nearby branch and landed on Gerda's shoulder.

"A timely messenger," I said, "for I must consult Unferth immediately about these runes. He may be able to see more deeply into the matter."

As soon as she heard my words, Gerda started down the path. Huginn flew off ahead, as if leading the way.

"We should not be gone long," I said to Runa. "Go on with the baking."

As we approached Unferth's hut, we saw him outside holding Muninn, poised as if waiting for us. He held out his other arm and Huginn flew down and perched there.

"I was again expecting you. What is it this time?"

"I need your wisdom, Lord Unferth. I have encountered a puzzling rune sequence I cannot interpret."

Unferth nodded and turned to Gerda.

"There's a bucket of grain inside the door. You may feed my birds, if you like."

Gerda peered into the dim interior, slipped inside, and reappeared with a small wooden bucket.

Cloak of Ashes

"Scatter a few grains on the ground," directed Unferth.

As Gerda did so, the ravens left Unferth's arms and flew down to peck at the barley. Gerda crouched down to watch them eat.

To me he said, "Take my staff and draw the runes in question," inclining his head toward a tall, oak staff leaning near the door.

Taking the heavy stave, I carefully drew Thurisaz, Wunjo and Pertho. Unferth watched me closely as I drew each line on the ground near his door.

"So... you have seen King Hrolf's sword," he said.

"Why yes, but Hrolf said you couldn't tell him... that is..." I faltered.

"Couldn't decipher the runes? That is both true and untrue, for the same runes do not always appear!" He gave a dry laugh.

"'Oh," I said in a small voice. "I did not know that."

"A clear evidence of strong magic," continued Unferth, nodding his head. "Different runes are revealed at different times."

I hesitated, but decided to ask anyway.

"Have you found them repeating in a pattern? I saw them — actually I felt them — repeating three times in the same order."

Unferth's head came up abruptly. His dark eyes bored into mine.

"Are you sure?" he hissed.

"Very sure," I said firmly.

"Hmmm. It may be that you see farther than I, king's daughter." He reached out to take the staff from my hands. "The pupil may have surpassed the teacher." With the end of the staff he erased the runes.

"But Unferth," I said earnestly, "Please tell me: how should one read these three runes aright? I fear they may portend danger to King Hrolf, and if so I would warn him!"

Unferth was silent for a time, then cleared his throat, looking straight ahead.

"The runes you have seen could work for or against the one who wields the weapon. The will of Odin would decide the outcome." He turned to Gerda. "Thank you, little sparrow. My birds and I must rest now."

He made a clicking sound with his tongue and the ravens immediately flew to his shoulders. Before he disappeared inside his hut, he gave a slight bow.

"I will see you tonight, king's daughter. Until then, fare you well."

Unferth did come to the mead hall that evening, and Vögg led him to the table where I sat with Olaf and Runa, near the front but off to one side, where we could speak with some privacy in the boisterous mead hall. As we all rose respectfully to greet him, I noted that he had taken some care with his appearance, for his beard was combed and he wore a clean tunic.

"Unferth," I said, "this is my dear friend Runa and her husband, Olaf. Olaf captains our ship."

Unferth nodded. "I remember Olaf, but this lady ... another seeress, is she not?"

Runa gave a modest bow. "Yes, your lordship, I have some gifts of that sort."

Unferth looked pleased. "Well-mannered, too!"

He took a seat beside Olaf, across from Runa and me. After ale had been served, he leaned toward me.

"My ravens tell me that you have travelled far in your lifetime, king's daughter, just as I predicted."

"Yes, Lord Unferth, I have: to the land of the Heathobards with my husband Ingeld, to Geatland, where Beowulf made his home, to Uppsala where I saw you at the Great Blöt, and most recently to the Brondings' country to deliver wergild."

"You are like your mother," he declared, taking a great gulp of ale, "not afraid to seek a new home when circumstances demand it."

This surprised me, for he had earlier refused to speak further of my mother.

"Perhaps Wealtheow's journey was a homecoming for her," I said lightly, "as this trip is for me."

Unferth eyed me suspiciously.

"I cannot say. But tell me of that little girl — the one who talks to my ravens. Who is she?"

I let Runa tell the story of our shipboard discovery, only adding that Gerda was a child with surprising ... insights. Unferth nodded.

"She sees keenly, that one, and listens with an inner ear. It might be wise to teach her rune lore. Either of you could do it."

Taken aback, Runa and I looked at each other, but made no reply.

"Lord Unferth," I said in a neutral tone, "what do your birds tell you of Wealtheow? Is she alive and well?"

"She is..." he paused, his mouth open. "I have visited the land of the dead... and saw her not," he concluded grudgingly.

For the rest of the evening Unferth refused to answer any more questions about Wealtheow. Instead, he spoke eloquently about Beowulf's long ago visit to Heorot, Beowulf's killing of the Grendel monster, and the loan of Unferth's sword to Beowulf when he sought out the monster's mother in the depths of the mere. To Unferth Beowulf was still alive, and I did not contradict him.

When Olaf helped Vögg walk Unferth back to his hut, Runa and I made our way slowly back to Drifa's longhouse. Although midsummer lay behind us, one could see a great distance in the soft, clear light — almost, I imagined, all the way to the burial mounds.

Later that night I lay awake long after the others were snoring. Even Gerda was sleeping soundly; her nightmares had not returned. Piece by piece I mulled over all I had heard from Hrolf, from Unferth and from Borghild in the last several days. According to Borghild Wealtheow was not alone when she left Heorot, but who could have gone with her? Could I have been mistaken about my brothers' deaths? Could one of them yet be alive? That might explain Wealtheow's excitement, as mentioned by Borghild, the oath of secrecy Wealtheow exacted from Unferth. Might that have been necessary to protect her son from pursuit by Hrothulf? My mind whirled with conjectures. One thing I knew for sure: I needed to return to my brothers' burial mound and try to determine exactly who lay there.

Chapter Ten
Departures and Arrivals

Amulet of Odin with his two ravens from Ribe, Denmark.

Gerda was up well before me, clearly anticipating another visit to Strongfellow, for she was trotting about the long house on an imaginary horse.

"We are riding today, aren't we, lady?' she asked, pulling up beside my sleeping bench.

"Yes, if our mounts are available — and yes, we'll visit the 'dead people'." I yawned and stretched and reached for the slit kirtle Runa had adapted for my riding. "But first," I admonished, "you must eat a big bowl of porridge; we may be gone for some time."

Both Strongfellow and Sunbeorht were waiting for us outside the door, as Bodvar had sent word to Sigrod of our intention. This time Sigrod had fashioned a make-shift saddle for Gerda from a leather bag stuffed with down, and added a proper bridle and reins. She squealed with delight as he hoisted her onto the animal's back.

"Wait for me," I cautioned as I saw her pick up the reins. "We will ride together, side by side."

Once in the saddle, I smiled down at this engaging child who had become so dear to me.

"Hold on tight, now — off we go!"

Mimicking my actions, she slapped the reins and smacked her heels against Strongfellow's broad sides, and we set off for our morning's adventure. We did not speak as we jogged along. Deep in my own thoughts, I still noticed Gerda rejoicing in the morning, lifting her voice in a high, thin, wordless melody akin to Runa's flute.

"What were you warbling, little sparrow?" I asked as she slowed to a stop in the wildflower meadow and slid down from her mount. She grinned up at me.

"I was calling to the birds, but none answered."

Gerda bent to pick a handful of dandelions, which she held up to me.

"For you, lady."

"Thank you," I said, accepting the flowers. "Now, how are you going to get back up on Strongfellow?"

"Jump?" She laughed.

I laughed too. "Even you can't leap that high! Let me help you."

I dismounted from Sunbeorht and swooped up Gerda, who giggled as she clung to me. I felt her soft lips on my neck and heard a whispered "Thank you for keeping me," as I swung her up, her rust-colored hair blazing in the sun.

Once settled on Strongfellow, Gerda said, "Lady, what is that mark on your shoulder? It looks like a feather."

I glanced to one side and saw that my kirtle had slipped down, revealing my birthmark.

"It's a gift from the goddess Freyja. She helps me when I call upon her — and sometimes gives me wings to fly to far places."

"I'd like to do that," said Gerda, her brown eyes glowing. "Could you teach me how to do that?"

"One day, perhaps. For now let's ride on — to visit the dead."

Agreeably, Gerda jiggled her reins and set Strongfellow going again. By the time we reached the burial mounds, I had made up my mind: I would call upon the goddess — and use the runes if necessary — to help me find answers. At the same time I would introduce Gerda to their powers. Runa had thoughtfully provided a packet of bread, cheese and water for our morning jaunt, so I had what I needed for an offering, and my rune bag was tied tightly at my waist, next to the knife I always carried. As I was thinking about how to proceed, Gerda called out.

"Look I think I see one!"

"One what? Where?" I looked up in alarm as Sunbeorht gave a snort.

"Oh, it's only a rabbit," said Gerda sadly. "I thought it might be one of the dead people."

"Gerda," I said sternly, "the dead do not come out of their houses."

"Then how can we visit them?" she asked, her face clouding.

"There are other ways, some of which I will show you now. Stop here and drop your reins so your horse won't stray. We are going to make an offering to the goddess."

Suiting action to words, I dismounted from Sunbeorht and removed the small bundle tied behind the saddle, as Gerda slid down from Strongfellow.

"Here. You may carry this bundle while I find a suitable place for our ritual."

With Gerda trailing behind me, I slowly circled the same mound that Hrolf had shown me the day before. It was not perfectly proportioned, for one side had sunk down noticeably lower than the other. Midway up I saw a level space.

"Up there," I nodded. "That's where we'll hold our ceremony."

Bending to negotiate the steep slope, Gerda dutifully climbed beside me in silence, but I could tell she was full of questions. When we reached the flat area and caught our breaths, she burst out.

"Do you know who lives here? Are we standing on top of them? Will it make them angry?"

"The answer to each of your questions is 'No'," I said calmly. "Put down the bundle and I will show you what we are going to do."

Gerda watched my every move as I took out my knife and, with the back edge, drew a wide circle in the turf around us.

"Sit still and stay inside this line," I instructed. "No harm will come to you."

Her eyes grew wide at this admonition, but she nodded obediently. Next I untied the bundle, handed the bread and cheese to Gerda, set down the jug and spread the cloth on the ground. Silently I lifted Gerda, holding the bread and cheese, and placed her in the middle. Picking up the jug of water, I walked around the perimeter of the circle, sprinkling the grass as I began my supplication.

"Goddess, come to us; goddess, be with us in this sacred space. Give ear to our pleas, receive our offerings, grant us the knowledge we seek. It is Freawaru who calls upon you, and her handmaiden, Gerda. Tell me, great goddess, reveal to me: who lies buried in this mound?"

Kneeling beside Gerda, I broke a piece of bread from the rough loaf and held it high in the air. To my astonishment the bread was snatched from my fingers by a large black bird.

"Huginn!" cried Gerda, forgetting to keep silent.

"That pesky bird!" I exploded. "What is it doing here?"

Gerda looked at me in surprise. "You called it, lady."

"Did I? Perhaps I did." The possibility slowly dawned. "The goddess uses many means to communicate. This may be one of them. But," I muttered, "this tells me nothing — nothing that I can understand."

Gerda had risen from her place and now held out an arm. Squawking loudly, Huginn immediately flew to perch there.

"He's talking to you, lady," cried Gerda. "He's talking to you."

"What is he saying? I don't understand!"

Frustrated, I stared at Gerda and the bird. She scowled, listening intently.

"It's a name; he's saying a name. All-rik... Aaal-reek... Aelric. He's saying Aelric!"

My mouth dropped open. I had never spoken Aelric's name in Gerda's presence. How could she –or the raven — know of it?

Gerda was beaming. "There is your answer, lady. Aelric — whoever that is — is buried here!"

She cooed at the raven and reached for another piece of bread to feed it.

Aelric. But if he is buried here, who is *not* buried here? Which of my brothers is missing from this mound?

Together the three of us finished the bread and cheese; then Huginn flew off toward the settlement.

Cloak of Ashes

"Lady, you forgot to thank him," chided Gerda, watching the raven's departure.

"I'll be sure to do so the next time I see him," I promised. "We have more work to do here. We will ask the runes for more information. Stay seated and watch what I do."

I untied the bag at my waist, opened it, and one by one drew out the runes, naming each as I laid it on the cloth.

"Fehu... Uruz... Wunjo... Ansuz... Raido... Kano..." I continued until all twenty-four lay before us.

"Listen carefully, Gerda, for what I now tell you is a wonder and a mystery."

She nodded solemnly, her little face intent and serious.

"The god Odin hung upside down on the world tree for nine long nights before he spied the runes, seized them and gave them to mankind. She who knows their meaning and uses has the power to see what is unseen, know what is unknown. But experience is needed to read the runes aright."

"When did you learn to read them, lady?" asked Gerda, meekly.

"When I was a girl—about your age." I smiled, remembering those long-ago days beside the oak tree with Unferth. "Now, I will return the runes to their pouch, settle myself quietly, then ask a question of the runes—but one must not ask it out loud. I will reach into the bag and let one rune find my fingers. After I draw it out and lay it on the cloth, it will give me an answer."

"Can they talk?" asked Gerda, wide-eyed

"Not in words, no, but each rune has its own meaning. When I have completed the process I will teach you the meaning of the rune I've drawn. This will begin your first lesson."

Gerda gave a tremulous smile and knit her brows, but nonetheless nodded acceptance.

"Now. We settle into silence."

Gerda shut her eyes tight and sucked in her breath.

I took deep breaths, gradually slowing my breathing. From the distant past I summoned an image of Hrothmund, my little brother, lover of bed-time stories and passionate player of board games. Although he had grown to young manhood by the time of his death, in my mind's eye I saw him as a boy: round-faced and smiling under a shock of unruly hair. I closed my eyes and breathed my question.

Hrothmund, dear Hrothmund, do you sleep in this mound?

Reaching into the rune bag I relaxed my fingers, stirring the runes gently. When one felt right I drew it slowly forth and laid it on the cloth. Opening my eyes, I saw... Raido.

"Gerda, you may open your eyes now... and breathe!"

She released her breath with a gasp, then stared at the rune on the cloth.

"I remember that one; you called it 'Raido.' What does it mean?"

"I am puzzling over that very question, Gerda. It means a journey — but it does not indicate who is taking the journey or where the journey leads. That's where interpretation comes in. Hmmm."

Mentally I considered the possibilities: Hrothmund's journey to the land of the dead? Hrothmund's journey with Wealtheow to a new home? The choice was not clear.

"I think, Gerda, it will be necessary to ask another question and to draw a second rune — but there's no need to hold your breath!"

Patiently Gerda closed her eyes and clasped her hands together, while I repeated the process. This time I focused on Hrethric, the lively young man who had loved to sail and ride to the hunt. His roguish eyes sparkled, his full lips opened in laughter as he repeated some rakish riddle.

Hrethric, dear Hrethric, do you sleep in this mound?

This time I was greeted by the birch tree rune, Berkana.

"Now, Gerda."

She opened her eyes and bent over on hands and knees, peering closely at the rune on the cloth.

"What is its name, lady, and what does it mean?"

"This is Berkana," I said, hope rising within me, "and it signifies growth, rebirth, new life, fertility — surely propitious signs!"

"I don't know what pro- pro-shus means, but you look happy!" observed Gerda.

"Yes, Gerda, for this could mean that one of my brothers yet lives! We must return to the settlement at once! I have more questions for Unferth, and this time I won't leave without answers!"

"Good," said Gerda, grinning. "This time can we ride like the wind?"

Returning to Roskilde, I let Gerda trot as fast as Strongfellow's legs could carry him — fast enough to satisfy her as she gleefully bounced

Cloak of Ashes

along. By the time we reached Drifa's long house she was ready to slide off and rub her skinny little bottom.

"I'm riding on to see Unferth," I called to Runa in the doorway. "Thank you for the provisions you packed—they were both tasty and useful!"

Runa nodded and waved me on as Gerda turned to her, bubbling with news of her morning's adventures.

When I reached Unferth's hut, the door was partly open, but Unferth was nowhere to be seen. After I tied Sunbeorht to the wattle fencing, I called Unferth's name, but received no answer. Perplexed, I stood listening. Finally a faint sound caught my ear. It seemed to come from behind the hut, so I walked cautiously in that direction. To my horror I found Unferth sprawled face down on the ground, his staff broken under him.

"Let me help you!" I exclaimed, kneeling beside him. "It's Freawaru."

Slowly, carefully, I helped him turn over. His lower lip was split, one eye was beginning to swell, and he had a bump on his forehead; otherwise he seemed intact.

"Don't try to get up. Rest awhile," I admonished. "Can you tell me what happened?"

Unferth blinked up at me. I had not noticed before how watery his eyes had become.

"My staff—old and brittle, like me—it broke—I fell and hit my head."

"How long have you been lying here?" I asked, gently rubbing his frail hands.

"Don't know—sent ravens—they found you?"

"Huginn, came, yes, but on a different errand. I've not seen Muninn."

"Sent him—to Gerda—she'll understand."

He closed his eyes and sighed as if the effort to speak had exhausted him. I waited in silence, watching him breathe hoarsely, his chest barely rising.

"If you think you can stand, Unferth, I'll walk you to your hut. You need rest, and nourishing food, and someone to take care of you!"

A faint smile passed over his features.

"And who would that be, king's daughter?"

"I will help you!" I declared in growing agitation, fearful that Unferth's collapse had been more than a simple fall. "You once saved my life, old friend. I will care for you now."

"Thank you — but won't be long — must see Beowulf — soon we have meeting — with Odin."

"No, no, you'll be fine in a few days."

Kneeling behind his head, I reached my hands under his shoulders and tried to lift him to a sitting position, but he was heavier than he looked. How was I to help him?

"Auk Auk! Auk Auk!"

A dark shape flew past my head and landed beside Unferth. Muninn! The bird's arrival was followed by shouts from the front of the hut.

"'Lady, where are you?"

"Back here — behind the hut."

Strongfellow's shaggy head appeared from around the corner; on his broad back sat Gerda and Runa. Immediately they slid down and hastened to my side. Together we managed to get Unferth to his feet and helped him shufflle slowly to the doorway.

Inside Unferth's hut the stench almost overpowered me, but I fought back my revulsion. The furnishings were sparse: two sleeping benches against opposite walls, a small low table, and a cauldron full of firewood for a make-shift hearth. Ranged along the walls at eye level were narrow shelves containing strange objects: bone fragments, pieces of fabric, broken bits of glass... and could that be... a skull? I shivered, remembering Unferth's long-ago attempt to talk to the head of Aeschere. He saw me staring and gave a low chuckle.

"Treasures from my ravens," he croaked, sounding like a raven himself.

After we got him positioned upright on one bench, I looked about for any signs of food or drink.

"How do you eat, Lord Unferth?" I asked gently.

He shrugged. "It is seldom necessary. Soon I'll be feasting — with Odin."

"Lady Freaw," called Runa, who had been searching among the shelves, "here is a pitcher of... something."

"Don't touch that!" commanded Unferth sharply. "It would be death for you — for anyone not accustomed to drinking it."

Shocked, I gazed at him accusingly.

"Are you still experimenting with mushrooms, old friend?"

Unabashed, he nodded and leaned toward me.

Cloak of Ashes

"They are the source of my strength — of my visions," he whispered. "With their aid I walk among worlds unknown to other men."

"They are also the source of your weakness!" I retorted loudly. "Unferth, you are slowly poisoning yourself!"

He shrugged again. "Perhaps. It is a bargain well made."

Gerda tugged at my sleeve; in her other hand she held out a piece of bread.

"Here, lady. I saved it earlier. He can have it."

"Thank you, child."

Taking the bread, I placed it in Unferth's bony fingers and helped him raise it to his lips. He chewed it slowly, then swallowed.

"Thank you, sparrow." He looked straight at Gerda. "Look after my birds when I am gone."

Gerda nodded solemnly, but I shook my head.

"No, Lord Unferth, you must stay and care for them yourself! I'll arrange for nourishing food and drink to be brought here — until you are stronger."

"And arrange for a good cleaning," muttered Runa in my ear. "This is not a fit place for a sick man."

I nodded. "Runa, please take Gerda back to the long house now and explain the situation to Drifa. I'm sure she will help. I'll stay here with Unferth for the time being."

Runa reached for Gerda's hand, but she hung back.

"'I'll feed your ravens — until you feel better," said Gerda earnestly. "Don't worry about them."

"I won't worry, sparrow, I won't worry at all."

While Unferth rested, his eyes closed, I walked to the open door to breathe in fresh air and to consider the situation. Learning that Unferth partook of mind-altering mushrooms helped explain his insistence that Beowulf was still alive, but it also complicated my search for the truth about my brothers. Could I believe anything this man told me? As I stood in the doorway, gazing outside, I heard Unferth's voice behind me.

"What is it now, king's daughter?"

Deciding to be direct, I turned, keeping my voice calm and clear.

"Unferth, do you remember Aelric, father's harper?"

"Yes, I do. A good man, Aelric, but not a good singer." He chortled and coughed.

"Can you tell me where Aelric is buried?"

"Of course I can. He lies beside Hrothmund, in the same mound."

Now I chose my words even more carefully.

"No, my lord, you must be mistaken. King Hrolf was clear that only two bodies lie in that mound."

"Hrolf is right," said Unferth, a note of irritation in his voice, "two bodies lie there: those of Hrothmund and Aelric."

"But what of Hrethric?" I asked, my own voice rising, "where does his body lie?"

In the light from the open door I saw Unferth's eyes begin to glow and he spoke with controlled intensity.

"Hrethric is not dead, Lady Freawaru. Hrethric yet lives!"

My heart leapt up, then sank as suddenly. Remember, Freawaru, you may be talking to a madman!

"How can that be?" I cried, incredulous. "I saw Hrethric die — I covered his face with my own hands!"

"Appearances can be misleading, king's daughter," said Unferth quietly. "Hrethric appeared to be lost in the sleep of death, but he later... recovered."

I stared at him, my mind racing, beginning to understand what must have happened.

"Did Hrethric leave with Wealtheow? Is that why she left Heorot — to save Hrethric from Hrothulf? Tell me what happened, Unferth, please!"

"Perhaps... it is time," he said slowly and sighed. "My own time may be short. Come closer."

He beckoned to me and I came to sit beside him, my heart pounding.

"Once Wealtheow knew that Hrethric lived, she planned their escape. A trading ship lay tied up in the harbor. She paid the captain to take her and the boy secretly on board. They left on the tide next morning."

"But what about the funeral pyre?" I exclaimed in puzzlement. "What about the missing body?"

Unferth smiled broadly.

"I had a hand in that deception. I substituted Aelric for Hrethric on the pyre. Each body was wrapped completely in heavy linen — because of their rapid decomposition, I'd said — so no faces were visible. Not Hrethric but Aelric lay beside Hrothmund. In the confusion at the time,

Cloak of Ashes

Aelric's death was overlooked, forgotten —especially by Hrothulf, still recovering from the blow to the head I'd given him."

I stared at Unferth in amazement, trying to take it all in. Finally I spoke.

"So... both Wealtheow and Hrethric fled... to the land of...?"

I looked at him in expectation, but he shook his head regretfully.

"I told you I gave my word to Wealtheow, but remember this: she was Helming's daughter."

"Helming's daughter? Is that a clue to her whereabouts?"

"I cannot say more."

We sat quietly for a time, staring into the gradually deepening dusk. Feeling a slight chill in the evening air, I roused myself to build a small fire in the iron cauldron and lay a sleeping robe over Unferth's knees. Soon the crackling flames sent shadows dancing over the walls and lighting Unferth's face. His eyes followed my every move, but his lips were still. Seating myself on the opposite bench, I leaned forward, elbows on knees.

"Unferth," I began, taking a new direction, "what news do they bring you — Huginn and Muninn? What news of the wide world beyond these shores?"

He cleared his throat and brought up a bony hand to rub one eye.

"They tell me of a great movement of peoples — over the whale road — and tribe against tribe, fighting for dominance. Thus it will ever be until the coming of Ragnarok," he declared in a voice unlike his own.

"Ragnarok? That tale about the destruction of the gods?"

Unferth snorted.

"Far more than a tale, king's daughter." His eyes narrowed and his look grew hard. "It is the reason Odin gathers the best of fallen warriors to his hall; they must fight at the world's end — against wolf and serpent and all the forces of darkness. But even the gods are doomed to fail," he sighed. "And so Midgard, our earth, will disappear into the sea in fire and flame — to be reborn in a later age."

I listened entranced to this ancient prophecy which seemed to issue from lips not merely mortal. In awe I gazed at Unferth's deeply lined and weathered face, the eyes now closed. I rose and crossed to his bench. Taking his hands in mine, I raised them to my lips.

"Thank you, Unferth, for all your gifts."

In a hoarse whisper he responded, "All may yet be well."

A light knock from the doorway alerted me to the arrival of Drifa's servants, young Eyvind and the matronly Erna. They carried a kettle of hot broth, a loaf of fresh bread and water for washing. I welcomed them gladly.

"Lady Freawaru, Eyvind will stay here tonight," said Erna. "Lady Drifa urges you to return with me after you've seen to Lord Unferth's needs."

An involuntary sigh of relief escaped my lips as I suddenly realized how spent I was in body and spirit. After Erna gently wiped his bruised face and dirty hands, Unferth took a few sips of broth from the wooden mug I held for him and a small bite of bread. Then he sank back against the wall.

"I am finished," he said. "Go now."

Looking around the dim interior I located the pitcher Runa had discovered earlier.

"'I'll just empty this outside, first," I said to Unferth, walking toward the door. "There, now. I'm ready," I told Erna. "Good night, Lord Unferth. May I find you better in the morning."

He nodded slightly, but made no other response as Erna and I slipped out into the dusk of late summer, leaving Eyvind to watch over his charge.

Back in the long house I took Runa and Olaf aside to tell them privately what I had learned from Unferth about my brother.

"If Hrethric is alive, he would be seen as a threat by King Hrolf," I said, recalling the words of Torgun: 'They will not return while Hrothulf lives.'

"Yes, you're right, my lady," said Olaf. "We must use caution here."

"In the morning," I continued, "I will have more talk with Unferth. Tonight I must rest. This day has been emotionally exhausting."

I was awakened once during the night when Gerda cried out, but when I rose and placed a hand on her shoulder, she sighed and turned over onto her stomach, settling back to sleep.

I rose early the next morning, but Runa was up before me. Together we made our way through the still-sleeping settlement to Unferth's hut. The door was ajar and I heard snoring, so I knocked lightly before pushing it open. Inside, Eyvind lay sprawled on one bench; Unferth's still form lay on the other. Something about that stillness made me catch my breath.

"Unferth? Lord Unferth?"

I touched his cheek. It was cold. A faint smile—the rictus of death—stretched his lips. With a wail I dropped to my knees beside the body. Eyvind woke with a start.

"Eh? What's wrong?"

Runa spoke quietly, standing beside me, her hands on my shoulders. "Lord Unferth is dead. He must have died during the night."

Eyvind gave a choked cry and sprang up from the bench.

"Lady, forgive me! I watched him, I did! He was alive—I'm sure he was—when I lay down to rest for just a moment!"

"It's alright, lad. You are not to blame," said Runa. "Lord Unferth's time had come. What you can do now is carry the sad news back to Lord Bjarki and Lady Drifa."

Nodding, Eyvind took up his sleeping robe and hurried from the hut. Runa knelt beside me to hold my hand as I wept, washing Unferth's cold fingers with my tears. When they subsided, she gently helped me rise.

"Do you wish to prepare the body yourself, my lady? I see there is water at hand."

I nodded, wiping my wet cheeks. "I'd welcome your help Runa—if you're willing."

"Of course."

Runa went to the cauldron, added wood to the embers and stirred up the fire. Together we carefully removed Unferth's filthy tunic and leggings, exposing the gaunt body. Kuna pointed to his left arm.

"Look, my lady."

Lines of dried blood that formed an arrow stood out against the pale flesh.

"That looks like a rune!" she marveled.

I bent closer to trace the uneven lines with my fingertips.

"It is a rune. It's Teiwaz, rune of warriors. Unferth must have cut it himself to ensure his entrance into Valhalla. And look—that old scar—that's where he cut himself long ago, using his own blood to bait a trap for the Grendel monster. There will never be another like him, not like Unferth."

Runa looked at me in awe as I nodded grimly, blinking back a fresh wave of tears.

While I washed Unferth's body, Runa took a brand from the cauldron and climbed carefully to the loft above. She came back with a tunic slightly cleaner than the one we'd removed. With difficulty, for the limbs had already begun to stiffen, we dressed him as best we could. Using Unferth's own knife, which I found on the floor beside him, I cut off a lock of my hair and tucked it inside his curled fingers.

"Good bye, old friend," I whispered, pressing my lips to his cold forehead. "May you feast with Beowulf in Valhalla. All may yet be well."

At Unferth's funeral pyre, King Hrolf stood close beside me. He appeared genuinely saddened by the loss of his long-time courtier and companion, but seemed unable to express it. As we watched the flames consume the body, Hrolf reached for my hand.

"Cousin, don't leave us. Stay here — and help me rule."

My thoughts were centered on Unferth and all he had meant to me over the years; stricken and speechless, I turned to the king, not understanding his words. At my blank look, he drew back.

"Forgive me," he murmured, "we will speak of this another time."

Giving my hand a firm squeeze, he bowed and left me among the assembled mourners — a small group, smaller that I would have wished, for few any longer knew or remembered the man who had been King Hrothgar's spokesman, the man who — with fire and poison, alone in the mead hall — had tried to kill the Grendel monster, the man who had been my mentor, my teacher, my dear, dear friend. I bowed my head and wept as smoke drifted about my head.

A tug at my elbow brought me back to the present. Gerda had begged to come with us and now stood at my side, pointing upward.

"Look lady, up there!"

Looking up I saw two ravens swooping and calling as they circled the pyre.

"It's Huginn and Muninn saying good bye," said Gerda. "They won't be back," she added sadly.

After what he apparently considered a decent interval of mourning, King Hrolf again invited me to his private chamber. I did not want to go. I felt raw, exposed, vulnerable — to what, I did not know. Losing Unferth had meant losing another link to my past, to the person I had once

Cloak of Ashes

been. Now I wondered: was it really so important to find my mother, my brother? Would I expose them to danger if I did find them? Would it be better to stay here and find my own place again? I felt myself to be at a crossroad, unsure how to move forward or where to go.

Runa searched my face that morning as I dressed for my visit to the king.

"You don't look well, my lady. What's wrong?"

"I have not slept, Runa, or rather, a certain night mare has returned which... wakes me." I smiled ruefully.

"Not... Lars?" she whispered.

"Yes, I think so, though the face keeps changing. What does not change is the feel of hot blood flooding over my fingers!"

"I'm sorry," said Runa simply. "We both battle that demon: memory."

I nodded. "But why now? What has the death of Lars to do with the death of Unferth? Or finding my mother? I'm not a child, like Gerda, afraid of the dark, yet I see a kind of darkness before me that I cannot penetrate."

Runa nodded sympathetically. "Patience, my lady, patience. Perhaps more light will be revealed to you."

"Perhaps," I echoed, "and perhaps King Hrolf will have some answers for me. I'll soon find out."

Rising, I set out, accompanied by Drifa's servant Erna as far as the mead hall. Apparently Drifa too was concerned about my state of mind.

By now Hrolf's chamber was familiar to me, and again a pitcher of wine awaited me at his table.

"Welcome, cousin, welcome!" he said, smiling broadly. "Your presence does me honor. Please be seated and take your ease. These have been dark days for you," he said soothingly, "and I would lighten the burden you carry."

Dark days? Burden? What does he know of my thoughts? Does he suspect something amiss?

Uneasily I let him seat me and pour me a glass of wine.

"What shall we drink to today?" he asked brightly, raising his glass.

"To finding Wealtheow," I suggested.

Hrolf frowned and lowered his glass.

"Do you still think to find your mother? Why not be content to stay here? Here you could be given a place of honor, here..."

"Do you have any information for me?" I interrupted. 'Have you searched your memory, as you promised?"

Hrolf's frown deepened.

"As it happens, I have. I can tell you two things: King Hrothgar sometimes referred to Wealtheow as 'Helming's daughter,' and boasted that she came from a royal line—the Wylfings, he called them, though he did not name their location. But cousin, set all that aside for a moment. I would speak with you about our line, the Scylding line."

He raised his glass again.

"Let us drink to the union of Freawaru and Hrolf. I ask you to be my wife, Freawaru, to rule with me over this kingdom."

He waited expectantly, his eyes wide and hopeful

I sat silent, stricken, my emotions in turmoil. Although I had had some inkling of his intention, now that it was stated openly, I had no answer to give him. As the silence deepened, his face changed.

"Perhaps I have misjudged the moment, cousin. You still grieve for your friend Unferth, do you not?" he inquired stiffly.

I nodded dumbly.

"Very well. I will give you time—but not too much time. I would make you my queen, Freawaru. Surely you know that I have always ... cared for you?"

I rose, my glass untouched, and suddenly found my voice.

"But King Hrolf, we are cousins. Would such a union not offend the gods? Like the union of your father and his daughter-wife?"

Hrolf's face relaxed.

"So, that is your only fear? Be at peace, cous ... Lady Freawaru. Many such unions have taken place in neighboring kingdoms with no adverse consequences. Why, I think the gods would smile upon the joining of two strands of the Scylding line!"

By now he was almost beaming, but I did not reveal my feelings.

"Even so," I murmured, "it might be best if I consult the goddess on this ... important matter."

Hrolf seemed to consider, but paused only briefly.

"If it will put your mind at rest, by all means—consult the goddess! I'm sure she will agree with me!" he declared smugly. "Now, shall we drink to ... future possibilities?"

This time I raised my glass.

"Yes. Future possibilities."

Chapter Eleven
Decision Time

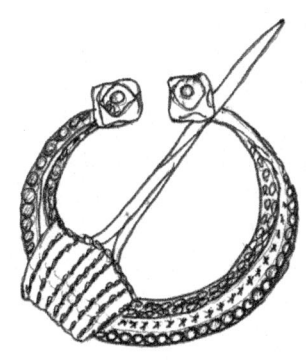

Bronze cloak pin with gilt and silver decoration. Gotland, Sweden.

I planned to consult the goddess the next morning, but something happened to change my plans: an unexpected summons from my mother.

I'd been so moody and out-of-sorts during the evening meal that even Gerda had kept her distance. Drifa politely inquired if I could use a purgative. I almost snapped my refusal, then hastened to apologize.

"I'm . . . not myself tonight, Drifa. Forgive me. You have been most kind to me and my people."

She looked at me appraisingly.

"Perhaps you will have better dreams tonight if you take a cup of chamomile tea. I've noticed your . . . restlessness of late."

"Thank you. A thoughtful suggestion, one I will follow," I said gratefully.

But even the herbal tea could not soothe my troubled spirit, and I fell again into a restless sleep. As I twisted and turned on my bench, I felt a sudden coolness on my sweaty cheek. What could be the source of such a welcome breeze inside the longhouse? Rising on one elbow, I peered into the darkness.

A soft light streamed from the doorway. Why is the door open? Did I not see Drifa close and bar it?

In the light a form appeared — a female form. It stretched out its arms to me and issued a command.

"Come!"

I rose and glided from my bench, not even touching the rough, planked floor as I hurried to follow the figure receding before me. Outside the long house we passed swiftly through the settlement, heading for the forest, floating over treetops as branches reached for my gown. Below me I recognized the sacred pool, the place of sacrifice, no longer filled with weeds and mud, but clear and sparkling in the moonlight.

Mother turned toward me — I knew it was she — and voiced an invitation: "Over the water, Freawaru. Come to me, over the whale road."

Without hesitation I stepped into the pool, shivering as cool water grasped my ankles. Deeper I waded, and deeper... "Mother, I'm coming!"

With a gasp I opened my eyes to find myself waist-deep in the swamp. A pale moon still hung in the sky, but no figure was to be seen.

How did I get here? What am I doing here? Turning around, I struggled to the shore. I must get back!

On bare feet in a sodden nightdress, it took me a long time to make my way back to the settlement. I kept to the shadows, hoping not to be seen by anyone and have to account for my presence — so late and so far from home, in such a condition.

Just as I reached the longhouse, the door opened and I was greeted by Gerda's little face.

"Lady, where were you? I saw your empty bench and was coming to look for you."

She glanced at my dirty feet and the nightdress clinging to my legs.

"You must be cold. Come inside and I'll warm you."

Leading me to her own bench, she sat me down and wrapped her sleeping robe around my trembling shoulders.

"Stay here while I close the door," she whispered.

As she padded toward the door, another figure came forward: Runa.

"What are you doing up, child?" she whispered, reaching for the door and closing it. "It's too early to go out."

Gerda nodded toward me, huddled on her bench.

"It's lady. She's back."

"Back?"

Runa turned with a start and hurried to my side.

"By the goddess, what happened? You look as if you've been dragged through the mire!"

Her exclamation roused Ginnlaug, sleeping nearby.

"What is it? What's wrong?" she yawned, sitting up and rubbing her eyes.

"Shhh. We don't need to wake the whole — whole household," I said through chattering teeth. "Apparently I've been . . . walking in my sleep."

Later, after another mug of Drifa's tea and a bowl of hot porridge, I told the women what I could remember of my night's adventure.

"It was definitely Wealtheow," I said. "I saw her face and heard her voice. She was as real as you are, Runa," I declared.

"This is serious, my lady!" cried Runa. "You might have drowned if you'd gone further and been sucked under in that swamp! You could have disappeared and we'd never have known what happened to you!"

Gerda's head jerked up.

"Don't do it again," she implored. "Don't leave us, lady! Don't leave . . . me!"

I grimaced. "It was not my intention to leave anyone, but Wealtheow's calls are growing stronger. She commands me to find her! But where did she go when she left Heorot?" I sighed. "In the few clues I've discovered, the name 'Wulfing' or 'Wylfing' comes up, and the phrase 'Helming's daughter'."

"Wulfing? I've heard that name before," said Lise, "from one of our young men — Alf."

"What?" I turned to her in astonishment. "What did he say?"

She reflected. "I think it had something to do with his uncle — the one who raised him as a boy — perhaps in another country? You'll have to ask Alf."

"I will, immediately! Where might I find him at this time of day?"

Lise wrinkled her nose.

He and Knud spend all their time at the forge," she said. "Whenever I see them, they're always black with soot!"

"Sooty or not, I will speak with him today!"

"Ooh, can I come with you? I'd like to see Alf all black!" Gerda's eyes sparkled as the women laughed.

We found Alf and Knud working beside Jörgen, the blacksmith. All three were sweaty and sooty in the heat that blasted from the forge. Jörgen was hammering something on the anvil, while Knud worked the bellows and Alf pushed wood into the roaring furnace. At our approach, Alf paused and reached up a grimy hand to wipe away the sweat that trickled down his face.

"Lady Freawaru! Sparrow! What brings you here?"

"I would speak with you, Alf," I called, "but please continue your work. We will wait — and watch — until you are finished."

"What are you making?" piped Gerda as we stepped back from the heat to observe.

"Sword blade," said Jörgen curtly, not looking up. He lifted his heavy hammer and brought it down on the metal with a resounding clang.

"Ooh," squealed Gerda, clapping her hands to her ears, "it makes a lovely big noise!"

Knud grinned, showing white teeth in a sooty face.

"Loud as Thor's hammer! Alf and I keep the fire hot to soften the metal, so Jörgen can hammer out a fine edge."

"Careful!" I cautioned Gerda as a shower of sparks flew out.

We watched in fascination as the men continued to work. Finally, Jörgen set down his hammer and nodded to Alf and Knud. Wiping their faces, they left the forge to attend us.

"We brought cold water for you," I said, reaching for the skin bag slung over my shoulder.

"Most welcome," declared Knud, lifting the bag to his lips for a long drink.

Alf took the bag and poured the remaining water over his head, to Gerda's delight shaking and spluttering like a dog.

"Thanks!" he gasped, wiping his face with his sleeve. "Now, how may I help you, my lady?"

I handed the empty bag to Gerda and faced Alf squarely.

"Alf, what do you know of a tribe — or a place — called 'Wulfing' — or perhaps 'Wylfing'?"

Alf gave another swipe to his dripping hair and grinned.

"That is an easy question for me for I grew up among the Wylfings — far to the south and east of here –and when I was old enough my father sent me over the water to be raised by my uncle, who called himself a 'Wulfing'." He looked at me quizzically. "With permission, lady, why do you ask?"

I could not speak. After all this time, to have the information I sorely needed handed to me so casually — it took me a moment to recover. Yet Alf had named two separate locations; one apparently reached by land, another "over the water." That's what Wealtheow had said: "come to me ... over the water."

"Alf," I said finally, "When you went 'over the water,' to what land, to what country did you go?"

He grinned again.

"So many of us Angles have been migrating there, most folks call it 'Angle-land'."

"Hmm. Do you know the way to this 'Angle-land'? If I wished to go there, could you guide me?"

This time Alf looked less certain.

"I have crossed the sea and back, but that was several years ago, and we did not leave from this place."

Knud, who had been kneeling beside Gerda letting her trace circles on his dirty face, now stood up.

"Lady Freawaru, I know something of Angle-land, if that's where you want to go. I went there once with a trading party. It would be a very long sea-journey from here — weeks, perhaps — but it could be done."

"Thank you Knud, thank you, Alf. I will consider what you have told me before making any decision." I raised my voice and turned toward the forge. "Thank you, Jörgen, for loaning me your workers. I'll return them to you now."

Later that day I found Bodvar Bjarki in the longhouse. He had just returned from a hunt and was refreshing himself with a mug of ale.

"Lord Bjarki!" I exclaimed, pleased to see him, for he usually did not return to the longhouse until late in the evening.

"Lady Freawaru," he said, putting down his ale. "The king tells me that you and he may soon be making an ... announcement."

"What? Freawaru, why didn't you tell me?" exclaimed Drifa, hurrying in from their bedchamber.

I frowned. "There is nothing to tell. I fear the king has been ... premature." I frowned again. "I hope word of this supposed announcement has not been spread about — has it?" I looked at Bjarki for confirmation.

"I cannot say. King Hrolf only spoke to me this morning as we were riding. He said that the two of you were considering a ... joint rule."

"Oh Freawaru, then you'd be staying here, not moving on," cried Drifa, clasping her hands, clearly pleased at the prospect.

"Nay, nay, there has been no such agreement," I said hastily. "I fear the king has misconstrued the situation. I still intend to locate my mother — and in fact have new information which may help me find her. Lord Bjarki, are you familiar with the sea route to Angle-land?"

Drifa's face fell at this turn in the conversation, but Bjarki answered calmly.

"Yes, I am. We sometimes trade with the Angles along the eastern shore of that land, but not all the tribes there are so friendly." He paused to take a swallow of ale. "Do you wish to go there?"

Slowly I nodded. 'Yes, I believe I do. Would a journey there still be possible this late in the summer? Knud said it could take weeks."

"Knud is right, but it will be a few months yet before the onset of winter storms. You could make it safely — if you left soon."

"No!" cried Drifa. "Don't go, Freawaru! Don't encourage her, Bodvar! We need her here in Roskilde!"

This time I shook my head.

"No, you no longer need me. I have told you all I could about Skuld. Dear Drifa," I said softly, embracing her shoulders, "you have been like a sister to me, and I treasure the time I have spent with you, but Mother is insistent. I must cross the sea to reach her."

Drifa sniffed, but nodded, her eyes bright with unshed tears.

"King Hrolf is sure to be ... disappointed,' said Bjarki mildly. "You might wish to tell him of your ... change in plans?"

"You are right. Has he returned to his chamber?" I asked, feeling uneasy at the prospect of facing him again.

"Yes, I left him there a short time ago. I'll send Eyvind to see if the king can receive you before nightfall. Speed would be best," he counseled.

I nodded gratefully. "Thank you, Bodvar. You have been most helpful — and understanding."

While waiting for Eyvind's return, I withdrew to my bench in the now-empty longhouse and opened my rune bag.

"Am I making the right decision?" I whispered to myself. "If I must go, let the rune I draw be 'Raido.' If I should stay, let it be 'Isa.'"

I closed my eyes, settled myself and reached into the soft skin bag. "Goddess, guide my fingers. Show me the path I must take."

A rune slid into my palm and my fingers closed over it. Drawing it forth, I opened my eyes. There in my hand lay . . . Othila!

Othila? Inheritance? What can this mean? Does it relate to my ancestry — to my connection with Mother? Or to the possibility of carrying on the Scylding line as Hrothulf's queen? But wait! Another meaning of this rune involves separation, severance, requiring the will to give up what has been held precious in the past.

I stared at the rune in puzzlement and wonder. Evidently the goddess was giving me no easy answers! I pondered my choices. Yes, I could stay in Heorot and enjoy a position of power and honor. But could I shut out my mother's voice? Could I be at peace knowing that I had ignored her summons — her need for me? Yes, that's what it was: need. Wealtheow needs me and I must go to her.

Sighing, I returned the rune to its bag.

Just then Runa entered the longhouse, carrying the nightdress I'd worn into the swamp. She saw me on my bench and hurried to my side.

"Most of the mud stains came out with hard rubbing," she said happily, "so you'll be able to wear this gown again . . . Oh, what has happened? Your face looks serious. Have you made a decision?"

I looked at her anxious face. "Yes, I have. Runa, we will soon be leaving for Angle-land."

"Angle-land? Where is that?" she queried, kneading the gown in her hands as if it were bread dough before dropping it on my bench.

"Across the ocean — many weeks away — but Mother is there and I must go to her," I declared with conviction.

"Oh. I see," said Runa, her face blank. "And the rest of us? Are we to accompany you — yet again — on this endless quest?"

"Why, Runa, what's wrong?" I asked, shocked at her unexpected response.

"It's just that... Olaf and I were hoping to settle down—finally. He's found a piece of land here, and Roald wants to trade his animals..." her voice trailed off.

"But Runa, you knew the purpose of this journey when we left Eaglesgard!" I chided. "It was always to seek out Wealtheow."

"I know," she admitted, "but I thought your search would come to nothing, that you'd give it up and find a place to settle... one day. Your search has now gone on for such a long time..." she concluded weakly.

We stared at each other in silence until a cough at the doorway drew our attention. Eyvind stood there waiting—for me.

"The king will see you now, Lady Freawaru," he announced cheerfully.

"I'll be ready in a moment,' I said, "after Runa and I have finished our conversation. Please wait outside, Eyvind."

He bowed and disappeared from the doorway, as I turned back to face Runa.

"Runa," I said earnestly, taking her hands in mine, "you have been my dearest friend for countless winters; we have shared many joys and sorrows, you and I. To lose you would grieve me, but you must understand: I have to go! I feel Wealtheow's call every day, stronger and stronger, and I must obey it."

Runa bowed her head and returned the pressure of my fingers, so that we stood as if locked in place.

"I owe you so much," my lady," she said quietly, "my freedom—even my very life! I should not have spoken as I did. Please forgive me."

"No, dear friend, there is nothing to forgive. You have been ever faithful, always putting my welfare above your own. You deserve your own life with Olaf. When I put the matter to Olaf and the rest of our people, there may be others who wish to stay here as well. It will be as Wyrd decides. Now," I released her hands, "the king is expecting me."

She looked up with a faint smile. "Thank you."

I had thought to face King Hrolf with my mind made up, certain of my next move, but Runa's response and the drawing of Othila had shaken me. Be resolute, Freawaru! If Hrolf detects any sign of hesitation on your part, he will use it to persuade you, to bend you to his will!

To strengthen my resolve, I pictured Wealtheow, glowing like the moon as she beckoned me onward—over the water. By the time Eyvind and I arrived at the mead hall, I felt calm and determined. Hrolf greeted me grinning with expectation, his own eyes aglow.

"Come in, come in, my lady! This is a joyful day, one we must celebrate together!"

Unlike the stained and sweated hunting attire I'd seen on Bjarki, King Hrolf had obviously changed clothes for our meeting. He wore a finely woven oat-colored tunic trimmed with rich black braid, and his dark beard was neatly combed and parted. I also noted that he had already poured our wine, in glasses of clear crystal.

"Wait... King Hrolf. You do not yet know the reason for my visit."

"Oh?" His grin faded. "Have you not come to give me your answer?" His eyes narrowed and he shut the door behind him with a sudden bang.

"Yes, but it may not be the answer you were expecting."

I made no move to sit down, and Hrolf too stood frozen, gazing at my face. Slowly he nodded, his own face darkening.

"I see. You have talked to the goddess and she gave you . . . bad advice!"

"No, not the goddess." I took a deep breath. "Wealtheow herself has come to me. I cannot ignore her summons. I must leave Heorot immediately and journey across the sea . . . to Angle-land."

"Angle-land? That's ridiculous! That's insane!" Hrolf exploded. "That would be a long journey, a hard journey even for seasoned sailors — a fool's journey! And what do you expect to find if you even get there? Wealtheow waiting with open arms? More likely Wealtheow dead and buried with no one to welcome Freawaru and her crew of misguided followers!"

My face burning, I stood and listened as Hrolf raged on, reeling off all the reasons why I should not go to Angle-land, including all the dangers I might face. When at last he ran out of words, I spoke quietly.

"I appreciate your concern, my lord. Nevertheless, I am going — with my crew of misguided followers as you call them." Whom I have not yet spoken to, I remembered. Will they indeed go with me?

Hrolf stared at me and suddenly gave a low chuckle.

"Cousin, cousin, sit down and let us discuss this, this mad plan of yours, over a glass of wine."

"I will be happy to sit with you, King Hrolf, but my mind is made up. The omens are clear. I must go to Angle-land," I said firmly.

"Yes, yes, so you say. Even more reason to grant me your presence here and now."

Hrolf came swiftly behind me and seated me at the table, then took his place across from me. He raised his glass.

"What shall we drink to this time, cousin?"

"To peaceful partings," I replied, mindful that Unferth no longer lived to help me make another escape from Heorot.

Hrolf chuckled again. "To peaceful partings."

We drank.

"I suppose a great king would not hold you against your will?" he asked, wiping his lower lip.

"Indeed, I was thinking the same thing," I said. "The great king Hrolf Kraki will be praised where ever I go — but cousin, I beseech you. Have a care for Skuld! I know she intends to do you great harm!"

"So! You do care for me –just a little?" He was half teasing, half serious.

"Yes, I do, but I cannot be your queen. Wyrd has other plans for me."

Hrolf reached across the table and took my hands in his. He raised my fingers to his lips and brushed them with a kiss.

"Thank you for that, Freawaru," he murmured.

"Hrolf," I said quietly, letting my fingers linger in his grasp, "for long years I . . . hated you, fostering the resentments of childhood and believing that you'd had a hand in my brothers' deaths. It was with great reluctance and apprehension that I returned to Heorot — and then only to seek news of my mother. During my stay here, however, I have been welcomed and feted, treated with great respect and honor. I have also seen you in a new light — in your role as king — and have come to . . . value . . . our connection. I am pleased and flattered by your proposal, even if I cannot accept it. I will . . . miss you."

As I gently withdrew my fingers, a great sadness settled over me, for I seemed to see the king as if from a distance, fighting for his life amidst a horde of phantom warriors and beast-like beings — in a battle he could not win.

"Nay, cousin, don't look so sad! I'm not angry," he said earnestly, relinquishing my hands. "You are a woman of wisdom and spirit and I respect you for that. In fact," he said, brightening, "if you are determined to follow the sea road to Angle-land, I will help you! Tell me what you'll need for your journey."

Surprised at this unexpected generosity, tears came to my eyes, but I blinked them back and took another sip of my wine. Better to show the strength Hrolf saw in me.

Cloak of Ashes

"Since none of my men have made the journey from Heorot to Angle-land, an experienced navigator would be must helpful — if you can spare such a person."

Hrolf nodded. "Let me think. I'm sure we can find a suitable man for that purpose."

I noted his use of the word 'we' and nodded, grateful for his cooperation. As I raised my glass to my lips, Hrolf too took another drink.

"We could even make it a fully-manned trading expedition, adding a second ship to accompany your cargo vessel — and get you there safely," he mused, stroking his beard in growing enthusiasm. He stopped suddenly, as if struck by another idea.

"Lady Freawaru, cousin, I'd like to make a second proposal — and please, hear me out before you respond!"

"Yes, my lord, I will listen to whatever you have to say," I assured him, wondering what could be coming next.

He leaned forward across the table, his eyes soft, almost pleading.

"If you don't find Wealtheow, if you don't find what you're looking for in Angle-land, would you return to Heorot and would you return... to me?"

The tenderness in his eyes was undeniable; I gulped as an answering tenderness rose within me.

"I... I cannot promise, but... yes, I would consider returning... to you."

Hrolf's face flushed and he rose, reaching out a hand.

"Please, Freawaru, let me see... your hair," he said hoarsely.

Silently I rose and reached up to pull off my kerchief. Shaking my head, I let my hair settle about my shoulders. Hrolf gazed at me as if in a stupor, then reached out to touch a lock beside my face.

"You are so beautiful, so beautiful," he breathed, now stroking my cheek.

"You honor me, King Hrolf. I shall hold this moment forever in my heart."

"'And I too, Freawaru. Forever," he echoed.

I lifted my own hand to take his before gently removing it.

"Now, my lord," I said briskly, "if you seriously wish to make this a trading expedition, we have planning to do."

"What?" murmured Hrolf, still gazing at me as if in a trance. He shook his head. "Oh, yes, a trading expedition. Planning. But Freawaru, did you really say what I thought I heard? You'll consider . . . coming back . . . to me?"

"Yes," I said, smiling broadly, "you heard correctly."

Before I left Hrolf's chamber we made preliminary plans. He agreed to provide a second ship stocked with men and supplies, trade goods and an able navigator to lead my group to Angle-land.

"Of course I must discuss all this with my people," I said, "but my lord, you have been more than generous. You have been absolutely . . . magnanimous!" I declared, flushed with happiness

"Magnanimous? I like the sound of that! It befits a great king, don't you think?" He smiled at me like a young boy.

"Indeed it does," I said, and began to laugh. "Suddenly I feel light as a feather . . . I feel like a girl again! What's wrong with me?"

"Nothing is wrong with you!" he declared, "but your mention of a feather emboldens me to ask another favor."

"What is it, great king?" I teased, feeling almost tipsy.

"Would you show me your mark of Freyja?"

The laughter died in my throat and I stiffened. Was this a move to seduce me? To get me into his bed? If I refused, would he take back his offer of men and supplies?

Hrolf instantly read my reaction and hastened to reassure me.

"I'm sorry, Freawaru. I've offended you. Forgive me, please, forgive me."

"You have not offended me," I said in a low voice, "but this is not the time. I should go now. I should tell my people what you have offered."

Hrolf nodded, though clearly disappointed. He swallowed and cleared his throat.

"Freawaru, I live in a world of men. In that world I know what to do and say. In your world, I am . . . less sure. I welcome your . . . guidance."

Startled and moved by his raw honesty, I hesitated, then slowly drew down the corner of my kirtle to expose my bare shoulder. I looked up at Hrolf's wondering face.

"There, by my shoulder blade. The mark of Freyja," I whispered, shutting my eyes.

I felt his lips brush my shoulder reverently, then the touch of his fingers as he slowly drew my gown back into place.

"Thank you, Freaw, thank you."

That evening I met with all my people in the same corner of the mead hall where I had last met Unferth. Runa had alerted Olaf to my decision, but the faces of the rest displayed a mix of apprehension, curiosity, and anticipation. After an initial round of bread and ale, I began to speak, standing at one end of the long table.

"Friends, you all know that we set out from Eaglesgard to seek my mother, Wealtheow. We stopped in Norway only to deliver wergild to Tor's family. Our sojourn here in Heorot was necessary to gather information on Wealtheow's whereabouts. That information has now been obtained. Wealtheow will be found in Angle-land among the Wulfings. Therefore, in a few days, I will set sail for Angle-land."

I waited for reactions, but there were none, so I continued.

"King Hrolf has generously offered a second ship with trade goods to accompany us, and an experienced navigator to lead the way. I hope that each of you is still willing to be part of my crew on this final leg of our journey, but if any wish to stay here, I will respectfully consider your request. Now. Let me hear your thoughts."

Suddenly several voices began speaking at once.

"Where is this Angle-land?"

"Who is the navigator?"

"How long will it take?"

I raised my hand. "One at a time, please. We have all evening to talk, and you will have until morning to give me your answer."

In the pause that followed, I saw my women, ranged along one side, looking at our men sitting across the table, as if waiting to see what their response would be. The men all looked toward Olaf, who slowly rose from his seat at the end of the table opposite me.

"My lady," he said, clearing his throat, "it has been my privilege to serve you for many winters, and I will not part from you now. Where ever you wish to go, Runa and I will go with you."

He gave a slight bow and resumed his seat.

"Thank you, Olaf, and Runa." I bowed in their direction. "I know this means some . . . sacrifice for you."

"Lady Freawaru?" A woman's voice sounded: Lise. "What can you tell us about this land, this Angle-land?"

"Those who have already been there can speak best," I suggested. "Alf, please stand and tell us what you remember from your boyhood days."

Alf rose awkwardly to look up and down the table. His face had been scrubbed clean of the grime from the forge, but I noticed a few streaks of soot on the back of his neck and arms.

"It's warmer—and greener," he began, "even than this place. My uncle kept many thralls to work the land—fertile soil, he said. Flat near the coast, lots of forest—and fens, big fens. Good hunting. I heard tell of mountains, but never saw any."

Alf sat down abruptly, as if he had told everything that needed telling.

Chuckling, Knud rose next.

"I too have visited Angle-land, but only with traders. I noticed that most of the settlements were built inland from the sea, along rivers that provided easy access. The people I met seemed much like us in word and dress—though the women were not as pretty!"

He winked at Lise, whose face brightened immediately.

"What about the men?" called out Vigo. "Should we expect opposition—resistance—if we try to settle there?"

Knud wrinkled his nose and shrugged.

"That would probably depend on . . . how we introduce ourselves. Since King Hrolf's men have already traded there, they could speak for us. But . . . since we have all sworn allegiance to Lady Freawaru, we should be ready to fight for her, if need be!"

The notion of fighting seemed to meet with approval from the young men, who pounded the table enthusiastically as Knud sat down, smiling smugly as if he had settled the matter.

"Nay, nay, ours is a peaceful mission," I said, "but thank you, Knud. Our challenge may come before we reach Angle-land, on the long sea voyage—longer than most of us have ever undertaken."

Lempi's quiet voice made itself heard.

"How long, my lady?"

"The better part of a month, from what I've been told. We'll need to sail north and west around the entire island of Danemark, then down along the coastline of the Frisians and Franks, before crossing the North Sea to Angle-land . . . across the whale road," I finished, my voice faltering as I envisioned the enormity of this undertaking.

"This navigator you spoke of, who is he?" asked Olaf.

"I have not yet met him," I replied, "but his name is Harig. King Hrolf told me he'd been severely wounded in a battle with the Swedes and no longer goes to war, but he is an experienced mariner who has made the voyage many times."

As it turned out, I did not have to wait until morning for the responses of my company. Everyone declared their allegiance and willingness to undertake the voyage. Even Ginnlaug, who had blanched at my initial announcement, cheerfully joined Roald in giving her consent. As she confided to me later, she had only waited for a signal from Roald—which came in the form of a sly foot under the table and a wink of his eye.

Gerda was still awake when we returned to the longhouse.
"When do we leave?" she asked cheerfully, sitting up on her bench.
"I laughed. "You seem sure that 'we' are all going!"
She nodded confidently. "Yes. You are the leader. Everyone follows you."
I gave her a hug and tucked her back under her sleeping robe.
"Get some sleep, little sparrow. Tomorrow will be a busy day."
She smiled up at me. "I'll help!"

Now that the decision had been made and we had the king's backing, we set to work preparing for the journey. For the women this meant re-packing our personal belongings in travel chests and preparing provisions for a lengthy sea journey—which included selecting livestock. Beside Roald's animals, King Hrolf insisted that we take a number of cows, pigs, goats and chickens from his herds and flocks. Most of these would be carried on Harig's ship along with the trade goods: leather, furs, skins, knives, axes, honey, fats and beeswax.

I was surprised to learn that Harig's wife and young son were to come with us. Harig himself was a tall, lanky Dane with sleepy eyes and a slow, deep voice that somehow inspired confidence. His grizzled beard and weathered face gave ample evidence of his days at sea. The only evidence of his battle wound was a pronounced limp. His wife Hedvig, a plump, fresh-faced woman with long yellow braids tucked under her kerchief, smiled constantly as she talked.

"Yes," she chirped, "Now that he's seven, we've decided to take Hans to stay with his uncle, my brother in Gaul—after we deliver you to Angle-land, of course. We'll winter over with my people, the Franks."

Hedvig and I were standing outside one of the storehouses for dried fish, where we had counted out the number needed for the voyage. I smiled at the word 'deliver,' as if I and my people were no more than cargo, but felt a prickle of apprehension at the mention of Franks — a sometime enemy of the Geats. Yet by the time we part from Harig and Hedvig, we will surely have found Wealtheow, in Angle-land.

Gerda had taken an instant liking to tow-headed Hans, as round-faced as his mother, with soft blue eyes and a dimpled chin. Hans was younger than Gerda, but a head taller. She, however, soon brought him down to her size.

On the day of their first meeting, down at the harbor beside the ship Harig was to captain, Gerda had taken the initiative. Looking the boy full in the face, she declared, "I'll be the leader — like Lady — and you can be my follower. We'll have adventures. Come on! They're loading the goats right now!"

As she dashed off, Hans hesitated and cast a questioning look at his mother, then ran to catch up with Gerda.

"Harig thinks I've mothered Hans too much," Hedvig had observed wryly. "Hans is used to taking orders from women."

I thought of this now as Hedvig and I piled dried cod into baskets.

"Will your son stay on with his uncle after you return to Heorot?" I inquired.

"Yes," nodded Hedvig, her habitual smile faltering. "Harig thinks the boy needs... the company of men... at this stage of his life."

"I see." I nodded. "King Hrolf was little more than Hans's age when he came here to live with his uncle — my father, King Hrothgar."

"Oh?" Hedvig brightened. "King Hrolf, you say? That's a comfort. He certainly turned out to be a man any mother would be proud of!" she declared, smiling.

Unless your son's father is also your own father. That curse can never be removed. Once again a sense of foreboding swept through me, but left just as quickly. I sighed.

Whatever lies ahead for Hrolf and Heorot, my own path is clear: I must go to Angle-land.

Chapter Twelve
Setting Sail

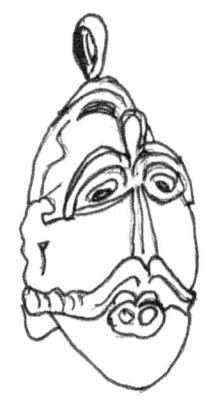

A silver pendant, perhaps a charm to wear in battle, from Aska, Sweden.

The morning of our departure a heavy mist lay over the fjord, hugging the shore. So, instead of an early start, we waited for the sun to burn it off.

"Is this a bad omen, my lady?" murmured Runa in my ear.

"No," I asserted, "only a brief delay."

I looked about me at the people gathered along the harbor shore: my own band of men and women, Harig's group, a mixed lot of young men jostling and joking, and old graybeards standing quietly, spitting and peering at the mist, Harig's wife giving instructions to her thralls, and Hans darting among clusters of men as he ran, chased by... Gerda.

"Gerda! Leave that boy alone!"

"Better let them run now, my lady," chuckled Runa at my side." On shipboard there'll be little room for running."

Gerda had asked if Hans could travel on our ship, but Hedvig was not ready to part with her son just yet.

"You can play together when we overnight on land," I'd told Gerda, and she had seemed satisfied.

Seeing Gerda and Hans together made me think of Inga as a girl and her little friend Toke.

Inga, my daughter, I have not forgotten you. Last night I drew a rune to determine your situation. I drew Berkana, signifying fertility and new life. As you experience motherhood yourself, dear daughter, may the goddess be with you.

Last night I had also said my goodbye to Hrolf, quietly in his chamber He had thoughtfully provided a farewell feast two nights earlier so that our men would not be sluggish from drink on the morning of departure. Again I had admired the consideration shown to me and my undertaking.

Seated across from my cousin for what would probably be our last meeting, I had tried to be calm and cheerful. Hrolf looked as if he were not well, his face so pale and drawn against his skull that it reminded me of the skeleton head used by Skuld to hurl her hate against me.

Hrolf had taken my hands and held them, fiercely gazing into my face as if to devour it, committing to memory every angle and curve. We spoke little and drank even less, our wine glasses largely untouched. When he did speak, Hrolf had one request.

"Freaw," he said huskily, "will you give me something of yourself? Will you give me . . . a lock of your hair?"

Nodding mutely I stared at him, tears springing to my eyes. Gently freeing my hands from his, I reached for the knife that hung at my waist. Drawing forth a curl from beneath my kerchief, I severed it with one quick stroke and laid it in his open palm. As his fingers closed over it, something also clutched at my heart.

"'What is it?" he whispered as the tremor passed through me.

I shook my head. "I do not know. Perhaps a premonition . . . of some grief to come."

"Nay, nay, let us not borrow future grief!" he declared. "There is enough to share right now, right here in this room."

I bowed my head to blink back tears before looking up.

Cloak of Ashes

"'I would not cause you grief, cousin, but our paths must part. I must go to Angle-land. You must continue to lead your people. You are a great king, who will one day be proclaimed in song in every mead hall in every kingdom: King Hrolf Kraki."

He sighed. "Thank you, Freaw, thank you for your encouragement and faith in me. I know the path I must follow."

He straightened in his chair, a slow smile starting on his lips.

"I too have a gift to bestow, but I cannot give it to you here. You will find it waiting for you when you board your ship tomorrow."

"A surprise? I love surprises!" I too smiled, my mood suddenly lifting.

And so we parted, in sorrow but with mutual affection and respect.

"Lady Freawaru! Wait!"

A panting voice behind me broke my reverie and made me turn.

"Borghild? What is it?"

Momentarily flushed and breathing heavily, the portly Borghild stood before me, holding out a bulky bundle.

"You need to have this, my lady. It belonged to your mother, it did."

"To Wealtheow? What is it?"

"Open it and see," directed Borghild, her eyes bright.

Slowly I unfolded what appeared to be an unfinished length of cloth, a weaving, that gradually revealed images: a building of some sort — perhaps a mead hall? — lines indicating waves of water... and above them, clearly flying... swans. I looked up in wonder.

"Where did this come from?"

Borghild gulped, still catching her breath.

"'My mother Torgun found it on Wealtheow's loom when your mother left Heorot. My mother took it off the loom and kept it —as a remembrance, you might say. She passed it on to me when she died, and I've kept it too. But it occurred to me last night that you should have it now — as Wealtheow's daughter. In case..."

"In case I never find Wealtheow?"

Borghild nodded.

"Never fear. I will find her. Thank you, thank you, Borghild for your thoughtfulness and generosity. I will treasure this always."

Borghild turned to leave, but I put out a hand to stop her.

"Wait. One gift deserves another."

Beckoning to Runa, I handed her the tapestry, then untied my head cloth.

"Here, Borghild. Take this small token in remembrance of Freawaru, Wealtheow's daughter."

Borghild accepted the cloth reverently and gave a slight bow.

"A true queen's daughter," she murmured. "May the gods go with you."

She turned again and this time disappeared through the throng waiting to board.

"My lady?" It was Olaf. "The mist is rising."

"Good. Give the signal."

Olaf put two fingers to his lips and gave a high, piercing whistle. Heads jerked up, faces brightened, and we all moved forward: down to the dock, up the gangplanks and onto our ships. From somewhere in the rising mist I thought I heard a whinny.

Our ship and Harig's were both modest-sized trading knorrs, with space for ten oarsmen. The heavy woolen sails lay furled on their racks amidships, the decks crowded with chests and barrels, sacks of seed and grain, casks of fresh water, tent frames, tripods and cooking cauldrons — and animals. Most of the livestock were penned in the hold of Harig's ship, so we had more room on ours to move about — an advantage on a long voyage. I knew we had Roald's cows with us for fresh milk and his two roosters, but I was not prepared for the sight that met my eyes in the hold of our ship.

As I climbed aboard, Gerda at my heels, I once again heard a whinny.

"A horse!" shouted Gerda. "Maybe it's Strongfellow!"

Down in the hold stalled next to the two cows stood a cream-colored mare with a white mane and tail.

"Sunbeorht!" I exclaimed, carefully lowering myself into the cramped space.

Hearing its name, the horse looked up and gave a whinny of greeting.

"So, my friend, we are to continue our journey together! What a welcome surprise!" Thank you, Hrolf, a surprise indeed, and most generous, I said to myself. As Sunbeorht nuzzled my face and blew her hot breath against me, I stroked her silky neck.

"I wish Strongfellow had come too," said Gerda, looking at me enviously, for of course she had scrambled down beside me.

"Don't worry; when we get to Angle-land we'll find a horse for you to ride," I promised.

"Like the wind!" beamed Gerda.

Runa and my other women had followed us on deck and now crowded around to look down at Sunbeorht.

"It is a splendid horse!" exclaimed Ginnlaug, kneeling and reaching a tentative hand to touch its nose. "King Hrolf must really like you!"

"It is not uncommon for royal families to exchange gifts on special occasions," observed Runa, archly.

"What did you give him, Lady Freawaru?"

Lempi's question was unexpected.

"That . . . is a private matter," I said, coloring.

"Ooh, we know what that means!" giggled Lise.

"Ladies! No more of this talk!' I admonished. "Heorot will soon be behind us. Let us turn our thoughts to . . . Angle-land." Taking Gerda's hand, we both made our way back up on deck.

"It will be hard to forget Drifa's comfortable longhouse and good cooking," said Lempi quietly, looking back toward Heorot.

"Or the day you lost your eyebrows, Lady Freawaru—to that witch woman!" shot back Lise, bridling at my reproof.

"They've almost grown back, my lady," assured Runa, frowning.

Ah, yes, Skuld again. At our parting this morning I had counseled Drifa and Skur to be highly vigilant in watching Skuld's activities for any potential threat. Lacking King Hrolf's personal attention to the danger, I could do no more.

We turned our faces to the sea, our men rowing out of the harbor to catch the morning breeze. As I lifted my head and shook out my hair, I looked back at the ship following ours. Olaf and Harig had agreed in advance that Olaf would lead the way in familiar Danish waters; Harig would take the lead when we reached Frisia. I felt a bit sorry for Hedvig, the only woman aboard her ship except for two female thralls, but she had declared it her customary lot when she accompanied Harig on trading expeditions, and said she was used to it.

As Heorot receded behind us, I wondered to myself: will I return here one day? Probably not. Despite the spark of attraction kindled by King Hrolf, I did not expect to see Heorot again.

Soon Olaf was shouting commands: "Ship oars!" followed by "stow oars!" and finally "up sail!"

Slowly the giant square sail was hauled up the mast and unfurled, its once brilliant red stripes somewhat faded and worn. Looking back, I noted the bright blue stripes of Harig's sail, blue as a winter sky. No matter. With the sail snapping and billowing above me, my heart soared too. As we plowed through the water, swans fluttering in our wake, I breathed in the salt sea air and gloried in the rhythm of the waves.

Perhaps this feeling is what Mother was weaving into her tapestry: escaping from land, skimming over water, rising, lifting, flying!

"Lady, I don't feel good."

Looking down, I saw Gerda's face, pale and miserable. She looked ready to retch. Hurrying her to the rail, I held onto her as she gagged and vomited, then apologetically wiped her mouth with the hem of her tunic.

"S-sorry," she whispered.

"You've never been sick at sea before, Gerda. What have you been eating?" I asked in perplexity.

She grinned weakly. "Hans and I were playing horses. We ate some grass."

I shook my head and chuckled. "Hedvig is probably holding Hans up to vomit right now! You two seem bound to get into mischief!"

That morning Gerda quickly recovered and scurried to make herself useful. She helped Mari and Berit take hay to Sunbeorht and the cows. She fed grain to the chickens in their wattle cages, and crowed with delight when she found that one of them had laid an egg, carrying it to me carefully as a precious prize.

"Thank you, but better to give it to Olaf," I directed. "He needs extra strength to manage the steerboard."

Grinning, she wobbled off in exaggerated fashion holding the egg before her in cupped hands as she headed for the stern. It took some time for her to return to the bow where I sat near Runa and the other women. Then she bubbled over with talk she'd heard among the men.

"Lady, is it true that the sea is full of sea-people? Anton told me he'd seen a mermaid!"

I laughed. "Most of such talk is just . . . talk. Sit down a moment, Gerda. I have something to say."

I patted the chest beside me and Gerda dutifully plopped down on it.

"I've been thinking: all this time we have on shipboard would be a good opportunity to teach you . . . the runes. Would you like to do that with me?"

Gerda glanced about wistfully, then looked up at me.

"Could I still visit Sunbeorht? And help the big girls?"

"Yes, you certainly may," I reassured her; "it will only take a part of each day. Now, let's see . . . you will need your own knife and pieces of wood for carving."

Her face drooped. "But I don't have a knife. I do know where there's a stack of wood, piled behind ropes and baskets of fish."

"Part of the cargo on Harig's ship is a packet of knives," I told her. "When we make camp tonight you may select one that suits you, and you can begin carving your first rune tomorrow — carefully."

Gerda jumped up and twirled in a circle.

"Ooh! Wait until I tell Hans! My very own knife!"

"Wait!" I put out a hand to caution her. "The runes will be a private matter between you and me. Remember what I told you earlier? Runes are a sacred gift from Odin — not to be taken lightly. Learning their secrets will cost you . . . your blood!' I paused to let that sink in. "Do you still want to study runes with me? By the way, it's alright to tell Hans about the knife, if you wish."

Gerda nodded enthusiastically. "I'd like that — getting a knife and learning the runes. Thank you, Lady. Now, may I go?"

"Yes, child. Run along."

I sighed as Gerda bounded off, almost tripping over Ginnlaug, who had extended her feet to hold the end of a tablet loom. One end was anchored by a big toe, the other fastened to the belt at her waist. Leaning over, I noted the mix of colorful threads she had chosen.

"What are you making?" I asked.

"It's a border." She looked up. "To add to my gray kirtle . . . for a special occasion."

"Special occasion?" Lise looked over from where she sat hunched on a grain sack, hugging her knees. "What occasion?"

Ginnlaug paused. "You have all been so busy lately. I couldn't find a time to tell you . . ."

"Tell us what?" called Lempi, biting off a thread on the tunic she was sewing, another tunic for Gerda, who was growing like a weed.

"It's Roald," said Ginnlaug shyly. "He — I — that is — we — want to marry. He was going to speak to you, my lady, the night you announced that we'd be leaving for Angle-land."

She flushed, then beamed at our exclamations of approval. Runa came up behind her and hugged her gently, careful not to disturb her weaving.

"It you want that red braid back, I'll be glad to remove it,' said Runa.

"No, not unless red is required for weddings in Angle-land. Is it, my lady?"

All turned to me, but I shook my head.

"'I know little about Angle-land," I admitted. "Hedvig, who has been there before, may be able to tell us more tonight. I'll speak to her. Ginnlaug, congratulations on your betrothal! Tell Roald to speak to me of his intentions. We can arrange the formal betrothal after we reach Angle-land."

Ginnlaug nodded and smiled. She still had all her teeth and looked almost pretty when speaking of Roald. I hoped he understood what a special woman she was. For the rest of that day we women shared our speculations on what life might hold for us in Angle-land.

That night we put into a familiar cove, familiar from our trip down from Breccasberg. Soon tents were unloaded, tripods set up and the smell of herb-seasoned stew bubbling in the cauldrons whetted our appetites — already keen from a day on the water, where dried fish, bread and cheese had been our fare.

That night everyone ate their fill of good venison stew. Roald and Vigo had brought down the deer a few days earlier, and Drifa had prepared the stew as a parting gift to us. After the meal I spoke to Harig about a knife for Gerda, in exchange for a piece of hack silver from my bag. He went back to his ship and returned with a sheepskin packet which he unrolled before us, displaying knives of various sizes. Gerda studied them intently, picking up each to get the feel of it before choosing a short blade set in a handle of antler.

"This one," she said, holding it up.

"A good choice — it fits your grip," declared Harig. "Hans has one very like it."

"Oh — he already has a knife?" she asked, frowning.

"Of course!" laughed Harig. "He doesn't always eat with his fingers!"

"Where is Hans?" asked Gerda. "I didn't see him after we ate."

"I sent him off with some of the men to gather wood for the fire," replied Harig. "That boy needs more work and less play," he said sternly, but winked at me.

That night at our first campfire, one of Harig's men told a story that appealed to Gerda and Hans, for it concerned Thor and the trickster Loki, a pair who often got into trouble together. Helmer, a tall, skinny fellow with a stubble of reddish beard, began by asking if anyone had heard of Thor's adventures in Utgard, home of the giants. Several around the fire smiled and nodded, but no one wanted to discourage Helmer's storytelling.

"That stew tonight put me in mind of an incident that took place when Thor and Loki were on their way to Utgard. As night was coming on, they stopped at a farmer's house to ask for lodging. In return for this hospitality, Thor slaughtered the two goats that pulled his chariot, boiled them in a pot, and invited the farmer and his family to eat. He warned them, however, not to break any of the bones. When they were done eating, they were to cast the bones onto a goat skin spread by Thor for that purpose. The farmer's son, however, used his knife to cut into one bone and get at the marrow."

"Ooh, Hans," said Gerda. "Did you find any bones in your bowl? I hope you didn't break them!"

"Next morning," continued Helmer, "Thor took his hammer and waved it over the pile of skin and bones. Lo, the goats were whole again—but one was lame. Thor flew into a rage so terrifying that the farmer and his household begged for mercy. Thor, seeing how frightened and repentant they were, agreed to take the farmer's son and daughter in payment for the goat's injury. So it was that Thjalfi and Roskva became his servants."

Gerda shivered and wrapped her arms around herself. *Oh dear, I hope this does not lead to more nightmares!*

Helmer stopped speaking and we all fell silent, pondering the story.

"So," said one of Harig's men, a bald-headed old fellow, "even a small transgression against the gods can lead to serious consequences."

"Is that all of the story?" piped Hans. "What about the giants?"

Helmer raised his head.

"There is much more to the story. Thjalfi, for example, becomes Thor's trusted companion, entering contests with him and even killing a monster — but those are stories for another night. We have a long voyage ahead of us."

"Aww," objected Hans, though his eyes were already heavy. Gerda too was nodding.

Rising, I excused myself and led a sleepy Gerda off to the tent we were sharing with Ginnlaug, who had already slipped into her bag. My visit with Hedvig would have to wait for another night.

Our first few days at sea were relatively peaceful, the calm waters allowing for domestic pursuits onboard. Being always in sight of land gave us a feeling of reassurance, though we sometimes encountered crashing waves below rocky headlands. Olaf was steadfastly on the alert, sharing helmsman's duties with Alf or Vigo when he needed to rest his arms or his eyes from the water's glare. For the most part we followed the current along the coastline, sliding smoothly through the waves.

Each morning Gerda and I settled ourselves in a section of the bow to pursue her lessons in rune-carving and rune-reading. Days before boarding I had asked Knud to provide me with several lengths of soft wood for Gerda to practice on, and I sharpened her knife with my own whetstone.

"A sharp blade is safer than a dull one," I told Gerda, "but you must respect it and use it properly. A knife is not a toy!"

She nodded solemnly.

"We'll begin with Fehu. You cut one straight line, then add two arms uplifted on the same side — like this." I demonstrated. "Now you try it."

We were using the top of a barrel as our work table, with Gerda standing on an overturned bucket. Earnestly she pressed her blade into the piece of wood and pulled, trying to keep the line straight. As I watched her, an unexpected chill passed through me; I seemed to feel again my own hand on the knife at Lars' throat.

"Try again," I advised.

When she could finally carve a fairly straight line, we moved on to the next stage: the two branching diagonals.

"Slant them a little higher — like this," I said, raising my arms in parallel to show her the correct angle.

Biting her lip, Gerda tried again, achieving a reasonable representation of Fehu.

"Good!" I crowed, smiling at her efforts. "Now you may carve it onto a fresh piece of wood and you'll have your first rune!"

Slowly and carefully Gerda worked at her task, then held up her hand with the finished piece in her palm for my inspection.

"Yes, that is Fehu. Now hand me your knife."

Puzzled, she did so. Taking her free hand I made a small cut across the tip of one finger. She yelped in surprise as bright blood welled up, and I pressed her finger against the newly-cut rune, intoning softly.

Know how to cut, know how to read,
Know how to stain, know how to prove,
Know how to ask and to sacrifice,
Know how to send and to destroy.

Gerda stared at me in shock, her eyes wide, then nodded ruefully.

"You said there'd be blood," she muttered.

"Yes, for the carver of the rune must make it her own. A small price to pay for knowledge!" I declared. "Now it will speak to you when you call upon it. This rune, Fehu, means 'cattle.' It speaks of wealth, possessions, and is associated with the goddess Freyja."

"Oh, the goddess who marked your shoulder with her feather?" asked Gerda.

"Yes. As you grow into womanhood I will tell you more about her. Freyja is a powerful goddess of love and fertility. It is her wealth that is found in gold and amber..."

I stopped, for I could see Gerda's attention wandering. She put her sore finger into her mouth, sucked it vigorously, then took it out and shook it. No more blood.

"Alright, Gerda, that's enough for today. Put your knife and the rune you've carved in my sea chest until tomorrow."

She climbed down from her perch, then paused to embrace me.

"Thank you, Lady. I'm going to whisper to Sunbeorht what I've just learned. Is that all right?"

"Yes, little sparrow."

When the weather was mild, after mid-day I took advantage of it to move about the ship, further reacquainting myself with our young men and asking them about their past adventures. When the seas were heavy, tossing the ship in a rolling motion, I stayed in the bow, dozing or talking quietly with my women. Everyone looked forward to our nights ashore.

One night Gerda asked a question about mermen that set off a contest between our men and Harig's men to see who could tell the most outrageous tale — or so it seemed to me. Many on Harig's ship were grizzled veterans with a great stock of yarns and fables, but our young men were not shy about offering their own stories and opinions. It reminded me of long-ago boasting matches in my father's mead hall.

Regin, a big bald man with a bushy beard and huge ears, started it off with the story of Thor fishing in the ocean for the Midgard serpent, a tale familiar to everyone at the campfire. But he did not stop there.

"You have to be careful when you're fishing in the ocean," he said, "for you could catch a merman in your net or on a hook. Since he'll be naked and cold, he'll expect you to give him clothes. You'd best do it, too, then throw him back in the sea, or he will take a terrible revenge. Above all, don't try to kill him!"

"What, Regin, afraid? Why I've always heard that catching a merman means you'll have good luck in fishing!" countered our Bram.

Before Regin could answer, a white-haired man with a very red face raised his voice.

"I once heard of a merman who visited folks on shore and challenged them to a duel of wits. If he got the last word, he took them captive. One night the merman came across a farmer and told him 'Tonight two sons have been born to you.'

'That's good,' the farmer said. 'It makes the family grow.'

'One of them died,' said the merman.

'Then they won't fight over their inheritance,' answered the farmer."

After the laughter that greeted this story subsided, our Anton rose to speak.

"Have any of you ever seen a mermaid?" he challenged. Without waiting for a response, he charged on. "I have! Once when I came back from a raiding trip, I found this woman lying on the shore, wrapped all in seaweed. She smiled at me. She had the most beautiful eyes I've ever seen, and she had long, golden hair that reached all the way down to her waist and glistened in the sun!"

A dreamy look came over his face as if he were recalling the sight.

"I knelt down beside her," he continued, "and was about to pull her onto my lap — when I saw her tail! I jumped up with a shout! She laughed and rolled down to the edge of the water and disappeared in the waves. I never saw her again," he concluded with mock sadness.

"Lucky for you!" called a young man with pimples all over his face. "She could have cast a spell on you!"

"No, Anton, here's what you should have done," cried his friend Eskil. 'You should have held on to her and made her answer three questions before you let her go!"

Old Regin shook his head.

"Best leave such folk alone, I say. And there be worse than mermaids and mermen in the ocean. There be monsters at the bottom of the sea, and there be revenants — draugs — spirits of the dead, people drowned at sea, who will come out at night and try to take over your ship."

"You're right about that, Regin," declared a squinty-eyed man with a sharp nose.

"Why, I once knew a captain who told me that he took the precaution of relieving his bowels over the anchor rope at night, for he'd heard of a draug in the area. Sure enough, one night he heard the draug come slithering up out of the sea. But the draug cried out, 'Damn, it's dirty!' and fled back to the water. The captain's shit had scared it away."

Amid hoots of laughter, I once again hustled Gerda off to bed, fearful lest the man's story give her bad ideas!

After our ship rounded the northern tip of what Olaf called 'Jutland,' we headed south — and were surprised by a sudden storm. It began with a freshening breeze, then heavy clouds darkened the sky, and a clap of thunder jolted us all in our places. Raindrops fell, soft and warm at first, then harder and harder, drumming like hail on the deck. We women reached for our sealskin bags and drew the flaps about our heads, but the men had work to do.

"Reef sail!" shouted Olaf as strong gusts sent the ship heaving to one side. Four men reached up to grab the bottom of the snapping sail and began to roll it, as a fifth man lowered the sail half-way down the mast. The cargo on deck was, of course, secured by ropes or nets, but as the gusts grew stronger and the waves grew higher, a few casks broke loose and began to roll across the deck.

"Our drinking water!" I shouted. "Don't let those barrels smash!"

Grim and Eskil nimbly ran forward to catch two of the three casks and wrestle them back under the netting, then captured the third. Rain streamed down their clothes and faces, but they looked cheerful and unconcerned.

"What about Sunbeorht? And Blæki? And the chickens?" cried Gerda in alarm.

"They are safe in the hold," I told her. "A little rain won't hurt them!"

But it wasn't just a little rain. As the gale increased, the wind rose to a roar. Our sail still beat wildly and the ship lurched to one side.

"Drop sail!" bellowed Olaf over the wind.

Several men ran forward, grabbing at ropes and pulling furiously to lower the wet, heavy woolen sail.

"Sea anchor!" shouted Olaf.

Someone—perhaps Gunnulf—stomped to the stern where he heaved out a heavy weight attached to a long length of rope. The ship began to slow perceptibly, but now huge waves billowed above us as we rode up the crests and down into the troughs.

Gerda clutched on to me, and I heard my women screaming.

"Bail!" shouted Olaf as water swept over the gunwales, drenching us where we sat huddled together, holding onto whatever was near. Dimly I saw several figures spring into action, bailing buckets of water as the drenching continued.

I tried to look back to see how Harig's ship was faring, but could not see it in the tossing waves and driving rain. Salt spray stung our faces, and we shook uncontrollably in the chilly blasts. Around us swirled the storm in all its fury.

How long it lasted, I do not know, for I was numb with cold and fear, bent over Gerda to protect her as best I could.

Stay strong, Freawaru. All may yet be well. What am I hearing? Unferth? Mother? Freyja?

"May all the gods protect us!" I cried aloud.

Valiantly we rode out the storm, thanks to the seamanship of our crew, and finally entered calmer waters. Harig's ship was close behind us, off to starboard. As soon as Olaf found a suitable place, we both put in to shore to assess possible damage.

It was still raining lightly as we women crawled out from under our bags, limbs cramped, rain-streaked faces white and drawn.

"By the gods," croaked Lise. "I never want to go through that again!"

"Where's Roald? I don't see Roald!" cried Ginnlaug, looking wildly around the deck.

"Over there," coughed Runa, gesturing. "He's safe."

"Sunbeorht! What about Sunbeorht?" exclaimed Gerda, "and Blæki!"

"We'll go see — right now." I answered, shaking off the paralysis that had gripped me.

Together we made our way to the hold, where Sunbeorht stood trembling beside the two cows who were bellowing in terror. Blæki too was shaking, but wagged his tail as we eased ourselves down.

"Easy, Solvi, easy Suka," I soothed, patting the frightened cows. "It's over now."

Gerda was simultaneously stroking Sunbeorht's mane and patting Blæki's coat.

"The hay is wet, Lady, and the grain — there's nothing left to feed them!" she wailed in distress.

"But they are alive — and so are we — that's what matters!"

Our inspection of the ship revealed no major damage: there were a few rips in our sail and the streamers on the weather vane had blown away, but the mast was still sound, and we had not lost any oars. More bailing was needed in the hold and some of the cargo would need drying out. Overall we considered ourselves fortunate to have survived in such good condition. Harig's ship was also largely intact, although the spar that held the sail had cracked and would need to be replaced.

"I've never seen such a storm at this time of year!" declared Harig to Olaf. "One might almost think the gods were angry at us!"

"Or they are testing us," I interjected. "If so, I'd say we passed the test. Well done, both of you! It can't have been easy to keep us on course and prevent capsizing in that ferocious storm!"

"I've seen worse," said Harig matter-of-factly, "but not in late summer."

Our men removed the heavy, wet sail and hauled it ashore, where they spread it out on the rocky beach to dry. Hedvig joined us to help mend the rips in the sail; we used some of our woolen blankets for patching. Harig's men searched the nearby forest for a suitable tree to replace the damaged yardarm. Gerda and Hans were put to work cleaning out the hold, along with the thralls and anyone else not already assigned a task. Several of Harig's older men busied themselves stuffing threads of tarred wool into leaks between strakes. Everyone worked diligently to restore order before darkness fell, but there was still much to be done before we could resume our voyage. Conferring with Olaf and Harig, I advised laying over an additional day — to which they readily agreed.

"I would also set a watch tonight, my lady," advised Olaf. "I don't know the nature of the tribes in this part of Jutland, but with our ships disabled, we are vulnerable to attack."

"Good thinking, Olaf. Roald's Blæki might be useful too — in case of wild animals."

That night we kindled several fires on the beach, both to dry out our clothes and belongings, and to cheer our hearts. Sitting cross-legged beside Hedvig, Ginnlaug asked her about marriage customs in Angle-land, specifically whether the color red was required for brides. Hedvig laughed heartily at the question.

"No, not that I've ever heard. Mind you, I've not witnessed such a ceremony there myself. I can tell you what I have noticed, however. Most of the women there don't wear oval brooches like you and me wear," she said, gesturing to her apron fasteners. "Round or square is what you'll see. Why, you can tell newcomers from old-timers just by looking at their brooches," she declared.

I could see Lise frowning in the firelight.

"So, we'll be marked from the start!" she sniffed.

Ginnlaug apparently had similar misgivings. "Thank you, Hedvig. I wish you were staying with us — to show us what's expected in this new land."

Hedvig patted her hand. "Harig and I will stay long enough to see your group settled somewhere –after all, King Hrolf will expect a report!"

As we sat around the fire that night, we women talked softly about the future homes we envisioned for ourselves, while some of our young men boasted of the gold and glory they hoped to gain in Angle-land. Older, quieter voices spoke of past joys in the mead hall, and the sight of sunlight on ripening grain. Could Angle-land possibly fulfill all these expectations?

Chapter Thirteen
Angle-land

Kitchen utensils, implements, and storage vessels from ship-burial at Oseberg, Norway.

Once the new yardarm for Harig's ship was finished, lifted into place and fastened, we were able to resume our journey, heading south toward the coast of Frisia. Frisia: the very name gave me a shiver of remembrance and apprehension. King Hygelac had been killed in Frisia during an ill-fated raid. But we were no raiding party, darting in to pillage and plunder. We would make landfall only to spend the night and find fresh water.

Day after day we sailed south, keeping a safe distance from shore. We were often wet and cold, as the long days of summer waned and the air turned chill, with sudden afternoon showers. One day we came to the mouth of a river which I recognized instantly, despite the passage of years.

"I once lived near here," I informed my women, "with my husband Ingeld." I could have added that I'd lost twin sons here, but did not speak of that. "He was chief of the Heathobards."

"Ingeld. Was he Inga's father?" inquired Lempi.

"Yes, but he died before she was born."

"Hedvig told me that the people hereabouts are called 'Saxons'," volunteered Lise. "She also said we'd see a lot of them in Angle-land — so many that one part of it is called the 'Saxon shore'."

Ginnlaug now joined in. "From what Alf has told us, many Angles also live in Angle-land. I do hope the Angles and the Saxons — get along," she concluded earnestly.

The adventures of Thor and Loki among the giants once again became our nightly entertainment, with Helmer doing most of the story-telling. One night he told of an eating contest between Loki and a giant named Logi, who devoured whatever was set before him. Loki later learned that his opponent in the hall had actually been fire itself, which consumes everything.

In another contest Thor was set three challenges. In the first he had to drain a giant drinking horn. Despite three mighty quaffs, he could not do it. Then he was asked to lift the giant's cat, but could only get one paw off the ground. Finally he wrestled an old woman named 'Elli,' but was easily thrown.

The next morning Thor discovered that the giant's drinking horn was connected to the sea, and his huge gulps had created a low tide. The cat he tried to lift was actually the monstrous Midgard serpent, and Elli turned out to be Old Age, which finally defeats every man.

Our young men delighted in such stories, and devised contests of their own to test each other at evening campfires, with wrestling the favorite activity. Our Bram usually won these trials of strength. At sea, when it was calm enough for wood-carving, Gerda's rune-lessons continued. One day she had difficulty carving Pertho, with its elbow-like projections top and bottom, just as I had difficulty explaining its meaning.

"It concerns hidden matters, magical forces," I began. "Its secrets are not easily revealed."

"My grandmother," added Runa, whom I'd asked to join me occasionally in Gerda's instruction, "saw Pertho as a rune of initiation, of introduction to a different way of life."

Gerda frowned at both of us, then slammed her knife down on the barrel head.

"I don't understand what you're telling me," she said crossly. "I don't believe it matters anyway. I'm tired of these lessons!"

Somewhat surprised, Runa and I looked at each other.

"Are we making a mistake? Is she too young to learn?" I asked Runa. "Yet Unferth saw special gifts in her . . ."

"I think Gerda is just feeling restless from this long voyage," said Runa. "We've been sailing for a very long time, my lady. I feel restless myself."

Nodding to both of them, I picked up Gerda's knife and placed it in my sea chest.

"We'll resume this lesson another day," I said quietly.

By the time we reached the string of islands that bordered Friesland, Olaf declared our journey more than half over, and let Harig take the lead. Thus we followed Harig's ship down the coast to the mouth of a great river, called 'The Rhine.' At our campfire that night Harig explained that in the morning we must leave Frisia behind us and make our way across the North Sea, sailing due west . . . to Angle-land.

"But how will you find the way?" queried Ginnlaug, clearly daunted at the prospect of losing sight of land.

"By day with the aid of the sun and the currents and different types of sea birds. By night the stars will aid us. Don't worry," he said confidently, "I have made the trip several times before. We may even encounter other ships taking the same route."

This seemed to cheer Ginnlaug, as it did me. Hedvig also added her assurance that Harig knew the route well, for she had often travelled it with him. The knowledge that we were now much closer to our destination lifted our spirits. Once again there were stories and laughter around the fire at night. I also heard Blæki barking and noticed Gerda and Hans chasing each other in the shadows, shrieking with abandon as the dog romped beside them.

Harig had estimated that it would take us two to three days of sailing to cross the North Sea, but it was actually late on the fourth day when we finally sighted land, a low, dark silhouette against the setting sun. Earlier that day a sea eagle had landed on our yardarm, screeching repeatedly before it flapped away to the west.

"It said we're almost there," reported Gerda, smiling.
"Oh," sneered Lise. "You understand bird talk, do you?"
"Yes," answered Gerda simply.
Lise's mouth opened, then closed as I gave her a warning look.
With nightfall looming, we looked for a place to shelter below the sea cliffs, but finally decided to anchor offshore and spend another night on board ship.
"So close," grumbled Lise. "I can't wait to set my feet on solid ground!"
I ignored her complaints as I stood at the gunwale, breathing in the scent of this new land, this... Angle-land. It smelled... softer, somehow, and... green.

We rose with the dawn, eager to press on. Alf had joined Harig's ship to locate the exact river mouth that would lead us to his uncle's settlement — home of the Wulfings. It seemed we had arrived on the coast slightly north of this river and must follow the coastline south to reach it. Both Alf and Harig spoke of treacherous sandbanks along this part of the coast, so we proceeded cautiously, keeping well offshore and posting a lookout in the bow of each ship.
As we made our way south, we sighted, high on a cliff, the gray ruins of what looked like a large fortification. Its massive blocks of stone made me shiver.
"Romans!" spat Vigo, coming up beside me. "My grandfather told me about them — tales he'd heard from his grandfather. Roman armies once overran every country to the south and enslaved the people. Good builders, though. We'll likely see more evidence of their time here."
I nodded, gazing in awe at the structure looming over the land. It looked like the work of giants.
As we continued southward, I could see that the ocean had been eating away the headlands, hollowing out caves and causing whole cliffs to tumble into the sea. Gradually the cliffs gave way to long stretches of shingle beach, with flat land beyond. In some places the land was somewhat higher, and covered with a purple vegetation. Its beauty struck me keenly.
"What is that?" I shouted to the crew in general, pointing inland.
"Probably heather, my lady," Olaf shouted back. "You've seen it before, just not in such quantity."
"It's beautiful," I exclaimed, breathing in its fragrance.

Darkness was nearly upon us when Alf finally sighted the river he was looking for. One of Harig's men signaled Olaf to veer to starboard. As he did so, we all looked forward expectantly. Sails were lowered and oars pulled out. Settling into their places, our men rowed us slowly along a broad river lined with reeds and rushes, alive with birds of every description.

Gerda and Blæki, who were pressed as far forward in the bow as they could get, responded excitedly, Blæki barking and Gerda echoing the calls she heard. Our men scanned the banks for any sign of a coastguard, but found none.

"It's very flat here," observed Runa, looking about skeptically.

"And damp," said Ginnlaug, her face suddenly beaded with sweat.

"And full of... bugs!" declared Lise, swatting her forehead.

Indeed, as the breeze subsided, a number of flying insects filled the air — and the ship. Lempi reached up and caught one of them. When she opened her hand, we gazed at it in curiosity, for it did not resemble anything we'd ever seen. It had a slender body as long as Lempi's thumb, marked with bands of bright blue and green, two large eyes and two sets of long, transparent wings that fluttered furiously between her fingers.

"Ooh, pretty," exclaimed Gerda, who had come up to see what was absorbing our attention. "But you're hurting it, Lempi! Let it go!"

Obediently Lempi opened her fingers and the creature flew off into the dusk.

"Even the bugs are strange here," muttered Lise, for now the winged creatures were landing all over the ship and Blæki was jumping up to snatch at them.

Just then Olaf gave a shout and our men stopped rowing.

"Oh, we're going to land!" cried Gerda. "I can't wait to tell Hans about the little dragons!"

"I'm sure he's seen them too," I said, smiling at the name she'd given them. "They are hard to miss. But let's get ready to go ashore. This will be our first night on the soil of Angle-land and I want to treasure every bit of it."

We were not to land just yet, however. After Olaf and Harig shouted back and forth about marshes, bays and inlets, Olaf sought my opinion.

"My lady, Harig — and Alf — think we'll find higher ground beyond this marsh, but it may take some time to reach it. What do you think? We could anchor here and spend another night aboard ship — or go on and probably have to make camp in the dark."

I glanced up at the faint half moon taking shape in the eastern sky, and at the hopeful faces of my women.

"If Harig thinks it is safe to proceed, let's go forward. We'll have some moonlight to help us. All are eager to be on land again."

"Right. I'll tell Harig to go ahead."

Once again our men leaned in to their oars. Gradually we pulled away from the little dragons in their marsh, much to Gerda's dismay. Low, sandy banks now rose alongside the river, dotted with scraggly trees and small shrubs. As I watched the landscape gliding past, I blinked and rubbed my eyes. Something strange was happening. Was the land rising or was the water level dropping?

"Olaf!" I cried, gesturing toward shore. "What's happening?"

"The tide — it's starting to go out!" he called. "We'll need to find a place to land soon, or we'll be stuck out on a mud flat until morning!'

A halloo from Harig's ship told us he'd come to the same conclusion. Both ships now turned toward shore, heading for a small inlet on the starboard side. First Harig's ship, then our own, came to rest on a low sandbar at the mouth of the inlet, the steerboards pulled up to allow for landing.

Despite no evidence of a coastguard, Harig sent a small party of men ashore to look out for any obvious dangers and to find a suitable campsite. We waited in suspense, watching their wavering torches as they trudged toward land and then disappeared in darkness, for low clouds now covered the moon. At last they reappeared, shouting and waving us forward.

Both ships were now rowed toward the dark shore line; ropes were thrown from the bow to the men on land to secure our crafts to the larger trees, and anchors were dropped from the stern. Gathering our gear, our tents and tripods and cauldrons, we streamed down the gangplanks, wading through the shallow water to a shore devoid of familiar features, but land nonetheless.

Each person set to work at his or her usual task. Although the moon had emerged, we still stumbled over roots in the dim light and blundered into each other's path. Everyone took it in good humor, eager to create at least a temporary home in this new place. By the time a fire was kindled, the half moon shone on our miniature settlement, set amidst the tall grasses and strange, twisted trees.

We had killed several chickens earlier that day, including — with Roald's permission — his two roosters. I wanted to serve fresh meat for our first night in Angle-land. Soon the savory odor of chicken stew rose from the cauldrons, a welcome change from the dried fish that had primarily sustained us at sea.

"Too bad there's no bread to go with it," muttered Lise. "I can't wait to get my hands into a batch of dough again!"

True, some of our grain had spoiled from wet and mold, but it would be harvest time soon — in this or any country — and we should be able to obtain more. If we find Alf's kinfolks, we may then find Wealtheow, whispered a tiny voice inside my head.

That night Hans begged for just one story before bed, despite the lateness and our weariness. This time Knud volunteered as we sat around the fire, almost hypnotized, licking the last remnants of stew from our bowls and handing them to the thralls to wash.

"This dark, strange place puts me in mind of an adventure Thor and Loki had on their way to the land of the giants," began Knud.

"Oh good," I heard Hans say to Gerda. "Another Thor story."

"After a long day of travel, Thor and Loki found themselves deep in a dark forest, and looked about for a place to spend the night."

Here Knud glanced briefly at the impenetrable darkness beyond the firelight.

"Loki spied an enormous opening at the foot of a small mountain, like the mouth of a cave. Thor led the way inside with his hammer raised, in case it might be a trap. He and Loki found five passageways leading off in different directions. After exploring all five and finding they led to empty rooms, Thor and Loki settled down to sleep in the room nearest the opening. But their night was not a peaceful one. Several times they were awakened by distant roars, and the very ground beneath them shook."

As Knud paused, I thought I heard something in the distance: a horse's whinny? A cow's bellow? Surely Mari and Berit had remembered to feed our animals? Beside me, Gerda and Hans shivered and hugged their knees.

"At first light," continued Knud, "Thor and Loki strode out of the cave. To their amazement, what they had taken for a mountain was the body of a sleeping giant! The roars and shaking had been his snores, and the room in which they had spent the night...? It was the thumb of the giant's glove!"

At this the children laughed out loud, as did my women, sitting nearby. An older man on the far side of the fire stood up.

"'I can add a trifle to that story," he declared. "Thor and Loki later had a falling-out, and Loki told anyone who would listen that Thor had cowered all night in the giant's glove, afraid—lest the giant hear him—to sneeze or even fart!"

To the sound of giggles and guffaws, the man sat down, grinning. Now I stood up and cleared my throat.

"Friends, comrades, I thank you all for your hard work and good humor on this expedition," I said, looking around the circle. "Now that we have landed safely in Angle-land, we can take our rest, looking forward to whatever adventures await us in the morning. Hopefully we won't encounter any giants!"

Nodding and chuckling, our group broke up, leaving a few men from each crew to keep watch and tend the fire. The rest of us drifted, yawning, toward our tents. We could not have dreamed what the morning would bring.

I was soaring above the river on outstretched wings, flying with the 'little dragons', when I heard the sound of a barking dog. It was Blæki. Blæki was barking. One dragon landed on my bare shoulder. A tingle, then a stab of pain shot through me. Suddenly I started to fall! I saw the little dragon flying away—clutching my feather mark of Freyja. No! No, come back! It was too late. I plummeted down, down...

"Wake up, Lady, wake up! Something's happening."

Gerda's voice and her insistent poking on my shoulder brought me fully awake, and I sat up.

"What is it? What's wrong?" I asked, rubbing sleep from my eyes. It seemed barely light, but I could hear a commotion outside.

"Strange men, and a strange horse," whispered Gerda, with a worried face.

Cloak of Ashes

I bolted from my sleep bag and grabbed a cloak to cover my nightdress. Ginnlaug still lay snoring in her bag, and I let her lie. As I parted the tent flaps, Olaf appeared before me.

"My lady, we have . . . visitors. You are needed."

His face told me nothing. Shaking my head to clear it of the dream, I stepped outside.

Beside the ashes of our camp fire stood a half-circle of our men with weapons drawn. In front of them stood Harig, gripping the arms of two strangers, skinny fellows with sullen faces, dressed in patched and dirty tunics, muddy leggings and leather skull caps.

"My lady, we found these two prowling about our ships early this morning," declared Harig. "We also found a horse on shore with an empty pack — a horse that looks too well-fed to belong to this pair."

They did not look dangerous to me. They looked like thralls. As I advanced, both dropped their eyes.

"Look at me!" I commanded. "What are your names and who is your master?"

Harig gave a jerk to the arm of the man on his right, who growled, "Ulf, but I serve nobody!"

"Really?" I frowned. "Everyone serves someone. What are you . . . exiles? Runaways? Thieves?"

"We didn't steal," whined the other man. "We was just lookin' for food."

"Shut up, Karl," snarled Ulf.

"Eskil, Anton," I called. "Come forward and pull the head coverings off these men. I want to see their hair."

Smiling grimly, Eskil and Anton came up behind the captives and pulled off their skull caps. Both men had shaved heads.

"Thralls — who probably belong to a master nearby," I said, my suspicion confirmed. "Well done, Harig. The return of these runaways may provide us with a warm welcome in Angle-land."

"Lady, may we touch the horse?"

It was Gerda, of course, now joined by Hans as our tents emptied and the rest of our group gathered to see what has happening.

"Yes, and I'll come with you — in a moment. Olaf," I said, turning, "be sure these men are fed, bound and well-guarded."

After a hurried meal later that morning, we caught the rising tide flowing upriver and continued our search for signs of a settlement. Our captives had refused to give any information, but it seemed likely they had not travelled far. Harig tied them to the mast on his ship, while the horse, a docile, dun-colored mare, joined Sunbeorht in our hold.

In the clear morning sunlight I could almost forget my troubling dream. We had enough breeze behind us to use the sail, so we were moving briskly up river. On both sides we could see broad stretches of untilled land and low grassy hillsides, interspersed with thickets of birch and alder and occasional stands of oak and elm.

"This looks promising," observed Olaf as I stood beside him at the tiller. "All the things you need for a settlement: fresh water, arable land, pasturage and a good supply of wood."

"Smoke! To starboard!" shouted one of the men from the bow.

Our heads swiveled to scan the horizon. A few small smoke wisps rose from what appeared to be a distant clearing.

"Look for the harbor!' shouted Olaf. "It must be nearby!"

Indeed we soon saw a long, finger-like pier jutting out from the land. At its end stood a man with a spear.

"'Just one coastguard?" I wondered aloud.

"More likely a fisherman," responded Olaf. "See? There's a line attached to one end of the spear."

As we neared, the man lifted a hand in greeting and Olaf went to the gunwale to shout a question.

"Are you missing a horse? Or two male thralls? We have both on board."

The man lowered his spear and scratched his head.

"What's the look of the horse?" he shouted.

"Dun-colored, a mare, about four years old," Olaf shouted back.

The man shook his head. "Not from here. Try Rendlesham — a half day's sail up river, when the tide is in."

"My thanks. May the gods be with you," called Olaf, waving an arm. "Well," he chuckled. "I hope all the locals are this friendly!"

Rendlesham announced its presence long before its piers came into view. The number of smoke spirals rising above it reminded me of Uppsala, capital of the Swedes and their evil king Eadgils. Could Rendlesham be the seat of an Anglian king?

"Good trade here," called Harig from his ship.

"I hope we can restock fresh water and meat here," said Olaf. "And I'd wager that someone here will recognize our... extra cargo."

We encountered not one but a series of coastguards as we neared the harbor. Each one asked our name and business and each one waved us on.

"With Gerda and Hans practically hanging over the gunwales, the guards can clearly see we are no war party!" smiled Runa beside me.

"This looks like a long-established settlement, a good place to ask about Wealtheow," I responded. I had pushed to the back of my mind the dream of flying with the little dragons, but suddenly felt a need for reassurance that I had not lost my special powers.

"Runa, would you please take a look at my shoulder? My birthmark has been... bothering me."

I pulled down the neck of my tunic and offered my back for her inspection.

"Hmm... perhaps the feather outline is a bit fainter, but it looks fine."

"Thank you."

Relieved at this visual confirmation and feeling a bit foolish, I turned my attention to the landing before us.

Pulled up at the piers extending from shore were a mix of longboats and cargo ships like ours, and several small fishing boats. Alf had recollected at last night's campfire that the river, called 'Deop', contained excellent fish, different in taste from the salt-water varieties we were used to. I had hoped that he would remember more about the location of his uncle's settlement, but he admitted that his memory was poor on that score, and also observed that the shoreline had changed since his previous visit.

A young guardsman signaled us to land at a particular pier, and soon our two ships were tied up side by side near a broad wooden walkway that extended along the shore in both directions. Beyond the walkway three paths led up a slight rise to the first level of houses. They looked much like the longhouses I was familiar with: timber walls, thatched roofs, and a smoke-hole at top. A line of trees prevented further observation of the settlement's arrangement, but the plumes of hearth-smoke indicated several rows of dwellings, each row set slightly higher than the one below.

Fortunately we had arrived before the tide started to retreat, shortly after mid-day. Leaving our crews on board ship, Olaf, Harig and I were escorted up the central path by a lad with a long spear who had the beginnings of a light beard.

"Is Rædwald still chieftain here?" asked Harig casually.

When the guard nodded, Harig turned to me and Olaf.

"Rædwald is the son of Tyttla, current ruler of the eastern Angles."

"Do you mean that Tyttla is king, or Rædwald?" I asked, uncertain.

"Tyttla," answered Harig, "although he was old and very sick the last time I came up this river."

"King Tyttla is well," said the guard suddenly, "but Rædwald will receive you. He will question you about your business here."

"Very good," I said, smiling at the serious young man. "We will be honored to meet him."

The guard relaxed his stiffness, and almost smiled in return.

Rædwald's hall, located at the top of the rise, surprised me with its size and grandeur. Although not as gold-adorned as Hrolf's hall, it was clearly the residence of a man soon-to-be-king.

Rædwald himself was likewise an imposing figure: a tall, regal man dressed in fine linen, with a cloak of scarlet. He was standing beside his high seat, talking to an older man, when our guard halted and bowed low.

"The strangers, my lord, as you ordered."

As Rædwald turned, he gave a smile of recognition.

"One of them is not a stranger," he said in a deep voice, "but Harig, I did not recognize your ship. What have you brought me this time? Are these two trade goods?"

Startled, I opened my mouth to protest, but Harig was already speaking.

"I see you still love a jest, my lord. No, not trade goods. May I present the Lady Freawaru and her captain, Olaf—come from the court of King Hrolf Kraki to seek a kinswoman."

Rædwald's face brightened and he took a step forward.

"Hrolf Kraki's court? I have heard much of that king. His fame has travelled over the waters. Well... welcome to Rendlesham! You must join me tonight in the banquet-hall as my honored guests. Then we can talk at leisure. For now I will leave you in the capable hands of my steward, as I have pressing matters that demand my attention."

Inclining his head politely in my direction, Rædwald turned and left the chamber. An older man now came forward and spoke in measured tones.

"Oswald, steward of Rædwald, at your service. What do you require?"

This time I took the initiative.

"Oswald, we have amongst our cargo two runaway thralls and a very likely a stolen horse, apprehended down river early this morning. Might they belong to someone here in Rendlesham?"

"Describe the horse!" said a voice behind me.

I turned to see a woman of about my age advancing from the doorway. She too was dressed in fine linen, her hair bound in a kerchief edged with gold thread.

"My Sandyfoot is missing," she declared, frowning.

"It's a gentle, dun-colored mare, very friendly," I said with a slight bow, feeling instinctively that this woman was a person of high standing.

"Very likely that's Sandyfoot. Where is she now?"

"Safe in the hold of our ship, my lady, next to my own horse, Sunbeorht."

"You ride? Splendid! Perhaps we can ride together one morning. Oh—forgive me—my name is Radegund, wife of Rædwald. And you are...?"

"I am the lady Freawaru, come from the Danish court to seek a kinswoman. This is Olaf, captain of my ship, and this is Harig, our guide on the journey to Angle-land."

Both men bowed deeply, as did I. Radegund's open, friendly manner charmed me immediately, as did the unexpected invitation to ride with her.

"You say you're looking for a kinswoman?"

I nodded as she continued.

"I know the name of every woman in every settlement along this river, so perhaps I can help you," she beamed.

She spoke so rapidly I found it hard to follow her, but I seized on her offer of aid.

"I do welcome your help, Lady Radegund. It is my mother I seek. When she was Hrothgar's wife, queen of the Danes, she was called 'Wealtheow.' She may have changed her name after she... left Heorot."

"Ah, I sense a mystery! How delightful! Let me think... Wealtheow, Wealtheow. I do not recall anyone of that name, but as you suggested, she may be called something different now. You must come to the banquet-hall tonight and tell me more about her. Yes, I insist! But now let us go see if that horse you found is my Sandyfoot. I've been at the loom all morning and would like nothing more than a brisk walk down to the harbor!"

As she turned toward the door, all three of us followed her — nay, four of us, for Oswald came too, saying he'd try to identify the runaways. Radegund chattered brightly as we walked, asking about our journey, but hardly pausing long enough to hear the answers. I noticed Oswald grinning at our bemused expressions and decided that the Lady Radegund was good-hearted but exceedingly talkative! She reminded me of someone in my past... and after a few moments it came to me: Willa. She reminded me of my old nurse Willa — long dead, devoured by the Grendel monster.

Radegund stopped abruptly. "What is it? You look... stricken!"

"Nothing, that is, nothing you can help — an old memory, a ghost from the past."

I managed a smile, but Radegund took my arm and tucked it under hers. For some moments she did not speak a word.

The mare was indeed Radegund's horse. It whinnied when it heard her voice, and trotted eagerly to her side once brought up from the hold by Anton, beside Sigrod leading out Sunbeorth.

"A beautiful lady's horse!" declared Radegund, appraising Sunbeorth's dainty proportions.

"Yes. She was a gift from King Hrolf," I said, adding — at her quizzical look — "he is my cousin."

"My dear, you come from royalty!" she exclaimed.

Thinking of my past — daughter of Hrothgar, king of the Danes, wife of Ingeld, ruler of the Heathobards, lover and almost wife of Beowulf, king of the Geats, I said simply, "Yes."

"Where are those slaves you spoke of?" demanded Radegund. "They must be severely punished for daring to touch my horse!"

Oswald came forward, followed by Harig's man Regin leading the two thralls, hands bound and ropes around their necks.

"Here they are, my lady, two of ours," said Oswald. "What shall I do with them?"

"Have them beaten soundly for running away, and cut off a finger on each hand for their thievery!" retorted Radegund.

Oswald nodded. "As you wish, my lady. You are most lenient, true to your generous nature."

Radegund smiled grimly. "I spare them because their labor will still be useful during weed month — despite fewer fingers."

As Regin gave them a kick to get them moving again, the one named Karl called out beseechingly.

"Wait! I know sumpin you want to know!" He jerked his head in my direction.

Radegund's lip curled. "How dare you speak to this lady, you miserable thief? Take them away!" she shouted.

As Regin dragged him away, Karl resisted, calling out desperately, "Wellthoo, Wellthoo! I know Wellthoo!"

"Stop, Regin!" I commanded. "I want to hear what this man has to say!"

Regin halted and I waited while Karl gasped for breath, recovering from the rope's choke-hold. When he could speak, he croaked, "She cured me, she did — back at my old master's farm. My master called her 'Wis... Wiswicca', he did, but her boy called her 'Wellthoo'."

I eyed the pathetic figure, wondering. Beside me I could hear Radegund slowly repeating the name: 'Wiswicca.'

"Of what use is this information to me?" I asked sternly, even as my heart beat faster.

"You was lookin' for her — I heard 'em say so on board ship. I kin tell you where to find er," he whined.

"So can I!" cried Radegund, "So can anyone, you fool! Take him away — now!"

As I started to protest, she put her hand on my shoulder.

"I know Wiswicca well, as does every woman on the river! She is our healer, our wise woman, and... if she is your mother... very much alive!"

As Karl was dragged off, still protesting, I turned to Radegund.

"If this Wiswicca is indeed my mother, perhaps... more leniency... for Karl?"

Radegund shrugged. "We'll spare him his thumbs."

Now Gerda and my women, who had held back during this interchange, surged forward. As Gerda ran up to clasp me about the waist, Radegund's face lost its sour look.

"Well, now, who is this curly-haired child?" she exclaimed, reaching out to touch Gerda's unruly locks.

"You can call me 'Sparrow,'" said Gerda boldly.

"Her other name is Gerda," I added, "and these are my women: this is Runa, wife of Olaf, and this Lise... Lempi... and Ginnlaug."

Each gave a bow—even Gerda—which brought a smile to Radegund's lips.

"Lady Radegund is wife to the chieftain here," I explained.

"You are all most welcome to Rendlesham," said Radegund graciously. "Please join us at the feast tonight. Now I'll get this rascal safely back in her stall!"

Taking Sandyfoot's bridle, she walked off with her horse, talking all the way.

That night in the banquet-hall Radegund told me—eventually—more about Wiswicca. I and my whole group were sitting at a front table reserved for guests. After several courses had been served, Lady Radegund came to join us, taking a place beside me. First she asked my opinion of the dish just placed before me—which I guessed to be some sort of waterfowl.

"The taste is new to me," I admitted. "What is it?"

"Eels—boiled in broth. The river is full of them."

I heard a gagging sound across the table and shot a warning glance at Lise, as she pushed away her bowl.

"They are very... tender," I said, for indeed they were.

"Much of our food comes from the river," said Radegund. "That's one of the reasons Rædwald's ancestors settled here. Game is also plentiful and the soil productive."

"How fortunate," I murmured. "When did his ancestors arrive?"

Radegund frowned, considering. "Several generations ago, I believe. They came over with Hengest when the Romans were still here. Rædwald has a brother with a seat nearby, two rivers to the south. Once you're settled, I can introduce you to his wife, and to other women in the area."

"You are most kind, Lady Radegund. Of course, my first goal is to find my mother. Apparently you have known her — if she is Wiswicca — for some years?"

"Indeed I have!" laughed Radegund. "She was midwife at the birth of both my sons, Rægenhere and Eorpwald. They have since grown to manhood, so it was some thirty winters past that I first met Wiswicca!"

I listened eagerly, wanting to learn something about my mother's life in this new land — if, as I sincerely hoped, Wiswicca turned out to be Wealtheow.

"Wealtheow's son would have come with her. What does she call him?"

As I had not previously spoken of my brother Hrethric, I was curious to get Radegund's reaction, but she spoke matter-of-factly.

"Erik. A strange one — sickly for many years. She keeps him out of sight for the most part — almost as if she is hiding him."

I nodded, understanding fully Wealtheow's need for secrecy, but not willing to reveal the reason to Radegund, or my brother's real name.

"Wiswicca currently lives at Helmingham," Radegund was saying, "and no longer leaves that settlement to minister to others. Those who seek her aid must now go to her."

"How far to Helmingham?" I asked. "Could I reach it in a day's time?"

"Yes, if you follow the tide." She gave a wry smile. "We are at the mercy of the tide here, but we've learned to use it to our advantage. The fish they are serving now, for example, were caught in a weir set on the river, easily harvested when the tide flows out."

Politely I picked up a morsel of the flaky piece on my trencher and slipped it into my mouth.

"Delicious," I murmured, but my thoughts were far from the food. "When you last saw Weal- that is, Wiswicca, was she in good health?"

Radegund considered as she picked the bones from her fish.

"Aging. Frail in body but clear in mind." Radegund licked her fingers and turned to look at me. "Why is it that you seek her now, after so many years?"

"She has called me . . . and I have come," I answered quietly.

"Called? How?" asked Radegund, clearly curious.

"We share a special gift," I began, "one which enables us to communicate over great distances — sometimes."

"Oh, you mean trances . . . and visions?" inquired Radegund bluntly.

"Yes, that," I conceded, "and also... dreams."

"I wouldn't put much trust in dreams," said Radegund curtly. "They often lead one astray!"

Now it was my turn to be curious, but I did not question her. Instead, the troubling doubts produced by my flying dream returned in full force, and I experienced again the moment of panic when I saw my powers disappearing.

"... for years, but the dream never came true," Radegund was saying with a note of bitterness in her voice.

"Your dream of...?"

"Having a daughter, of course. Now I'm too old. It will never happen. The goddess can be cruel at times," she murmured, lifting her goblet to her lips.

"The goddess?" I echoed. "Tell me. Do you lead the women here in worshipping the goddess?"

"Yes, I do. In fact Wiswicca herself taught me the necessary rituals."

"That sounds like Mother," I said happily, recalling our trip to the sacred pool at Heorot. "Lady Radegund, thank you for your hospitality and all the information you have given me. I will leave for Helmingham on the morning tide!"

After our warm welcome at the home of Rædwald and Radegund, we were not prepared for the brusque reception we met with Helmingham, where two burly men were posted at the end of the long pier. They hailed us as our ships approached, demanding our names and our business. This time I answered, calling out in a sure, strong voice.

"I am Lady Freawaru, daughter of... Wiswicca, come from across the whale road to answer her summons."

"Wiswicca sees no one," shouted one man. "You have wasted your voyage."

"And she has no daughter," added the second man in a growl.

"May we put in here to discuss the matter?" called Olaf.

The two guards conferred briefly, seeming to disagree. Finally, one beckoned us forward.

"Come ahead, but you'll have to leave on the next tide," he shouted.

As our men maneuvered the ships alongside the pier, I turned anxiously to Runa.

"This does not bode well. Perhaps Weal- Wiswicca is sick, even dying — otherwise why would she refuse to see visitors . . . supplicants?"

"Perhaps," suggested Runa, "she is only weary from the demands made upon her and is taking a respite . . . My lady, it might help to tell these men that Lady Radegund has sent us."

Indeed, the guards did lose their frowns at mention of Radegund's name, but still refused to believe that I could be Wiswicca's daughter. They had boarded my ship when we were moored to speak directly to me.

"Please," I pleaded, "just carry my name to Wiswicca. Tell her that Freawaru has answered her call. Please."

Grudgingly the older man turned to the younger.

"We'd best inquire further. She could be telling the truth. You go, Heinrich, but apologize for disturbing her. Tell Wiswicca what this woman has said." Turning back to us, he growled, "People will go to great lengths to be in Wiswicca's presence and receive her help. We have to protect her from the many needs of others!"

I looked about the harbor, largely empty of boats, and wondered if he were telling the truth. Then an idea struck me.

"Wait! I have something to give her — something that will prove I am her daughter Freawaru!"

Hurrying to my sea chest, I pulled out the unfinished tapestry given to me by Borghild, which I had wrapped in fine linen. Carrying it carefully in both hands, I held it out to Heinrich.

"This is Weal — that is, Wiswicca's own work, brought from her former home by her daughter, Freawaru, who bears the mark of Freyja on her back. Tell Wiswicca that!"

Heinrich hesitated, then accepted the bundle, repeating to himself the words I had just spoken. Apparently satisfied that he had them fixed in his mind, he turned, walked down the gangplank and headed for the settlement.

While we waited for Heinrich's return, I looked about me. Helmingham sat above a bend in the river, on gently sloping banks dotted with trees and low-growing vegetation. It looked to be a smaller settlement than Rædwald's. A dozen or more smoke spirals rose from houses ranged along the hillside. From their direction I heard myriad animal sounds: dogs barking, pigs grunting, cows bellowing and the occasional whinny of a horse. Our own dog Blæki, paws on the gunwales, joined in.

The older guard, who identified himself as Frans, looked about the deck of our ship, then fixed his eyes on me.

"You say you've come from across the whale road . . . exactly where did you come from? Whose court?"

I hesitated. If I said we'd come from the court of Hrolf Kraki, would that raise an alarm? Would Mother have asked these folk to warn her if strangers arrived from that court? I was spared the necessity of an answer by Heinrich's return — almost at a run.

"Let them come ashore!" he shouted. "Wiswicca will see them!"

Chapter Fourteen
Wiswicca

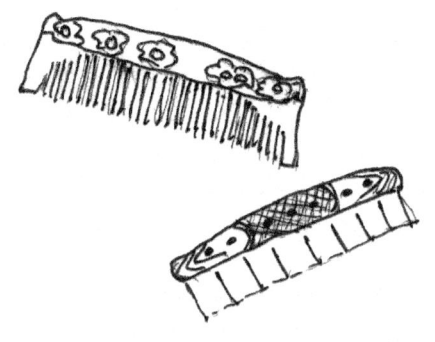

Combs carved from deer and elk antlers, held together by iron or bronze rivets, were prized possessions, often found in female graves.

"Wait!" commanded Frans as we headed for the gangplank. "Not all of you. Just this lady and one of her attendants. I don't want to overwhelm Wiswicca with too many people."

At my nod, Runa joined me and we followed Frans as he left the ship and headed toward Heinrich, waiting on shore. My heart beat faster as we hurried along behind the two men.

Will this woman be my mother? Wealtheow at last? What if it's not Wealtheow? What will I do? Where will I go? Oh Freyja, goddess, be with me. Help me find what I am seeking!

We passed several modest homes, some half-timbered, some with stave walls, with children running about outside. We passed garden plots where a few women were gathering herbs — their fragrant scents reminding me of Heorot — then more houses and more gardens. Finally we stopped in front of a large structure set apart from the rest. It resembled a mead hall with its high gabled ends and central doorway flanked with carved wooden pillars.

"This is our great hall," said Frans, "but we've given it to Wiswicca for her use as long as she wants or needs it."

"How generous!" I said, awestruck by the honor done her.

"Some of us owe our very lives to Wiswicca," said Frans simply as he pulled open the heavy door.

As we stepped over the raised threshold, I could barely see into the dim interior. We had just entered the hall when a young woman bustled up to us, frowning.

"No. She can't see you now. Wait outside, please."

"What's wrong, Minna?" grunted Frans, stopping so suddenly I almost bumped into him.

"Wiswicca is not . . . ready for visitors."

"But I'm her daughter!" I protested. "She wants to see me!"

"She will see you — just not yet," said the girl, glancing back over her shoulder.

I heard what sounded like a muffled howl in the darkness, and stiffened. Mother? Frans turned abruptly and motioned for me and Runa to exit ahead of him. Heinrich stepped aside to let us pass. Coming into the bright sunlight, I squinted. Neither man spoke as we stood silently, waiting.

What is happening? Why am I being kept out? Is something wrong with Wealtheow?

Even as my anxiety grew, the door opened suddenly and Minna's face peered out.

"You may enter now. Wiswicca is ready to receive you."

Mystified yet eager, I once again followed Frans into the great hall.

Inside, a fire burned brightly in a raised rectangular hearth. By its light I could see the usual arrangement of benches and tables, with the chieftain's high seat visible beyond the hearth. What most drew my eyes, however, were a double row of soapstone lamps on the floor leading to one end of the hall. Their flickering flames lit a path to an ornate wooden bed on a raised platform.

As I drew nearer I saw a still figure swathed in rich furs, leaning against a large cushion. In the lamplight her face glowed like the moon, full and luminous. Wiswicca.

I caught my breath, trembling in anticipation. Frans and Heinrich bowed respectfully and stepped aside, motioning me forward. For a moment I could not move. Runa nudged me gently, whispering, "Go on, my lady."

Taking a deep breath, I approached the platform and sank to my knees, praying to all the gods and goddesses: let the figure before me be my mother! When I raised my head, I beheld a face of such sweetness and serenity that all my doubts and fears faded away.

"Whom do you seek?" asked a gentle voice. Did I know that voice?

"My mother, Wealtheow," I whispered, hope rising in my heart. "I am Freawaru, come to answer her call."

"Wealtheow . . . I remember that name. It once belonged to me," said the voice, now increasingly familiar. "Rise, my daughter, and come to me."

Blinded by sudden tears, I nonetheless rose and mounted the platform to take my mother's hand. Raising it to my lips, I kissed her fingers tenderly. Behind me I heard a sigh of happiness from Runa.

I looked deeply, hungrily, into the face before me, a thin, pale face with warm brown eyes. Her hand in mine felt almost weightless, the bones nearly visible through the skin, but her grip was firm.

"Show me the mark you bear, my daughter," commanded my mother's voice.

Obediently I loosened the neck of my gown and knelt before her. When I felt her fingertips on my skin, lightly tracing the outline of a feather, I trembled. Deep within me something hard began to dissolve. She stroked my shoulder gently, then spoke words that sent a shock through my body.

"I am glad to see the goddess' mark is still intact. I had dreamed . . . or was it a vision? . . . that dark forces had wrenched it from you!"

As I absorbed this information, she bade me rise and sit beside her on the bed. For a time we were silent, engrossed in this moment of reunion.

"You come at last," she said. "I did not know if you would hear me."

"Yes, Mother, I heard you," I whispered, my throat thick with tears. "Across the whale road, I heard you. I am here now and I will not leave you." Is she dying? Is that why she has summoned me? To say goodbye? As if divining my fears, Wealtheow spoke.

"I won't leave you either — not yet. This is one of my... bad days... others are better." She paused as if to gather her strength, then spoke slowly.

"There is work to be done, my daughter. The goddess needs us — needs you — to resist the coming evil, an evil which may destroy Mother Earth if not resisted, an evil which even now is crossing the whale road..."

She broke off in a fit of coughing that wracked her frail frame. Suddenly other figures appeared beside the bed: two young women dressed in white who spoke to me accusingly.

"You've made her talk too much!" charged one, her dark eyes stabbing me as she lifted a cup that smelled of herbs to Wealtheow's lips.

"You must leave now. She'll need rest," said the other, whom I recognized as Minna. She nodded at me sympathetically.

Regretfully relinquishing Mother to the care of these attendants, I rose, but had an important question to ask before I left.

"Where is... Erik? I would speak with him."

I would not have recognized my brother had I met him in other circumstances. The once rosy-cheeked boy had become a tall, gaunt man with slightly stooped shoulders who appeared weighted down with cares. Dark eyes peered out from a sallow face with sunken cheeks.

"My sister, you say? From the court of Hrolf Kraki?" He spat. "The man who murdered my brother... and almost killed me!"

We were sitting by the hearth in the home of Wilhelm, Alf's uncle. Wilhelm was chieftain here, a descendant of the Helming in my mother's family line. After all the uncertainty, all the searching, it had been surprisingly easy to find Wealtheow — and Hrethric. Extraordinary coincidence or the will of the gods? I chose to believe the latter.

Convincing Hrethric/Erik that I was really his sister took some time, despite initially showing him the feather birthmark. As I recounted episodes from his childhood, he began to warm to me. When I produced the very game board he had given me as a present upon my marriage to Ingeld, Hrethic smiled broadly, handling the whale bone playing pieces with affection.

"Yes, Freawaru, I do remember you," he said finally.

Now that I was in his confidence, I asked earnestly, "What is wrong with Mother? Is she dying?"

"I cannot say," he answered soberly. "She has been gradually fading for years, but worsened this past summer."

"And what of your own health?" I continued. "It is still hard for me to believe that you are alive!"

Hrethric smiled grimly.

"Mother is an amazing woman. Miraculously she was able to neutralize the effects of the poison and slowly nursed me back to . . . a kind of health. But look at me! I'm not fit for battle — no warrior! Instead of ruling Heorot as the rightful king, I work for Wilhelm as his steward — all I'm fit for now. I'll never have a chance to take my revenge on Hrothulf!"

"Hrolf, that is, Hrothulf," I said slowly, "swears that he had nothing to do with your . . . poisoning."

Hrethric gave a snort.

"Who else could have done it? And now he reaps the reward of his deed . . . Oh, I've heard all the stories about the great king Hrolf Kraki! He must cast a spell on everyone he meets!"

I lowered my eyes, realizing that it might be true in my own case. Raising my head, I introduced another subject.

"What is this great evil Mother speaks of?"

Again, Hrethric shook his head.

"I cannot say. She is never specific, just rambles on about men in dark robes, temples burning, losing the goddess." He shrugged

Losing the goddess? Just as I dreamed of losing my feather — the mark of the goddess? A chill passed through me, but I shook it off.

"Lady Radegund," I ventured, "thinks that Mother's mind is still clear, though her body is much weakened."

Hrethric shrugged again.

"That may be. The women hereabouts treat Wealtheow like a goddess. They would never find a fault in her!"

I pondered this statement for the rest of the evening as I and my companions shared a last meal with Harig and his crew. They planned to depart on their ship in the morning, Hedvig and Hans with them. Gerda was disconsolate at the prospect of losing her playmate.

"I'm going to marry Hans when I get big," she had confided to me. "Then we will always be together."

"If the gods are willing," I had responded, thinking of Ingeld and Beowulf. "If the gods are willing."

Wilhelm proved to be a most generous host. Upon discovering that I was Wiswicca's daughter, he wholeheartedly welcomed us all to Helmingham, finding places for everyone to stay — temporarily — and inviting me and Gerda to live in his own home until I could make better arrangements. His wife Gudrun, son Walthar and daughter Lark were equally gracious, and I felt that the gods were definitely smiling upon me.

In this small settlement — which I judged to be roughly the size of Hrethelskeep back in Geatland, about twenty families in all — hosting would impose some inconvenience. Concerned that we not be viewed as a drain on the community, I had already instructed Olaf to seek out available spaces for purchase, including a place for my horse and his animals. Places were found for Mari and Berit with Wilhelm's thralls in the loft above the cattle byre. Our young men could sleep aboard ship and take their meals with the various households hosting my women, but this solution could be only temporary. Much depended on what I would learn from — and about — Mother.

The next day Mother was feeling stronger and I was able to spend more time with her. This time when I entered the hall she was seated on the high seat dressed all in white, her long white hair unbound, falling softly about her shoulders. Seeing her like this, I could well believe that she was revered as a goddess. Again I took her hand and kissed it gently before speaking.

"Where are your attendants this morning?" I asked.

"I sent them away so that we could be alone," she answered quietly. "They are dear girls, but at times overly attentive. Now. Draw up that bench. We have much to speak of. You may begin by telling me about your life since you left Heorot."

For the rest of the morning I told my story: the birth of Inga, my love for Beowulf, the Great Blōt at Uppsala, war with the Swedes, the deaths of Herdred and Hygd, the dragon raid, the recent death of Unferth, and finally I spoke of the death of Beowulf himself, my beloved. She listened intently, asking few questions. When I stopped speaking, however, she leaned forward and extended her hand.

"So many deaths. It is the way of Wyrd. But is there not one death you have omitted?" She gazed at me mildly but searchingly.

I blanched. How could she know? Shocked, I once again felt a man's hot blood streaming over my hand...

"Yes," I said, swallowing hard. "The death of Lars. I... killed him."

"Tell me what happened," she said softly.

With an effort I related the events of that horrible morning: my arrival at the herb shed... seeing Runa anguished and helpless, sprawled on the floor... Lars hulking over her... drawing my knife... Shuddering, I finished the tale and fell silent.

"You are strong, my daughter," said Wealtheow approvingly. "You rescued your friend. Now lift your head and look at me!"

Surprised at her commanding tone, I raised my eyes to Mother's face. Her own eyes flashed as she spoke.

"Freawaru, the goddess marked you at birth. Much is demanded of those chosen by the goddess, but she gives strength when needed — even the strength to kill!"

"But Mother," I objected, 'you have always been a healer, saving lives, not taking them!"

"The fact that you have taken a life, my daughter, puts you in a better position to know its value," she said firmly. "My own life is coming to an end — no, do not protest — I know my thread is nearly unraveled, but you have years before you, and I must lay a charge upon you!"

"Whatever you command, I will attempt, "I told her, adding, "no matter the cost."

"The goddess!" cried Mother, rising from her seat, "Do not desert her! She will be attacked by powerful forces, her worshippers reviled, her rites debased... When she is driven from the earth, the earth itself will sink into darkness, darkness and... death."

Suddenly Mother crumpled; I barely caught her as she collapsed.

"Help me! Minna, Käthe, help!" I shouted, hoping that Mother's attendants were hovering somewhere nearby. The sound of hurrying feet on the wood floor told me I was right.

"What's happened?" cried Minna, rushing to assist me.

"Let's get her back to bed," directed Käthe. "I knew she should not have left it this morning!"

Both cast sidelong glances at me as we supported Wealtheow and helped her walk slowly to the platform where her bed lay ready.

"I'm not dying... yet," she gasped as she sank down on the cushions. "Brew me a strong tonic of mint and borage," she commanded.

Minna and Käthe looked at each other.

"I'll do it!" declared Minna. "You keep watch."

She hurried toward the door as Käthe tucked furs around Mother and gently rubbed her hands.

"She gets cold easily," explained Käthe, with a look that suggested she knew better than I how to care for my mother.

Minna was soon back with the hot drink and we all watched anxiously as Mother sipped from the steaming bowl. At last she handed it back and smiled.

"Much better. Thank you. It has been an exciting morning. Now I must rest."

Nodding approval, the three of us bowed and left quietly. I noticed that Käthe had tears in her eyes.

"We can't lose Wiswicca, we can't! We all depend upon her," she quavered as we left the hall.

Minna nodded. "She's been a second mother to us ever since she brought us into the world."

"She cured our father when he was so sick with swamp fever," declared Käthe, sniffing and wiping her eyes.

"Swamp fever? There is a swamp nearby?" I asked in surprise.

"The Great Fen," nodded Minna. "A dangerous place, too. Folks say..." she dropped her voice, "folks say that monsters inhabit the fen."

"Really?" I paused, remembering the swamp monster of my youth, the Grendel. "I'll be sure to stay far away! But, to return to Weal — Wiswicca's condition. Do you fear for her life? She is clearly very weak, but otherwise...?" I let the question hang in the air.

Minna and Käthe looked at each other. Minna spoke first.

"I hate to admit it, but I think she has held on to life because she's been waiting — for you."

"Perhaps," suggested Käthe, managing a smile, "your presence will help revive her!"

"May it be so!" I said emphatically. "Her health and well-being are of the utmost importance to me! But, tell me. Has she spoken to you of a great evil which she fears?"

They looked at each other questioningly.

"Not in words we can understand," muttered Minna ruefully.

"She sometimes goes into a kind of frenzy," said Käthe, "as if she is being attacked. I have seen her recoiling in horror from some unseen assailant, crying out for the goddess."

"We don't know what sets off these . . . spells," added Minna, "but they became more frequent over the summer. We feared . . . we feared that your sudden appearance might make her worse — but perhaps you are exactly what she needs. She seems less . . . desperate . . . since your arrival," she concluded reluctantly.

"I am glad to hear that." I nodded. "Tell me, please. Has Mother still been able to lead the women here in worshipping the goddess?"

Again they shook their heads.

"Wiswicca gave that responsibility to Gudrun when summer began," said Käthe, "but somehow . . .

" . . . it never happened," finished Minna.

"Then I must speak to Gudrun. Perhaps taking part in such a ritual would help heal Wiswicca, or at least help her recover some strength."

Both girls brightened.

"A splendid idea!" exclaimed Minna, as Käthe nodded agreement.

By this time we had walked half way through the settlement and were near the house I now shared with Wilhelm's family. Before reaching the door, I turned and took each girl by the hand.

"Thank you for your tender care of Wiswicca. Please know that I am not here to replace you. It is clear to me that Wiswicca needs you and cares very much for both of you."

As I smiled at them, they smiled back. Releasing their hands, I turned and entered Wilhelm's dwelling.

Gudrun and Lark were standing at their looms at one end of the room, Lark singing a wordless melody that dipped and soared as her hands flew back and forth with the shuttle. She was small like her mother and every bit as quick. The two of them reminded me of little birds. As I entered, Gudrun paused and turned to greet me.

"So, Lady Freawaru, how is . . . your mother?"

"I fear she exhausted her strength this morning. She is resting now. Thank you for your concern."

Lark stopped singing and turned as well.

"Your Gerda went off with . . . Runa, is it? . . . to look at some horses."

I laughed. "That child is smitten with horses. She visited my Sunbeorht in the hold every day when we were at sea!"

"I like horses too," said Lark. "See what I'm weaving?"

Going closer to examine her loom, I made out what had to be the legs of a horse, galloping on a sandy shore.

"That is fine work for one so young!" I exclaimed. "Gudrun, you have taught her well."

As mother and daughter glowed at my praise, I thought it a good moment to ask a special question.

"Gudrun, would it be possible to hold a ritual celebrating the goddess . . . sometime soon? I'm thinking it would be sure to raise Weal . . . Wiswicca's spirits."

"Oh, Mother, could we?" exclaimed Lark, almost dropping her shuttle. "The moon will be full soon — the harvest moon — and it's been a long time since we danced in the moonlight!"

Gudrun laughed, then frowned.

"I don't think Wiswicca should be out of doors after dark, weak as she is, and with the nights getting so cool . . ." She glanced at me apologetically.

"Perhaps we could use the great hall itself, so Wiswicca could take part comfortably," I suggested.

Gudrun paused to consider the idea as she resumed weaving.

"Of course we'd have to move the benches and such out of the way, but it could be done, I suppose," she said slowly. "I have not led a ritual in a very long time, and asking Wiswicca is out of the question . . . but wait!" She gave a chuckle. "You are Wiswicca's daughter. You have led many such rituals, am I right?"

As I nodded modestly, she frowned again.

"Of course it would not be a space that's been kept sacred for women's use; before Wiswicca was set up there to receive the sick and needy, that hall was a rowdy place full of men drinking and carousing!"

"I understand that," I soothed, "but Wiswicca herself is now sick and needy. I think the goddess would understand, given the . . . special circumstances."

Gudrun regarded me doubtfully.

"Would you be willing to lead the ritual there, given the . . . special circumstances?" she asked.

"I would gladly do so," I answered. "We can hold the ceremony on the night of the full moon, and replicate it indoors with more of those wonderful lamps."

"Oh, you like the lamps?" asked Lark, beaming. "Those were my idea." Now she too frowned. "I used to help Wiswicca with many things before ... before Minna and Käthe took over!"

"Are they sisters?" I inquired mildly.

"Twins!" declared Gudrun, "though they don't look alike. They belong to Katrin and Stefan in the next house over. Only girls in that family — even Wiswicca couldn't help Katrin conceive a boy child!"

"Well, that means more maidens to worship the goddess," I said lightly, not wanting to concede more value to men than women. "But getting back to our plan: how many days do we have until the next full moon?"

Gudrun bobbed her head, counting silently.

"Ten, I'd say."

"Will that give us enough time to prepare?" I asked cautiously.

"That depends on what you have in mind, but ... yes, I'd say so," responded Gudrun.

"Good!" shouted Lark. "And Lady Freawaru, I'll be your helper!"

I had not yet introduced Gerda to my mother, so I took her along on my visit the next day. Wealtheow was again sitting in the high seat, draped in furs, Minna and Käthe hovering nearby.

"Is that lady a queen?" whispered Gerda as we approached. "She is very beautiful!"

"She was once a queen," I whispered back, "but she has no kingdom now."

Or does she? Wiswicca is treated with great respect, even reverence, by the folk here.

Aloud I said, "Mother, this is Gerda — or 'Sparrow' as she is sometimes called. She is my charge, and my delight."

Gerda bowed low, then sprang up with a smile.

"I can talk to birds!" she said brightly.

"Come closer, child," said Wiswicc, smiling. "Let me see you."

Obediently Gerda stepped forward and Mother reached out one slender hand to touch Gerda's halo of russet hair.

"Glorious! A blazing sunburst! The goddess has blessed you!" she declared, still smiling.

Then she drew back, breathing deeply. Her face darkened and her eyes flashed as she looked wildly about the hall.

"We must save this child from the coming evil! We must not allow her to be torn from the arms of the goddess!"

Wealtheow's voice was rising, out of control, as she herself rose in her chair, furs falling to the floor. Minna and Käthe hurried to her side, each seizing a hand.

"Calm yourself, Lady, calm yourself," begged Minna.

"My lady mother, Wealtheow, hear me!" I cried, advancing to lay my own hands on her trembling shoulders. "Be at peace. On the next full moon the women of Helmingham will gather to honor the goddess. I will need your help in leading the ritual. Together we shall banish this evil that affrights you. Together we will champion the goddess!"

Mother stared at me, and gradually relaxed, sinking back down in her chair. She nodded wearily.

"I was right to call you, my daughter. You will uphold the goddess — as you uphold me." She nodded. "Now I must rest."

Shakily she allowed Minna and Käthe to assist her in rising from her chair and walking to her bed at the far end of the hall. Gerda watched her departure with a troubled face.

"What is the matter with her?" asked Gerda softly.

"Perhaps the goddess has spoken directly to her," I replied quietly, "or perhaps she is being attacked by... demons of the mind. I do not know yet the foundation of her fears. We may learn more when we address the goddess."

Gerda lifted her face to mine. "Would it help to ask your runes?" she offered.

I considered. "Yes, the runes might help," I agreed.

When Gerda and I returned to Wilhelm's house, no one else was about. Going straight to our sleeping benches, I took one of the keys hanging from the keeper at my waist and knelt to unlock the chest below the bench. As I withdrew my rune bag, Gerda, eager to help, removed a white cloth from the chest and spread it out atop the bench. I stood up, holding the bag aloft to make my invocation, Gerda's eyes fixed upon me.

"Goddess, Freyja, hear me! Nerthus, Earth Mother, hear my plea! Reveal to me the danger which Wealtheow fears. Reveal to me the dark evil of which she speaks."

Together Gerda and I settled into silence, seated on the bench with the cloth between us. After a time, when I felt calm and receptive, I closed my eyes, opened the bag, and reached inside. Immediately my fingers were drawn toward one shape that felt almost... hot. Snatching it out, I dropped it on the cloth and opened my eyes.

"What is it, Lady?"

"Othila," I answered slowly, "rune of inheritance."

"What does that mean, 'heritants'?" asked Gerda earnestly.

"It means... anything of value passed down from generation to generation, family to family," I began, then realized that the rune was pointing away from me. "Wait! This rune is reversed! It means a loss of inheritance, a break with the past, a departure from old ways..."

I stared at the rune, my mind reeling with staggering possibilities: loss of the rituals that bind us together, loss of the strength provided by the goddess, loss of Earth Mother's life-giving powers, loss of connection, of community... loss, loss, loss.

"What's wrong, Lady?" implored Gerda, gripping my arm. "You look ... terrible!"

I struggled to clear my head, but could not free it of these dire thoughts.

"'It's what Wealtheow has been trying to tell me. Our whole world may be under attack — our gods destroyed — our rites forbidden..."

I rose, tumbling Othila back into the leather pouch and drew the strings tightly shut.

"I must see Mother again — as soon as she is able to receive me!"

At this moment Gudrun and Lark entered, carrying large willow baskets piled high with apples.

"A good harvest," declared Gudrun. "These will be a tasty treat this winter!"

She held out her basket piled high with apples of different sizes and colors.

"Please try one, if you like."

"My thanks, but not just now," I answered, my mind flooded with the warnings generated by Othila. "Gerda might like one."

Beaming, Gerda reached for a small red apple and took a big bite.

"Ooh — good!" she gurgled, her mouth full.

"We were lucky not to have the three windy days we usually get during this month," said Gudrun. "As they say, 'September blow soft, 'til the fruit's in the loft'." She chuckled.

"September? What does that mean?" I asked in puzzlement.

"Seventh month — probably a Roman naming for the time of barley harvest," answered Gudrun

"Lady Freawaru, see what I have?" Lark proudly displayed a basket filled with rough-textured greenish-brown balls. "Walnuts!"

"Walnuts? What are they?" I asked, curious in spite of myself.

"The nuts are inside. You have to break off this hard green part, then crack open the shell. It 's hard work, but the nuts are delicious — my favorite!" she said.

"My lady, I'm not surprised that you're unfamiliar with walnuts," said Gudrun, setting down her basket on the table. "Only a few such trees grow here — near the ruins of an old villa."

"Villa?" I wondered aloud. "What is a villa?"

"Oh, that's what rich Romans called their houses, according to my old grandam. That was long ago, but we still harvest the nuts," said Gudrun.

Gerda reached into Lark's basket and pulled out one of the greenish balls.

"Ugh! They don't look good!" She wrinkled her nose in distaste.

"Just wait," said Lark, chuckling. "They'll need to dry for several moons. Then you can help me crack them — if you're still here."

"Lark!" scolded Gudrun. "That was a rude remark to make to our guests!"

Her face contrite, Lark set down her basket and turned toward me.

"I'm sorry, Lady Freawaru, if I have offended. Please forgive me."

"No apology necessary," I said, smiling, "and you've raised an important issue: our future here in Helmingham. Gudrun," I said turning, "where did Wiswicca . . . live before she took up residence in the great hall?"

Gudrun looked down, then raised her head.

"I am embarrassed to tell you that she once lived in a small hut — near that villa I spoke of. Apparently she wanted privacy when she first arrived, and lived a very humble life — she and her boy — in that hut. The plain truth is . . ." said Gudrun, lowering her voice, "folks thought she might be a witch—living almost alone at the edge of the forest. Of course that was before we learned of her healing powers! Since then, she's assisted at the birth of most every child in the settlement!"

"Lady Freawaru, if you want to see Wiswicca's old hut, I could show you the way," volunteered Lark. "I go exploring there sometimes."

"Oh, I like exploring too," said Gerda. "What do you find there?"

Lark shrugged. "Not much yet, though I did once find an old Roman coin buried in the dirt."

"What's a coin?" asked Gerda.

"A small piece of metal used as money," I said. "Lark, I will be glad to accept your offer later, but right now I must see Wiswicca herself. May Gerda stay here with you two while I'm gone?" I glanced at Gudrun.

"Of course," said Gudrun. "And take one of those yellow apples to Wiswicca. She likes those best."

"Thank, you, I shall. Now I must go. When I return, perhaps we can make further plans for our celebration of the goddess."

"Of course," nodded Gudrun. "Of course."

As I left the house I reflected: If I am to help Wealtheow banish the evil she fears, I must know a great deal more. What form does it take? What must I watch for? Glancing down at the golden apple in my hand, I suddenly remembered an old tale told by my nurse Willa about the apples of immortality. Guarded by the goddess Iduna, they were eaten daily by the gods to renew their vigor. When the apples were stolen by Loki, the gods languished and almost died. Hmm . . . golden apples . . . apples of life. Perhaps we could use them in the ritual.

Chapter Fifteen
Roman Remains

Gold buckle from ship burial at Sutton Hoo, England.

Although reclining on her bed, Mother yet received me eagerly, her eyes bright with expectation — or was she feverish? Gently I reached down to touch her brow, but found it cool. When I proffered the yellow apple, she smiled.

"From Gudrun, of course!" she said, taking the apple in both hands. "In her own way Gudrun knows as much about healing as I do. She feels a deep connection to the Earth Mother."

"Before we speak further of the Earth Mother," I said quietly, "I need to know more about the evil which threatens her. Tell me, please, what has been revealed to you in your dark visions?"

Wiswicca's face sobered immediately.

"Sit down beside me, my daughter, and I will tell you what I have seen."

As I settled myself on the side of the bed, Mother placed the apple on a low table beside it and sat up straighter. She looked down the row of flickering lamps and gave a deep sigh.

"I wish I could see the future as clearly as I see the present, but only scattered fragments have come to me — brief glimpses. In one recurring image..." she took a deep breath, "... hooded, dark-robed men advance in waves, crushing women underfoot. These men bear before them wooden talismans — like weapons..."

She stopped, breathing heavily. I reached for her hand, but she pulled away, shaking her head.

"There is more. I also see a circle of women dancing and singing in praise of the goddess..."

"As we will soon be doing," I interjected, but Mother kept right on.

"As they dance in the moonlight, a great darkness arises and spreads, swallowing up the moon. Under this darkness every woman is shriveled to nothing!"

She shuddered, and I leaned forward to pull up the fur robe which had slipped from her shoulders.

"Most terrible of all," she whispered hoarsely, her eyes wide as if gazing at unspeakable horrors, "I see fire, fire, women burning — old grandmothers, young girls, bound to crossed stakes, being burned alive as punishment for serving the goddess. Oh, my daughter!" cried Mother, seizing my hands, "Death and destruction are upon us!"

Caught up in her anguish, I felt the icy grip of dread and despair on my own heart, and understood why Mother could no longer shake off the cold that chilled her to the marrow. With effort I pulled myself free.

"Not yet, Mother, not yet!" I protested. "It has not yet come to pass! We can still act to avert what you have seen, or at least ... blunt its impact...?"

I trailed off, unsure how to comfort my mother, or myself. As we sat in silence, my mind travelled back to the places I had visited on my journey to this moment, places where the goddess was sometimes neglected, her rituals forgotten, her blessings taken for granted.

That must not happen here! The message of the rune Othilla was clear: preserve your heritage! If the Earth Mother were no longer honored, what would happen to the earth itself? Would it be destroyed?

Might not Ragnarok arrive in an unexpected form? If men turn against women — the very source of life — what hope will be left?

Confused thoughts swirled in my head as I stared wordlessly at my mother's stricken face. When I lowered my eyes, my glance fell on the yellow apple.

"Apples of life, Mother, apples of life! We must elevate the goddess in a ceremony which will leave an indelible mark on every woman present. We will start here in Helmingham and work to assert the primacy of the goddess in every settlement. We will honor and defend the Earth Mother with all our strength!"

A little color seemed to creep back into Mother's pale cheeks as I spoke, and she gave a wan smile.

"Yes, my daughter, yes. We must plan a powerful ceremony... but now, again, forgive me. I must rest."

As I walked slowly back to Wilhelm's house, I pondered all that had passed between Mother and me, suddenly realizing that I had promised to celebrate the goddess in every settlement! 'Goddess, give me strength!' I prayed inwardly. Well, Helmingham would be a start!

Deciding to involve as many local women as possible in planning the celebration, I first consulted Gudrun and Lark, who were inside cleaning up from the morning meal.

"As it is harvest time," offered Gudrun, drying her hands, "we could show our appreciation for the bounty of the goddess by asking each woman to contribute something for the feast. There will be a feast, won't there?" she asked hopefully.

"Of course," I laughed, echoing Gudrun's oft-used phrase. "I also think we should invite women from Rendlesham and other settlements along the river. What do you think?"

Gudrun nodded enthusiastically. "I'm sure Lady Radegund will want to attend — and if she comes, others will come too. Wilhelm's men could carry the invitations this very day!"

Now Lark chimed in. "Lady Freawaru, don't leave me out! I'm old enough to help!"

"Indeed you are, and Gerda will help too. Speaking of Gerda, where has she gone this morning?" I looked about the room, empty save for the three of us.

"Off with Runa again," said Lark. "They were going to inspect a house left vacant after its owner died — old Ermengard's place."

"Isn't that where Sunbeorht is being stabled?" I asked.

"Yes, in the byre at one end," said Lark. "Gerda was taking apples."

I nodded. "I want to use apples somehow in the ritual — perhaps as a parting gift to each woman to take home, to plant the seeds? Each woman could thus mirror the role of the goddess in bringing forth life."

Gudrun nodded too. "We could also roast apples in the hearth to serve at the feast. They would be a tasty addition to bread and beer."

"Bread and beer? Hmmm. I like that idea," I said. "Both come from the grain produced by mother earth, and both are blessed by Freyja herself."

A broad grin spread across Gudrun's face.

"I always say, if you have good food, the rest will take care of itself!"

"Not quite," I cautioned. "For the ritual before the feast, I will confer with Wiswicca. I know she will have ideas about it."

"Of course!" said Gudrun. "And you'll get all the help you need from the women hereabouts. We all honor Wiswicca!"

Indeed this seemed to be the case. That afternoon when I spoke to Gudrun's neighbor, Katrin, she promised her aid and that of her five daughters — including Minna and Käthe. Both girls were present in the great hall when I visited Mother again, but they remained at a discreet distance as we talked. Mother again lay on her bed and I sat beside her.

"A spiral dance — leading to the heart of the goddess and out again — that's what I suggest," Mother offered. "that is, after the establishment of a sacred space and ritual purification."

I mused on this, looking about at the hall itself.

"What should we use to symbolize the heart of the goddess? Perhaps ... a cauldron ... on the hearth?"

Mother raised up on one elbow to peer down the length of the hall.

"That would do," she murmured.

"And what about the sacrifice? " I continued. "What would be a suitable sacrifice to offer the goddess?"

A strange look passed over Mother's face.

"Must there always be a sacrifice?" she said slowly. "Perhaps we should leave that up to the goddess. She will provide."

"But . . ." I started to protest, then fell silent, watching Mother's face as she stared into some distant place.

"I am coming," she whispered. "Soon."

Slowly her gaze returned to me and she smiled.

"You must attend to the details, my daughter. Again, I need to rest." She sank carefully back on her bed and closed her eyes.

Minna and Käthe followed me out of the hall, their faces filled with concern.

"Won't this ritual you're planning be too much for Wiswicca?" asked Minna, frowning.

"We're losing her, aren't we?" whispered Käthe, her voice breaking.

"No, and no," I said firmly. "Wiswicca wants this ceremony to take place. She wants to reaffirm her — and our — connection to the goddess. We must all join her in this public declaration of devotion."

"It's Wiswicca herself I'm devoted to," said Käthe, almost sobbing.

"Then you can express that devotion by taking an important part in the ritual," I suggested.

She raised her eyes, brimming with unshed tears. "Tell me what I must do."

"And me," said Minna solemnly. "Tell me what I must do."

I looked at them carefully, two girls who had sprung from the same womb.

"Both of you can help me create the circle. Minna, you will speak for the powers of the North, the power of earth. Käthe, you will speak for the powers of the West, the power of water. I will ask Lark and Gerda to speak for the East, air, and the South, fire. Together we will create a healing circle, a powerful circle of devotion, a circle to embrace the goddess!"

Awed, Minna and Käthe stared at me open-mouthed, then turned to each other gleefully.

"I'm earth — you're water," declared Minna. "Wait till Mother hears!"

"Let's tell her now!' proposed Käthe.

As the two hurried off, Käthe looked back.

"Thank you, Lady!"

Gerda and Runa were back in Wilhelm's house by the time I returned. Lark and Gerda were equally enthusiastic about being given a role in the ritual, but Runa looked at me quizzically.

"How may I help, my lady?"

"As I have done before," I began, "I will beat a rhythm for the dance on my drum and you are needed to play your flute."

"With pleasure," smiled Runa. "It has been many a moon since I put the flute to my lips. And, my lady, I think Olaf and I have good news: a house to live in — if the price can be arranged."

"Wonderful!" I exclaimed. "I can help you there, if necessary."

"Lady," interjected Gerda, coming up to stand between us, "Where are *we* going to live? After the ritual, I mean."

"I have been thinking about that," I said reassuringly. "I'm hoping Lark can show us that hut at the edge of the woods this afternoon."

"Oh, Mother, may I take them?" Lark implored Gudrun. "I've done all my chores!"

"Yes, yes, you may," said Gudrun, "though I don't know if it's suitable for a lady of your station," she added, glancing at me apologetically.

"Since my mother found it suitable for her needs, I'm sure it will be fine for me," I said.

So we set off, Gerda and I following Lark through and beyond the settlement, past fields where the hay had already been cut and fields where thralls were harvesting barley with sickles and carts. As we neared the edge of the wildwood, I heard the grunting and snorting of swine rooting for acorns.

"Will those pigs hurt us?" quavered Gerda, suddenly taking my hand.

Lark shook her head and smiled. "They're too busy eating. Besides, we're almost there."

We were following a narrow but well-worn path through the woods, albeit somewhat overgrown in places. Oak leaves crackled and crunched beneath our feet. Whenever she spied an acorn, Gerda tried to crush it under her bare feet, but found the nuts only sank into the dirt beneath her heels. Two gray squirrels darted across our path and ran straight up a nearby tree to perch chattering on a limb.

"Sorry!" shouted Gerda. "You can have the acorns!"

When the path reached a fork, we took the turn to the left and soon emerged into a small clearing fringed with large oak trees.

"Oh, look, Lady!" squealed Gerda, dancing forward, "Our new home!"

I shared her instinctive reaction, for the structure that met my eyes was far more than a simple hut. Admittedly a modest dwelling constructed of staves set upright in the earth, it yet had a look of coziness and contentment about it. Vines had grown up and over the thatched roof, making the hut seem part of the forest itself. Strangely, the grass in front of the hut was clipped short, and only a few oak leaves dappled the ground.

Gerda stopped and drew an exaggeratedly deep breath, inhaling a sweet scent that filled the air.

"Mmm...pretty...and they smell good enough to eat!" she declared, pointing at a bush of late summer roses arching over the doorway. "I'll pick one for you, Lady."

Running ahead, she stood on tiptoe to pluck a fragrant blossom.

"Ooh, it bit me!" she cried, jumping back to put a bleeding fingertip in her mouth.

"Roses do have thorns!" laughed Lark, then turned to me with an air of authority.

"Lady Freawaru, Wiswicca added to the hut over the years. There's an herb-drying shed attached on the right, and at left a wing where she sometimes housed the sick. Beyond are the gardens where she grew herbs and other things. Oh, there is also a separate cook-house out back. I'll show you everything!" she said, glowing with importance. "Let's go inside."

Carefully I lifted and pushed aside the mass of thorny roses. The heavy oak door did not yield at first, but gradually creaked open as the three of us pushed together. At first I could see nothing in the sudden darkness, though a thin shaft of light from the roof hole fell on the hearth. It smelled of ashes and dampness.

I leaned back against the door to be sure it stayed open.

"Gerda, Lark, please gather a few small, dead branches and some dry leaves for a little fire," I instructed. "We need more light."

As they ran back out to do my bidding, I let my eyes adjust to the dim interior. In one or two places I could see daylight through the thatch above me. Repairs would be needed. The floor of beaten earth had been swept clean by someone. A broom still stood propped against the wall beside the door. A single table and two benches were the only furnishings. Cobwebs brushed my face as I moved cautiously through the space, looking for signs of my mother's previous occupancy.

Gerda and Lark reappeared, their arms full of leaves and dry twigs. Using the fire starter that hung from my waist, I soon had a small fire crackling in the hearth. Now I could see that a few wooden bowls and mugs were arranged on shelves above empty clothes pegs. Beside the hearth sat a heavy iron cauldron, and other cooking utensils hung on the wall nearby. I saw no loom, and wondered if Mother had abandoned her weaving when she abandoned Heorot.

Gerda skipped around the fire, waving her arms to create dancing shadows on the walls.

"Just big enough for the two of us, Lady, but where will we sleep?"

"I'll show you," said Lark, pointing to one end of the house. "Follow me."

Together the three of us turned a corner and found ourselves in a separate room filled with sleeping platforms and another small hearth. Again, light streamed down through holes in the ceiling.

"It's like a byre — for people!" observed Gerda, climbing up on one platform and stretching out full length. "All I'll need is a bag of straw to sleep on."

Seeing my look of doubt, Lark quickly offered a suggestion. "If you'd like a real bed, my lady, Walthar could make one for you. He's very good at wood-working."

"Thank you, Lark. I may well employ him for that purpose. Now let's look at the drying shed you mentioned."

Again, Gerda and I followed our guide back past the hearth to the opposite end of the house, where a left turn took us into a shadowy space fragrant with the collection of herbs still hanging from the rafters.

"Ahhh." I inhaled deeply, closing my eyes and breathing in old, familiar scents: mint, dill, rosemary, sage... Now I could almost feel Mother's presence, and see her sorting and tying these bundles: herbs for medicinal use, herbs for cooking, herbs for magic...

"Do you want to see the gardens?" asked Lark at my elbow.

"Yes, in a moment," I answered, opening my eyes.

"There's a door back here that goes to the outside," said Lark, leading the way.

The girls were outside before I even reached the door, and I could hear Gerda exclaiming: "Apples! Lots and lots of apples!"

When I emerged, both girls were down on their knees, piling apples into the apron fronts they held out before them. Just a single gnarled apple tree stood in one corner of Wiswicca's garden, but its branches hung heavy with golden fruit — all we could possibly need for our goddess ritual.

"Thank you, Wiswicca, thank you, Earth Mother," I breathed. "Thank you for the bounty you have given us."

The rest of Wiswicca's garden was less appealing, its separate plots overgrown with weeds and vines.

A thorough cleaning-out is needed here! But there will be time enough to put everything in order — if this becomes my home.

"What's that?" Gerda was up and running again, apples tumbling from her apron as she headed toward a small, three-sided structure at the edge of the clearing

"The outdoor cook-house," said Lark, retrieving Gerda's fallen apples. "Wiswicca used it in hot weather. That's where I found the Roman coin — in the dirt there."

"Speaking of Romans, is that ... villa ... nearby?" I asked Lark. "The one with the walnut trees?"

"Very near," she assured me. "Do you want to see that too?"

"Yes, I'd like to see what a walnut tree looks like — and a villa," I answered. "You girls may want to leave your apples here while we explore further."

Quickly Gerda took off her apron and spread it on the ground. Lark arranged the gathered apples in the center and tied the cloth into a bundle.

"There. Now, follow me!"

She sprang up and headed for the trees, Gerda right behind her.

"Wait! I'm not as fast as the two of you!" I exclaimed. "Wait for me, please."

As Lark stopped abruptly, Gerda ran into her backside and giggled loudly as I approached and took each girl by the hand.

"Lady Freawaru, it gets tangly up ahead," warned Lark, looking up at me. "We may have to crawl in a few places."

"Crawl? Perhaps not," I retorted. "Better to use my knife to cut through — or find another way!"

Lark shrugged. "Still, you'd best let me lead the way."

Lark was right: as we made our way further into the forest, we encountered a tangle of thick vines, fallen trees and prickly plants that caught on our clothes. In the heat of the afternoon I began to sweat, and paused frequently to wipe my face with a corner of my apron.

Gerda hopped and bounded over every obstacle like a forest rabbit, while Lark slid over or ducked under. I found the way exceedingly difficult and soon began to lose interest in villas or walnuts. My knees had ached when I woke that morning, and now the constant bending and climbing were making them feel worse, but doggedly I kept on.

"Almost there," called Lark over her shoulder. "See? There is one of the walnut trees!"

I looked up at a stately tree of great height, which cast a heavy shade with its spreading branches. The ground beneath it was littered with the green balls I'd been shown earlier.

"Ooh, that tree would be fun to climb!" exclaimed Gerda.

"It is," said Lark, "but if you want to see the villa, we'll have to go on — and now comes the hardest part, where we'll have to crawl — through a gorse thicket."

She gestured toward a mat of overlapping branches and tangled vines that stretched before us like a giant spider web. Chuckling, I took out my knife and sliced at the nearest strand. Quickly realizing that the limbs were dry and brittle, I began to snap the smaller ones with my hands. Soon I'd broken an opening wide enough for us to slip through, Lark in the lead.

We emerged into a clearing much like the one which held Wiswicca's hut, but much larger. I looked about and shook my head in awe at the towering roofless ruin which met my eyes. A row of majestic gray columns stood before crumbling walls, all partially hidden by vines and small saplings — remnants of an age long past. I thought again of the huge fortification we'd seen along the coast. Indeed the work of giants!

Gazing up at the pillars, I felt both exalted and diminished, much like the sensation I had felt at viewing the ancient rock carvings on the cliff face near Breccasberg. Despite the day's warmth, I shivered.

Lark and Gerda were already inside the enclosure, poking at the earth with sticks. Silently I walked among the massive pillars, which seemed to form a sort of terrace, wondering who had once lived here and why they had gone away, leaving their home to be reclaimed by nature.

"Look, Lady." Gerda came up to me holding out a piece of what appeared to be broken pottery, though the edges were even and the top smooth. What held my gaze was its color: bright blue.

Gerda turned to Lark. "What is it?"

"I'm not sure," said Lark, "but I think it's part of a picture. I've found a few other pieces like it — in different colors — all buried in the ground. I've never had enough time to dig for more."

"Lady," said Gerda, turning back to me, her eyes shining, "If we lived in the forest hut I could come here every day and dig!"

"Wait, wait. I've not yet decided about the hut," I cautioned, though deep in my heart I knew the decision had been made. "We'd best return to the hut, retrieve our apples and go back home. We have been gone so long Gudrun may be worried. Lark, please lead the way."

By the time we reached the hut all three of us were scratched and dirty, with sweat streaking our faces. We were certainly in no condition to meet strangers — yet, beside the open door of the hut stood a tall young man dressed in rough work clothes, hands on hips, a frown on his face.

"Who are you?" he demanded, showing a missing front tooth. "The ones who walked off and left a fire going? I saw the smoke from my field and came to see what was burning."

I glanced at the smoke hole, where a thin wisp still drifted upward.

"It was only a small fire, a safe fire, and as you can see we have returned to extinguish it! I am Lady Freawaru. Who are you?" I countered, lifting my shoulders and staring him straight in the face.

"I am Johan, son of Jacob. I live in Helmingham, but I've never seen you before," he answered evenly, staring back.

"Johan," said Lark, stepping forward, "You know me — Lark, Wilhelm's daughter. This lady is a guest in our house. She is the daughter of our healer, Wiswicca."

"Wiswicca?" Immediately the man's face softened and he pulled off his leather cap. "Forgive me, lady. I only wanted to ensure that no harm came to Wiswicca's cottage. I used to help her with the heavy work here — hauling water, digging herb beds and such."

"Well, Johan, you may be called upon to do such work again — if I take up residence here," I said coolly. "Tell me, please: where did Wiswicca get water? The river is too far away."

"I'll show you,' said Johan, inclining his head toward the back of the clearing.

He led us to a circular wooden platform raised a hand's width off the ground.

"Wiswicca told me to dig here," said Johan. "I did, and found water only a few feet down. It's safe to drink. I built the well myself," he concluded, almost shyly.

"I can see that you have been a great help to my mother," I said, smiling to show my approval. "Thank you."

Johan nodded. "I am freeborn, but always ready to serve Wiswicca. Speaking of the lady, how does she fare in the great hall? I've heard that she is . . . ailing."

"My mother is weak in body but strong in spirit," I answered. "Shall I carry your greeting to her?"

"Yes, please. Tell her that Johan is available whenever she needs him. Now I'd best get back to my fields."

He gave a slight bow and turned to go.

"Are those your men harvesting barley?" I inquired.

"Yes."

"Then we may become neighbors, Johan — soon. If you wish to help Wiswicca, repairing the holes in the thatch would be a start."

He nodded, bowed again, and left the clearing.

By now the sun had almost disappeared and a light, chill breeze rustled through the oaks as we made our way back to the settlement. A flock of crows passed overhead, flying toward the barley fields. Gerda echoed their calls, waving them on.

When we entered Gudrun's home, a cauldron of lentil soup was bubbling on the hearth.

"Mmm, good!' pronounced Gerda, lifting her upturned nose. "I'm hungry!"

Lark proudly presented her mother with the bundle of apples from Wiswicca's garden.

"And there are more, Mother, many more," she exclaimed. "Lady Freawaru says we can use them in the goddess celebration."

"Well, well, I'm glad to hear it, but now it's time to wash up for the evening meal." Gudrun turned to me with a quizzical look. "What did you think of Wiswicca's hut?"

"I think it would suit me — us — perfectly," I said, "and with an addition across the back there would be room enough for my women, if they wish to join me. Should I speak to Wilhelm tonight about taking possession?"

"That is for Wiswicca to decide. If she agrees, Wilhelm will support her decision."

Wiswicca did agree when I went to see her first thing, shortly after dawn. Wrapped in furs on her platform bed, she listened with closed eyes to my recounting of the previous day's adventure. By the flickering lamplight I could not read her expression, but she readily gave her consent.

"Yes, of course you may live there," she said, clearing her throat with difficulty. "It has everything you will need, and Johan is a good man who will serve you well."

"That Roman ruin nearby—the villa—feels like a place of power. Did you ever make use of it in any way?" I asked, recalling the sensation I had experienced there.

"No, I was too busy tending to the needs of the settlement. You may be the one to unearth its secrets."

I laughed. "More likely Gerda. She can't wait to go exploring there again!"

"Ah, Gerda." Mother opened her eyes. "The spirit in that child is strong—very strong."

"She is learning how to cut and read runes. Runa and I began teaching her aboard ship, but we've not had time to give her a lesson of late. After the goddess ritual..."

"Yes, after the ritual," echoed Mother, closing her eyes again.

That night I woke unexpectedly, stirred by something in my dreams. Groggily I sat up, remembering that I had found myself in a large clearing surrounded by women dancing. Yawning, I rubbed my eyes, trying to recall more of the dream. There had been something strange about that clearing... what was it? Was it the tall trees that lined the edge? No... those were not trees... those were pillars, ghostly guardians, white columns glowing in the moonlight. Aha! The Roman ruin!

Now fully awake, I looked about me in wonder and confusion. Was this a message from the goddess? If so, what was she trying to tell me? I was seized with a sudden strong need to return to that ruin. Yes, yes, I must go back! There is something powerful in that place! This time I'll take all my women; together we will clear away the vines and underbrush to see what may be revealed.

Filled with excitement, I slept no more that night, and when Gudrun arose to stir up the fire, I was already dressed and ready to help her start the porridge. She blinked at me in surprise.

"Couldn't sleep?"

"I did sleep some—but that is no matter. Tell me please, Gudrun, who owns that ruin Lark showed me yesterday? Is it part of Wiswicca's holding?"

Gudrun considered, then shook her head.

"No, I think it's part of Johan's land. His people have farmed that area for generations. Wilhelm can tell you more."

"Thank you. I'd like to go back again today to see both hut and ruin."

After the morning meal I sent Gerda to the houses where the rest of my women were lodged, with instructions to meet me at Gudrun's home. While Gerda was gone I conferred with Wilhelm, who revealed some surprising background as we sat at table over a second mug of barley water.

"Johan won't tell you this, but his people once worked for the Roman overseers. When the masters departed the workers often took over their empty villas. Of course such grand houses could not be maintained without a host of slaves, so the buildings gradually fell into disrepair and decay. I'd say they're mostly a reminder of bad old days for Johan's family."

"Why didn't they pull down the remaining structures and put the land to the plough?" I wondered aloud.

"Someone tried that long ago and was crushed to death by a falling pillar!" Wilhelm shrugged. "Since then people have kept away, believing it to be a dangerous place, perhaps haunted by malevolent spirits—though it's mostly just a forgotten relic of the past." He eyed me keenly. "What is your interest in it?"

"I am not yet sure, but I think I may have a use for it. I must speak with Johan today, if possible."

Wilhelm rose.

"You'll pass near his house on your way to the ruin. Just take the right fork. Now I also have work to attend to."

"Thank you, Wilhelm. You have been most helpful."

Gerda and Lark were eager to return to the villa site; to my surprise Minna also asked to join our expedition.

"It's Käthe's turn to stay with Wiswicca today," she explained, "and Lark told me you were going to visit the haunted villa. I've always wanted to see that place!"

We were standing outside Gudrun's doorway on a crisp autumn morning, although the day held a promise of warmth. Mari and Berit had been working in the fields with Wilhelm's thralls since our arrival, but today I allowed them to join us. They carried rakes and digging tools. Lise, Lempi and Ginnlaug were laden with shears and small axes. Lark and Gerda carried brooms and cleaning rags. When Runa emerged with a well-packed basket and a large earthenware jug, she handed the jug to Minna.

"Here. You can carry this if you're coming with us. Be forewarned: it may be a very long day!"

I had told my women to be prepared for sweaty, heavy, dirty work, and all looked ready to meet the challenge. Minna nodded happily and fell into step beside Ginnlaug as we set off, Lark and Gerda in the lead, Runa and I behind them, Lise and Lempi behind us.

This time the path was familiar to me and we moved along briskly, so that Wiswicca's hut came into sight sooner than I'd expected.

"I've been here before with my mother," declared Minna, setting down the jug. "She came here to see Wiswicca shortly before my baby sister was born."

The other women stood back, looking at the hut appraisingly, for I had told them this might become their new home.

"It's not very big," observed Lise, frowning.

"But the roses are lovely," said Lempi, lifting her nose to sniff.

After I pushed open the heavy door, my women crowded in behind me, eager for a look inside. The cold ashes of my previous fire lay in the hearth and cobwebs still hung from the thatch, but I noticed that most of the holes in the roof had already been patched.

"Ugh!" squealed Lise. "I hate spiders — and it's dark and stuffy in here!"

"Get a fire going," I said. "It will look better after a thorough cleaning. You women can make a start while I go to see Johan, who lives nearby. Then we'll continue on to the villa — if Johan approves. Runa, you will be in charge while I'm gone. And Gerda — don't go wandering off!"

"I won't," she promised already waving her broom vigorously at the cobwebs.

Leaving the women to begin their work, I made my way through the dimly-lit forest, looking for that fork in the trail, and soon found it. When I emerged from the trees I came upon fields divided by hedgerows, and saw a spiral of smoke rising beyond a slight ridge. Ah, that must be Johan's house.

To my astonishment I suddenly found a paved surface beneath my feet, a surface which stretched both left and right. Could it be a road? On the other side I saw a path leading toward the ridge and followed it, wondering about what I had encountered. When I came within sight of Johan's hut, two black dogs came bounding toward me, barking loudly but wagging their tails. They were soon followed by Johan himself, looking a bit startled. He stopped abruptly when he recognized me.

"Lady Freawaru! What brings you here?"

"Good day to you too, Johan," I said calmly. "First, thank you for those roof repairs, but I have come to ask you about the ruined villa."

He stared at me for a moment, than inclined his head toward the ridge.

"Please come into my house — my lady. It's humble, but it's clean."

"Thank you, I will. I have a proposition to put before you."

When I emerged from Johan's clean and humble dwelling, I had not only been given permission to clear out the ruin, but I had also been told that the Roman road — for so it was — led past the front of the villa and was wide enough to accommodate an ox-cart. No crawling through gorse thickets would be needed to reach the villa from Helmingham!

The goddess is indeed smiling upon me, I thought, my mind racing with possibilities.

If the villa's interior is large enough, and not too rough underfoot, we may not have to hold our ritual in the great hall after all!

I could picture a circle of women dancing in the moonlight — just as in my dream. But first, much hard work lay before us.

When I returned to the hut, I found it free of cobwebs, its few furnishings scrubbed clean, the pots polished and a cheerful fire crackling in the hearth.

"Well done, everyone!" I exclaimed. "Please take some bread and cheese from Runa's basket before we go on to the villa. There's water in the jug as well. Oh, and I have asked Johan to add another section to the back of the hut, so there will be ample room for everyone who wishes to live here."

After a brief respite, and after carefully extinguishing the fire, I personally led the group away from the hut, headed in a new direction.

"Lady Freawaru, where are you going?" asked Lark, hurrying up beside me. "The villa is *that* way!"

I looked in the direction of her pointing finger and shook my head.

"According to Johan, the road to it is *this* way!"

"Road? Oh, he told you about the road," said Lark, flushing and avoiding my eyes.

"Yes, he did. Why didn't you tell me there was such a road?" I asked in some exasperation.

Lark hung her head, then looked up apologetically.

"That way takes longer, and it's not as much... fun."

"Fun? Do you think crawling through gorse thickets is fun?" I gazed at her severely.

"I'm sorry, Lady Freawaru. I wanted to make it more of an... adventure. Gerda likes adventures," she said meekly.

Coming to her friend's defense, Gerda quickly piped up. "It *was* an adventure, Lady — you said so yourself!"

"Yes, yes, I suppose I did," I admitted, smiling, "but today is different. Today there is work to be done... so, let's take the road!"

Quietly the girls and women followed as I strode ahead, retracing my steps to the roadway. Soon our feet were treading on square-cut blocks of stone, fitted neatly together. The road was wide enough to let four people walk abreast, with shallow ditches alongside for drainage. Another Roman marvel!

Although the roadway was fairly smooth, we still had to watch our footing, and with the sun now high overhead, we were all sweating by the time we came upon a row of walnut trees, a signal to me that the ruin was near.

"Almost there!" sang out Gerda, dancing in a circle. "Come on, Lark, hurry!"

Leaving the road, the two girls dashed ahead, scrambling up an embankment toward the line of pillars which now shown bright in the mid-day sun.

"Oh!" said Minna, stopping to gasp. "So, my grandam was telling the truth about this place! I thought it was just a bed-time story."

She gazed in awe at the tall sentinels lining the clearing and the traces of crumbling walls.

"My lady," said Runa, standing stock still. "I feel it — the power of which you spoke. We must tread carefully here lest we displease some ancient force. What gods and goddesses did the Romans worship?"

"Many, I imagine, but all people owe their existence to the Earth Mother. It is she we must celebrate — and preserve."

I turned to look for Gerda and Lark, who were poking in the dirt again with sticks.

"Girls, exactly where did you find those colored pieces? We will start in that place and work our way out to the columns."

When Lark indicated the place, we set to work with rakes and digging tools, carefully removing the growth at our feet, then kneeling to pull up layers of grass, roots and dirt. Gradually we uncovered more colored pieces revealing an eye ... another eye ... hair worn like a crown ... and an inscription in marks unknown to me. They were similar to runes, but not runes: a curved line like a lightning bolt, two lines that met in a point at the bottom, similar lines on their side, one straight line, and another lightning bolt: S-V-L-I-S.

Soon the face of a woman gazed up at us, framed with ribbons, in a circle twice the size of an oxcart wheel. Her wide-lipped mouth was unusually large

"Who can she be?" marveled Lempi. "She looks ... dangerous."

"No," countered Lise. "She looks proud — and powerful!"

"Perhaps she lived here," suggested Ginnlaug. "Perhaps she was head of the household in this ... villa, is it?"

"Those marks could be her name," said Runa. "Perhaps this Johan you've met could tell us more."

"Perhaps," I agreed. "For now we must continue our work. It is possible that the entire floor of the villa is covered with these small pieces of stone. If they are, we don't want to damage any of them."

As it turned out, the face of S-V-L-I-S was the only image we uncovered, but the whole floor was indeed paved with small stones, mostly intact and still perfectly level. A perfect place for dancing!

By mid-afternoon we had uncovered the entire floor and moved on to the pillars, stripping off the encircling vines, which left fine lines of tracery on the stone. We found one pillar that had toppled outward, its individual segments still intact and laid out in a straight line on the ground. Inwardly I shivered, thinking this must be the pillar which had crushed its would-be destroyer.

"How big they are!" marveled Ginnlaug, reaching her arms around one huge block. "Look! My fingers don't reach!"

As we stripped away their coverings, I inspected each column carefully for signs of cracking or shifting. To my relief I found none; this work of giants looked ready to endure . . . forever. As shadows began to lengthen, I called a halt.

"Enough! We will return tomorrow to finish our work here. Take a good look at what we have accomplished!"

As we stood, sweat streaked and dirty, I drew in a deep breath.

This place is so beautiful . . . so peaceful yet powerful . . . indeed it is fit for the worship of a goddess. The ancient pillars remind me of the standing stones in our circle at Hrethelskeep. Also like that place, this one is open to the trees and sky and far removed from daily human activity. I think we have found our sacred space! But . . . will the local women come to this 'haunted villa'? Could Wiswicca herself come? And I still have no clear idea of what the sacrifice should be!

Chapter Sixteen
Calling the Goddess

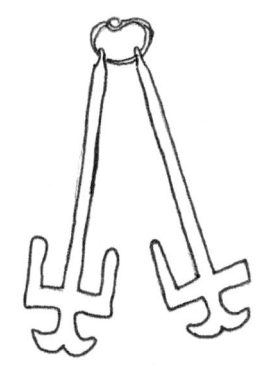

Girdle hangers from Soham, Cambridgeshire; may have been worn by women as symbols of authority. British Museum.

Although darkness had fallen and owls were calling, I visited Mother that same evening. I found her still awake on her high bed, staring at the ceiling. When I told her what we had discovered at the Roman villa, she lifted herself on both elbows.

"A face, you say? The face of a Roman goddess?"

"Perhaps. Here, I will draw on your palm the marks we found. You may know their meaning."

Gently taking Mother's hand, I used my fingertip to trace one by one the strange marks: S-V-L-I-S. She watched intently, recognition showing on her face.

"Yes, I do know those marks. They signify Sulis Minerva, goddess of growth and fertility. She was worshipped at sacred springs by the Romans. Johan's grandam told me about her."

We stared at each other, unspoken questions hanging in the air. Finally I broke the silence.

"Mother, what if we held our ritual in that place? It has the feel of a sacred space. An old Roman road leads directly from Helmingham to the villa, and we could carry you there by ox cart. I do not want to tax your strength, but..."

Wiswicca raised her hand to stop the flow of my words.

"Before we talk about that, I too have made a discovery today."

"A discovery? Of what?" I asked, taken aback.

"About the sacrifice," murmured Wiswicca. She sat up straight in the bed and fixed her eyes full upon me. "The goddess has revealed to me what we must sacrifice: blood!"

"Blood? What blood?"

"Our blood," she declared emphatically. "Each woman at the ritual must offer a drop of her own blood. That will bind us together and connect us to the goddess — to Earth Mother. It is essential that the sacrifice be significant."

Wiswicca's face glowed with color as she spoke these words, and I gazed at her in approval.

"Yes, our blood." I nodded. "And I have the very vessel in which to capture it: a sacred silver bowl once given to me by Beowulf!"

"And I have the blade," said Wiswicca, reaching beneath a cushion.

She produced an object which I instantly recognized: the small, golden sickle she once used to cut mistletoe, the sickle she used to cut locks of hair for an offering. It had once severed one of my own curls. She smiled, touching a finger to the blade's tip.

"It is very sharp. I honed it myself. The merest touch will cut."

As proof she pressed lightly against the point and a drop of red blood appeared on her pale finger.

"Yes, it is ready."

We locked eyes and looked at each other for a long moment. Suddenly all my weariness fell away: I felt charged with energy.

"The goddess will prevail, Mother. I feel it in every fiber of my being!"

Wiswicca placed her stained fingertip on my forehead.

"As will you, my daughter, as will you. Hold the ritual where ever you wish. The goddess will give me the strength I need to attend and to do my part."

The next day Wilhelm's men carried the message up and down the Doep to every settlement on the river, inviting each woman to honor Wiswicca in a goddess celebration on the night of the next full moon. It was my idea to make Wiswicca the focus of the invitation, hoping to draw more women. The enthusiastic response justified my decision. Lady Radegund immediately promised to attend, along with every woman in her court, and other households would follow.

"We'd better make sure to have enough food and drink," exclaimed Gudrun when she heard her husband's report.

"I will leave the food up to you, Gudrun," I said, my thoughts taken up with the ritual itself.

Again and again I went over in my mind each phase of the ceremony: creation of a sacred space, purification of the participants, summoning the goddess, transformation through the spiral dance, closing the circle, and feasting. The one component which had eluded me — the sacrifice — was now settled. As Mother had promised, the goddess had provided the answer.

As the night of the full moon drew near, Mother herself seemed to wane rather than wax, for she grew thinner and paler each day. Despite my pleas she refused all food, subsisting on the herbal teas prepared for her by Minna and Käthe.

Taking my hand, she whispered, "It is for the best, my daughter. I must be prepared . . . to meet the goddess."

"Oh, Mother," I protested, catching my breath, "Mother, I have just found you. Don't talk of leaving me again!"

"All is as Wyrd decrees," she countered. "Do not fear. I have the strength I need to perform my role in the ritual." She sighed. "Freawaru, we each have our parts to play in this world. After that . . ." Her voice trailed off. "Who can say?"

At last the day of the harvest moon dawned, fair and full of promise. As anticipated, women from all along the Doep began coming into Helmingham on the afternoon spring tide. Lark had explained to me earlier that "spring tide" had nothing to do with seasons of the year, but everything to do with the full moon, for the tide then is much higher than usual.

Our local men were waiting at the docks to catch the mooring topes thrown by arriving women, some accompanied by their older children. What a glorious hubbub! Shouts and cries and laughter, the splash of oars, the bumping of wooden boats echoed in the crisp autumn air.

Lise, Lempi and Ginnlaug had joined Gerda, Lark, Runa and me as part of the onshore welcoming party, greeting each arrival and directing or leading them to their temporary lodging. Helmingham would be full to bursting by nightfall with visitors quartered in every longhouse of the settlement.

"Hundig says she can take two more, but that's all," announced Gerda, running up to me breathlessly.

"Good. That means this lady and her daughter will follow you to Hundig's house," I said, smiling at a plump woman who stood patiently before me, her arms clasped around a basketful of root vegetables. Her daughter carried a small sack of grain and nodded shyly when I asked, "Barley?"

Lady Radegund and her party had arrived on the morning tide and were already settled at one end of the great hall, where special accomodations had been set up for their use. She had been deep in conversation with Wiswicca when I'd left them to help at the harbor. Gudrun was supervising food preparation at the great hearth, for we had decided to return to the hall for feasting after the ritual at the villa. Earlier I'd sent Mari and Berit to bring dried herbs from Wiswicca's hut to strew on the floor of the hall. Thralls now rushed back and forth with supplies as each boatload brought fresh offerings, and a growing number of children ran gleefully about. All of Helmingham was abustle with activity.

Surveying the scene at the harbor, I paused to stretch my arms and rotate my head, hoping to relieve the ache in my neck and shoulders — no doubt due to the heavy weight of responsibility I felt for tonight's ritual — then turned to toil up the slope, which seemed to grow steeper with each climb.

"Here, Lady Freawaru, may I assist you?"

It was Roald with Blæki at his heels.

"Where are you headed?" he asked cheerfully.

"To the great hall. Thank you for your timely offer."

I reached down to pat Blæki's shaggy head before gathering my skirt with one hand and taking Roald's arm with the other.

At the top of the rise we paused while I caught my breath, then continued on to the great hall. As we walked I questioned Roald.

"How are you and the other young men faring thus far?"

"Well enough; we have kept quite busy helping with the harvest, but come winter I don't know what Wilhelm will ask of us. Hopefully we'll be invited to join some hunting parties. Too bad we don't have any horses," he added regretfully.

I stopped and turned to him.

"After tonight's ritual I will be free to attend to other matters," I began. "Our ship, for example, needs maintenance. Why, we may even want to build a new one. And I intend to breed Sunbeorht — if we can find the right stallion. Perhaps, Roald you could seek out a suitable candidate?"

His face brightened.

"It would be an honor, Lady Freawaru, an honor."

By now we had reached the door of the great hall, where a string of thralls were exiting. Bidding Roald good day, I stepped inside. Immediately the scent of herbs crushed underfoot met my nostrils, reviving my flagging spirits. Gudrun and Katrin stood at the hearth stirring the contents of two large cauldrons, sending up aromas that made my mouth water — but I would take no food until after the ritual.

After greeting Gudrun and Katrin, I turned toward Lady Radegund and her group of women, clustered to my right around a table at one end of the hall.

"Honored guests, do you have everything you need?" I inquired politely.

"Almost," said Radegund, beckoning me toward her end of the tale. "We are all wondering: where will the celebration take place? Is it to be here?" She gestured toward the hearth, where two thralls were stacking more wood beside the fire.

"Only the feasting," I replied, coming to her side. "The ritual itself will be held outdoors in a special place we have prepared."

At these words several women turned questioning faces toward me.

"Is it far?" asked one with a frown.

"A pleasant walk in the moonlight," I said quietly, "over the old Roman road."

Lady Radegund regarded me with some alarm.

"Surely Wiswicca cannot be expected to walk! She seems quite frail."

"No, no, she will not walk. Wiswicca will ride in an oxcart, with all of us as her attendants. Speaking of Wiswicca, I must confer with her about some of the details of the ritual. Please excuse me, honored guests."

Bowing, I left the group chattering behind me.

Wiswicca lay on her bed, already arrayed in the white robe she had chosen for the ritual, her long white hair spread over her shoulders. She looked as pale as death, but greeted me warmly, reaching out both hands.

"Daughter. Our time has come. Again, tonight, we meet the goddess."

"Yes, Mother. Tonight, together, we will meet the goddess."

I leaned down to kiss her forehead, which seemed overly warm.

"Are you well?" I asked, rising.

"Well enough," she answered. "Sit beside me and listen carefully to what I say."

"Yes, Mother." Obediently I sat down on the edge of the bed.

"Freawaru, during my time in this country I have learned of many things. One in particular I wish you to know. It concerns the lines of sacred power which lie across the countryside, travelling underground like streams of water. The hut where I chose to live lies on one such line. Holy wells and groves, even ancient standing stones are often connected by these hidden lines of sacred power.

As a servant of the goddess, you must seek out these sources and lead your people in using them wisely. You may already have found such a place in this villa you uncovered. Tonight we will discover more. Tonight the powers of the goddess may be revealed." She sighed. "That is all I have to say. Please go now and let me rest."

"Yes, Mother. Just one question: at the ritual tonight do you wish to make the invocation to the goddess, or shall I?"

Mother regarded me sagely as she sank back on her cushions.

"I will summon the goddess. She will speak through me."

"As you wish, Mother. Rest well."

Shortly after sunset we gathered before the great hall: women young and old, women in fine embroidered kirtles and women in humble working clothes, but all women who had come to honor Wiswicca by celebrating the goddess. As was customary during a women's ritual, the men and thralls were left at home.

Four of Katrin's daughters carried Wiswicca out on her bed and carefully settled her on the oxcart beside the door. Gerda and Lark brought extra cushions for support. The cart had already been loaded with the few supplies needed for the ritual: oil lamps, a jug of water, a bundle of brands, and a special chair for Wiswicca, constructed by Walthar. Also carefully stowed were Wiswicca's staff and small sickle, my silver bowl, and my drum to which I had attached a hanging strap. The moon had just risen, golden as one of Wiswicca's apples.

Minna and Käthe took their places beside each ox, ready to lead them forward when I gave the signal. Lark and Gerda seated themselves on either side of Wiswicca as her most immediate attendants. Radegund and Gudrun and I would lead the rest — but first I must give a few words of instruction. Taking a torch from one of the thralls bringing out brands from the hearth, I raised it aloft and stood beside the oxcart to address the throng.

"Women of the River Doep! We are gathered tonight to honor your healer, your wise woman and my mother, Wiswicca. It is her wish that we celebrate this night the goddess, the Earth Mother, who gives us life and sustains us in our trials. Tonight we go to a special place, a sacred space, where our prayers and offerings will be hidden from others' eyes. As we walk together, let us sing praises to the goddess: 'Goddess bless us, goddess guide us. Giver of all life and joy.'"

Torches were being distributed as I spoke, and soon the evening dusk was punctuated with flickering light. Glancing down at Mother, I saw her face illuminated by both torchlight and moonlight.

"It is time!' I cried in a loud voice. "Let us depart!"

Minna and Käthe gave a tug to the horns of the oxen and the great beasts plodded forward, causing Gerda to squeal with delight and Lark to admonish her gently. Radegund and Gudrun fell into step on either side of me as we set off, my heart beating faster in anticipation of what the night might bring.

When we reached the Roman road, the wheels of the oxcart made a great rumbling on the stone. I worried lest the noise and jarring would upset Wiswicca, but she smiled serenely up at us, as if she felt no discomfort. I glanced back to see if I could detect Runa and my women at the rear, but saw only a trail of torchlights wavering in the slight breeze.

The moon shone ever brighter on the stones beneath our feet, so that we seemed to be walking on a river of light.

"Goddess bless us, goddess guide us," came voices behind me, and I smiled in relief. We are well begun; may the evening end as successfully as it has begun.

Long before we reached the villa Wiswicca had closed her eyes, but they blinked open when the oxen stopped abruptly near the line of walnut trees.

"This is the place," I called out cheerfully. "Take a moment to look about you, everyone, but do not yet go beyond the pillars."

The scene was indeed breath-taking: The towering ancient columns glowed in the moonlight like shafts of bone, and the stones of the villa floor reflected enough light so that the whole floor seemed to shimmer before our eyes. Exclamations of surprise and wonder broke out among the women as they arrived in small clusters, taking in their new surroundings.

"What—what is this place?" gasped one woman.

"It's—it's magical!" cried another.

"Lady Freawaru," murmured Radegund beside me, "are you sure this place is... safe?"

"Have no fear,' I replied calmly. "My women and I labored long to prepare this space for tonight—with no interference from anyone—or anything."

"So this is the place Lark keeps talking about," said Gudrun, looking around appraisingly. "Looks alright to me."

"Come. Let us assist Wiswicca from the cart and help her into her chair," I directed.

Gerda and Lark had already scrambled down from the cart, their arms full of cushions, while Minna and Käthe were looping the oxen's lead ropes around a nearby tree. Gudrun and I helped Wiswicca slip down off her bed and supported her while Minna and Käthe set up her special chair: a clever device with a high back, arm supports, and folding legs.

When Wiswicca was comfortably seated and Runa had come up to assure me that everyone had arrived safely at the site, I raised my hands for silence.

"Women of the River Doep! In this place we will meet the goddess, but first a sacred circle must be created. Space yourselves evenly outside the colonnades, while Wiswicca is conducted to the place of honor. Then extinguish your torches in the dirt. After that the ritual will begin."

As the women moved to take up positions, Katrin's daughters lifted Wiswicca's chair and carried her to the place I indicated: at the head of the large circle containing the Sulis Minerva image. I instructed Radegund and Gudrun to take places outside the colonnade on the side facing Wiswicca. Runa helped Gerda and Lark place small oil lamps around the perimeter of the stone image, while Minna and Käthe brought the water jug, Wiswicc'a staff and the packet containing our ritual implements.

When all were finished I handed Wiswicca her ashwood staff. Then, turning slowly, I addressed the women who stood in suspense beyond the pillars, waiting to see what would happen next.

"Women of the River Doep, we now create a sacred space in which to hold our ritual. I call upon the powers of earth, air, fire and water to establish the four corners of our world, to enclose us here in sacred space."

I nodded at Minna, who stepped forward holding a lamp, which I lit with a brand from my torch.

"Hail to the north, corner of all powers. We invoke the powers of earth: stone, mountain, fertile field. Send forth your strength. Be present here."

Lark approached next to have her lamp lighted by my brand.

"Hail to the east, to the powers of air. We invoke you, corner of all beginnings, rising sun and whirlwind. Send forth your light. Be present here."

Next Gerda came to face me, holding up her lamp.

"Hail to the south, corner of fire and passion. Oh spark of life, send forth your flame. Be present here."

Last of all, Käthe held out her lamp.

"Hail to the west, corner of the waters. Rain maker, send forth your flow. Be present here."

At my nod, the four girls turned and walked solemnly to their respective corners. Then I raised my torch aloft and intoned loudly, turning slowly to face everyone present.

"Earth and sea of ill stay free. Fire and air draw all that's fair. Round and round the circle is bound."

Bending, I used a brand to light the lamps at my feet, creating a ring of flickering fire that illuminated the image of Sulis Minerva. Several onlookers gasped in surprise, "It's a face!"

Rising, I intoned again.

"The circle is cast. We stand between worlds, beyond the bounds of time, where night and day, birth and death, joy and sorrow meet as one. The fire is lit. The ritual is begun. All may now enter."

Hesitant, the women hung back at first, until Radegund and Gudrun stepped boldly forward. Gradually a circle of forty or so women and girls formed beyond the circle of fire and stood expectantly, waiting. Now it was Wiswicca's turn. Using the chair's arm supports, she rose slowly and stood erect in the flickering firelight. With surprising volume, she spoke.

"My dear friends, we must come before the goddess with clean hands and hearts. Hold out your arms, that you may be purified."

Taking the jug of water, I circulated slowly, trickling a few drops of cool water on their outstretched fingers and cupped palms, until all were purified. When I returned to her side, Wiswicca raised her arms to the moon, its light bathing her face with a luminous glow.

"Dear, dear friends, now hear me. Listen to the words of the goddess, whom I have served all my life long: 'I who am the silver moon among the stars, the bright beauty of the green earth, the mistress of all waters, the guardian of all hearth flames, I call upon you now to rise and come to me. Maiden, mother, crone, I am within you. I have been with you from the beginning and I am that which is attained at the end. Plant, animal, blood and bone, earth, air, fire and water. I am life and death and life again. From me all things proceed and to me must all return'."

Turning slightly toward me, Wiswicca held out her hand. In it I placed her small, golden sickle, which she held aloft for all to see.

"To confirm our connection to the goddess, I now call upon each of you to make an offering: a drop of your blood. One at a time, come from your place to touch the tip of my blade. I myself will be the first to make an offering."

As Wiswicca pricked her finger, I was ready with my silver bowl to catch the drops. Without hesitation Radegund stepped forward and approached Wiswicca, her eyes shining.

"I honor you Wiswicca as I honor the goddess. You are one and the same to me," she murmured as she extended a finger.

Gudrun came next, followed in turn by the rest of the women, each ready to offer a precious part of herself to the goddess. When all had returned to their places in the outer circle, I made my own sacrifice, adding my blood to that of the others. Handing both bowl and sickle to Runa for a moment, I helped Wiswicca lower herself back down on her chair, then took the bowl with its crimson content.

Walking straight to Lady Radegund, I dipped the tip of my forefinger into our communal blood and touched her forehead. I did the same to Gudrun, then made my way around the circle, marking each woman. When finished, I returned to Wiswicca's side and then turned to address everyone.

"Women of the River Doep, we are bound each to each and to the goddess. To her I now pour this libation."

Raising the bowl, I held it out over the image of Sulis Minerva and slowly poured the remaining blood into the open mouth of the face. Here and there a few gasps escaped from the circle of women, but Wiswicca nodded in approval.

"Now," I continued, exchanging the bowl for my drum, "we will celebrate our union in a spiral dance, weaving our way into the heart of the goddess. To the sound of flute and drum, follow the corner girl nearest you, circling the ancient image embedded in the floor. We dance in honor of the goddess!"

At my nod Runa lifted her flute and blew one high, piercing note, followed by a lilting melody that called to mind the rocking of an infant's cradle. The girls at the four corners had been previously instructed on when to begin and how to form a single spiral. Minna set out first, nearby women falling in behind her, a hand on the shoulder of the woman before.

As Minna's line circled wide of Wiswicca and the Sulis Minerva, Lark set out, adding her line to the chain. Then Gerda's line connected, and finally Käthe's. Soon the villa floor was filled with a moving form that wound up into the circle and out again. At the heart of it all sat Wiswicca, erect and regal.

Gradually I increased the speed of my drumming, and Runa's flute kept pace, the music swirling above us. Women with smiling faces, ecstatic faces, snaked past me, as the spiral coiled and uncoiled. High above us the moon shone on as we danced in its transformative light.

Rising abruptly from her chair, Wiswicca gripped the staff before her in both hands and called out. "The goddess smiles upon us!"

Surprised, I involuntarily broke off drumming, as Runa's flute played on. A moment of confused hesitation rippled through the line of women before I resumed the tempo; then all surged forward. Gradually I relaxed the beat: slower — slower — slower — finally stopping altogether. Runa played one last lingering note, and the dance came to a halt. Silently each woman returned to the place from which she had started. Mother, however, still stood like one transfixed, she and her staff bathed in moonlight.

I was about to speak, to begin a formal closing of the ritual, when Wiswicca shuffled forward, advancing inside the circle of lighted lamps, crossing over the face of Sulis Minerva. Holding her staff upright in front of her, she stopped before the open mouth, still wet with our mingled blood. Extending her arms at full length, she raised her staff and again called out.

"Great goddess, show yourself! Goddess, come forth!"

With unexpected strength Wiswicca drove the staff down squarely into the mouth of the image at her feet. Startled cries and exclamations of shock echoed around the outer circle. As we stood, frozen in bewilderment, all watched as Wiswicca, still clutching her staff, slumped against it and then, in a twisting descent, sagged to the floor. A low, rasping sound escaped from her throat.

"Mother! Moth..." I cried, dropping to my knees beside her. I turned her body toward me, gripped with fear. There was no life in her face.

Chapter Seventeen
Sacrifice and Sorrow

Memorial stone with runic inscription from Sjuota, Skokloster, Uppland, Sweden.

Utter silence. Then shrill cries and the sound of rushing feet as women hurried forward, full of concern.

"What's happened?"

"Do you need help?"

Clasping Mother to my breast, I clung to her body, slack and still, too shocked for tears. Someone knelt beside me, her hand on my shoulder. Runa. Above her Gudrun's face appeared, then Minna's and Käthe's. More and more women were flooding into the center.

"She... she's gone," I groaned, looking up at Runa.

"Gone?" Minna picked up the word and began to wail loudly. "Gone! Wiswicca's gone! She has gone to the goddess!"

As if from a distance I heard cries and shouts of disbelief. Still cradling her body in my arms, I whispered through my sobs.

"Farewell, dear mother. You have... left your Freawaru... for the last time. May you rest now... in the arms of the goddess."

Gently I lowered her upper body to the dancing floor and closed her eyelids. A faint half smile lingered on her lips. By now I was surrounded by a tight knot of women, some sobbing, some struck dumb as they bowed their heads in grief. A single voice broke through abruptly.

"Lady Freawaru — look!"

It was Radegund's voice, but I could not comprehend her command until Runa added, "Look, my lady, at the staff — at the ground."

Welling up from its base came bubbles of water, forming a pool that spread slowly over the dancing floor. As I watched, awestruck, one of the small stones that formed the lips of the Sulis image broke loose — then another and another — pushed upward by the water. More water flowed forth, wetting the feet of the nearest onlookers, who cried out in amazement and hastily stepped back.

Still kneeling, I dipped my hand in the gathering stream and tenderly bathed Mother's pale, thin face.

"A sacred stream!" announced Radegund, looking about at the women. "Wiswicca summoned the goddess and she has come — showing herself in the form of this sacred spring!"

Suddenly every woman was dipping her fingers in the freshet, wiping them on her own or a neighbor's face, filling the night with hysterical sobs and laughter.

"Yes!" I proclaimed, slowly rising. "A gift from the goddess! And a gift from Wiswicca! Let us give thanks for her sacrifice — her life. We will call this place 'Wiswicca's Well,' and honor it always. Praise be to the goddess!" I shouted.

"Praise be to the goddess!" came the heartfelt response.

"Friends," I continued, "I declare this circle broken. Let us accompany Wiswicca back to the great hall. There we will celebrate her life and praise the goddess for the gift she has given. We now return to Helmingham."

"Lady Freawaru, with your permission may I address the women?"

It was Radegund, her face a mixture of wonder and sorrow.

"Why, yes, if you wish."

Radegund bent to pick up one of the lamps surrounding the Sulis image and held it aloft.

"Women, sisters," she shouted, "a word before we leave this place. We all mourn Wiswicca's passing and will always miss her, but despite our grief we must now show our appreciation and respect for this great gift from the goddess. We must honor her with feasting and celebration — just as Wiswicca had planned. Let our hearts be filled with gratitude — even joy — as we return to Helmingham. Let the fullness of our hearts be heard in the fullness of song, as we bear Wiswicca... home."

Her voice caught on the final word. Lowering the lamp, she handed it to me and I raised it high again. As the assembly broke up and groups of women headed toward the road, a few tentative voices began to sing.

"Goddess bless us, goddess guide us..."

As we were leaving, I thought of my mother's staff, still standing in the villa floor.

"Gerda, child, please run back and fetch Wiswicca's staff," I charged her.

"I will," she cried and was gone in an instant — but she returned empty-handed.

"It's stuck! I can't pull it out," she declared, crestfallen.

"Oh, very well. We'll get it later," I said, distracted with thoughts of all that lay ahead.

Next beckoning Katrin to my side, I said, "as soon as we get back to the settlement, my brother Erik must be notified of Wiswicca's death. Could you send your husband to find him?"

"Yes, of course, my lady. He will be glad to help."

On our return journey waves of emotion swept through the throng, some women singing, some sobbing. Wiswicca's still form in the oxcart was accompanied by Minna and Käthe, looking red-eyed and solemn. Lark and Gerda now led the oxen, pleased to be given this responsibility. I walked wearily behind the cart with Radegund and Gudrun at my side. Radegund put her arm on my shoulder, but kept a respectful silence; Gudrun, however, needed to talk.

"My lady Freawaru, your mother came to this settlement as a stranger and changed all our lives. I have a feeling you may do the same. Why, you've already begun, you have."

"Thank you, Gudrun. I will do what I can, but I understand that I could never replace Wiswicca," I half sobbed.

"You don't have to, my lady, but once you've settled in Wiswicca's old hut, folks will be coming to you. Everyone needs help from time to time."

She turned from me to gaze at Wiswicca's body, reclining as if asleep against a stack of cushions in the cart.

"Besides us, Wiswicca's funeral pyre will draw all the men from these parts. They'll want to honor her as much as we do," concluded Gudrun, nodding emphatically.

It was after midnight when we reached the great hall. We carried Wiswicca on her bed to the platform she had formerly occupied at the far end of the hall. There I smoothed out her long white gown and lifted a damp wisp of hair from her brow. Leaning over, I kissed my dear mother on the forehead, her skin chill against my lips. Picking up a light linen coverlet, I spread it over her slight frame and gently drew it up to her chin.

"Rest in peace," I whispered, stepping down off the platform.

Minna and Käthe were lighting lamps and placing them around the platform's base, ringing Wiswicca with light.

"Soon you will sleep in the flames, dear Wiswicca, but tonight we will keep watch beside you," murmured Minna. Käthe nodded, unable to speak. I saw Katrin slip out the main door to find her husband and convey my message.

We found everything in readiness for the feast. I had thought I could not possibly take food or drink, but suddenly found myself ravenously hungry and thirsty. Gudrun took charge immediately, waking the thralls who had slumbered by the hearth and directing them in serving out the bread and soup — first to Lady Radegund and her party. Soon all the ritual participants were seated at tables, their mugs filled with barley beer, their bowls full of rich, hot vegetable stew.

Amidst the bustle of serving, a babble of voices rose in the great hall.

"Did you see it? Feel it? Wiswicca brought the goddess, she did!"

"I can't wait to tell my husband!"

"What a marvel we have witnessed!"

"I would never have believed it had I not seen it with my own eyes!"

When all were served, Radegund rose to speak.

"Sisters: we have been truly blessed by the gift of Wiswicca's life among us. Even in death we are blessed by her. Because of her the goddess will always be with us. Let us celebrate the life of Wiswicca and the gift of the goddess."

"Wiswicca and the goddess!" came back the response from all in the hall.

We ate and drank and drank again, but watchful Gudrun saw to it that no one had too much barley beer, for there was still the walk back to the longhouses where the women were quartered. When everyone had finished, I signaled for Gerda, Lark, Minna and Käthe to help me once again.

This time each girl picked up a basket of yellow apples, as I rose from the head table to speak.

"Women of the River Doep. The apples these girls carry were gathered from a tree in Wiswicca's garden. Take them home. Plant the seeds beside your door. When a seedling emerges, water it well. In time you may have your own Wiswicca apple tree. Blessed be Wiswicca. Blessed be the goddess."

"Blessed be Wiswicca. Blessed be the goddess," echoed through the hall, as eager hands reached out to receive the proffered fruit.

When I sat down again beside Runa, she leaned over to murmur in my ear.

"Well done, my lady, well done. Wiswicca would be proud."

Suddenly I was choked with emotion, my eyelids stinging with salty tears. This time I let them flow.

"Nothing will ever be the same," I sobbed.

"It never is, my lady. It never is."

When I could recover and find my voice again, I bid the assembly make their formal farewells to Wiswicca, one at a time. As they filed slowly past Wiswicca's bed, I heard over and over again words of gratitude for what she had done.

"Thank you, Wiswicca, for saving my husband."
"That wonderful potion — thank you."
"Dear friend, thank you for my healthy child."
"Your advice made our way clear. Thank you."
"Thank you ... thank you ... thank you."

Gradually the hall emptied as everyone sought their beds. Although exhausted, I chose to stay in the hall beside Mother on a nearby sleeping bench. I sent Gerda home with Lark, and my women back to their beds, but Runa insisted on staying with me.

"Your brother has not come, and you should not be alone tonight, my lady."

"Alone? Lady Radegund and her women are settled at the far end of the hall," I demurred, nodding in their direction.

Runa gazed at me reproachfully.

"They are strangers. They do not love you as I do," she broke off with a sob.

I sighed. "Very well, dear friend. Of course you may stay."

Before I could lie down for the night, I went to Mother's side once more. Sinking to my knees, I reached for her hand under the coverlet.

"Mother, dear Mother, I hope we accomplished this night all that you wanted. I believe that you and the goddess will never be forgotten. For my part, I will do all I can to defend against the dark future you envisioned. May your spirit ever be with me. Good night, Mother, good night."

The next morning I had barely opened my eyes when I heard a commotion at the main door of the hall.

"She's my mother too!" shouted a loud male voice.

Hastily throwing back the sleeping robe, I slid off the bench and reached for my gown.

"Where is she? I want to see her!"

Hurrying to the door, I found Runa trying to hold back a raging Erik.

"It's alright, Runa. Let him in. I'll take him to see Mother."

As Runa stepped aside, Erik charged into the hall like an angry ox, almost knocking me over.

"What happened? What did you do to her?" he cried, glaring at me wildly.

"Calm yourself, brother. I sent a messenger for you last night, but you were not to be found." I took his arm to lead him to Wiswicca's platform. "Our mother died during the ritual, at the height of her powers, at a moment of glory. She sleeps with the goddess now, but will be forever revered and honored by the folk of the River Doep. I swear it!"

When we reached Mother's bedside, Erik gave an anguished cry and fell to his knees clutching at the coverlet.

"It's true, true! She's gone! She's left me — alone!"

"Alone? I am here, Erik, your sister."

"You?" He turned to look up at me, his face flushed and distorted. "What good are you? You can't help me! Mother promised I'd sit on a throne one day. Now she's gone — and I'll never be a king!"

"What's all this?"

Lady Radegund's voice, cold as an icy river, sounded behind us.

"Rædwald will be the only king here — Rædwald, my husband! Do you dare to question his right — or his authority?"

Her voice cut like a whiplash and Erik cringed.

"No, no, Lady Radegund," he pleaded, getting to his feet. "My throne awaits me across the whale road — in Denmark. There I would be king... one day. I meant no disrespect to you or to Rædwald."

"Really?" Radegund's face relaxed slightly, but still wore a frown. "Instead of raving at her bedside, you could better serve your mother by seeing to the construction of her funeral pyre. I will return with Rædwald to attend — shall we say in three day's time?"

"Yes, my lady," muttered Erik, backing toward the door. He glanced at me sourly. "We shall speak more of this later — sister."

When Erik was gone, Lady Radegund approached and embraced me tenderly.

"My dear, pay no heed to your brother's disparaging words. You are the true daughter of Wiswicca, and as such will always be welcome here. In fact..."

She held me at arm's length, gazing into my eyes. "In fact I think you should be given a new name to reflect your status: 'Freawicca.' What do you think?"

I bowed low before her, my eyes brimming with tears.

"I would be honored by that name, my lady, deeply honored."

"Rise, then, Freawicca, and let us be sisters. I welcome your friendship."

Respectfully I embraced Radegund, remembering that I had once been the blood sister of Queen Higd of the Geats, a bond not only strained but broken. Would Radegund prove to be a true friend?

Lady Radegund and her party left on the morning tide, promising to return for Wiswicca's funeral pyre. Word of Wiswicca's death would spread quickly along the river as the rest of the women returned to their homes. In Helmingham a cloud of sorrow hung over the settlement. Wilhelm led the men in paying their respects to Wiswicca as they filed solemnly past her platform. Willing hands joined Erik in constructing the funeral pyre.

At first the sudden appearance of the sacred spring was spoken of only in whispers, as everyone mourned the loss of Wiswicca, but gradually those who had witnessed it began to marvel out loud. When their men heard of it, they came to me for confirmation, Johan among them. On the second morning after Wiswicca's death, he appeared at Wilhelm's door seeking me, and I stepped outside to greet him.

"Good morrow, Johan."

He wasted no time in preliminaries.

"Is it true, my lady? This spring?"

"Yes, it is true. If you go to the villa you can see for yourself."

"That's just what worries me — that others will flock to the villa to see for themselves — over my land!"

"Oh," I said, taken aback. "I had not thought that far ahead. So... you think this spring will create a problem?"

"I do," he said earnestly, "unless you agree to become the guardian of the spring — a sort of gatekeeper, if you will."

As I stared at him, absorbing these words, Johan continued.

"Anyone coming to visit the spring must pass through Helmingham. You could let it be known that they must first visit you before being admitted to the spring — and then only if they bring an offering — which you could share with me."

I recoiled in sudden understanding.

"An offering? No! This spring is a gift from the goddess, to be enjoyed freely by all who come to it. No offerings! None!"

Johan frowned, then shrugged.

"I thought you might say that. You're just like your mother. She would never accept payment for her help — though many thank-offerings appeared at her door over the years."

He grinned, showing his missing front tooth.

"No offerings. No offense. But... you do need to be prepared to deal with those who will come to worship here, once the word gets out. Thank you, my lady. Good day."

Johan had barely disappeared down the path when Erik approached.

"Good morrow, sister. Decisions must be made."

"Good morrow, brother." I was glad to note that he sounded more civil this morning. "Please come inside."

Gudrun and Lark were clearing away the morning meal, but removed themselves when Erik and I sat down at table. He came straight to the point.

"The pyre is ready and Wilhelm has sent messengers down river to announce the burning for tomorrow. My question is this: what ornaments, what costly objects, could be added to the pyre to show our mother's royal status? She had little left of her own after long years of nursing me," he concluded bitterly.

I regarded him thoughtfully, making a mental inventory of my goods.

"I am glad to hear that you wish to honor our mother, Erik. In my chests I have fine garments and precious jewels, all fit for a queen. Tell me, what will you cast on the pyre?"

Erik looked down, then up to face me. The naked anguish in his eyes smote my heart.

"The only thing of value I have left: my horse."

"Your horse?" I echoed, wondering if that was the cause of his anguish. "A sacrifice indeed — I commend you!"

Erik nodded ruefully.

"Helmingham must be shown that we come of noble stock — you and I," he muttered. "Our father was a king!"

"So he was," I murmured, "but that was long ago. Now we must each create our own place in the world." I sighed. "Fear not, Erik, Mother will be arrayed in queenly fashion. The honor of the Scyldings will be upheld."

True to her word, Lady Radegund and her husband Rædwald were among the first to arrive to witness Wiswicca's final rite. Radegund had brought with her a finely decorated urn which she presented to me, saying solemnly, "The royal burial ground at Rendlesham — I thought you might like to place your mother's ashes there."

I nodded.

"Yes. Thank you. That would be most fitting."

And, I thought to myself, it would appeal to my brother's pride.

Wiswicca's pyre had been constructed near the river bank, a short distance from the landing. She was carried out of the great hall by four men of the settlement, high on her pallet, even in death a regal figure. On her silver-white hair I had arranged the circlet of gems given to me by Ingeld at our betrothal: a lustrous pearl, a blood-red garnet, and a stone of deepest blue. On her arms I had wound spirals of gold. Bedecked with herbs and late summer wildflowers, she could be mistaken for the Earth Mother herself, a queen in all her glory.

As chief of the village, Wilhelm would lead the procession along with Gudrun, Walthar and Lark. Erik and I took our places immediately behind the bier, accompanied by my people. Next would come Rædwald and Radegund with a large party of courtiers from Rendlesham. Everyone else would follow after.

As we began to walk quietly, I was aware of bird songs around me. Then a different, familiar sound floated on the midday air: music. Runa was playing her flute. As the soaring notes soothed our sorrowing hearts, a sigh of release rippled through the procession. By the time we reached the river, I felt almost uplifted.

Suddenly Gerda tugged at my arm, crying out.

"Look, Lady! On the river!"

All heads turned to stare. A single white swan, its head held high, sailed serenely on the sparkling water.

"Is it another sign, Lady?" asked Gerda, her face filled with delight. "A sign from the goddess?"

"Yes!" exclaimed Radegund behind me. "Yes!"

As the sound of the flute soared even higher, I remembered that Runa's flute was made from the leg bone of a swan. The swan stayed abreast of our procession until we reached the pyre. Then it lifted its great wings and slowly ascended, leaving us to look up in wonder.

Runa's flute fell silent as Wiswicca's pallet was lifted onto the wooden framework, high as our heads. Together, Erik and I took the torch handed to us, lit the pyre and stepped back. After a wisp of smoke and a few crackles, a tiny tongue of flame licked through the dry branches inside, feeding on the fat smeared over them. We all stood silently, watching, drawn to the devouring flame.

The fire leapt and danced, then with a roar enveloped the pyre in a great ball of flame. I wailed and staggered back from the heat. I could no longer see Mother's body through the smoke and fire. Reaching out

Cloak of Ashes

I took my brother's hand and gripped it hard. Great sobs escaped my throat. Someone was screaming.

Another hand grasped mine — a tiny hand yet one that tugged at me fiercely. Opening my eyes, I looked down to see Gerda, tears streaking her cheeks.

"Oh, Lady, don't leave me! Don't ever leave me!"

With a cry I snatched her up, burying my face in her cloud of unruly hair, as she clung to me: a motherless child ... just like me. We stood, Gerda and I, clinging to each other as the fire raged on, devouring and purifying. When the pyre had been reduced to a heap of glowing embers, Gerda spoke again.

"Lady, your queen mother ... will she soon wear a cloak of ashes?"

"Yes, Gerda, as will I one day. Death comes to us all."

At the funeral feast — largely produced from the supplies brought earlier for the goddess celebration — Radegund announced my new name, 'Freawicca,' to the company assembled in the great hall. This was greeted with approbation, though I saw a frown appear momentarily on Erik's face.

I noticed that Mother's platform had already been removed. Now replaced by tables and benches, the place where she had spent the last days of her life bore no trace of her presence, save for a lingering scent of mint and borage.

As beer flowed freely, the matter of the sacred spring soon became a topic of animated conversation. When Johan proposed that I be named guardian of the spring, this met with general approval, but again I saw Erik frowning.

'Ungrateful man!' I thought to myself, 'especially after I saved your stallion from the flames!'

Shortly before the funeral pyre Roald had told me that he considered Erik's stallion Bludroyal to be the best candidate for breeding with my Sunbeorht. With this in mind I had suggested to Erik that he sacrifice a different horse at the pyre, a horse I would purchase from its owner. Wilhelm had arranged the transaction with Stefan, Katrin's husband, to the satisfaction of all involved — or so I had thought.

'Erik, why can you not accept me and love me as your sister?' I stormed inwardly. 'We have no family now — only each other.'

At the conclusion of the feast, Wilhelm proposed that he and a party of village elders accompany me to the spring for a first-hand look. To this I readily agreed, asking only that we make the trip on a different day. Truth to tell, I was near the limit of my strength.

When Rædwald and Radegund rose to leave, she came to embrace me.

"Sister, you must come soon to Rendlesham — and bring your horse! We can ride together through the countryside, and I will show you the beauties of this land."

"It would be my pleasure, Lady Radegund. Thank you for your support and your friendship. Fare you well."

When everyone had left save Wilhelm's family and my own people, I felt suddenly bereft. I had come from afar to Helmingham seeking my mother. I had found her, but now she was gone again, this time... forever. What could I possibly do to fill this void? A soft hand on my arm drew me back to the present. Gerda's face, her eyes questioning, looked up at me.

"Don't be sad, Lady. You still have me!"

I nodded, swallowing hard.

"Yes, Gerda, and I love you dearly, my treasure. You comfort me — and I have you to care for, you, Runa, and all the rest of my men and women. I must set aside despair and look to my people. After all, I am Hrothgar's daughter; I am Wiswicca's — Wealtheow's daughter. I am a Scylding. I will carry on."

Even so, my body was suddenly wracked with shudders and I fell to my knees. A great gulf seemed to open before me, a gulf which had swallowed my mother and now threatened to swallow me. As I stared into the abyss, unseeing, I gave myself up to darkness and despair.

How long I lay, a prisoner of my grief, I do not know. When I came back to myself I was sitting up, surrounded by familiar faces: Gerda, Runa, Gudrun, Lise, Olaf, Ginnlaug, Lark, Lempi... 'Not all are lost to darkness,' I told myself. 'Not all. Together, we will carry on.'

Chapter Eighteen
Starting Over

Matronae with fruit; small clay sculpture from 1st or 2nd century AD. Bonn, Rheinisches, Landesmuseum.

Autumn was a busy season for everyone in Helmingham. Harvest time continued, from cutting grain in the fields to gathering herbs in the gardens. It was also time to dung the fields for next year's growing season — and we could smell the odor when wind blew from the east. Weather continued dry and warm, despite the daily changes in leaf color. Gudrun told me that this part of the country often experienced a 'second summer'. She warned me, however, that an abundance of bright red berries in the hedgerows indicted heavy frost and bitter cold in the coming winter.

I employed several of our young men to build an addition onto Wiswicca's hut, providing room across the back for all my women, including our two young thralls. Johan directed this construction, as he had experience in such matters. While watching Johan at work one day, I was curious to note that he marked several timbers with an X, the Gebo rune, signifying a gift, and others with a V, like one of the marks in the Roman name SVLIS.

"So, you know runes, Johan?"

When I pointed at the X, he looked at me blankly.

"That's not a rune, my lady, that's a measurement."

"Oh? What does it mean?"

"Mean? It means what it says: ten. Each of those planks measures ten arm-lengths."

"What does that signify?" I pointed to the V.

"Five. Half of ten. Those are pieces for your end walls."

"Is this a system of your own making?" I asked, intrigued.

He shrugged. "My father used it and his father before him. Family lore, I guess. Now I should get back to work."

"Just one more thing, Johan. Before you erect the ridgepole, I'd like to carve a rune on it — for protection."

Gudrun had given me a shoot of elder to plant near the garden door to guard against evil, but additional protections could not hurt.

"As you wish, my lady. The ridgepole is lying yonder beside Knud."

"Thank you, Johan."

Fortunately, although an undercurrent of grief seldom left me, the need to make immediate decisions and execute long-range plans kept me fully occupied each day. Now that I was fully committed to making Helmingham my home, others could make plans as well. Runa and Olaf were eager to set up their own household; Roald and Ginnlaug wished to marry as soon as possible. And now that Wiswicca no longer resided in the great hall, it resumed its former function as a place to house young warriors — although most of the men in Helmingham were farmers, not fighters.

Noting that our cargo ship needed extensive repairs and maintenance, I suggested that we build a new ship — partly to give our men a substantial project, partly to enhance our status in the area. At first Olaf shook his head at the idea, declaring a second ship unnecessary, but our men were eager for real work, and gradually Olaf gave in. Soon the wildwood rang with the sound of axes and falling trees as they set to work, followed by the creak of ox carts hauling heavy timbers. Alf and Vigo oversaw the ship-building, with unexpected help from Wilhelm's son Walthar, who was skilled in wood carving and construction.

Daily Lark and Gerda made their way down to the harbor to watch the men at work. I sometimes joined them to marvel as the ship took shape, strake by overlapping strake. One day I was unexpectedly joined there by my brother Erik.

"Planning to leave soon?" He asked without a greeting.

"Leave? No, not at all!" I replied, wrinkling my nose at the smell of fresh tar being applied to the seams. "Why do you ask?"

"I'd leave if I could," he said bitterly. "There is nothing here for me."

I gazed at my brother, at his scraggly beard and sallow face, wondering—not for the first time—if his brain had been poisoned along with his body.

"Have you friends here in Helmingham?" I asked, then instantly regretted my words as Erik's brow furrowed.

"I sometimes drink a mug of ale with Frans and Heinrich," he growled, "if that's what you mean."

"I was just wondering . . . what pastimes you enjoy when . . . when you're not busy supervising Wilhelm's men . . . Hunting, perhaps?"

Erik looked at me quizzically, his shoulders in their usual slump.

"Do I enjoy killing, you mean? Not usually—although it is nearly time to collect hawks for training. No one in Helmingham does that better than me!"

"Really!" I exclaimed, glad to have found a topic of interest to him. "I know three young men who are keen on falconry: Grim, Eskil and Gunnulf. They had a bit of practice at Heorot before we came here, but I'd wager they would welcome more instruction."

"Oh? Which three are they?" he inquired, glancing toward the work crew swarming over the vessel under construction.

"Him . . . him . . . and him," I replied, pointing to each man.

"Perhaps . . . perhaps I'll speak to them tonight . . . in the great hall." Erik nodded with a slight smile. "Thank you . . . sister. And by the way, my stallion is available when your mare is ready."

He turned without another word and walked away, but it seemed to me that his back was straighter and his head held higher.

Well before 'blood month', when animals are butchered before the start of winter, my women and I were settled in our new home, Wiswicca's old hut. Besides the addition across the back, the whole roof had been renewed with fresh thatch, and a byre created for our milk cow — one of the animals given to us by King Hrolf. The rest had been added to Roald's livestock, under the care of Runa and Olaf. They had moved into the longhouse left vacant by Ermengard's death, with the understanding that Roald and Ginnlaug would join them there after they were wed. We fixed upon Yule as a good time for their wedding ceremony, hoping to further secure our position as accepted residents of Helmingham with a lavish communal celebration.

As soon as the hearth fire was lighted and our chests and goods were stowed away in our new home, I made a pilgrimage to the site of my mother's death. I had intended to go alone, but Gerda would not be parted from me.

"If Runa were here, you'd take her!" said Gerda earnestly. "She's not here, but I am. Take me!"

Hands on hips, face in a frown, she stood in the doorway, looking defiant.

"If you don't, I'll ... I'll fly after you!"

I sighed. "Alright, sparrow, you may come with me. Get your cloak; I don't know how long we'll be gone."

As Gerda turned to pull her cloak from a peg near the door, Ginnlaug emerged from the herb room.

"Take your time, Lady Freawaru — that is, Freawicca."

"Don't worry, Ginnlaug," I laughed. "My old name will do. And we'll be back before nightfall."

"Very good, my lady. We'll have the evening meal ready when you return."

Although it was mid-day, the pale sun barely penetrated a haze that still hung over the river, remnant of an early morning fog. Before we set out I wrapped my shawl about me and picked up a small leather water bag.

"What's that for?" asked Gerda.

"I thought we might bring back some water . . . from Wiswicca's Well," I answered quietly.

"But we already have water in the back!" said Gerda.

"Yes, but the water from a sacred spring may have special properties — healing powers, for example."

Gerda was silent as we walked along the road together, but as we neared the villa she looked up with anxious eyes.

"Will she still be there — as a — as a ghost?"

I stopped and took her hand.

"No, Gerda, probably not. Her ashes lie in the burial ground at Rendlesham. Only her staff remains here. I thought I might bring it back with me... as a remembrance. You may carry it."

Gerda nodded and her face cleared. As we moved past the walnut trees, now bare of leaves, the colonnade of white pillars beyond did present a somewhat ghostly appearance, bleak and forlorn in the damp, misty air.

On my earlier visit with men from the settlement, I had explained that the villa floor was now a sacred space, reserved for women's rituals. The men had respectfully stopped just outside the colonnade, looking in at the fountain of water flowing from the mouth of Sulis Minerva.

"By the gods, a strange and wondrous sight!" exclaimed Wilhelm. "Gudrun did not exaggerate."

The other men were equally in awe of the site, some speaking in hushed tones, others muttering uneasily about the alien power they sensed here.

"You women cleared this place... all by yourselves?" queried Frans, gesturing toward the dancing floor.

"Yes, we did. The goddess gives strength when strength is needed," I had answered.

"Look, Lady! There's the spring!' cried Gerda. "And the staff still stands inside it."

"How strange," I murmured, moving quickly across the stone-paved floor. "I thought the flow of water would have dislodged the staff by now — but it is not so."

Indeed, the base of the staff appeared to be still securely planted inside the mouth of Sulis Minerva, at the head of a bubbling stream. As I reached out a hand toward the staff, Gerda gave a warning cry.

"Stop, Lady — don't touch it"

"What? Why not?" I asked, in surprise and some irritation.

"She doesn't want you to!"

"Who doesn't? Mother? Sulis Minerva? The goddess?"

"All of them," declared Gerda. "They are looking after it. We are not to touch it."

I stared at Gerda's earnest face.

"How do you know this, little sparrow?"

"I just know. Don't you feel it? It's alive!"

Perplexed, I turned back to the staff before me and studied it closely. Something about it did seem different. Were those tiny swellings ... near the top? Surely not ... surely this is dead wood. The staff must be older than me!

Without further comment or question, I knelt to dip my water bag in the bubbling spring, careful not to touch my mother's staff. Gerda was now floating walnut leaves on the stream, crooning a little song: "Down to the river, down, down, down, all the way to Helmingham."

Leaving Gerda to her play, I rose slowly and closed my eyes, invoking my memories of that night — the night Mother had summoned the goddess and given up her own life. As images of that night passed before me, I made my silent supplication:

Mother, dear Mother, I am here. Your Freawaru is here — now Freawicca. Be with me, Mother, now and always. Never leave me. Guide me as I go forth bearing your name. May I be worthy of that name. Bless me, Mother, bless me.

Tears welled up and streamed down my cheeks as I gave vent to my grief here, — almost alone — with no need to maintain a public face. When the tears finally ceased, I opened my eyes and looked about. Gerda still knelt by the stream, but her eyes were fixed on me. Slowly she rose and came to my side, then took my hand.

"Let's go home," she said.

On the walk back I asked Gerda not to say anything about the staff to anyone.

"It's best to wait and see what happens, if anything," I cautioned.

She nodded cheerfully. "Whatever you say, Lady." She squeezed my hand gently.

We had been settled in our new home for less than a month when the first visitor arrived seeking my aid. It was Eskil with a nasty gash on his leg, suffered when splitting timbers for shiplap, he said. Lise fussed over him like a hen with a wayward chick, leading him into the house and seating him on a bench to remove the dirty cloth wrapped around his leg.

"How came you to be so careless?" she chided as she propped his leg on a stool.

"I guess I got distracted when Minna came walking by," he answered, winking at me over Lise's head.

"Minna? Huh! Why didn't she tend to you, then? What made you walk all the way out here?"

"To see you, for one thing," said Eskil. "And I'd heard that Lady Frea ... wicca keeps a magic potion for healing cuts: water from Wiswicca's Well."

"What?" I exclaimed, "Who told you that?"

Eskil shrugged, then winced as the last of the dirty cloth was removed. "Everybody says so," he answered evasively.

"Well, I wouldn't want to disappoint you, so I will bathe this wound with water from that source, but I think a compress of yarrow leaves will do the most good. Hold still."

Eskil willingly obliged while I carefully cleansed the wound and bound it with the herbal compress. I was just finishing when Gerda came bounding in from outside.

"Who's hurt?" she exclaimed. "There are spots of blood leading right up to our door!"

Lise stepped aside to reveal Eskil, who greeted Gerda affectionately.

"Hello there, sparrow. It's only me — and you were right about that magic potion! I feel better already!"

"Gerda? What have you been telling people?" I demanded.

Gerda's face fell, but she answered bravely.

"You didn't say not to tell about the water, just about the ..."

"That's enough!" I quickly interrupted. "Go find Mari and Berit and get more water from the well in back. You three can scrub the blood off our doorstep."

"Yes, Lady," she sighed, eyes downcast.

As soon as she left the room, I addressed Eskil.

"Is Gerda the 'everyone' you spoke of earlier?"

"Yes," he admitted, "but everyone does believe you have special powers and potions. Why, you're the Wiswicca now!"

"So I am, and I will try to deserve that title, but let's have no more idle talk. The powers of the sacred spring — if powers they be — have yet to reveal themselves."

I sent Eskil back to the village after instructing him to return in a few days so I could look for possible infection. As it turned out, the wound healed perfectly, leaving only a slight scar.

As the time of Yule neared, we folk from Geatland got our first taste of winter in Angle-land. Despite Gudrun's warning, the cold that set in seemed very slight in comparison to what we had experienced at our previous home. Indeed we welcomed the first crisp, frosty morning and the soft, powdery snow. When I asked Gudrun if the river ever froze over, she laughed.

"Not in my lifetime, though I've heard it has happened."

I was glad of this, for Yule looked to be a time of merry-making both up and down the river. Here in Helmingham the wedding of Roald and Ginnlaug was near at hand, and I had also been invited to spend several days with Radegund and Rædwald in Rendlesham.

Shortly after moving into the hut we had set up our looms in the new addition, and spent many days there weaving bedclothes and blankets for Ginnlaug. I found it increasingly tiring to stand for long periods of time, so left most of that work to my women. Instead, I used my time to resume Gerda's lessons in rune-carving and interpretation.

On mild days we sat outside in the garden, for enclosing the fourth side of the square had created a sheltered bower. My knees ached less there and Gerda always preferred being outdoors, so we both found it an agreeable place to take on what were sometimes difficult tasks.

I usually selected the rune to be studied each day myself. Strangely, day after day, the same rune met my fingers: Hagalaz — rune of radical change and disruption, even destruction. Each day I put it back, unwilling to expose Gerda to the darker runes just yet. Still, it made me uneasy. Could something be amiss back at Eaglesgard? No, Berkana — rune of new life — came to my fingertips each time I focused on Inga. I rejoiced for her and the child she must be carrying eight months after her wedding.

Erik occasionally came to the hut for brief visits, sometimes bringing a small rabbit or waterfowl killed by one of his hawks. At such times he seemed less moody and resentful. Once he even laughed outright at one of Gerda's antics. Later she had observed to me, "He's just lonely, Lady."

In preparation for the upcoming wedding of Ginnlaug and Roald, I walked to Gudrun's house one morning to ask her about two important elements: a hammer of Thor to hallow the marriage, and a supply of mead for the honey moon afterward.

"Speak to Ulrich about the hammer — our blacksmith — although we've never used such a thing for weddings here to my knowledge. As for honey, the best bee-keeper hereabouts is Johan."

"Ulrich? I know the location of the forge, but I've not yet met the smith."

"You'd better let Wilhelm introduce you. Ulrich doesn't like women around his work place."

"Thanks for the warning! I'll speak to Wilhelm later. In the meantime I'll go talk to Johan."

"Oh, Lady, may I go with you? I'd love to see the bees!"

Gerda's face appeared at my side, glowing with anticipation. She had come with me to visit Lark, but found her busy at the loom this morning, absorbed in her weaving.

"Yes, yes you may come — but I don't want you doing anything to upset Johan's bees — that could be dangerous!"

"I won't — I promise," she declared.

I was curious to see where Johan kept his bees, as I had not noticed any skeps on my previous visits. He led Gerda and me around the back of his house and across a small meadow, all of us crunching frosty grass underfoot. He stopped several feet away from a row of buzzing hives, coiled straw skeps set on wooden platforms.

"Quiet now, so I can listen!" he instructed, putting a finger to his lips.

Gerda, who had been asking a steady stream of questions, immediately clamped a hand over her mouth.

The hives gave off a soothing hum, and Johan nodded with satisfaction.

"They are feeling calm and happy, they are. Now I must introduce you," he said, glancing back at Gerda and me. "Bees," he called out, "this is Lady Frea ... wicca and her girl Gerda. They wish to use some of your honey for a marriage couple."

He stopped and listened again. I could detect no difference in the sound.

"That should do it." Johan nodded his head. "Despite the time of year, they've made more than enough honey to feed themselves this winter and have some left over for you. Best swarm I've had in years — big producers, they are."

"I like their little houses," said Gerda softly. "They look so ... cozy. But why do you talk to the bees?"

Johan laughed. "Bees are just like people — but smarter. I treat 'em with respect, and never get in their path when they're flying back from gathering nectar. I'd get stung for sure! Now if they come in low to their hives, they've most likely come off a field of clover, but if they've been working fruit trees, they'll come in much higher."

"Fruit trees? Like the apple tree in our garden?" asked Gerda.

"Exactly. You'll see that tree buzzing with bees come spring."

"Johan," I said, "when I was a girl, Wealtheow, that is, Wiswicca, once told me that bees carry the souls of the dead up to the gods. Do you believe that?"

He regarded me solemnly.

"I told my bees when Wiswicca died, I did. My old grandam also told me that the bees bring the thread of life to all living creatures — at birth."

We stared at the hives in fascination, awed at the power of these small insects.

My visit to Ulrich's smithy got off to a bad start. When Wilhelm and I arrived at the forge one drizzly morning, Ulrich was in a foul mood. One of his thralls had let the fire go out overnight, causing a delay in beginning the day's work. The arrival of a woman did not improve his temper.

I eyed the smith with some alarm. Ulrich was a short, squat man with no visible neck but powerful arms and shoulders. Beneath a thick leather apron that covered his chest and hung to his knees, he wore a rough woolen tunic flecked with burn holes. Blackened with soot and smoke, he looked more like a monster than a man.

"What now?" he growled as we approached. "What do you want?"

Wilhelm stepped forward to intervene.

Cloak of Ashes

"This is the lady Freawicca, Ulrich, Wiswicca's daughter. She's come to commission a special piece from you for a wedding ceremony."

"No time," he grunted. "I'm behind as it is: tools to make, swords to finish, horses to shoe..."

"Horses?" I asked in surprise. "You make shoes for horses?"

Ulrich eyed me with an expression of mixed pity and disgust.

"Yes. Iron shoes, of course."

Beside me Wilhelm hastened to declare, "Ulrich is the best farrier on the river, my lady." Dropping his voice, he added, "Some even say he is a horse-witch."

Ulrich apparently heard this, for he flashed a sudden smile that lit up his grimy face.

"I just talks to 'em in their own language, I does." He paused. "What is this special piece you're wanting?"

"A hammer of Thor," I answered quickly, "but not an amulet. I need a full-sized hammer... to hallow the marriage of two of my people."

Ulrich stared at me in disbelief.

"Full size? That would take a lot of iron! What do you have to offer?"

"Offer? I can pay you in gold or silver..."

"No, what do you have that's made of iron? A cauldron, perhaps? I'll need iron for the hammer — if I decide to make it."

"Oh, I see. Yes, I could spare a cauldron. Would that be enough?"

He nodded. "How soon would you need it?"

"Before Yule, if possible"

He paused again, peering at me. "Say, aren't you the sister of Erik the Steward?"

"Why yes, I am," I said, wondering what possible significance this could have for Ulrich.

"Good man, Erik. Knows horses." He nodded. "Get me your cauldron and I'll see what I can do."

Abruptly he turned back to his work and I understood that I was dismissed.

Walking back to Wilhelm's house, I asked him about Erik's reputation as a horseman.

"He can draw or jade a horse better than any man in the settlement — save for Ulrich."

"Really? I had no idea!" I marveled; I also had no idea what 'drawing' or 'jading' meant.

"Ask him to show you sometime," suggested Wilhelm.

"I will. Now I must go home and arrange for that cauldron to be delivered to Ulrich. Thank you, Wilhelm, for your assistance this morning."

He laughed and gave a slight bow.

"Don't worry about your hammer, my lady. Ulrich will make it for you."

Later that same day Erik brought his stallion to breed to my mare, now housed in a stable near Olaf and Runa's house. After we left the two horses together, I asked him about 'drawing' and 'jading.'

"It is easier to show than to explain. I could demonstrate with your Sunbeorht, if you like — perhaps tomorrow?"

"Agreed. May I bring Gerda? She loves horses."

"Bring anyone you want," he said expansively.

The next day several of us trooped over to witness Erik's demonstration. Besides myself and Gerda there were Lise and Lempi, Ginnlaug, Runa and Olaf, and Lark. Erik was waiting for us in front of the stable, looking pleased and confident. Sunbeorht stood quietly in her stall, facing the open door.

"I will begin with jading," he said. "That means to make a horse stand still and refuse to move. Watch me."

Walking up to Sunbeorht, he stroked her mane and whispered in her ear.

"Now call your horse, my lady," he said, backing away.

Calmly I walked forward, reaching out a hand to touch her nose. "Come, Sunbeorht."

She did not move a muscle. Clucking my tongue, I reached up to her halter rope and gave it a gentle tug. "Come, Sunbeorht." Again, nothing.

"She will not move until I release her," said Erik. "Step aside, please."

As I did so, he walked forward, stroked Sunbeorht's mane again, then lifted one of her front hoofs and tapped it sharply with his knuckles.

"There. Now she'll go. Try her."

I held out my hand and clucked my tongue. Immediately Sunbeorht stepped out of the stable, but turned to follow Erik, who was walking away. I heard gasps of surprise behind me. Indeed, I myself was astonished.

"Brother, what power is this you possess?" I exclaimed.

"Apparently one you do not!" he retorted.

I stared at him in wonder as he picked up the halter rope and led Sunbeorht to me.

"Take her. She's yours again."

Now the onlookers pressed forward to encircle us.

"That was amazing!" burst out Lise.

"How did you do that?" queried Lark.

"Secret words of power?" guessed Runa.

Erik shrugged and gave a wry smile. "Secrets are secrets," he said, "or you could just call it 'horse sense.' Now you must all excuse me. I have work to tend to."

He walked away, whistling, leaving us to stare after him.

Back in our hut, I realized that Gerda had said nothing during the entire performance — most unusual for her. When we were alone, I asked, "Do you feel well, sparrow?" smoothing back the hair from her forehead.

"Lady," she said earnestly, her face thoughtful, "He had something in his hands. I was watching."

"Who? Erik? Are you sure?"

She nodded vigorously.

"Well, perhaps he did, but I doubt we'll ever learn his secrets."

Like many of my predictions of late, this one was to prove wrong.

The wedding of Ginnlaug and Roald brought out all the inhabitants of Helmingham. Despite several dreary days of cold rain, the atmosphere inside the great hall that night was warm and festive. Earlier, both bride and groom had bathed to ritually cleanse themselves, then dressed in their best attire. Ginnlaug wore a new kirtle of undyed linen, edged with the red rose braid she had once given to Runa. Beneath the wreath of fresh evergreens on her hair, Ginnlaug's plump face glowed with happiness. At her side she carried a sword newly fashioned by Ulrich.

Roald wore a deep blue tunic and trousers that set off his blue eyes and fair hair, so that one scarcely noticed the scar across his cheek.

He carried an ancestral sword brought from his family home back in Norway.

Seated on the high seats on either side of me, for I was acting as priest, they rose to exchange the wedding gifts placed beside each of their chairs.

"Ginnlaug, I give you this handgift as I oathed to do."

He handed her a handsome fur, representing the livestock he owned.

"Roald, I give you this brydgifu as I oathed to do."

She presented him with a finely woven coverlet, a sample of the goods in her chest. Next came the exchange of swords.

"Ginnlaug, I give you this sword for our sons, to have and to keep."

"Roald, you must bear a blade to keep us safe. I give you this sword to protect our home."

After they sat down, I rose, carefully lifted the hammer of Thor, and held it aloft for all to see. Ulrich had done a fine job on it, even decorating the broad, heavy head with designs incised in the metal.

"Having witnessed these vows and the exchange of gifts between Ginnlaug and Roald, I now hallow this marriage."

Carefully I touched the hammer to Roald's chest, then laid it carefully in Ginnlaug's lap.

"Before the gods and all present here, I declare that Roald and Ginnlaug are husband and wife! Bring in the bridal cup!"

Beaming with importance, Gerda carried in a large wooden cup of foaming ale, treading carefully lest she spill it. Taking the cup from her and holding it between them, Ginnlaug and Roald offered toasts to the gods, which were hailed by everyone in the hall.

"We drink to Freyr and Freyja!"

"Wes heil!"

"We drink to Thor and Braggi!"

"Wes heil!"

"We drink to Odin and Frigga!"

"Wes heil!"

When they had emptied the cup, I raised both arms high.

"Let the feast begin!"

The feast that followed lasted for nine days, with intervals for sleep and replenishment. Meats, roasted or cooked in pies and stews, graced every table: chicken, pork, venison, rabbit, pigeon. There was barley beer

Cloak of Ashes

and bread aplenty. Hazelnuts. Dried and boiled fruits. Eggs and pottages of mixed vegetables. Most of the dishes were familiar to me, except for the shellfish that were urged upon Ginnlaug.

"Swallow it raw! Each one guarantees a fine son!" came the shouts.

I noticed that Ginnlaug got one down, but declined further consumption of the slimy things.

"What are those?" I murmured to Gudrun, seated beside me at the head table.

"They're called 'oysters' — a gift from the sea. You'll soon get to like them."

"Ugh!" I shivered. "Perhaps not soon."

Mead was not served at the feast, as Johan's honey supply would barely cover the couple's honey moon, but I did not miss it, for I was enjoying a refreshing drink made from apples.

"Cider, you call it? This is excellent."

"Made from Wiswicca's apples," grinned Gudrun. "The best."

Given the raw weather outdoors, our entertainment was restricted to the great hall, but everyone entered in with gusto. Wilhelm employed no scop, no harper, but when someone produced a lyre, our Knud plucked the strings and began to sing a plaintive lay about the kings of old. Sigrod and Anton turned out to be jugglers of some skill. The locals favored riddles, however, which came from all corners.

> *Head down, nose to the ground, I belly and grub.*
> *Driven by a bent lord who hounds my trail,*
> *Who lifts and lowers me, rams me down.*
> *I bite and furrow, sowing seed.*
> *My ways are weird; one flank of my trail*
> *Is gathering green; the other black.*
> *What I slash falls in a curve of slaughter*
> *To one side. What am I?*

"That's an easy one," called Frans, lifting his beer mug. "It's a plough."

"Here's one for the ladies," called a voice I did not recognize.

> *This small miracle hangs near a man's thigh.*
> *Full under folds, it is stiff, strong and bold.*
> *When a young lord lifts his tunic over his knees*
> *He wants the hard head of this hanging creature*
> *To greet the hole it longs to fill. What is it?*

Snickers and loud laughter greeted this riddle, but no one ventured a guess until Ginnlaug boldly rose and shouted, "It's a key!"

"And we mus' be off . . . to see if it fits the lock," cried Roald, rising drunkenly to seize his bride by the waist.

To the applause of the company, they lurched out of the hall, leaning on each other. I saw Olaf and Runa follow them out, and knew they would see the new couple safely to their abode. I wondered if Ginnlaug would be able to notice her morgengifu tomorrow: Roald's bridal gift for the morning after. He had sworn me to secrecy, but I knew that Blæki had given birth to a litter of tiny elkhounds, and one of the bitches was to be his gift to Ginnlaug, along with a plough share, signifying the land he would farm with Olaf.

The Yule festival began with a blast of icy air from the sea. Even with fires burning on both hearths, my knees sometimes ached in the damp, cold weather. I would gladly have stayed at home beside my own fire, but Gudrun insisted that I take part in the observance of Mothers' Night, to be held in the great hall.

I had heard other women speak of this celebration during my sojourn at Wulfhaus on the River Elbe, but did not take part myself because of my miscarriage. I knew it involved the worship of three female figures — or 'Matrons' as they were called — who somewhat resembled the Norns known to us speakers of Norse.

Gerda was keen to go, hoping to see Lark there; Lise and Lempi wanted to see Ginnlaug and Runa. So, we all wrapped ourselves in our warmest cloaks and set out. We carried baskets of dried apples, as Gudrun had said that fruit would be a suitable offering. By the time we reached the great hall, my toes and fingers were numb, and even Gerda's teeth were chattering.

Inside the hall I was surprised to see a large gathering — most of the women who lived in the settlement. Katrin greeted us warmly as we entered and ushered us to places at the head table. A kind of shrine had been erected in front of the high seats, with three carved wooden female figures. One held a basket of fruit, one cradled a baby, and the third — in the middle — wore her hair loose, indicating maiden status.

"You're here at last — we've been waiting for you," exclaimed Gudrun, rising from her seat. "Place your offerings at the feet of the Mothers. Lark will help you."

"Those are Mothers?" queried Gerda, pointing at the wooden figures.

"Yes. In the old country they would have been carved of stone, but we don't have much of that here," said Gudrun, somewhat apologetically.

"What's that strange smell?" asked Lise, lifting her head to sniff the air.

"Incense," declared Lark. "Father gets it in trade, but we only use it on Mothers' Night."

"What's incense?" asked Gerda.

"Something that's burned to make a pleasant odor," I told her, looking around to locate the source. In all four corners of the hall I saw hanging bowls emitting an aromatic smoke.

"Lady Freawaru, do you like it?" asked Lark.

"Yes, it's most... unusual," I replied politely.

By now we had added our offerings to the shrine and returned to the table.

"Lady Freawaru," said Gudrun, "Tonight we women gather to honor the Earth Mother and our ancestral mothers, both living and dead. As your own dear mother has recently joined the holy ones, we wish to do her special honor on this night, the birth of the new year."

For a moment I was speechless, looking about me at the loving faces of these women of Helmingham

"Thank you, thank you, dear friends. Instruct me. Tell me what I must do."

The rest of the evening passed in a kind of blur, as I followed the others in a series of rituals and sacrifices. At one point each woman lifted up the name of an ancestor whose guidance and protection she sought. Some made specific requests or gave thanks for past favors. When it came my turn, I named Wiswicca, inwardly asking her to come to me in a dream or vision, as she used to do when alive. Her death had created a great emptiness in me, a blank space that I longed for her to fill.

"Wiswicca!" echoed the women around me, followed by individual voices.

"Holy one," "Wise one," "Giver of the sacred spring," "Guardian of our homes and families."

Gudrun concluded the paean of praise.

"Wiswicca, this night we honor you above all others. Be present at our hearths. Be with us through the coming year."

The evening ended with each woman approaching the three Mothers, touching them one by one, and bowing low in reverence. I saw tears in the eyes of many as they returned to their tables.

That night Wiswicca came to me — not as a pale figure in a dream but as a beautiful woman in the prime of life, a queenly figure bathed in light. She carried a golden crown which she held out to me, a single word on her lips: 'Erik.'

Erik? A crown for Erik? How can that be? Bewildered, I shook my head and backed away, but again Mother extended the crown. 'Erik,' she insisted. Reluctantly I reached out to take it from her, but when I touched the cold metal, both crown and Mother disappeared. I awoke to find myself clutching one of the keys at my girdle.

Chapter Nineteen
Rendlesham

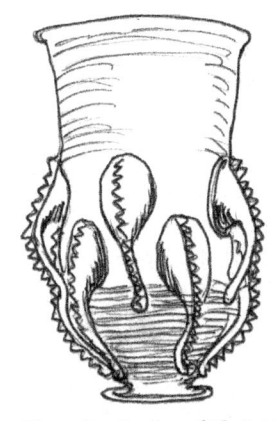

Glass claw beaker of Rheinish manufacture.

Yule brought unexpected news from Runa, who came to visit us at the hut one wintry morning. After she removed her cloak and handed it to Berit, she turned to me with a glowing face.

"Lady Freawaru, the goddess has smiled upon me! I am carrying Olaf's child!"

"Runa, how wonderful! And you thought you were too old for motherhood!"

I embraced her warmly and led her to a bench beside the hearth. "How long have you known?"

"I would say I am three months along — and I've felt the first kick!" She smiled broadly. "You must admit, my lady, that I am past the usual age for child-bearing. Because of that Olaf wants me to be very, very careful. Why, he hardly lets me lift a finger at home! That's another reason I've come: to ask if I may borrow one of your thralls to work for us."

"Of course, and you may keep her as long as you need. Which do you prefer: Mari or Berit?"

"The older girl, I think — Mari."

"As you wish. Berit!" I called, turning, "fetch your sister and tell her to bring her things. She is to serve Runa this winter."

Berit's face crumpled, but she nodded silently and left to do my bidding. She returned shortly with Mari and her small bundle of clothes. Both girls looked as if they'd been crying.

"Don't be sad," soothed Runa. "You'll get to see each other often. We all live close by."

Gerda rushed in, her face full of concern.

"What's happening? Why is Mari going away?"

"Good news, little sparrow: Runa is going to have a baby!" I explained, reaching out to draw Gerda close to me. "She'll need extra help for a while."

"A baby? I love babies! I'll help you too, Runa," she enthused.

Runa smiled. "We'll have at least six months to wait — perhaps until Midsummer — but I will welcome the help of all my friends."

Now Lise and Lempi appeared, carrying pails from the morning's milking.

"What is it? What's all the excitement?" demanded Lise, frowning.

"Runa's having a baby, Runa's having a baby," chanted Gerda.

Lempi set down her pail and embraced Runa carefully. "Congratulations, dear friend," she murmured.

Lise was blunt. "What luck! Pregnant at your age!"

Runa laughed heartily and we all joined her, delighting in her happiness.

I had thought of inviting Runa to go with me to Rendlesham, but realized that Olaf would be loath to let her travel just now. Therefore, Gerda became my companion on the trip down river to celebrate Yule at the king's hall. Lise and Lempi had agreed to stay home to do the morning and evening milking, and to keep Berit busy at the grinding quern — after I promised to bring back every detail of life at the court.

During my earlier trip to take Mother's ashes for burial, I had not taken time to see much of the hall itself or the rest of the settlement.

Rædwald and Radegund had respected my grief and need for privacy, not pressing me to stay, but this trip was to be different. This time they wanted me to experience all the pleasures of a great hall at a time of celebration. For my part, I was ready to relax and enjoy myself, free — at least temporarily — from cares and responsibilities.

The visit started well, with a warm reception from our hosts. Gerda and I were housed with three of Radegund's women: Berta, Hannah and Gertrude. Their faces were familiar to me from the goddess celebration, and I welcomed the opportunity to know them better. Gertrude was especially gracious, offering to supply whatever we might need during our stay.

A great oak log had been dragged in from the forest and lay on the main hearth, ready for burning in the Yule fire. That night's feast was to feature a boar's head on a platter. Gerda was excited at being allowed to attend, and actually paid some attention to her hair and dress in preparation. She was wearing a new undyed kirtle decorated with tablet braid she had woven herself in a mixture of red, blue and yellow threads. I had given her a string of brightly colored beads from my jewelry chest to wear about her neck.

"How do I look, Lady?" she inquired, peering down into a bowl of water as she tried to tame her hair with a wet comb.

"You look fine, dear one. How do I look?"

Gerda lifted her head and scrutinized me critically.

"Your hair has gotten much lighter — almost white around your face!" she declared.

"Really? Let me look in that bowl!"

Gerda was right. My hair was whiter. I looked almost like . . . my mother.

Rædwald and Radegund made a regal pair as they presided over the feast that night. Radegund had chosen a gown of deepest red heavily embroidered with gold thread. She had shown me the costly thread earlier: pure gold foil wound around a core of horsehair and flattened. I also noticed that her tight-fitting sleeves were fastened at each wrist with clasps of silver, and at her waist hung two large girdle-hangers, shaped somewhat like keys. I knew that Lise, especially, would be interested in such details of dress.

King Rædwald — for king he was in practice, his father being aged and infirm — was dressed in a dark leather tunic and leggings, over which he had draped a bearskin cloak, fastened at the shoulder with a clasp of gold and garnet. On his left hand he wore a large gold ring set with a black stone; the standing figure carved into it portrayed a Roman god of good luck — so Berta told me. She seemed happy to extol the riches to be found at Rædwald's court, pointing out a pair of ornately decorated drinking horns on the head table, used for toasting the gods. Rædwald and Radegund drank their wine from strange claw-footed glass beakers, which Berta told me were imported from the Rhineland. Rædwald's court also had its own scop, a man named Gunter, who strummed a fine lyre made of beautiful maple wood. As I came to discover, there was no dearth of such luxurious items in Rendlesham.

Gerda too took note of the magnificence of Rædwald's hall, looking about in awe as we followed Berta to our table near the throne chairs.

"It's so *big*!" she declared, "and ... beautiful."

I had to agree, for I had never seen a finer hall. Not even my father's Heorot or Hrolf's hall at Roskilde could compare with it in size and grandeur. Every surface was carved or painted or hung with tapestries. The huge central hearth where the Yule log lay was flanked by smaller hearths that helped to warm and light the cavernous space. What seemed an army of thralls ran in and out, bringing bread and ale to each of the many tables ranged throughout the hall. Gunter was singing something to King Rædwald, but in the hubbub I could barely catch the words — something about a boar's head.

"Look, Lady!" shouted Gerda, pointing toward the main doors where four young thralls had entered, bearing a platform on their shoulders. On the platform rested an enormous pig's head, its bristly ears wrapped with holly and a rose red apple lodged between its gleaming tusks.

"Oooh, it looks scary," said Gerda, shivering.

I laughed. "Probably not as scary as the giant boar that King Eadgils sent to attack Hrolf Kraki and his men," I said, recalling Bodvar Bjarki's story of that confrontation in the Swedish court.

Hrolf ... Bodvar ... Drifa ... I wonder if you are celebrating Yule back in Denmark as we do here in this far-away Angle-land? As I said these names to myself, a sudden cold clutched at my heart, and all the light in the hall disappeared. Gasping for air, I reached out blindly, crying out, "No! No! Spare them!" Then darkness swallowed me.

When I came back to myself I was no longer sitting in Rædwald's great hall. I was lying on soft coverlets in a high bed, and Radegund herself was bending over me.

"Freawicca, Lady. Have you returned to us?"

I gazed at her, not comprehending my situation.

"What... what happened?" I asked weakly.

"That is for you to tell us," said Radegund kindly. "Your Gerda says you suddenly fainted. Are you ill?"

I turned to see Gerda staring at me, her face full of concern, her hands knotted.

"Ill? No, I'm not ill, but I have seen... a terrible vision."

Radegund stood up and spoke to others in the room whom I could not see.

"Leave us, all of you, except for Gerda."

When the sound of shuffling feet and whispers had subsided, Radegund spoke again to me.

"What have you seen? Tell me, please. Does it portend aught of evil for the court of Rædwald?"

I tried to focus, with difficulty summoning the ghastly vision.

"No," I whispered, my throat dry, "No, not this court... but across the whale road... in King Hrolf Kraki's court... I see... death."

Radegund gave a slight shiver, but seemed somewhat relieved.

"May death not travel across the whale road," she murmured, then spoke briskly. "Can you sit up? I'll send for wine to help you recover from the shock you've had. Then, perhaps you can tell me more of what you saw?"

I nodded and rose up on my elbows. "I'll try."

After a few sips of the strong red wine Radegund offered, I searched for words to describe what I had glimpsed in that one terrible moment.

"Hrolf... Bodvar... Hjalti... Svipdag... and many other warriors: I saw each one fall, hacked and bloody, falling before the relentless advance of a ghostly force—led by a figure with the head of a horse."

As I spoke these words a burning sensation spread across my face, and I reached up to touch my scarred eyebrows.

"Skuld," I whispered. "Skuld is behind this."

"Skuld? Who is he? And those others you named—who are they?" asked Radegund, wrinkling her own brow.

Before I could answer, Gerda burst into tears.

"Don't let her hurt you again, Lady! Stop her!"

"What are you two talking about?" exclaimed Radegund in complete bewilderment.

Briefly, while I stroked Gerda's hair to calm her, I told Radegund what had taken place during my stay at Heorot. When I finished she was quiet for a time, reflecting on what she had heard.

"Lady Freawicca, is it possible to interpret your vision in a different way? Perhaps there has been some sort of... conflict, but surely no woman — not even this evil Skuld — could destroy a whole court of able warriors!"

"I hope you are right, Lady Radegund. There is only one way to find out. I must go to Heorot."

"Go? Now? You can't!" cried Radegund. "It's the dead of winter — no ship can cross the icy seas at this time of year."

"I do not need a ship to carry me there," I said quietly. "I need only a flute and a drum."

Gerda's head jerked up in alarm.

"No, don't do it! Skuld might kill you!"

Radegund's face grew suddenly grave.

"I think I understand your intention, Lady Freawicca. If I and my women can shield you from harm in this undertaking, please call upon us. After all, we are sisters now."

"Thank you, Lady Radegund, for your offer. I welcome your aid. I know that tonight you must return to your duties as hostess, but perhaps tomorrow... in the morning?"

"Yes," nodded Radegund emphatically. "We can use my chamber for privacy, but I think Rædwald should be told of whatever we learn there. Events in one court have a way of affecting other courts — witness the presence of young Edwin here, visiting from Northumbria."

"Edwin? Have I met him?" I asked politely, though my mind was far from Rendlesham.

"He's the handsome young man who sat on my left at the king's table. Edwin may be a king himself one day, if he can regain his throne."

Instantly my thoughts flew to my brother. If it should be true that Hrolf no longer ruled in Heorot, there might be a chance... for Erik... that golden crown...?

Cloak of Ashes

"I must leave you now, sister," said Radegund. "Sleep here tonight. You will be safe — you and Gerda — I'll see to that. On the morrow I hope all your questions will be answered, for worse or for better. I hope for the better."

"It will be as Wyrd decrees," I said soberly. "Thank you for your care and hospitality... sister."

Sighing, I lay back on the soft cushions which Gerda had already plumped for my head.

After the morning meal next day, we assembled in Radegund's chamber, a small group of women including Berta, Hannah and Gertrude. Gerda would beat my drum to set the rhythm for my turning. Lacking Runa's flute, Radegund introduced a bent old crone named Beornwyn who assured me she knew all the ritual chants used for vision quests in her native Frisia. She reminded me of my old neighbor Gunilla back in Hrethelskeep — now long dead — and I warmed to Beornwyn immediately.

"I'm too old to travel," she quavered, "or I would have come to honor your mother's passing. Fine woman, Wiswicca."

"Yes, she was," I said. "Thank you, Beornwyn. Oh... what is it you have there?"

Beornwyn was holding out something wrapped in a piece of linen.

"It's to aid you on your journey," she said, unfolding the wrapping.

Inside lay two swan feathers — one white, one black — and a third feather I did not recognize.

"It comes from a gannet, a seabird," she explained in response to my questioning look.

"Most fitting," I acknowledged, "for I will fly with Freyja across the seas to Denmark."

"... and back again, Lady, for you must return!" asserted Gerda, frowning ferociously. "I wish I could fly with you!" she added.

"I need you here, little sparrow, to keep a steady beat and drum me home again. Now, let me reveal to the rest of you what is required."

The women listened intently as I explained the steps of the ritual: drumming, chanting, turning — until I could leave my body and fly across the sea. They were to receive me when I returned, to catch me if I fell.

"Have no fear," I reassured them, noting several anxious faces, "I will return."

I did not add that I might not be quite the same person when I returned, but that was a risk I must take. Fastening the three feathers to the braided belt at my waist, I pulled it tight. My empty stomach rumbled in protest, as I had taken no food that morning, and I wore only my linen under shift to leave my body free of impediments.

After each woman took her place in a circle around me, I led them in an invocation to the goddess. Lifting my arms high overhead, I called out.

"Great goddess! Freyja! Be present here. Aid Freawicca in her journey!"

"Great goddess! Freyja! Be present here. Aid Freawicca in her journey," they echoed.

Three more times I repeated the invocation, each time echoed by the chorus of women's voices.

"Gerda. Sound the drum!"

Confidently Gerda's hands set up a steady rhythm on the deerskin drum: *Pum*-pah-pah, *pum*-pah-pah, *pum*-pah-pah. Slowly I began to revolve, turning sunwise in my own circle. Gerda gradually increased the tempo as Beornwyn began to chant: deep-throated words in a language unfamiliar, yet one I understood: "lift me on your wondrous wings, oh mother of the morning." Borne aloft by these powerful words and the reassuring drumbeat, I gave myself up to the unknown.

A blast of cold air scattered the warmth of the bed chamber and sent me swirling through mist and fog, rising, rising, swept along by gusts of wind. My breath turned white before my eyes, and I blinked back icy tears. How long I hung suspended, numb with cold, I do not know. I could no longer feel my body, but still heard the steady flap of my wings, bearing me onward through the darkness. All around me great crystalline stars glittered in their vast domain, and far below me the whale road frothed and billowed.

Slowly, slowly, the air grew warmer and I felt myself descending, spiraling softly down onto a barren peak high above a fjord. I knew that fjord. "Closer, closer — I must go closer!" I implored. Wearily my wings responded, carrying me down ... down to a snow-covered plain heaped with strange boulders and scattered fires that sent up acrid smoke. It stung my eyes and filled my nostrils with the stench of ... death. Closer

... closer... Bodies! Those strange rock piles are heaps of bodies — yet to be burned! Closer... closer... With a shriek, I fell to earth.

"Lady! Lady! Come back! Please come back!"

Groggily I opened my eyes, but could see nothing. Someone was bathing my forehead with cool water, while others stroked my hands. I could feel soft cushions beneath me.

"Lady, it's me!" sobbed a familiar voice.

"Gerda? Where are you?"

Reaching out with both hands I touched her hair, tangled as always, and felt one cheek wet with tears.

"Why are you crying, little sparrow? And why can't I see you?"

"Lady Freawicca?" A different voice sounded this time: Radegund. "Can you see my hand?"

"Hand? No, I see nothing but darkness. Where am I?"

Gasps of alarm sounded around me.

"In the hall of Rædwald at Rendlesham. You have returned from a long journey," said Radegund's voice.

"She's taken a shock," growled a deeper voice. "Let her rest. You can ask questions later."

"Beornwyn speaks wisely," said Radegund. "Come, ladies, let us leave and give Lady Freawicca time to... recover."

Her voice seemed to break on the last word, as if she were almost sobbing.

"I'm staying!" asserted Gerda defiantly. "I'm staying right here beside her."

I felt her warmth as she suddenly embraced me. Wearily I closed my eyes and drifted off again.

Am I dreaming? I seem to see Drifa... and a large animal. She is bending over a great white bear. She is crying. Drifa, don't cry! Drifa, I'm coming...

Sometime later I opened my eyes again. Hearing the sound of soft breathing near my face, I turned my head.

"Gerda, is that you?"

"Lady, you're awake! Yes, it's me. Can you see me?"

"Come closer, little one. The light is so dim..."

"No, Lady, no. All the lamps are lit and I'm right beside you." Her voice trembled. "Are you... are you blind?"

The possibility struck me as ridiculous. "Of course not — I just can't see."

Gerda gave a strangled laugh. "And your hair, Lady — it's white, all of it."

"Oh?" I reached up to feel for a lock of hair and pulled it across my face. "I do see something... a sort of shadow."

"Did you see Skuld again? Did she blast your eyes?" persisted Gerda.

I considered. "No, I did not see Skuld. I saw only destruction... and death."

"Lady Freawicca?" Radegund's voice sounded from a distance. "We heard voices. Are you awake?"

"Yes. Please come in. I am stronger now."

This time when Radegund passed her hand over my eyes I was able to detect the motion, and told her so immediately.

"Thank the goddess!" she exclaimed. "Perhaps — in time — your sight will be fully restored." She paused. "Do you feel well enough now to tell us of your journey?"

"Yes, but who else is with you? I sense others present."

"The same ladies who attended you during the ritual, and... the king."

I raised a hand. "King Rædwald, I wish I had more details to give you, but this much I know: a massacre has taken place in Denmark."

"A massacre?" No answering hand met mine. "I am sorry to hear it," he said gravely. "Who are the Danes' fiercest enemies?"

"Why... the Swedes, after Hrolf's humiliation of King Eadgils."

After a long, silent moment, Rædwald spoke gruffly.

"Eadgils is no favorite of mine, but I am allied to that royal house. My Scylding ancestors came from the region of Uppsala."

"I too have kin in Uppsala," I murmured, thinking of Aunt Ursula, "although raids and wars have sadly reduced the number."

"To get to the matter at hand," said the king, "What did you see on your... journey?" Rædwald's voice was kind but commanding.

I told him all that I had witnessed.

"How many bodies would you estimate?"

"That's hard to say, but several score," I answered, "or at least scores of body parts." I gulped as the image of severed heads and arms came back to me.

"Radegund told me earlier about King Hrolf's sister — a sorceress, I believe. Do you think she played any part in this . . . event?"

"Something tells me that she did, but for that matter, Odin himself had a grudge against Hrolf and his men."

"Odin, you say? What do you mean?"

As I recounted the tale of Hrolf's encounter with the one-eyed 'Hrani,' I realized that Rædwald's image was slowly coming into focus. By the time I finished, his face stood out: brow furrowed, lips set in a straight line.

"Why, King Rædwald, I can see you clearly!" I exclaimed, smiling with relief.

"Praise the goddess! Your sight's restored!" declared Radegund, coming forward to take my hand.

I blinked. Yes, I could see both Rædwald and Radegund — and Gerda, her own eyes shining, but not with joy.

"Oh, Lady," she croaked hoarsely, "no more drumming, no more leaving, please. I won't help you hurt yourself again."

"The child may be right," said Radegund quietly. "You are . . . visibly diminished." Gently she pressed my hand.

Rædwald, however, was stroking his beard with a thoughtful expression on his face.

"Lady Freawicca, the Danes are not the only tribe with enemies. Each season brings invading Saxons to these shores, and the kingdoms already established on this island are sometimes at war. Your presence as a seeress could be very helpful to my court. You could warn us of impending attack, see into the enemy camp, give us an advantage . . ."

"By putting her own life at risk?" exploded Radegund. "Nay, she is my sister, my friend!"

"Friends help their friends," said Rædwald shrewdly, his eyes narrowing.

"King Rædwald, I would not want you to rely exclusively on my visions," I said earnestly. "As you have witnessed, they can be . . . incomplete . . . ambiguous. A wrong interpretation could also lead one astray."

The king's expression remained unchanged.

"When spring arrives," he said, "I predict that we will hear more of this . . . envisioned massacre. Then we can better judge the veracity of your report."

Radegund nodded. "In the meantime, let us put aside all troubling thoughts and enjoy the Yule celebration."

"I will try," I promised, though I did not expect the horrific vision to fade easily.

The rest of our nine-day stay at Rendlesham passed without further incident. Radegund and her ladies took special delight in showing me the beauties of their court. I admired and praised their tapestries, their table linens, and other fine products of their looms.

Radegund also led me into a large room adjoining the great hall where Rædwald's court worshipped the gods — that is, the male gods. Tall carved posts representing Thor, Freyr and Odin stood on one side of the space, with a low stone altar placed before the three figures.

"We used to worship in the oak grove nearby," explained Radegund, "but after a wind storm damaged several old trees, Rædwald had them cut down and built this temple with their wood. There is an outdoor entrance on the far side."

"How clever," I murmured, "a temple-house for the gods." I paused. "Where do you worship the goddess?"

Radegund made an apologetic gesture.

"We don't have a space as grand as your Roman villa, but we women of Rendlesham gather occasionally at a small channel off the main river to perform our rites and ceremonies."

"I am glad to hear it," I commented, smiling. "The goddess must never be . . . forgotten."

I had almost said "neglected," but did not wish to offend my hosts.

The king himself led me on a tour of his workshops, where I saw craftsmen working in gold and silver to create exquisitely detailed jewelry, belt buckles and garment clasps, harness mounts and decorated serving ware. Others worked in wood, producing elegant drinking cups of maple or finely carved posts and panels for bedsteads and wagons. Among the products of the metal workers I especially admired a large, circular serving piece with a small fish sitting inside on the very bottom.

"That's a trout," chuckled Rædwald, "my favorite fish."

"How clever," I murmured. "It is only revealed when you reach the bottom of the bowl."

"Yes," said Rædwald. "A surprise is sometimes ... welcome." He gave me a sidelong glance. "Have you considered my invitation ... to join us at court?"

"Thank you, King Rædwald. You do me much honor, but I have obligations to fulfill first in Helmingham. And, as you said, the coming of spring may help decide the question."

In truth I was eager to return to Helmingham for many reasons. Primarily I wished to impart my grim vision to my brother Eric and its possible implications for him. Thus I was not regretful when it came time for Gerda and me to bid our hosts farewell and board ship for home.

A thin skim of ice had formed along the edges of the river and a chill wind whipped at our faces as we arrived at the harbor in Helmingham, laden with gifts for our household and friends. Grim caught the mooring rope thrown by one of our escorts, and Eskil secured it, our boat hull crunching through the shoreline ice.

"Welcome back, Lady Freawaru—I mean, Lady Freawicca," called Grim, grinning from ear to ear as he helped Gerda and me climb out of the boat.

"Thank you, Grim. Don't worry about remembering my new name. Is all well here?"

"Nothing new," volunteered Eskil. "A few fights, but no serious injuries."

"What? Do you jest?" I asked in surprise and consternation.

Eskil shrugged. "Not much else to do in winter time."

"Don't worry, my lady," added Grim. "Your brother keeps a tight rein on the younger lads."

"Eric? He does? Where is he now? I would speak with him."

"Can't we go to the hut first?" asked Gerda, touching my elbow. "Lise and Lempi will be waiting for us."

"Eric's longhouse is on the way," I pointed out, "if he's at home."

"He is," said Grim, tousling Gerda's hair—for she never wore a cap or kerchief—"and he has news for you."

To myself I thought: news for me? Nothing like the news I have for him!

"Grim, will you and Eskil please take our things to the hut while Gerda and I pause to visit Eric?"

"As you wish, my lady."

The two young men gathered up our bundles and set off for the settlement, as Gerda and I, at least one of us chilled to the bone, picked our way over the frozen ground.

Eric was surprised to find Gerda and me at his door.

"Judging from your attire, you have just returned," he said as he admitted us.

"Yes. We haven't even been home yet. Brother, I have important news for you!"

"And I for you, sister. Your Sunbeorht will be foaling this spring!"

"Ah, welcome news indeed. I wish my news were as good — though it may lead to good."

Pulling off my heavy cloak and fur cap, I handed them to Gerda.

"By the gods, what's happened to you?" burst out Eric. "You're suddenly an old woman!"

Startled at his reaction, I said, "Just wait. I will tell you all — as soon as I'm warm."

Eric ushered me to a bench beside the hearth and shouted at a young female who stood gaping by the fire.

"Bring hot ale!"

"I'll help your girl. What's her name?" asked Gerda, who had hung our wraps near the door.

"The thrall? I call her 'draggle-tail.' Won her from Heinrich in a game of dice."

"Why Eric, she's just a child!' I admonished, holding my hands out to the welcome flame.

"Old enough to work," he growled. "Now what is this important news of yours?"

Starting with the apparition that came to me in Rædwald's hall and finishing with the scene of carnage I'd witnessed in my vision quest, I laid out for my brother the likely situation in Denmark. Eric listened in silence, his eyes gleaming. When I stopped speaking he gave a harsh laugh.

"So ... my old nemesis has finally gotten what he deserves — a just retribution! May your vision prove true!"

"Alas," I exclaimed, "there are those I love in the court of Hrolf Kraki. The innocent may have suffered along with the guilty — if guilt there was..."

Eric stared at me in disbelief.

"Sister, how can you feel sorrow for anyone in that court? They made me suffer — in exile — me and Mother — for years! But Mother must have foreseen that my time would come. She somehow knew I would one day wear the crown in Heorot!"

Eric was exultant, shouting and pacing about the room. I recalled my dream with Mother holding out a golden crown.

"Perhaps," I said slowly. "But brother, if that day should come, you must be ready — ready to fight, ready to be a leader of men. You must prepare!"

Eric stopped pacing and turned to me, his eyes ablaze.

"That new ship you built — was that built for me? Do you, too, believe that I am destined to take my father's throne?"

Now it was my turn to stare in disbelief. Yet . . .

"Wyrd will have its way," I whispered.

Chapter Twenty
Raido: Return

Two warriors in boar helmets; a 7th century metal die for making helmet plates. Torslunda, Oland.

That winter seemed to pass more slowly than any other winter of my life. Of course there were happy events to look forward to: Runa's coming child, the foal in Sunbeorht's belly—even Roald's Blæki gave birth to another fine litter of elkhound pups, and Roald let Gerda choose one for her own—but the sense of dread which hung over me would not dissipate.

I tried to present a serene face to my household, but they knew me too well. I had given Lise and Lempi a brief description of my vision at Rendlesham, but asked them not to share it with others. After all, what if I were mistaken? Aches in my joints increasingly plagued me, and I spent most days sitting beside the fire in our hut. And it seemed to me that it took longer every morning for my vision to clear.

Runa came often with Ginnlaug; their visits helped to brighten the gray afternoons. Gudrun and Lark came as well, usually bearing a pot of fish stew or a round of crusty bread. Lise and Lempi cooked and baked well enough, but we all welcomed these gifts from loving friends.

Lark and Gerda decided to name the new puppy 'Elki,' and spent many an afternoon playing with the animal. The dog slept with Gerda at night, though on occasion I tried to entice it into my own bed. Since my spirit journey to Denmark, I was continually cold. Would I ever feel warm again?

From time to time people came out from the settlement to seek my aid for their ailments and accidents, or advice for other problems. Most of these complaints were easily addressed with herbal remedies, but others were more challenging.

One desperate young woman sought my help for her husband — or so she said. She told me that they had no children and she despaired of ever having any, for her husband no longer lay with her, preferring to drink himself into a stupor night after night or, worse, seek another's bed. After delicately probing for further details about their relationship, I decided that an extreme measure was needed.

"The next time your moon blood comes," I said to her, "catch some of it in a basin or mug ... and pour a few drops at a time into your husband's ale."

The woman, whose name was Editha, gave me a blank stare.

"Do I dare do such a thing?" she quavered.

"Yes," I said firmly, "if you want to bind him to you. Continue adding the blood until your husband returns to your bed."

Rising, she shyly embraced me.

"Thank you, Lady Freawicca. I will do as you advise."

"May the goddess go with you," I said, as she walked toward the door, "and forgive me for staying at my hearth. Within the coming year I will expect to attend the birth of your first child."

When Editha was gone, Lempi approached me tentatively.

"I heard what you told that woman from back in the herb room, my lady, and I'm wondering ... can you also recommend a ... a love potion?"

"I can, but who would be the recipient?" I asked in surprise.

Lempi looked down, talking to the floor.

"I've given up on Grim; he'll never grow up. But there's another man here who has ... shown an interest in me."

"Lempi, my dear," I exclaimed, taking her by the shoulders, "any man would be lucky to have you as his wife! Do I know this fellow?"

She nodded, blushing slightly. "It's Johan."

"Johan? Well! He is a steady man, a dependable man . . . but I don't think you will need a love potion to win him. Let things take their course. Spring will soon be here, and then we shall see. Anything might happen."

The possibility of returning openly to Heorot galvanized Erik into action. Without revealing his motivation, he began working with the young warriors, including the group of thanes I'd brought from Geatland. They in turn expressed to me their surprise and delight at Erik's interest in their training and conditioning.

"It feels a bit like old times, my lady," declared Anton one evening when I visited the great hall. "Beowulf once kept us in fighting trim, ready at any moment to meet the Swedes."

"I remember," I said, my eyes momentarily misting. "But is life here so dull for you?"

Anton gave a rueful grimace.

"Beg pardon, my lady, but . . . yes. Erik, however, has let it be known that he might lead a raiding party come spring. If he does, I want to go with him."

"I see. And how do the rest of our young men feel about this?"

Anton considered. "Now that Olaf and Roald have taken wives, they might be content to stay at home, but as for the rest of us . . . we'd go — with your permission, of course," he added hastily.

Ah, I thought to myself. Someone else yearning for spring. Whose hopes will be realized?

Early one morning, well before daylight, I heard a nightingale singing outside the hut. Rising from my bed, I wrapped a shawl about my shoulders and went to the door to listen better. When I opened the door a crack, I felt a soft breeze, much warmer than any we'd experienced for several months. Could spring be on its way at last?

"What are you doing, Lady?"

Gerda's voice startled me and I swung around to face her.

"I heard a lovely bird song. Why are you up so early?"

She yawned and stretched, shaking herself like a little dog.

"I had a dream," she said, her eyes half-closed. "I dreamed I was dancing . . . with you and your mother. We were singing and laughing and dancing . . . and then I woke up. Lady, could we visit your mother's well today? Elki has never seen it . . . and he needs exercise."

"Today? Why today? We have not been there all winter," I answered.

"That bird you heard singing? I heard it too," said Gerda, "and it told me 'go to the well, go to the well.' Besides, it doesn't smell like winter today," she said, poking her nose through the opening at the door. "It smells like . . . sunshine and dragon flies!"

I had to laugh at this, but also admit to myself that something did feel different.

"We'll see . . . after we break bread. Perhaps it's time we all got out of the house."

Later that morning we set out: Gerda with Elki, Lise, Lempi and I, with Berit carrying jugs to be filled. The ground was damp from melted snow, and a few icy patches lingered in shadowy places, but the air felt fresh and clean — a welcome change from our smoky hearth. I had wrapped myself in layers of clothing, but welcomed the sunlight warm on my cheeks.

Gerda and Elki frisked ahead, running back from time to time to urge the rest of us along. It was Berit's first time to set foot on the Roman road, and she stopped to gawk at its unexpected surface.

"I never seen nothin' like this afore," she exclaimed, stepping gingerly along on the stones.

"Just wait til you see the villa!" called Gerda, beckoning Berit to catch up. "We dance on the floor!"

"Lady Freawicca," said Lempi at my elbow, "will you be leading us in more rituals this spring?"

"I hope so, but that may depend on . . . news from across the whale road," I answered soberly.

Lempi looked at me in alarm. "Surely you wouldn't think of . . . leaving again?"

Before I could answer, Lise joined the conversation.

"I, for one, want to stay right here!" she declared. "We have a comfortable home, a cow that gives good milk, and Heinrich says . . ."

"Heinrich? What has he to do with us?" I asked, curious.

Cloak of Ashes

Lise flushed. "Lempi's not the only one who has an... admirer. Heinrich says he has been saving up to afford a wife, and he'd like that wife to be... me!" she concluded, almost defiantly.

"Well, well! It seems everyone is making their own plans," I said quietly.

"Oh, Lady Freawicca," said Lempi quickly, "We mean no disrespect. You are our mistress and our leader, but... Runa has a husband, and now Ginnlaug, so we thought..."

"You are quite right," I admitted with a smile. "When the time comes I will provide dowries for both of you, but I'll need your company a bit longer... at least until the situation in Denmark is clear."

"Thank you," chorused the women. "We can wait."

By this time we had reached the walnut trees that bordered the villa, their branches stark and bare against the sky.

"Almost there, Berit," called Gerda. "Look for tall white pillars."

"Pillars? What are them?" questioned Berit.

"Over there! See? A line of them shining in the sunlight."

All eyes turned to follow Gerda's pointing finger. The site looked quite different in the light of early spring. No green yet softened the few tendrils wound around the towering columns, and the villa floor was hidden under a layer of sodden leaves. And Wiswicca's staff? Had it survived the rigors of winter? As she ran ahead with Elki and Berit, I heard Gerda splashing in the spring.

"Lady! Come quick!" she shouted. "It's alive!"

Hurrying on ahead of Lise and Lempi, I found Gerda dancing excitedly around a small tree at the head of the spring, its delicate branches swollen with leaf buds.

"It's alive, it's alive!" she shouted gleefully. "Just as I told you before!"

What? Can it be Wiswicca's staff? This little tree? I paused to examine it more closely, stepping carefully to avoid the flowing water. It has the right height... and it's in the right place... but there were runes carved on Mother's staff: Kano, Berkana and Inguz. Peering at the trunk of the slender sapling, I made out faint but distinctive marks. Stooping and using my fingers I traced each one, revealing... Kano, Berkana and Inguz.

In wonder I looked up at the faces now peering at me.

"It's a second gift from the goddess," I breathed. "A sacred tree to complement the sacred spring. Thank you, Mother, thank you!"

In awe, Lise and Lempi stared at the little tree. Gerda reached out a tentative finger, then drew it back.

"What's wrong?" cried Berit. "You all look so ... scared."

"No, not scared," I said quietly, steadying myself on the slender trunk, "but amazed and filled with reverence, respectful and grateful for the honor bestowed on us by the Great Mother. This is a wonder! Wiswicca's staff of dead wood has become a living tree!"

"I can't wait to tell Lark!" exclaimed Gerda, her eyes shining.

"Yes, we will tell Lark and Gudrun and Runa and Ginnlaug and all the women of the village — and beyond," I exulted. "This will become a place of veneration for all women! Here the goddess has unmistakably revealed herself!"

On the walk back home we were silent, wrapped in our own thoughts. Gerda's puppy nipped playfully at our ankles for attention, until I asked Gerda to carry him the rest of the way, and he fell asleep in her arms. I too felt weary after the exhilaration of our discovery, but directed our steps toward the settlement, to spread the marvelous news.

Gudrun met us at her door, smiling as usual, but her face filled with surprise when she saw ours.

"What is it? What's happened?"

Drawing us inside, she called for Wilhelm, who came out from the byre, holding his hands out before him. Lark and Walthar were right behind him, looking very happy.

"We have a new calf!" announced Lark proudly.

"We have a new tree!" countered Gerda.

"What's this all about?" rumbled Wilhelm as he dipped his sticky hands in the water bucket and wiped them on a rough towel.

"Wiswicca's staff," I answered. "It's no longer a staff but a living tree. It has been transformed!"

Wilhelm's family stared at me as if I were demented.

"It's true!" burst out Lise, followed by a declaration from Lempi. "We all saw it — earlier this morning — at Wiswicca's well.'"

"By the gods," said Wilhelm, placing both hands on his hips, "nothing has been the same in Helmingham since you arrived, Lady Freawicca. First Wiswicca dies, then a spring suddenly appears, and now ... this!"

He did not look altogether happy as he spoke these words.

"What kind of tree is it, my lady?" asked Walthar mildly. "An oak?"

"No," I said, "it's an ash — like Yggdrasil, the world tree."

"Yggdrasil?" exclaimed Wilhelm. This reference seemed to make him even more uncomfortable. "Magic, that's what it is! A place of judgment! Beset with snakes and serpents! Meddling with magic is for the gods, not plain people like us!" He drew a deep breath, then blew it out loudly. "Lady Freawicca, I'd advise you not to tell anyone else about this!"

I could not believe what I was hearing.

"But Wilhelm, this is an honor, a gift! The goddess, the Earth Mother, is showing great favor to Helmingham! Gudrun," I exclaimed, turning to her, "help me make Wilhelm understand."

Her face, however, showed conflicting emotions.

"I don't know, my lady," she said slowly. "Wilhelm may be right." She paused to reflect. "You surely know that the ash tree is the last to leaf out in spring. For one to be budding now is ... unnatural!"

Dumbfounded and exasperated, I turned to leave.

"Oh, Lady, may I see the new calf?" begged Gerda.

"Father, may I show her?" begged Lark.

Wilhelm fixed me with a look of great intensity before he opened his mouth to speak.

"Lady Freawicca, when a calf is born I know where it comes from and how it got here. But a miraculous spring and a magic tree? Who can say if it's a gift from the gods or ... a curse? It's best to be cautious." Looking down at the two girls, he growled, "Go see the calf."

Squealing, Gerda scampered off with Lark to the byre at the far end of the longhouse. For an awkward moment the rest of us stood staring at each other.

"Lady Freawicca, will you and your women take a cup of ale?" asked Gudrun politely as Wilhelm and Walthar turned away.

"No, thank you. We are on our way home with water from Wiswicca's well. We stopped here because we wanted you to be the first to know of our ... discovery."

With difficulty I swallowed the lump of anger and disappointment that had risen in my throat.

"We will visit Runa and Ginnlaug next," I said stiffly, "but I will not speak to anyone else in the village about ... Wiswicca's staff-turned-tree." I paused. "Anyone who goes to visit the spring will see the tree for themselves."

"But not all will recognize the tree as Wiswicca's former staff," said Gudrun quietly. "Why, the shock of her sudden death had put that staff quite out of my mind," she declared.

"That is good to hear," said Wilhelm gruffly, returning to stand beside his wife. "The less said the better. We don't need strange folk flocking to Helmingham to gawk at this . . . this new wonder!" He nodded emphatically.

"I understand your position, Wilhelm, but I think that such a gift from the goddess should not be scorned," I countered.

For a moment Wilhelm looked troubled; then his face cleared.

"Lady Freawicca, you are already the keeper of the spring, so to speak. Why not become the guardian of this tree as well? You can see that no harm comes to it, and show it . . . due respect."

Gudrun beamed at this suggestion, and when Lark and Gerda emerged from the byre, they found us talking in quiet agreement.

Ginnlaug greeted us warmly at the door to the house she and Roald shared with Olaf and Runa.

"What a welcome surprise! Come in, come in!"

She ushered us to the hearth where Runa sat weaving a tablet braid beside the fire. We had left Elki outside with Berit.

"Don't get up." I smiled at Runa, noting that her belly now protruded noticeably beyond her waist.

"Ooh, can I touch the baby?" asked Gerda as she took off her cloak.

"Yes, but don't get him started kicking! He kept me awake most of the night," said Runa.

"I'll be careful," promised Gerda, placing her hands reverently on the swollen belly.

"What brings all of you out today?" asked Runa, setting aside her tablet.

"We have amazing news!" I cried, "But first I have a question for you. Do you expect a boy? Just now you spoke of your baby as a 'him'."

Runa laughed. "Olaf started doing it," she confessed, "and I picked up the habit, but it's too early to tell."

"Speaking of Olaf, where is he today? And Roald?" asked Lise, looking about the spare but neatly kept interior.

"They've gone out to see if the soil is still too wet for ploughing," said Ginnlaug. "Roald has more experience with farming, so he is ... assisting Olaf," she concluded proudly.

"It's hard for me to envision Olaf as a farmer," I observed dryly, "but we did not come to speak of farming. Friends, listen!"

As I told Runa and Ginnlaug of our wondrous discovery at Wiswicca's well, both reacted with delight and surprise.

"Amazing! That's miraculous!" cried Ginnlaug, clapping her hands excitedly.

"My lady, it's almost as if your mother is reaching out to you," observed Runa. "She is providing a place of solace and refreshment for you."

"I wish Wilhelm saw it that way," I said sourly. "He has advised me not to tell anyone in Helmingham about the tree, and even suggested that it might be evidence of dark magic!"

"Many fear what they do not understand," said Runa calmly. "Time will reveal if it has supernatural powers."

She was about to say more when we heard voices outside. Ginnlaug opened the door to reveal Olaf and Roald, scraping mud from their boots.

"We saw your thrall and knew you were here," exclaimed Olaf, striding forward to embrace me warmly yet respectfully.

"Good day, my lady," said Roald shyly, bobbing a sort of bow. "We've been inspecting the farmland you helped us acquire. Too wet to break ground yet, but we came back with some interesting finds. Look!"

He opened a grimy hand to display what looked like a curiously dome-shaped rock with a striped pattern on its sides.

"It's flint," he said, "only found in these parts, where it turns up in the soil. Folks here call this a 'fairy loaf' or a 'shepherd's crown.' They say there will always be enough to eat in a house where this charm is kept."

He grinned as he wiped the object against his tunic and handed it to Ginnlaug with a bow.

"For us. For good luck in this house and plenty to eat!"

"I too have a find," declared Olaf, reaching for a pouch inside his tunic.

Opening the drawstring, he upended the pouch, tumbling several long, slender needle-like objects onto the broad oak table-top.

"I believe Wilhelm collects these," said Olaf, holding up one of the dart-shaped cylinders. "He says some folks call them 'Thor's thunder-bolts,' but he thinks they are elf-shots that cause disease in cattle."

"He would!" I snorted. "Wilhelm seems to be suspicious of anything out-of-the-ordinary... such as Wiswicca's tree!"

"Wiswicca's tree?" echoed Olaf. "What tree is that?"

Quickly I told him of our morning discovery and of Wilhelm's reaction. Olaf nodded sagely.

"Wilhelm is a good man. I can understand his caution. The chief of a village must consider the safety and well-being of everyone in it."

My conscience smote me at these words, as I thought of the disaster I had envisioned in Denmark and its possible consequences for my own people in Helmingham. Here were Olaf and Runa, settled and with a baby on the way, and Roald and Ginnlaug, happy to be together at last...

Feeling a sudden need to consult my runes about what might lie in all our futures, I spoke.

"It is time for me — for us — to go."

"Lady Freawicca, I meant no offense," said Olaf, raising his eyebrows. Runa too looked startled.

"What is it, my lady? What's wrong? I can tell by your face that you are troubled."

I paused, pondering how much to reveal, yet these were two of my oldest and dearest friends.

"While at Rendlesham," I confessed, "a vision came to me revealing disaster in Hrolf's kingdom. Until that vision is confirmed or dispelled, my mind is not at ease."

Runa and Olaf exchanged troubled looks.

"My lady, how may we help you?" whispered Runa.

I shook my head. "Until the seas are once again suitable for travel, we can only wait — but I intend to consult the runes again. Perhaps they will reveal more."

Back at the hut I went directly to the herb-drying room to be alone with my runes. First I spread a white cloth on the table where we sorted and tied herbs. Breathing in the fragrance of the hanging bundles to calm my spirit, I closed my eyes and reached into my rune bag. Immediately a single rune met my trembling fingers. Drawing it forth, I laid it on the cloth and opened my eyes.

Raido. Reversed.

Raido, the journey rune ... but if reversed, not a journey. What could this mean? I pondered possible interpretations: is another journey required? Is a journey forbidden? Would it be a journey from Angle-land to Denmark or a journey from Denmark to Angle-land? Would it be a physical journey or a journey of the spirit? As I sat with head in hands, my mind busy with possibilities, I heard a soft knock on the door frame. Lifting my head, I saw Gerda silhouetted in the dim light, holding a pitcher.

"Water from your mother's well," she said, carefully extending the heavy jug. "I thought it might ... help."

"Dear child." I rose to take the jug from her. "Come in. You are ever mindful of my comfort and well-being."

Spying the rune lying on the cloth, Gerda eyed it suspiciously as I took a deep draught of the cold, clear water.

"Don't do it!" she said suddenly. "Don't go and leave us again!"

"Ah, you remember your rune lessons," I said approvingly as I put down the pitcher, feeling refreshed.

"Yes," she said soberly, "I do remember the journey rune ... and I don't like it!"

"Did you also notice that it's upside-down?" I queried. "Perhaps this time it means that someone else will make the journey — coming to us."

Gerda nodded vigorously.

"That's better. I hope they come soon — and 'set your mind at ease' as you said earlier."

"So do I, little one," I said fervently, "So do I."

Barely a month later, a loud knock on the door of our hut commanded everyone's attention. We had just finished our morning porridge and Berit was clearing away the bowls. Lempi raised her hand to her throat, and Lise jumped up, spilling her mug of milk. Gerda's eyes were wide as we stared at each other in turn, all seized by a premonition of misfortune.

"I'll go," I whispered, rising from the table.

Is this the summons, the sign, the answer to the riddle of my vision? As I covered the distance from the table to the door, I held my breath. Slowly I lifted the bar and pulled open the door. There stood ... Wilhelm.

"Good morrow, Lady Freawicca. You have visitors — in the great hall — people from Denmark."

Wordless, I nodded and reached for my cloak beside the door. Gerda scrambled from the table to join me, followed by Lise and Lempi, grabbing for wraps. Silently we followed Wilhelm down the path to the settlement. As we walked, my ears were filled with the sounds of birds, blithely cooing, chattering, whistling and trilling in celebration of spring — a sharp contrast to the cold fear that gripped my heart.

Inside the great hall a fire had been lit, its warmth bathing our faces as we entered. Squinting, I searched for figures in the semi-darkness. A small group at the front table rose and turned to face us — only four people: two men and two women.

"Lady Freawaru?" called a familiar voice.

"Drifa? Is that you?"

Hurrying forward I walked into her outstretched arms. As we embraced, she sobbed out my name.

"Frea, oh Frea, Bodvar is dead! And Father is gone!"

Another hand touched my back as a bitter voice declared, "Svipdag is dead too — all our men are dead, murdered by Skuld, that evil witch!"

Shuddering to hear that name, I opened my arms to include Skur in our embrace. For a time we three stood locked together, swaying in our shared grief. When we disengaged, Drifa and Skur were staring at me.

"Lady, what's happened to you? You are . . . changed," exclaimed Skur, reaching out to touch a lock of my hair.

"I saw the massacre in a vision," I whispered. "It happened at Yule, did it not?"

Drifa and Skur nodded mutely.

"All winter I have waited for news, dreading what I might hear, fearing the worst. Now I know my vision was true, and my heart breaks for you both."

Spontaneously we again embraced.

"Lady Freawaru," said Skur, looking me full in the face, "We need you! You can defy the sorceress, you can counteract her powers, you can help us reclaim our homeland!"

Now the two men stepped forward. I recognized Harig, the shipmaster who had brought my own group to Helmingham, and Vögg, one of King Hrolf's men.

"Lady Freawaru," said Harig, bowing respectfully, "I brought these ladies to Helmingham at their request, along with several other survivors from the massacre, including Vögg, here."

Vögg knelt and took my hand to kiss it.

"Lady Freawaru, I was not able to save my king, but I promise you I will fight to the death to avenge him!"

"Rise, Vögg. We have much to discuss before any action can be taken. I should tell you," I said, addressing all four, "that here I am called 'Freawicca,' after my late mother, Wiswicca."

"Oh," gasped Drifa. "Harig had told us that you finally found your mother... but you have already lost her?"

"Yes, she too is gone," I gulped. "Loss has visited each of us."

My women, who had stood in respectful silence a short distance away, now came forward to greet our visitors. The first words out of Gerda's mouth were directed at Harig.

"Is Hans safe? Did he come with you?"

"He is safe, at home with his mother in Frisia—to which others fled after the massacre at Roskilde."

"Oh," frowned Gerda, "then he won't get to see my new puppy."

"Not this time. Perhaps on another trip."

Wilhelm cleared his throat to get our attention.

"Lady Freawicca, would you like your guests to be lodged in the great hall? If so, I'll have arrangements made."

"Why yes, Wilhelm, that would be most fitting. Thank you for your thoughtfulness."

As he left, I turned back to our visitors. "We have much to talk about, but first I must introduce you to a very important person you've never met: my brother."

"Brother?" echoed Skur, her mouth agape. "Then you are not the last of the Scylding line?"

"No. I have a younger brother who is very much alive, living right here in Helmingham. After we get you all settled, I will bring him here to meet with you. I think you will find his help more useful than mine."

On my way to Erik's house I heard only the cawing of carrion crows. I found him inside his longhouse, getting ready to shave.

"What do you think?" he asked as I entered, "Should I take off the whole beard in preparation for warmer weather?"

"Brother, put down your blade. We have newly-arrived refugees from Denmark in the great hall. Heorot has fallen. King Hrolf is dead."

Erik paused, taking in the news as he put down his knife. Then he gave a whoop and rushed to lift me straight up into the air, spinning me with surprising strength.

"At last, sister, you bring good news!" he cried, looking up at me.

"Yes and no," I replied as he set me back down on my feet. "Two of the survivors are Hrolf's daughters — and my friends. They will not take kindly to any gloating over Hrolf's death — nor will I!"

A pang of grief suddenly assailed me as I thought of the courtly figure who had treated me with such tenderness and respect, the generous man who had given me Sunbeorht, the king who had asked me to become his queen...

"What's the matter with you?" growled Erik. "This is what we have been waiting for!"

"What *you* have been waiting for," I corrected. "I have no wish to return to Heorot, but vengeance must be taken, and the kingdom restored to its rightful rulers."

"The Scyldings!" said Erik with grim satisfaction. "On that we can agree. Don't worry," he added, "I will try to be respectful of your grieving friends."

I urged Erik to change into his finest tunic before meeting our visitors, and I took a shears to personally trim his beard.

"Ashamed of me?" he muttered as I held his chin steady.

"No, of course not," I retorted. "I just want you to look your best — to look... kingly." Mentally I pictured how Hrolf had looked, tall and regal in a gold-embroidered tunic.

"That will come later — after the fighting," said Erik. "If I can destroy the witch and regain my kingdom, I will look kingly enough!"

"You will need help to do that!" I observed dryly, laying aside the shears. "Do not underestimate Skuld's powers! But come — let's go to the great hall. They are waiting to meet you."

Erik straightened his shoulders. "Do I look kingly enough now?"

I nodded.

When we entered, Wilhelm was standing near the doorway with several of his men, including Frans and Heinrich."

"So, Erik, you are the son of a king!" trumpeted Heinrich. "And all these years we never knew!"

"Lord Erik, you have my backing," said Frans, extending a hand.

"Before anyone rushes into anything," declared Wilhelm, "we need to hear the full story of what happened at . . . Roskilde, is it? I propose we let our visitors speak first."

"Indeed!" said Erik, immediately striding forward to greet the group standing near the head table.

"Good morrow, lords and ladies," he said, bowing in turn to Drifa, Skur, Harig and Vögg. "Welcome to Helmingham. I am Hrethric, son of Hrothgar and brother to Lady Freawaru. I was cousin to your late father and king. My sympathy for your losses."

Astonished at such a speech from my usually laconic brother, I hastened to join him and introduce each of our visitors.

"Have you taken bread?" asked Erik, gracious as any host.

"Yes, thank you," said Drifa. "Wilhelm's wife saw to that."

"Then I propose we all be seated," said Erik smoothly, "and listen to your account of the horrendous . . . and heartrending . . . events at the court of King Hrolf."

He beckoned to Wilhelm and his men. When everyone was seated, Erik asked, "Who will begin?"

"I will," said Harig, "for I saw the preparation for the battle, though I did not realize that's what it was at the time. It was near the end of the day and I had just come up from the harbor when I saw Skuld and her husband Hjorvard arrive with many wagons. I supposed they contained the tribute due to King Hrolf at Yule, but as was later revealed, they contained men, armor and weapons. Tents were pitched outside the stronghold, tents which were large and long and strangely outfitted. Skuld's tent was black as midnight and I caught a glimpse inside of a tall platform like a scaffold. I thought this strange, but had business to attend to elsewhere and shortly returned to my ship."

Now Vögg picked up the story.

"King Hrolf and most of his champions were in the hall that evening, drinking deeply at the Yule feast, when Hjalti burst in to sound the alarm.

'Wake up, my lord!' he shouted at King Hrolf. 'Your sister Skuld with no small army has circled your fortress!' To the champions he cried, 'Rise up! Arm yourselves!'

All leapt up, reaching for war gear. King Hrolf too sprang to his feet and without a trace of fear shouted, 'Let us now take the finest drink to be had, to be cheerful before battle. Let us strive to make our bravery so superior that it will never be forgotten. Vögg! Go! Tell Skuld and Hjorvard that we will drink to our own satisfaction before going forth to receive their 'tribute'."

Vögg's eyes filled with tears and he gulped back a sob.

"I carried out my king's orders. Skuld, that shameless deceiver, did have the decency to admit that King Hrolf her brother was a man like no other and it was a shame to lose such men. Nevertheless, she said, what had been set in motion by the gods must go on to its fated end."

Skur, who had been listening with bowed head, now raised it.

"I was in the back of the hall with Drifa when Svipdag and Bodvar and the others donned their armor. We heard the first clash of arms as the men rushed outside, and watched in horror through a crack in the wall as helmets were smashed, mail coats split, and men thrown from their horses. Suddenly, a great bear appeared, advancing in front of King Hrolf's troops."

A bear? Like the one I saw in my dream? With Drifa crying over it?

"The bear used its weight to crush Skuld's men and horses; it killed as many men with one paw as five of the king's champions. No one in Skuld's army could stand against this wondrous beast!"

"Ach!" cried Drifa, a crazed look in her eyes. "If only Hjalti had let him sleep! That bear was Bodvar, in a trance in the king's chamber while he sent his animal double to fight! But Hjalti ran back to find him and cursed him for cowardice, so Bodvar needs must go — though he told Hjalti 'I can now offer the king far less support than before you woke me'."

"Alas, it was indeed so," muttered Vögg. "The disappearance of the great bear gave heart to Skuld's forces — which included draugar, revenants, creatures from the dead who could not be killed, but rose up again after being cut down!"

Vögg shuddered.

"Skuld besieged the king's shield wall with a storm of enchantments, until finally ... it fell. King Hrolf died gloriously amidst his champions."

We sat in silence, absorbing this tale of treachery and disaster. I was gripping Drifa's hand so tightly my knuckles were white. With tears coursing down my cheeks, I rose to deliver words of praise for my cousin Hrolf, once king of Denmark — and my would-be husband.

"A light has gone out in the northern world," I declared, "but King Hrolf and his men will always be remembered for their courage — as Skuld will be for her wickedness."

"Svipdag once told me," said Skur looking up, "that father and his champions were fated to be gathered to Valhalla, that Odin had marked them as the ablest warriors to fight beside him at Ragnarok. He was proud when he said it." She smiled faintly. "Since Svipdag had only one good eye, he sometimes likened himself to Odin."

"Odin!" I spat out the name. "That faithless dissembler who grants favors with one hand and takes life with the other!"

"My lady, it does no good to curse the gods," came Wilhelm's calm voice. Turning to our guests, he asked, "What may we do to benefit you most?"

Before any of them could answer, Erik rose to speak.

"As son of the former king Hrothgar, I have a claim to the throne of Denmark. But first this fiend, Skuld, must be overcome. For that we will need men, ships, armor and weapons. I, for one, pledge my support — should you ladies agree to accept it," he concluded, bowing to Skur and Drifa.

They looked at each other.

"We have also sent messengers to the brothers of Bodvar," said Drifa, "to Elk-Frodi and Thorir Hound's Foot, King of the Gauts."

"Likewise to Hrolf's mother, Queen Yrsa in Uppsala," added Skur.

"Surely you don't expect help from the Swedes after what Hrolf did to King Eadgils!" I burst out.

"King Eadgils no longer lives; he died after a fall from his horse," said Drifa quietly.

"Indeed?" I intoned. "Much has happened in the past months! But, tell me... were you able to give proper burial to the men who fell in this fateful battle? Did Skuld have the decency to allow it?"

Harig cleared his throat.

"I myself was part of the group tasked to erect funeral pyres, but we were not able to build memorial mounds over them because of the frozen ground."

A voice which I recognized as belonging to Frans called out, "How did you escape from Roskilde and come here?"

Vögg lifted his head.

"Skuld's army, along with her husband Hjorvard, was completely destroyed — save for a few shirkers. She now relies on her enchantments and supernatural creatures, her rabble and ruffians, to maintain a shaky control. Fortunately we were able to slip out of the harbor on Harig's ship during the night."

"Who else is onboard now?" I asked.

"Only my usual crew," answered Harig. "We left the widows and children who came with us in Frisia. Hedvig took charge of finding homes for them all."

"Did you stop at Rendlesham on your way here?" asked Wilhelm.

"No, we came directly to Helmingham," said Drifa, "for Harig said that this was the place where we would find Lady Freawaru."

"I think," said Wilhelm slowly, "that Rædwald should soon be told what has happened in Denmark. He may have an interest in the matter."

Erik nodded. "I will take the news to him myself, while our guests here recover from their long sea journey. I am sure my sister will see to their comfort."

He cast a sidelong glance at me. What is Erik scheming? Does he think to persuade Rædwald to back him in reclaiming his kingdom? Or does he expect me to finance his attempt?

"It will take time to gather the forces you have called upon," Erik was saying to Skur and Drifa. "There are also men here in Helmingham eager to make a name for themselves — and I am willing to lead them!" Erik's face shone with a kind of dark joy.

"Hold on, hold on," said Wilhelm, getting to his feet. "Planting time is almost upon us — the busiest and most important time of the year. We can't afford to have all our young men running off to fight in a foreign war!"

"All of them won't be needed, Wilhelm," came Erik's easy reply. "The twelve men who accompanied my sister to these shores were once the bodyguard of Beowulf himself. They would be more than ready to take on this challenge!"

Now I too rose to speak.

"Physical strength alone will not avail against Skuld and her enchantments," I cautioned. "She must be taken by surprise if she is to be captured — a feat which will take careful planning."

"Oh, Freaw," exclaimed Drifa, rising to her feet. "So you will help us!"

"I will do what I can, but I am not going back to Denmark," I said firmly. "My place is here now. I must carry on the work my mother left for me. No, don't despair," I continued, seeing Drifa's face. "Powerful forces have arisen here in Helmingham which may help us counteract Skuld's dark magic."

Drifa and Skur stared at me, their eyes full of questions. Behind them I saw Wilhelm lift his head and nod at me with a look of understanding and consent.

"When you've both had a chance to rest, I will take you to a remarkable place sacred to the goddess," I said. "There we will seek guidance."

All this time Gerda and my women had been waiting back in our hut, eager for news of what was transpiring in the great hall. When I returned with Drifa and Skur, they were greeted warmly and given a brief tour of our modest home.

"What's been decided?" asked Lise when we had all returned to the hearth. "About Skuld?"

"Nothing yet — at least nothing definite," I replied. "I thought Drifa and Skur should visit the villa first, to see the gifts of the goddess."

"Oh, may I go with you?" entreated Gerda. "I could carry the jug if you want to bring back water."

"Yes, you may, sparrow. Lise, Lempi — please prepare food for our guests while we're gone. I don't want to further burden Gudrun."

"As you wish, my lady," said Lempi.

On the walk to the villa I gave Skur and Drifa a detailed account of events on the night of Mother's death. They listened with downcast eyes, perhaps recalling their own recent losses. Both women were initially startled by walking on a road made of stone, but when we came to the ruined villa with its gleaming pillars and paved floor, they were astonished.

"Who were these Romans you speak of?" queried Skur. "Surely they must have used strong magic to create such wonders."

"As to that I cannot say, but I have witnessed two wonders in this place which could only have come from the goddess herself, from the Earth Mother. Behold! Here is the water which first sprang forth when

Mother's staff was thrust into the earth . . . and here is the staff itself, transformed into a living tree!"

Awestruck, Drifa and Skur stared at the flowing stream and the tree which stood at its head.

"Wonders indeed," murmured Drifa. "Amazing marvels."

"This is a place of power!" announced Skur. "I feel it!"

"Lady!" marveled Gerda, setting down her jug to reach up into the leafy branches of the young ash. "See how it's grown?"

Indeed the tree was at least a head taller and it had filled out remarkably since our last visit. For a time we all stood simply gazing at it, as Drifa and Skur absorbed the magic of the place. A linnet swooped down to perch on one of the slender branches, then flew away, taking our gaze with it.

"But Lady Freawaru," said Drifa, like one emerging from a trance and wrinkling her brow, "how can these things — marvelous as they are — help us fight against Skuld?"

"I have been thinking about that, and I have some ideas," I responded. "With her army mostly destroyed, Skuld must resort to her black arts for defense. She will be casting runes to divine the future, and dispatching her creatures to gather information — all to warn her if opposition threatens. Why, even now some dark raven might be winging its way over the seas to spy on us!"

Gerda glanced up ueasily, then turned to me.

"Lady, the other birds would tell me if that happened," she said earnestly.

"Thank you, child. We are blessed by your special gifts," I assured her. "But we won't sit passively and wait. No! I propose we weave a counter spell against her enchantments, a spell of binding designed to block her spells, to blind her sight, so that she is not aware of the forces coming to envelop and destroy her!"

Three mouths gaped at me as I finished this declaration.

"Can you do such a thing?" quavered Skur.

"I am going to try!" I said firmly.

In preparation for weaving the binding spell, I cut several thin strips of green bark from the lowest branch of Wiswicca's tree and plaited them together to form a tiny, nest-like basket. Drifa and Skur watched with keen interest, periodically taking sips of spring water from Gerda's jug.

"Into this web I will place three runes, also cut from the ash bark: Nauthiz for constraint, Hagalaz for disruption and Isa for standstill."

Gerda nodded solemnly, recognizing the binding nature of the runes I had named.

"I will soak the basket in water from Wiswicca's well and bury it during the dark of the moon. Thereafter I will chant over it each night, calling on the goddess to block Skuld's spells and blind her sight."

The three watched in silence as I used my knife to incise each rune on a piece of bark and slip it inside the tiny receptacle.

"Lady Freawaru," said Drifa suddenly. "Would you have any use for that kerchief of Skuld's? I brought it with me on the journey — in case you might need it."

"Yes! Perfect! Where is it now?"

"Back in the hall, in my sea chest," she answered, a smile spreading across her face.

"We'll get it tonight. A wonderful idea, Drifa! Together we will overcome this evil sorceress... despite her great powers!"

Since Drifa and Skur were so directly involved in the conflict with Skuld, I invited them to join me in weaving the spell against her. Working in the herb-drying room of my hut, the two sisters and I took turns tearing Skuld's kerchief into long strips of cloth, then winding them tightly around the ash bark basket containing the binding runes. As we worked, we chanted:

> *Skuld shall not see.*
> *Blind shall she be.*
> *We blank her eyes*
> *Against surprise.*
> *Draw the mask tight*
> *To cover her sight.*

When the ball of cloth and bark was finished, we packed it inside a clay jar, then filled the jar and sealed it with mud from Wiswicca's spring. Now we had only to wait a few nights for the moon's disappearance.

We buried the jar in the garden at the base of Wiswicca's apple tree, so as to have easy access for my nightly incantations. It was a cool spring night, but I felt no chill as we worked together. Once, looking up through the still bare branches, I saw the stars of Freyja's Girdle hanging high above us.

'Freyja, dear Freyja, hear us. Wiswicca, Mother, hear us,' I breathed to the sky. One star seemed to flicker in response — or was it merely a trick of my old eyes? In unison we chanted again the spell of binding:

> *Skuld shall not see.*
> *Blind shall she be.*
> *We blank her eyes*
> *Against surprise.*
> *Draw the mask tight*
> *To cover her sight.*

Chapter Twenty-One
Giving Birth

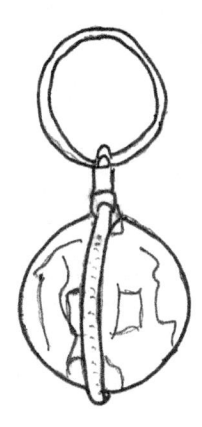

Crystal ball from Chessel Down, Isle of Wight. Found in graves of upper class women in Kent. British Museum.

On a fresh morning in May — the month Gudrun called "three milkings" — we bid farewell to Erik, to eleven of our young men and to our visitors from Denmark. Hawthorns were now in bloom, their white blossoms scenting the air. Lark had brought a flowering branch to our door the day before — 'for good fortune,' she'd said. The morning felt full of promise, but also edged with the pain of parting — sharp as the thorns on the hawthorn tree.

As Anton had predicted, Olaf and Roald chose to remain in Helmingham with their wives, but the rest of the men seized this opportunity to regain their reputation as warriors. Erik and Alf captained my newly-built long ship, with Erik's stallion onboard as cargo. The ship was my contribution to the enterprise, for I felt that I must fully support my only brother, now almost the last of the Scyldings. Harig's crew and his cargo of Danish passengers was augmented by several young thanes from Rendlesham, who had obtained permission from King Rædwald to join in the attempt to liberate Roskilde

On the night before their departure, we discussed strategy in the great hall. I stressed the importance of surprise, advising the men to take Skuld from behind and cover her head immediately so she could not use her eyes or mouth. At this suggestion the young men stole cautious glances at each other, but Vögg spoke up immediately.

"I will do it, my lady, if I have the chance. I would gladly die to entrap the killer of my king."

"You're a brave man, Vögg, and loyal unto death. It is my hope that the spell I've been casting will keep Skuld in ignorance of your approach, and give you an advantage. But, you must act quickly! Bind her, muzzle her, shackle her securely!"

Vögg nodded somberly, then croaked, "How does one ... kill ... such a witch?"

"Others may have a say in that," I observed, "since Hrolf's mother and two brothers are among the avengers. But, after Skuld is dead, dismember her body and bury the bones in far places, that she may never return to haunt the living."

I had a sudden vivid recollection of the extreme measures taken at Heorot to dispose of the Grendel monster's head — cut off long years ago by Beowulf.

Vögg nodded again, grimly. "It shall be done, my lady."

Now, as the boats slid away on the tide, bearing my former companions, my heart went with them. Whether or not they were successful in re-taking Roskilde, I doubted that I would ever see any of them again. Would I never again take Drifa's soft, plump hand in mine? Or feel the pressure of Skur's slender embrace? Was I sending these women — these sisters — back into certain danger, even ... death? As I watched their ship recede, pulled inexorably by the outgoing tide, my heart felt as heavy as the clay jar buried in the garden.

As usual, Gerda was at my side to comfort me.

"Don't be sad, Lady. I'm still here," she said softly, taking my hand.

"Yes, little sparrow, and I am grateful," I said as I squeezed her hand gently. "Let's go visit Sunbeorht to see how that foal in her belly is developing."

"Oh, yes! Let's!" echoed Gerda, stepping away and pulling on my hand.

So we set off for Runa's house, where Sunbeorht was stabled. Runa herself had grown quite large, and we suspected she might be carrying twins — a possible danger in a woman her age, but one we did not speak of. Wilhelm had appointed Olaf as his steward to replace Erik, and Olaf was happy to be given this responsibility. He and Roald had come to the harbor to see our friends' departure, but had quickly returned to the fields to supervise and assist with the planting. I could hear shouts in the distance where thralls with sticks were scaring off the birds that followed the seed-sowers.

Earlier, special plots of woad and madder had been planted for use as dyes, and flaxseed for our linen had long since been put in the ground. The late spring had delayed ploughing and planting, so now our men were working to catch up, mindful of the need to sow when the moon was waxing.

Gerda and I stopped first to greet Runa and Ginnlaug, both visibly relieved that their husbands had not gone off with Erik and the other men. Runa was having back pains, for which I prescribed a shaving of dried mandrake root boiled in water, or a tincture of ginger.

I had cautioned Runa earlier to avoid salt during her pregnancy, remembering Hygd's terrible death and my suspicion that salty pork had contributed to it.

"What I crave most," she sighed, "are fresh greens. How I'd love a big mouthful of garden greens!"

I considered. "Nothing in the garden is ready yet, but my women might be able to find some young nettles for you to eat or brew in a tea."

"That sounds good," said Runa. "I'm getting rather tired of chamomile and peppermint — though they do help with the nausea and vomiting."

"Vomiting? So late in your pregnancy? That is worrisome..."

As my eyes roved from Runa's very pale face to her distended abdomen, a buried memory surfaced: Twins. Dead. Born too early. Strangled by their cords. Shivering and shaking my head, I said huskily, "As soon as I get back home I'll send Lise and Lempi out to search for nettles. In the meantime, try taking small bits of food at frequent intervals — to see if you can keep it down. You must get nourishment both for yourself and your babies!"

There: the word: "babies." Runa smiled weakly but said nothing.

Sunbeorht whinnied her pleasure as Gerda held up a dried apple, and delicately ate it from her palm.

"You're looking well, my girl," I murmured, stroking her soft muzzle. "Your coat is shiny and I see that you have clean straw. Mari is taking good care of you."

"How long before she foals, Lady?" asked Gerda, climbing up on the gated partition to reach Sunbeorht's head and give it a pat.

"Erik estimated two more months — about the same time Runa's baby is due," I said.

Erik had also told me something else: the secret to his skill at drawing and jading horses. He had taken me aside after a visit to assess Sunbeorht's pregnancy, and entrusted me with his secret methods.

"When the foal is born," he said, "you must immediately remove the milt from its tongue before it can swallow it. Once dried and powdered, this milt can be mixed with a drawing oil and used as an allurement to attract or 'draw' a horse. It is the horse's keen sense of smell that enables one to control it."

"What? Then all that business about lifting the leg and knocking on the hoof was just . . . for show?" I asked indignantly.

Erik smirked and nodded.

"Yes. Now, to do the opposite — to stop the horse literally in its tracks — substitute something with an obnoxious smell which you hide on your person."

"Well! So it wasn't magic after all." I frowned, somewhat disappointed.

"And is all your so-called magic really magic?" countered Erik shrewdly. "I doubt it. Making the beholder believe in what you've done is the only real trick."

I stared at my brother with a new appreciation of his insight, and — for the first time — thought 'I will miss you.'

"Lady, may I help Mari brush Sunbeorht's coat?"

Gerda's eager face drew me back to the present.

"Of course you may. I'll visit a bit longer with Runa and Ginnlaug."

Every night before retiring I pronounced the binding spell over the jar buried in the garden, fervently praying that the spell would do its work. I knew it might be many months before news from Denmark reached us again. In the meantime, repeating the ritual was all I could do, and it gave me a measure of comfort.

During the day I was drawn outdoors to work in the garden with Lise and Lempi. Besides the herbs needed for cooking and medicine, we had planted a large variety of vegetables: peas, beans, carrots, parsnips, turnips, leeks, onions, cabbage, lettuce, summer squash — and two vegetables new to me: radishes and cucumbers. We were growing extra food for Runa's household, so all the work would not fall on Ginnlaug's shoulders.

Runa had taken to her bed — a fine, wide bed with a high headboard. Olaf had asked Walthar to construct it out of oak using my high bed as a model, the bed where I once slept with Beowulf. Alone in her bed Runa slept — or tried to sleep, for the heavy weight pressing on her insides made it difficult to find any comfortable position.

The separate bed chamber also spared her from the nausea induced by cooking smells. Each day I sent Gerda over with a pitcher of fresh water from Wiswicca's well, for Runa had found that she could tolerate only very cold water. Her problems caused me considerable anxiety, and I started at every knock on the door, sure that it must be a call for help.

Although Midsummer was still more than a moon away, I began to prepare my birthing bag, stocking it with clean linen cloths and several small packets of herbs — including chamomile to relax and soothe the birth canal after delivery, and a tincture of red raspberry leaves mixed with yarrow — from Old Elsa's garden in Breccasberg — in case of excessive bleeding. Last I added a ball of rawhide string and a pair of small shears. Thus I was prepared when the knock came, late one evening.

It was Roald, breathing heavily, his eyes round as the moon rising overhead.

"Come quick, my lady! Ginnlaug says to tell you that the wa ... wa ... water has broken and she's in pain — Runa, I mean. Olaf doesn't know what to do!"

I reached for my cloak. "Don't worry, Roald, this just means that the baby is on its way ... a bit early. My bag is ready; here, you may carry it."

I handed down the leather bag from its peg by the door and called to the others in the next room, who were laughing and preparing for bed.

"Lise, Lempi, Gerda, I'm off to Runa's with Roald. The baby is coming."

Bare feet hit the floorboards and three excited faces appeared in the door frame.

"Can I go with you, Lady?"

"Do you need our help?"

"No, and no, but thank you. I probably won't be home until late morning—if then. You three get a good night's sleep. Runa will need your help later." Especially if she has twins, I added to myself.

When Roald and I reached their house, we found Olaf supporting Runa as she sat up on the bed, gasping and panting. Ginnlaug stood beside them, rubbing Runa's back.

"When did the pains begin?" I asked, removing my cloak.

"Shortly after the evening meal," answered Ginnlaug, "but they were far apart and Runa thought it might be false labor. Then, later, her water broke and we sent for you."

"Un...tie, un...tie," grunted Runa.

"Untie what? What is it you want?" I touched her sweaty forehead, lifting a strand of dark hair matted over one eye.

"Knots...all knots," she gasped.

"Ohhh, yes, of course. Olaf, that's something you and Roald can do. Go through the house, the byre, the stable, looking for knots—in clothing, harness, anything—and untie them all. It will ease Runa's mind," I added, seeing Olaf's dubious look. I well remembered that Runa had insisted on performing this service for me when I was giving birth to Inga—a remnant from Runa's Finnish upbringing.

As Olaf and Roald hurried out of the bedchamber, I turned to Ginnlaug. "Put water to boil and get out several bowls for mixing herbs. I should have everything else we'll need in my bag."

Next I turned to Runa. "Now, dear friend, let's take a look at you."

Parting her legs and lifting her nightshift, I made a brief but careful examination.

"Only slightly enlarged," I reported to her. "We have a long wait ahead of us. In the meantime, let's get you washed up."

Opening my bag, I pulled out a stack of clean linen towels and several packets of herbs, all the time talking in a conversational tone to distract Runa from the spasms that gripped her at irregular intervals.

"I'm going to crush thyme, comfrey and plantain together and add them to boiled water to make a cleanser. And these towels were bleached in the sunlight, so all will be clean and safe to receive your baby."

She nodded and gasped out, "Th . . . thank you," then frowned and squirmed.

"Do you need to pass water?"

When she nodded, I called Ginnlaug, and together we eased Runa off the bed to walk to the waste bucket in the corner, then helped her return.

"Ginnlaug, I can use those bowls now, and the boiled water."

When she reappeared with the bowls, I used one in which to crush the herbs, adding them to the basin of hot water that came next, using Runa's low clothes chest as a tabletop.

"When this cools a bit, I'll bathe your groin area," I told Runa, "and we'll put fresh towels under you. Everything looks fine," I assured her. "By morning you will be a mother."

As the night wore on, Ginnlaug and I took turns counting to measure the intervals between contractions, while each of us gripped one of Runa's hands. After one particularly arduous series, I had an idea.

"Olaf!" I called, raising my voice to be heard over Roald's snores.

His face appeared in the doorway almost instantly.

"Is something wrong?"

"No, but I need your belt — and Roald's belt. Bring them, please."

He reappeared shortly, belts in hand.

"Fasten one to each bed post," I instructed, "so that Runa can pull on them as she bears down."

Olaf did as I directed, bending low to brush Runa's sweaty brow with his lips as he placed a belt end in each hand.

"Courage, dear wife," he murmured. "I love you dearly. Courage."

"Go back and rest if you can," I counselled Olaf. "The baby is not yet ready to come."

Runa herself dozed occasionally, exhausted by her effort to bring the baby forth, although the belt straps did help her during each push. Ginnlaug prepared chamomile tea, and I set out my tincture of yarrow and red raspberry, hoping it would not be needed. As we waited, thoughts of my first meeting with Runa sprang up. Years and years ago at Eaglesgard, she — a mere slip of a serving girl — had offered me lingonberries, saying they were good for a woman with child, though I had not yet revealed my pregnancy. We had faced so many challenges together, shared so many joys and sorrows... Dear Runa, dear friend, ever faithful, ever loving... May the goddess help me deliver you safely of a healthy child.

Toward morning Runa's contractions grew more frequent and more intense, and I knew delivery was near.

"Wait, wait, hold back a bit," I cautioned "Slow and easy, so you don't tear yourself."

"I'm... I'm... trying," gasped Runa through gritted teeth.

"The crown — I can see the crown of the head!" I cried. "Easy now — one long, slow push."

With a tremendous effort Runa bore down, her arms taut on the belt straps.

"Uhhhhh..."

The baby's head emerged, face down. Grasping it carefully in both hands, I eased out first one shoulder, then another.

"One more push, Runa, one final push!"

"Uhhhhh...!"

The whole baby shot out into my arms, and I turned it over, sticky and slippery with blood and mucus. It was very small, but fully developed.

"It's a boy, Runa, a boy. You have a son."

"Olaf," she mouthed, "tell Olaf."

"In just a moment. Ginnlaug, I'll need your help with the cord. Please hold the baby while I see to it." Lifting the cord, I tied it off close to the baby's navel and again near the mother, then used my shears to snip the interval, severing the baby from his mother. The infant did not wail, but blinked and rolled its eyes, its tiny mouth opening and closing as if saying farewell to the body which had nurtured and sheltered it for so many moons.

"I know you'll want me to bury the cord later," I said to Runa as I took the infant and laid it tenderly on her breast.

"And the afterbirth," she croaked hoarsely, reaching out to take her new son in her arms.

The afterbirth did not immediately reveal itself, so after a short time I placed a warm towel on Runa's belly and began to massage it gently. Something under my hands did not feel... right.

"Runa, I think there is another baby in your womb," I said quietly. "You may have more work to do — as we both suspected earlier."

Runa's eyes grew wide, but she smiled weakly. Just then Olaf entered the bedchamber, his eyes shining as he saw the infant on Runa's breast.

"A boy! A boy, my dear! Just as you said, just as..."

"She's not finished yet, Olaf," I interrupted. "I suggest you and Ginnlaug take your son into the next room and clean him up, while I attend to the second birth."

Dazed but happy, Olaf carefully picked up his son, who gave a little cough and began to wail.

"There, there, little one," crooned Ginnlaug. "We'll soon have you back with your mother."

As soon as they were gone, I returned my attention to the afterbirth. A trickle of blood announced the release of the birth sac, followed by an additional length of cord, and finally, the sac itself.

"Good, good," I breathed in relief. "Now let's see what else we have to attend to." Setting the sac aside, I peered again into the birth canal.

"It's still quite enlarged, Runa, and I see something near the opening ... I think it's a ... foot."

A foot? A breech delivery? Dear goddess, guide my hands! And this foot looks strangely deformed, almost flat!

Carefully grasping what appeared to be the ankle of a foot, I pulled down, feeling with my other hand for a second foot. Yes... there it was...

"Ginnlaug!" I shouted, "I need your help!"

She rushed into the bedchamber but stopped short when she saw what I was holding.

"Hand me a clean towel so I can get a better grip on this... baby."

Dumbly she did as I asked, staring.

Slowly I worked out the legs, instructing Runa when to push and when to hold back. As the body emerged, it became immediately clear that something was horribly wrong.

"What is it? What's wrong?" cried Runa, her eyes on Ginnlaug's stricken face.

"It's... it's dead!" blurted Ginnlaug before I could stop her.

Alas, it was true. When the head was finally expelled, what I held in my arms was a shriveled semblance of a baby, not a living, breathing child.

"Runa, I'm so sorry. She must have died in the womb — some time ago." Quickly I wrapped the body in another towel before Runa could see it.

"She? A daughter?" Runa lay back on her pillows, pale and panting.

"Ginnlaug, quick! A cup of that chamomile tea for Runa!"

Shaking herself as if from a trance, Ginnlaug hastened to bring a restorative cup to Runa, while I waited for the second afterbirth. At least Runa had been spared the kind of bleeding which once, long ago, had almost taken my life. She had survived, and she had a son.

With the ordeal over, a trembling seized me and I sank to my knees beside the bed. This time it was Runa who called for help.

"Olaf! Husband! Come quickly! Lady Freawaru needs you!"

Although faint with exhaustion, I smiled to hear Runa use my old familiar name; I made an effort to rise, but could not.

"I'm alright," I protested as Olaf first handed the baby to Ginnlaug, then slowly helped me to my feet. "Just a momentary weakness."

I saw Olaf glance at the small bundle beside the bed.

"The second child — where is it?" He frowned at the bundle on the floor.

"Olaf, it was dead before its birth — a girl. For your sake, don't ask to see it," I said in low tones as he led me to the only chair in the room. "Better to rejoice in your boy." Raising my voice, I asked, "Have you and Runa picked a name for your son?"

"Yes," said Olaf, brightening. "Sverre. It was my grandfather's name." He held my hand as he lowered me into the chair.

"Sverre. A strong name," I said, "and it is good to honor one's ancestors."

A sudden howl from Sverre made us all laugh.

"Give him to me," called Runa, holding out her arms. "He must be hungry."

When Ginnlaug laid the baby on Runa's breast, the infant rooted blindly for a few moments, then latched onto a nipple and began to suck greedily.

"That boy is a survivor!" I chuckled.

Olaf stood beaming down at Runa and the baby.

"My wife. My son. I'm sorry the other child did not survive, Runa, but Sverre is... perfect. You are a strong woman, my dear. Thank you, thank you, dear wife."

Slowly I rose from the chair and took Ginnlaug's arm.

"Come. Let's leave the little family together — alone. They don't need us at this moment."

Silently we left the bedchamber.

Runa and I buried the afterbirths beneath Wiswicca's apple tree, along with a small pot of ashes. Runa told me that she had folded back the bloody towel to view her daughter's body, and to say farewell, but after that the dead child was never spoken of. The white petals of apple blossoms that covered the ground beneath the tree put me in mind of a blanket over a sleeping child. Forever afterward I thought of Runa's stillborn baby as a bud that had never come to flower.

During the days that followed, Gerda, Lise, Lempi and I spent more time at Runa's house than we did in our own hut, for Sverre soon became the center of a circle of adoring women. Runa complained that she barely got to hold her own child except for feedings — but I saw the dark circles under her eyes and observed how slowly her appetite returned. This birth had cost her more than she was willing to admit.

One day I was surprised to receive a messenger from Rendlesham — a young man with a fringe of beard who finally found me at Runa's house.

"My Lady Freawicca," he said formally, bowing, "King Rædwald and Lady Radegund request the honor of your presence at their Midsummer celebration — and you're to bring your horse," he concluded, smiling and bowing again.

"That won't be possible," I said. "My horse is due to foal at any time. I really shouldn't leave her."

Olaf had come in from the fields to fetch something and overheard my response.

"You mustn't hesitate on that account, my lady." He grinned, wiping a dirty kerchief across his forehead. "I have a lot more experience with horses than I do with women—and Roald is here to help me if I need him."

I still hesitated, unsure where my duty lay in this instance. Then Runa came in from the bedchamber and handed her husband a clean square of cloth.

"Olaf is right, my lady. You deserve a respite. Why, you've been here every day! You've played the mother hen long enough; your chicks can survive a few days without you!"

Her amused smile took some of the sting from her words, yet . . . Was I being a nuisance? I had not considered this possibility. Suddenly my decision was made. Drawing myself up to full height, I extended one hand to the messenger.

"Tell your lord and lady that I accept with pleasure their kind invitation. I will come to Rendlesham for Midsummer."

After a moment's hesitation the young man made a slight bow and lifted my hand to his lips.

"I shall tell them, my lady—and it is understood that you may bring your women to attend you."

"Thank you. I shall bring at least one companion."

To my surprise Gerda was not keen to come with me this time, as she would rather see Sunbeorht give birth to her foal. Lempi, too, engrossed in helping Runa with the baby, showed no interest in being my companion. Lise, however, seized at the chance to visit Rædwald's court. We were standing at the table in our hut, chopping vegetables for soup, when I broached the subject.

"I'd love to go, my lady! What should I pack?"

"Your best clothes." I smiled. "Rendlesham is noted for its love of splendor and display."

"Oh, I wish I'd finished embroidering the hem of that new kirtle," she said. "Perhaps if I work on it every evening—or Lempi might help me."

"Don't fret," I advised. "You'll look lovely in whatever you wear."

To my surprise, Lise burst into tears and dropped her knife.

"Whatever is the matter?" I asked, genuinely at a loss.

Wiping her eyes, Lise sobbed, "I thought you never paid any attention to me—or to what I look like. You're always off with Gerda, or Runa, or someone. I'm just . . . glad to know you think I'm . . . pretty."

"Why Lise," I said, wiping my hands on my apron and taking her in my arms, "I have always thought you attractive. More importantly, you are a woman I count on in any situation. I'm sorry if you have felt . . . neglected. So much has happened of late . . ."

"I know," she said, raising her head and sniffing, "and I'm sorry to act like such a child. Please forgive me."

"If you like," I suggested, holding her out at arm's length, "I can help you finish that embroidery."

On the afternoon Lise and I stepped aboard the boat for our trip downriver to Rendlesham, Sunbeorht had still not foaled, though her belly had dropped. Gerda had bid me a hurried farewell and rushed off to join Olaf and Roald in the stable. Bathed in the heat of summer, the river shimmered and hummed, alive with insects, but once underway a breeze cooled our faces.

"Reminds me of our arrival last year," said Lise, swatting at a swarm of gnats. "Bugs. Lots of bugs."

"There are fewer over the fast water," volunteered one of the young lads rowing our boat, a lad who looked scarce older than Gerda.

"Have you lived here all your life?" I asked pleasantly.

"Yes, I have. My father works for King Rædwald. Oh, excuse me, my lady! I am Per, son of Anders."

"It is good to know you, Per, son of Anders. What sort of work does your father do?"

"He's a goldsmith — the best!" declared the boy proudly.

The boat gave a sudden lurch and one of the other oarsmen growled at Per.

"Here now, mind what you're doing! You can talk later!"

The boy subsided into silence and I made no further effort to engage him in conversation. We were moving with the current, pulled along by the outgoing tide. Our oarsmen had little more to do than keep our boat aligned with the current. When we came closer to shore — as we often did after rounding a bend — our progress slowed. At one such place, Lise cried out in alarm.

"What's that?"

I looked up to follow her trembling finger. Ahead of us the air was filled with flying insects, clouds of them seeming to rise straight out of the water.

"Day flies," said Per. "It's their mating season. Don't worry—they'll soon be gone."

"Gone? But they're here right now!"

Lise shrieked and slid down to the bottom of the boat, trying to pull her apron up over her head.

"Calm yourself," I said, though I too did not relish passing through such a swarm.

"Eek! They're on me! They're on me!" screamed Lise, batting at her head and clothes.

Many soft wings brushed lightly across my face; I shook them off, trying to remain calm.

"Pull hard, lads!" shouted the oarsman next to Per.

As they leaned into their work, we pulled away, back to the main channel, leaving the insect horde behind.

I put a hand on Lise's shoulder.

"They're gone. You're safe. You can come out now."

As the day wore on, large puffy clouds drifted over the sun, bringing welcome relief from its intensity. Lise and I dozed on our seats, lulled by the rhythm of the rowing. We followed the river around bend after bend after bend, until at last we reached familiar landmarks.

"Lise, wake up. We are almost there."

"Was I asleep?" Lise yawned and stretched, then looked about. "Where are we?"

"Look to your right—to the east bank. Do you see those three spurs of land extending into the river? Just past the first one lies the long, low, flat-bottomed valley which leads up to Rendlesham."

Lise squinted in the sunlight. "I only remember that it was a long walk up from the harbor when we stopped here before—with that stolen horse."

"Yes," I nodded, smiling at the memory of Radegund's horse. "And that long ridge in the distance is an even longer walk. That's Hoo Hill—the royal cemetery, where Wiswicca's ashes are buried."

"Hoo Hill," repeated Lise softly. "What a lovely name."

"It's also the place where the bale fires will be started," volunteered Per. "You can see them all along the river."

"Ah, bale fires. My favorite part of Midsummer," murmured Lise, sighing.

Midsummer ... Could it be only a year ago that we had celebrated the solstice at Heorot? With Hrolf and his court? A pang of grief assailed me as I recalled my first sight of Hrolf as a king: tall, commanding, richly dressed, at ease among his courtiers. Now Hrolf was gone, brought down by his own half-sister. I shivered despite the summer heat, but Lise took no notice.

Soon our oarsmen were rowing hard against the tide, heading for the series of piers that marked the main harbor. Once again there were longboats and cargo ships tied up at the wharf, with several small boats like our own bobbing at anchor in the sheltered bay. The broad wooden walkway that stretched along the shore was crowded with moving figures.

"Apparently we are not the only visitors," observed Lise. "I hope I brought the right clothes!"

One of the figures turned out to be Gertrude, one of Lady Radegund's women, waiting to greet us. As we disembarked, she called out.

"Welcome to Rendlesham, Lady Freawicca." After we embraced, she added, "I trust you had a pleasant journey?" Her broad face wore a cheerful smile.

With a warning glance at Lise, I replied, "Yes, thank you, we did. This is my woman Lise, a valued member of my household."

"Welcome Lise. I will take you both to your quarters. My lady, I hope you won't mind sharing a room with me. We are so crowded with guests just now ... I apologize for any inconvenience."

"On the contrary, Gertrude, I shall relish the opportunity to know you better."

We smiled again and exchanged slight bows.

After Gertrude sent two of our oarsmen ahead with our travel chests, we began the gradual ascent toward the settlement. I sometimes found it necessary to take Lise's arm as we climbed, and Gertrude politely paused at brief intervals. By the time we reached the great hall I was winded, but gratified that I could still manage.

Gertrude ushered us into a cool, dark chamber fitted with sumptuous hangings and dark, heavy furnishings. When she lit the wall lamps, gold threads gleamed from the tapestries, adding a richness to the room that made Lise gasp.

"It ... it's beautiful! And ... real beds! I get to sleep on a real bed!"

"I'm glad you approve," said Gertrude, suppressing a smile. "Now I will leave you to rest and refresh yourselves. There will be a banquet tonight to welcome all our guests. Lady Radegund will greet you then."

"Thank you, Gertrude. You have been most gracious."

As soon as Gertrude left us, I collapsed on the nearest bed, but Lise immediately began unpacking her travel chest, laying out each change of clothes on a bed.

"Oh, dear, what should I wear tonight? The tunic? The new kirtle?" She turned to me with a troubled expression. "My lady, what are you going to wear?"

"My one good dress — you've seen it many times." I sighed wearily. "Lise, I suggest you wear your best attire in the evenings and your plainest during the day. That will heighten the contrast."

Lise stared at me, chewing her lip, then nodded and gathered up her garments to return them to their chest.

The feast that night was every bit as magnificent as I had expected. Every table was set with trenchers made of bread, and real glass goblets. Every bench was covered with soft cushions. And the food . . . ! Three courses — or "sendings" as they called them here — were carried in by young boys all dressed alike. The first included roasted meats, cheeses of different kinds, and birds baked in pies. In the second sending several varieties of fish were served, along with vegetables fresh from the garden. The final sending featured baked fruits, fresh berries and bread sweetened with honey. Ale flowed freely throughout the evening as everyone partook of Rædwald's bounty.

He and Radegund initially sat in high seats at the back of the hall where they received their guests, later taking places at the head table. With Lise's hand clutching mine, I could feel her trembling as we bowed low before Rædwald and Radegund.

"Where is your Gerda?" asked Radegund, after greeting us warmly.

"At home waiting for my horse to foal," I answered.

"So, my Sandyfoot will be denied her favorite companion! You must tell me more . . . later."

'Later,' as it happened, would be the next day, for I did not see Radegund again until morning. Lise and I were seated with Radegund's women, two rows below the head table, but close enough to have a good view of those seated there.

"Who are those handsome fellows?" inquired Lise, pointing to a pair of young men who flanked Rædwald and Radegund.

"The king's sons," replied Gertrude. "Eorpwald is the older, the dark-haired one, and — being first born — Rædwald's heir. His younger brother Rægenhere, however, is his mother's darling, and a general favorite here at court."

I studied the two young men. Eorpwald certainly resembled his father, with the same strong jaw and serious expression. Rægenhere seemed more relaxed, perhaps at that very moment sharing some jest with his mother, for both were laughing.

I recognized the person seated to my far right at the end of the table as Oswald, the king's steward, but not the man and woman opposite him.

"That richly dressed couple — who are they?" I asked.

"The king's brother Eni and his wife Eadburh," said Hannah. "They've come down from their seat at Snape to attend the festivities."

"I see. Quite a family party."

"King Rædwald revels in entertaining his family and friends," noted Berta. "He is a very generous man and highly respected in these parts."

"And what of his father, Tyttla? Is he too aged and infirm to take part in the celebration?" I asked, curious about the king I had never seen.

Gertrude nodded ruefully. "Exactly. The poor old man has lost his sight, his teeth, and can no longer walk unaided, so he is cared for in his own chamber. I sometimes accompany Lady Radegund on her daily visit." She leaned forward and lowered her voice. "Each time I am surprised to find him still alive."

Ah, I thought to myself, like Brecca, another king facing a 'straw death.' At least Beowulf died in battle, a warrior to the end. His reputation is secure. His fame will endure.

I decided to leave the banquet early that night, for I needed to chant the binding spell against Skuld alone, in the dark of night. Lise, however, begged to stay.

"Oh, my lady, the scop has just begun to sing and I want to hear the story — something about two lovers named Waldere and Hildeguth."

"It is an absorbing story," I admitted, for I had once heard it in my husband Ingeld's hall, "but I need to take my leave."

"If it please you, my lady, let Lise stay with us," offered Gertrude, nodding at Hannah and Berta across the table.

"Very well. Thank you, Gertrude. No — I can find my own way."

I motioned for her not to get up, excused myself, and made my way past the rows of tables crowded with revelers. When I slipped through a side door, I found myself in Rædwald's temple, empty save for the carved wooden figures of Thor, Freyr and Odin, standing tall behind a stone altar. As I passed I bowed to each, then found the outside door and pulled it open.

As the cool night air washed over me, I drew in deep breaths, filling my lungs to clear my brain and prepare myself to address the goddess. A crescent moon hung low above me, and beyond it a sprinkling of stars. Slowly sinking to my knees, I pressed my palms firmly on the earth and began to chant.

"Skuld shall not see, blind shall she be . . ."

Three times I repeated the incantation, each time more fervently. Just as I finished, a long dark cloud passed over the moon. I looked up and smiled.

"Perhaps the goddess is answering me. Thank you, Earth Mother."

With an effort, I rose to my feet.

When I woke the next morning, Lise was already up and dressed.

"Balefires today!" she crowed. "The others have gone ahead, but I thought you needed sleep. Gertrude left bread and porridge for you. Please hurry!"

I smiled at her eagerness — excited as a child — and felt a moment of longing for Gerda. Would she be dancing around a balefire today? Or still holding vigil for Sunbeorht's foal?

I did my best to dress and eat quickly and was soon ready to join Lise for the climb up Hoo Hill. To our surprise we found Radegund's son Rægenhere waiting outside the chamber to escort us. He flashed an engaging smile and bowed slightly.

"Mother tells me that you are a very special guest, Lady Freawicca, and I am to take very good care of you. Please, take my arm."

So we set out, Lise fluttering behind us like a moth drawn to flame, repeatedly muttering, "I should have worn better clothes."

I was grateful for Rægenhere's support as the path grew steeper, but at last we reached the crest of the ridge. Already three giant bonfires were blazing, making the air around them quiver with heat.

"Welcome my sister, welcome!" called Radegund, advancing from a rough table festooned with garlands of greenery and stocked with mugs and pitchers. "Would you like a drink of cold cider after your climb?"

She extended a mug which I took thankfully and drank eagerly. When I turned to thank Rægenhere for his help, he had already disappeared.

"Your son is a charming young man," I said, following Radegund toward a bench. "On the way up he entertained us with stories of his . . . exploits at court."

"His pranks, you mean," said Radegund, smiling broadly. "Full of mischief, that one. But come. Sit and tell me about your life at Helmingham. It has been long since we talked."

"Lady Freawicca, have I your permission to join the other women?" asked Lise at my elbow.

"Of course. Go, go enjoy yourself. Today should be a day without care."

For the remainder of the morning Radegund and I conversed happily as if we were old friends.

"First, I must tell you a marvel," I began. "Wiswicca's staff—the staff that brought forth a spring of water at the goddess ceremony—has bloomed into a living tree."

"What? Can this be?" Radegund leaned closer. "Tell me everything."

When I finished recounting the details of our discovery—not omitting Wilhelm's reaction—Radegund's face reflected both dismay and delight.

"So . . . the goddess has revealed herself in powerful ways!" She smiled smugly and nodded her head vigorously. "Bertha has nothing to compare with this!"

"Bertha? I don't believe I've met anyone of that name."

"No, you haven't—but I'll speak of her later. Please tell me: what else has been happening at Helmingham? Have you had any more visions? And how did you part with your Danish visitors?"

Radegund listened intently to my telling of the binding spell I'd concocted with Skur and Drifa, and of the jar we'd buried in my garden.

"Lady Freawicca, you are an extraordinary woman," she marveled. "The goddess has blessed you with great powers of your own!"

"Yes, I am blessed," I said humbly, "and I do what I can, but Wyrd will have its way. I could not, for instance, save Runa's baby."

As I described in detail the birth of Runa's twins, Radegund shuddered.

"I almost lost Rægenhere at birth, and he was a sickly child for years afterward. But — as you can see — he has grown into a fine, strong young man. Rædwald thinks I spoil him." She smiled. "But it's hard not to!" She paused as her face grew somber again. "I'm glad your friend did not lose both babies."

"So am I," I said, thinking back to my own loss of two sons.

For a moment we sat in silence. Then Radegund's face brightened and she reached for my hand.

"Lady Freawicca, I hope you will stay with us for several days this time. Rædwald is planning a visit to Kent, and I'd very much like you to come with us."

"Kent? What and where is Kent?" I asked in surprise.

"Kent is the kingdom to the south of us — about one day's journey by boat. I'd like you to meet Aethelbert and his wife Bertha, the rulers there."

"Oh . . . I had not planned to be gone for so long from Helmingham," I replied slowly. "I am honored by your invitation, but . . . I'll think on it."

The rest of that day — day of the year's turning — passed in a haze of heat, with feasting and frolicking around the balefires, and intermittent toasting to the gods. I drank to Freyja, to Frigga, and to Earth Mother, respectfully pouring most of each libation on the ground as an offering.

Late in the day, when the sun had briefly set and risen again, I made my way to the burial ground where I had planted an apple sapling on Wiswicca's grave. After watering the little tree with a mug of cider, I knelt to repeat the binding spell. This task completed, I sat back on my heels surveying the valley below and the River Doep winding snake-like beyond it.

Alone in this solemn place, I summoned up an image of Wiswicca as I had first seen her at Helmingham: a white-robed figure with luminous face, the skin almost transparent over delicate bones, and soft brown eyes liquid with love. A sob caught in my throat as I felt her gentle touch and heard her voice in urgent admonition: 'Do not desert the goddess! Uphold the goddess!'

"Oh, Mother," I called, "It is Frea . . . waru, who seeks your counsel. Guide my path, help me find the best way to serve the goddess and to forestall the evil you envisioned."

Once again her description of this evil came back to me: hooded, dark-robed men... bearing before them wooden talismans. Who or what could they be? I had seen no such men in this new land.

"Lady Freawicca? Is that you?"

I turned to see Lise advancing, her face pink with exertion.

"Have I been missed?" I asked, struggling to my feet.

Lise stopped to catch her breath. "Lady Radegund sent me. She said you might be here. She's waiting for your answer."

"Oh? And what do you know of the question?"

"Nothing, my lady, but Radegund said to tell you that Wiswicca once travelled to Kent."

"Indeed? I see... yes, I see."

Is this your charge, Mother? Is it your will that I go to Kent?

"Lise," I said, placing a hand on her shoulder, "we may not go directly back to Helmingham. We may take a... little excursion... with Radegund and Rædwald."

Radegund was most pleased with my decision and quick to share it with her husband, who called me to his council chamber the next morning. As I entered, he cleared his throat and gave a slight nod. The king was dressed in a simple light-colored tunic edged with gold braid, and secured with a handsome leather belt, the bronze buckle set with garnets. Gold gleamed from his muscular arms and long, slender fingers. Below bushy eyebrows, his grey eyes regarded me steadily.

"Welcome, Lady Freawicca. I trust you have found our hospitality satisfactory?"

He motioned for me to take a seat across from him in one of several elaborately carved, high-backed chairs. As I sat down, I ran my fingers lightly over the arm pieces.

"Yes, my lord. Indeed, Rendlesham affords nothing but the best."

"And yet my wife tells me that you have marvels at Helmingham not to be found here," he said in measured tones.

"All are gifts of the goddess, my lord. We have been fortunate to be so honored," I said blandly, wondering where this conversation might lead.

"Wilhelm tells me that unusual things have happened since your arrival in Helmingham," continued Rædwald, "which leads me to think that your own gifts have played some part in producing these... marvels."

"If so, it is solely as an instrument of the goddess," I responded.

"A most valuable instrument," said Rædwald, stroking his chin. "Lady Freawicca, to be frank, in order to rule my kingdom well I have need of many eyes and ears. A woman with gifts such as yours could be very helpful to me."

"So . . ." I said slowly, "am I being invited to visit Kent as a guest . . . or as a spy?"

Rædwald stared at me for a moment, then burst into hearty laughter.

"By the gods, a woman of spirit! Radegund told me as much, but I wanted to see for myself before I asked if you would serve me."

"My lord, I am the daughter of a king. I serve no one but the goddess!" I declared hotly.

"Nay, nay," said Rædwald, raising one hand. "I mean no disrespect, but everyone serves someone. My overlord is Æthelbert of Kent, though we rule our separate domains—an arrangement advantageous to us both."

Rising, and coming toward me, Rædwald placed his palms on the arms of my chair and leaned forward.

"Lady Freawicca, at Yule you foresaw a massacre in Denmark. Four months later, survivors from Denmark arrived to confirm your vision. Such divining is beyond the power of anyone else in my court. I need you." He bent closer. "The peace and plenty you enjoy here were achieved through years of struggle and constant vigilance. Beyond the borders of Rendlesham lies a world of treachery and conflict."

His tone had become increasingly stern as he spoke, but his face was sad, even . . . kindly.

"I need you," he said again. "Will you help me?" He stepped back, regarding me expectantly.

"My lord, what runes did you touch when you placed your palms on this chair?" I asked calmly.

"Runes? What runes?" Rædwald stepped forward to examine the marks on both arm pieces, but looked up blankly.

"I do not know," he admitted. "Does it matter?"

"Perhaps not, but the carver of these runes was naming the qualities of the person for whom the chair was intended."

"And what qualities do you find there?" asked Rædwald, his face alight with curiosity.

"Generosity—Gebo—and strength—Uruz—indicating a man of honor."

"By the gods, a rune mistress! Lady Freawicca, now I know you must join me! Move to Rendlesham immediately! I will give you a place of honor as my most trusted advisor, I will give you..."

Now it was my turn to protest.

"Nay, nay, my lord. I will accompany you to Kent, but I make no promises beyond that."

He took my hands in his, still smiling.

"Agreed."

We were a large party on our trip to Kent. Rædwald left his older son Eorpwald behind in his place, along with his steward Oswald, but Rægenhere came with us, as did three of the king's councilors. Rædwald introduced me to Haugen, Grima and Edvard, all of whom bowed respectfully. Radegund brought Gertrude and Hannah as well as Lise and me, plus all the servants required to support such a group. Added to the seamen needed, we were some forty in number.

We boarded early in the morning to catch the out-going tide. A slight mist lay over the water, obscuring my view of the countryside, but it gradually burned off as the sun rose ever higher. Sometimes I walked to the bow of the ship and stood near the rail to catch the breeze on my face. I was standing there when Rædwald joined me, at mid-afternoon, when we had reached the open sea and were following the coastline to the south.

"What do you know of the peoples of this country, Lady Freawicca?"

"Little more than what I know of those who live along the River Doep," I answered, turning to smile up at him.

"I have a map back in Rendlesham which I can show you later, but I'll give you a brief explanation now," he said, returning my smile. "As you know, we are headed for the kingdom of Kent, or Cantware. Æthelbert has his primary seat at Canterbury, with another at Rochester, where his son Eadbald holds sway. We Angles have long enjoyed friendly relations with the Jutes of the Cantware. Unfortunately that is not true of the other kingdoms."

"How many kingdoms are there in this country?" I asked in astonishment, "Is Angle-land not made up of Angles?"

Rædwald looked out to sea, musing, before he replied.

"Many peoples have occupied this island over time. You probably know of the Romans, who long held it as their own, and the Britons, who still control large territories to the west. Of most concern now are the Saxons to the south and the northern tribes of Mercia, Deira and Bernicia."

As I absorbed these strange names, all new to me, Rædwald continued.

"Each king seeks to protect his own kingdom and to extend its borders as far as he can. Thus, conflict is inevitable."

I sighed. "This sounds familiar: like the Geats fighting the Swedes, or the Franks, or the Frisians."

Rædwald shrugged. "War is a warrior's life. Your Beowulf knew that."

The unexpected introduction of Beowulf's name caught me unawares. Tears sprang to my eyes, but I blinked them back.

"While Beowulf lived, there was peace in the North! He sought to avoid war," I declared, "though he never backed down from a battle when it was ... necessary."

Was facing the dragon necessary? Did you have to die, my beloved? Rædwald nodded.

"That is my aim as well. That is why I need you to listen for me, to hear what I may miss." He paused and looked around to see if anyone else were near. "As you know, my lady, not all challenges are physical. Here in Kent you'll find new ideas, different ways of thinking that challenge the old ways. I would welcome your reactions — privately — to what you see and hear."

Mystified, but gratified by the king's trust, I nodded.

"I will do what I can."

During the voyage I asked Radegund to describe the court at Kent, but she demurred.

"We — Rædwald and I — want you to form your own impressions." She smiled apologetically. "I will tell you that Queen Bertha prefers to be addressed as 'your ladyship.' She is a Frank, and fond of ceremony."

"Do you ... like ... this Bertha?" I queried.

"Like?" Radegund considered. "I don't dis-like her. Again, you must judge for yourself."

Hampers of food were unpacked in the late afternoon and we all ate heartily, our appetites whetted by the bracing salt air.

"It will be late when we reach Canterbury," said Radegund. "After we leave the sea we still have to row up the River Stoor."

"Another river settlement?" I asked, taking a second portion of bread.

"Much more than that!" exclaimed Radegund. "Canterbury was once a Roman city, with walls and gates. You'll see."

It was after midsummer dusk by the time we reached our destination, drawing up to a landing crowded with other vessels. From the size and number of ships, I judged Canterbury to be a major trading center, more resembling Uppsala than Rendlesham.

"Leave your travel chests here," instructed Radegund. "The thralls will bring them up. We still have a bit of a walk to reach the gate."

I was glad to stretch my legs after a day aboard ship, but Lise was less eager.

"Remind me: why are we here?" she grumbled as we followed Radegund's women down the gangplank.

"You wanted to see more of court life, did you not? Radegund says that Queen Bertha sets the style for dress and decoration for all of Angleland. No doubt you can learn much from her example."

Lise frowned at me, unsure whether I were jesting or chiding.

"As you say," she mumbled.

After toiling up a long gradual incline, we reached a great stone wall that stretched to the right and left almost as far as I could see. Our party halted before a huge arched gate where a watch man emerged to ask our identity. When Rædwald stepped forward, we were immediately allowed to pass through and given an escort.

Once inside the city walls, we were conducted to the royal residence, a tall timbered building much like Rædwald's hall in Rendlesham.

"Don't worry," puffed Gertrude beside me. "We are expected. They'll have beds ready — after we've been formally welcomed by the king and queen."

"That is good to hear," I answered, rather short of breath myself.

Indeed I was too tired to take much interest in my surroundings, though I did notice one large structure built of some reddish-brown material not familiar to me.

Inside the hall I noticed an impressive display of swords and shields hung on the walls, interspersed with tapestries — just like Rendlesham. Carved and painted columns supported the roof timbers — just as at Rendlesham. So, I thought to myself, Rædwald may be an under-king, but his hall is no less magnificent than Æthelbert's. The thought gave me pleasure.

Æthelbert appeared to be a man approaching middle age, for his light hair and beard were only slightly streaked with gray. Shrewd blue eyes swept over our group as we advanced to the throne. He wore a tunic of deep blue shot through with silver threads, his legs encased in white leggings that accentuated his muscular calves.

Beside him sat a woman so diminutive that at first I mistook her for a girl. Great dark eyes gazed out from a milk-white face, its delicate features framed with dark hair. A black and silver gown fell loosely around her slender frame.

Beside her chair stood a tall, gaunt man dressed in a simple black robe. Around his neck he wore a silver chain from which dangled some sort of amulet — in the form of crossed sticks. What most drew my attention, however, was his head: shaved on top and below the ears, with a fringe of hair encircling it. A thrall? Surely not. He clearly stood in a position of some importance. As I was contemplating this scene, Rædwald and Radegund stepped forward and made deep bows.

"Welcome, Lord Rædwald! Welcome, Lady Radegund! Please rise," bellowed Æthelbert. "It is good to welcome old friends."

"Welcome friends," piped Bertha in a high, thin, reedy voice that reminded me of Runa's flute. "Welcome to zee court of Æzelbert."

Now Rædwald and Radegund were each discreetly handed a small carved chest. Rædwald presented his to Æthelbert, Radegund gave hers to Bertha.

"Tokens of appreciation for your hospitality," murmured Rædwald, bowing slightly.

Opening the lid, Æthelbert lifted out an ornate gold belt buckle set with garnets.

"Ah, another example of Anders' fine workmanship! You do me honor!" exclaimed Æthelbert, smiling.

Bertha carefully opened her chest and cried, "My favorite — zee honey of East Anglia! Zank you."

These preliminaries over, Rædwald and Radegund introduced each member of their party — starting with me.

"Queen Bertha, may I present my friend, Lady Freawicca of Denmark — now resident in Helmingham."

As I bowed, Bertha repeated my name, slowly.

"Frea-wicca. Does 'wicca' not mean 'magic' in your language?" Her eyes narrowed.

"Yes, your ladyship. It was my mother's name. She was a healer and a servant of the goddess."

The dark-robed man at her side reached up to touch the crossed-stick amulet at his chest, as Bertha bid me rise and gestured to her companion.

"Lady Freawicca, zis is my priest, Bishop Liudhard. I am sure he will wish to talk wiz you." She gave a thin-lipped smile as she dismissed me.

Somewhere in the back of my brain a tiny alarm sounded, but I was too fatigued to attend to it.

Chapter Twenty-Two
Canterbury

Silver pendant from Foss, Iceland, representing Thor's hammer. The dragon head may represent the Midgard serpent. The maker or owner has cut a Christian cross into the middle. University Museum of National Antiquities, Oslo.

After a night of uneasy rest, I woke to unfamiliar surroundings: rows of sleeping forms on benches and pallets in a strange high-timbered room. Rendlesham? No. Raising up on both elbows, I looked about me. In the flickering light from wall-hung oil lamps, I saw Lise to one side of me, on her back, her mouth open, snoring lightly. Beyond her lay Hannah, and beyond her, Gertrude.

I blinked, trying to shake off the feeling that remained from a dream — a dream just out of reach. I only remembered dark, heavy clouds approaching, pressing relentlessly down on me so that I gasped for air. A quiver in my loins made me sit up. Perhaps I just needed to find the latrine!

Folding back the light coverlet, I slid off the bench quietly, hoping not to awaken others. Another form down the row also rose: Gertrude. She beckoned me to follow; together we made our way silently past the sleeping women and out through a side door, to find the wattle and daub enclosure adjacent to our quarters. Although the sun was still low, we were suddenly enveloped in the warmth of a midsummer morning.

"Ah, here it is."

Gertrude politely waited outside while I stepped into the enclosusre. When we had both finished, we decided to stroll a bit before returning to our quarters. Moving away, we strode through the dew-spangled grass, wriggling our bare toes and giggling like girls.

"So, what do you think of Canterbury?" asked Gertrude.

"The walls are ... awesome!" I replied. "I've never seen anything like them!"

"Yes, well, I meant the court," said Gertrude, stopping to peer at me.

"I was not expecting ... the priest," I said, frowning. "What role does he play at court?"

"From what I've heard," said Gertrude, lowering her voice — though no one else was in sight — "Queen Bertha insisted on bringing him with her to the marriage. It was one of the conditions Æthelbert had to agree to. The priest is her confessor."

"Confessor? What is a confessor?" Surely a queen would have little to confess — to anyone.

"I'm not really sure," said Gertrude, 'but she tells her sins to her priest and he forgives her — or something like that."

"Sins?" Again I was bewildered. "These are strange words to me, Gertrude. In my understanding a priest is someone who leads the people in honoring and sacrificing to the gods."

Gertrude nodded. "At Rendlesham Rædwald acts as the priest on public occasions, just as you led us women in praising the goddess at Helmingham." She shrugged. "I think Queen Bertha prefers private ceremonies. She has her own temple here — I'm sure she'll show it off to you today."

Gertrude was right. After the morning meal Queen Bertha led our group from Rendlesham to visit her private temple, just outside the walls a short distance to the east; it was the strange reddish-colored structure I had noticed the night before.

"It's made of Roman brick from the local clay," murmured Radegund beside me. "Æthelbert allowed Queen Bertha and her priest to restore this abandoned temple for their own use."

"Welcome to St. Martin's Church!" caroled the queen as her priest ceremoniously opened the heavy oak door—located at one end rather than in the middle of the structure.

Inside, under a high peaked ceiling, an open space preceded a high altar covered with a white cloth. On it sat two silver vessels, gleaming in the dim light: a platter and a goblet. Towering behind the altar stood a wooden rood, a cross with a naked figure affixed to it.

"Oh!" I exclaimed, glad to see something familiar—something I could identify. "It's Yggdrasil, the World Tree, with Odin hanging from the branches! But why is he not upside-down?"

The priest, Liudhard, blocked my view.

"It is zee Christ!" he hissed. "Do not blaspheme!"

"Lady Freawicca," purred the queen, coming up to join her priest, "as a pagan you would not know zat I serve zee one god and his son, zee Christ. I have brought zee true religion to zis country."

Speechless, I stared at them in confusion. Their words made no sense to me. I cast about for some response, coming up with a question.

"Who is the St. Martin for whom you named your . . . church?"

The queen's expression softened.

"Zee favorite saint of my childhood. I have seen his relic—a piece of his cloak—preserved at Tours, where my sister was a nun."

Saint? Relic? Nun? I knew not the meaning of these words. Rædwald had warned me that I'd encounter new ideas in Kent. He was certainly correct! Suddenly I realized that Bertha was still speaking.

". . . and zee Pope has sent us holy men to explain zee true faith to all. You will meet zem tomorrow."

Later, without the queen present, we women strolled through her gardens—a series of strangely clipped hedges forming different designs. I asked Radegund to explain some of the terms I'd heard.

"A saint is a person who has lived a good and pure life," she began, "always serving others ahead of himself."

"Like Beowulf!" I exclaimed, smiling.

"Not quite. A saint must believe in one god—as Queen Bertha does."

"Which one? There are many gods," I objected.

"Not according to Queen Bertha." Radegund shook her head. "I can't explain it well, for I don't understand it myself."

"What is a relic? And what is a pope?" I persisted.

"A relic is something that belonged to a saint, like a piece of a cloak, or even a bone from their body."

"So... Beowulf's sword could be a relic," I surmised, but Radegund responded with "only if he were a saint."

"And a pope?"

"He's sort of the high king of the church. The pope lives across the seas on the Continent, in Rome. Now..." she sighed, "dear friend, please ask me no more questions! Let us relax and enjoy the day before us."

"All right. Thank you, Radegund — or 'zank you', as Bertha would say."

Radegund's eyes shot me a look of disapproval, but her lips curved in a smile.

That night in the great hall we heard more about Queen Bertha's "holy men" from Æthelbert himself. He was talking to Rædwald and Rægenhere when we ladies arrived to join them at table.

"I met them after they first landed, just off our coastline on the Isle of Thanet," he was saying. "My councilors advised me not to meet these men in any house, lest they use magic to harm me, so I met them in the open air."

Queen Bertha gave a 'hrumph' at this, but Æthelbert took no notice.

"They approached my party from the shore's edge, all dressed in black — forty of them. One carried a silver cross as their standard, another a large board on which was painted a man's head crowned with thorns. The leader, who called himself Augustine, offered a prayer 'to the one true god,' he said. Then the whole group began to sing — or rather chant, like forty scops reciting at once! The effect was strangely ...thrilling."

"Why have these men come to Kent?" asked Rægenhere, wiping foaming ale from his lips.

Æthelbert glanced fondly at Queen Bertha.

"My dear wife has long wanted our people to know more of her faith — or as she puts it, 'to hear the Christian message.' Augustine and his men have come as preachers and teachers."

"Will you support their effort?" asked Rædwald, his face blank.

"Yes, within limits," said Æthelbert. "When they arrive tomorrow I will give them a place to stay and my permission to speak to my people. I myself will not accept baptism into this new faith, but I will grant others the freedom to do so."

Baptism — another new word. I wonder what it means?

At that moment servers arrived with the evening meal, and there was no more talk of preachers and teachers for the rest of the evening.

As we were preparing for bed that night, at the far end of the chamber, I asked Lise for her observations of the court.

"The queen seems . . . stiff, but her women are friendly — and so finely dressed!"

"Really? Tell me what you have noticed."

Lise regarded me with some exasperation.

"Surely you've seen their brooches: square-headed or long and angular instead of oval and circular like ours? And the way they dress their hair? I've never before seen gold fillets worn over the forehead — but it's most becoming, don't you think?"

"Lise, Lise," I chuckled. "You are a delight. I am glad you are here as my companion."

Lise flushed and bowed her head. "Thank you, my lady."

The next morning I decided to pay more attention to the women of Bertha's court. Several shared the look and speech of Bertha herself, so I judged them to be Franks. Others more resembled the women of Rendlesham and Helmingham. One in particular caught my eye: a tall, large-boned woman with reddish hair and a ruddy face, who moved with the grace of a cat. Something about her put me in mind of Runa.

Runa . . . how is she faring? She and her babe? And Gerda? Sunbeorht?

"Are you well, my lady?" said the very woman, gliding to my side as I seated myself at table. "I saw your expression just now."

"I'm fine, thank you. I just had a moment of . . . sadness, longing for my little girl. Please join me, if you like."

She did like, for she slipped in beside me, introducing herself as Gwyneth.

"How old is your daughter?" she asked pleasantly.

"Ten winters — and she's not really my daughter, but I love her dearly. We have not been parted like this since we first met, over a year ago."

With a pang of conscience I realized it had been much longer than that since I'd seen my actual daughter, Inga.

"Where is she now?" continued Gwyneth.

"Back in Helmingham, waiting for my horse to foal. I'm sure it must have happened by now." Without my presence, I thought regretfully.

"Girls and horses share a special bond," observed Gwyneth. "I was once smitten with horses. When I was young I rode with my father almost every day."

"How fortunate for you! Do you still ride?"

"Rarely. The queen used to ride out beyond the walls with a group of her women, but now that she is pregnant . . ." Her voice trailed off and she shrugged.

"So, how do you spend your days at court?" I asked, genuinely interested.

"The queen and some of her attendants attend mass daily, but I am not of their . . . faith," she said delicately.

"Mass? What is that?" So many new words to learn.

"It's a ritual held in their church — with chanting and prayers and . . . incense." Her nose wrinkled as though smelling it. "Myself, I prefer to worship in the open air."

"And do you worship . . . the goddess?" I inquired, lowering my voice.

Gwyneth smiled. "It's alright to speak openly. The king grants freedom of worship to all his subjects. To answer your question, yes I do worship the goddess, as did my mother before me. Have I not heard the same of you?"

With this bond established, Gwyneth and I were soon deep in conversation, barely pausing to eat when the porridge was served. Two other women joined our table, nodding at Gwyneth and looking at me with open curiosity.

"Are you zee witch?" asked one, bluntly but matter-of-factly.

"Lady Freawicca is a healer and a servant of the goddess," said Gwyneth before I could summon an answer. "She is . . . a special guest."

"Oh. Welcome," said the woman. "I am Marguerite, and zis is Eleanor." She gestured to her companion, who nodded a greeting.

"Are you ladies attending mass today?" I asked sweetly.

"Zat was hours ago!" declared Marguerite. "We get up early to start zee day with prayer. Zee queen sets us a good example."

"She seems most... diligent," I observed, then added, "When is her baby due?"

Marguerite and Eleanor looked at each other. Finally Eleanor answered.

"Some time after Christ-mas, I zink."

"Christ-mas? When is that?" I asked.

"It's what you'd call 'Yule'," said Gwyneth, then changed the subject, addressing the two across the table. "I've discovered that Lady Freawicca is a horsewoman. Perhaps we could show her something of the countryside today — on horseback."

"Ooh, yes!" squealed Marguerite, sounding a bit like Gerda. "Zat would be most pleasing."

Later that morning we four were joined by Radegund, Hannah and Gertrude for a leisurely jaunt around the city walls. Lise had declined the invitation, preferring to visit the weaving sheds. It was a cloudless day, the sky a brilliant blue. As I felt the sun on my cheeks and the motion of the horse beneath me, the heaviness I had felt of late seemed to rise and float away.

The settlement at Canterbury looked to be even larger than Rendlesham. We passed rows of barns and houses and storage sheds; I also saw a number of sunken huts made of wattle and daub or wooden planks, all with thatched or turf roofs.

"What are those?" I asked Gwyneth, gesturing.

"It varies. That near one is a bake house; the next, larger one is a pottery workshop. Several are sheds for spinning and weaving. The forge for iron-working is located at some distance," she added, "and most of our fields and pastures lie outside the walls."

Gwyneth also pointed out several Roman ruins both inside and outside the wall, including a curious structure of tiered seats — all made of stone — which she called a 'theater.' By now I was used to hearing new words, and just smiled as if I understood.

Besides the St. Martin's Church I had visited the day before, we saw several other Roman temples — all in a tumble-down state — and I marveled at what a populous city this must have been in Roman times.

"My ancestors once fought the Romans," volunteered Gwyneth.

We had paused beside the riverbank, for part of the Stoor flowed through Canterbury; another part followed outside the line of the wall.

"Were your ancestors . . . Britons?" I ventured, remembering Rædwald's overview.

"Yes. I am proud of my heritage!"

"My mother may have been of that race," I said softly. "She is gone now."

Unbidden, Mother's face rose before me, her eyes imploring, 'Do not forget, do not forget . . .'

"Lady Freawicca?"

"I'm fine. Perhaps we should be getting back? I'd like to refresh myself before the banquet tonight, when we are to meet Augustine and his men."

"As you wish."

Gwyneth wheeled her mount, her red hair flying, and we set off back to the hall.

Once again our group from Rendlesham was honored with places at the king's table. I found myself seated between Radegund and Liudhard, anticipating an awkward, even difficult, evening ahead. Æthelbert informed us that he had invited Augustine's group to feast with us, but had been told that they were men of simple tastes who would join us later, after something called 'Vespers.'

This announcement did nothing to lessen our own appetites; soon we were enjoying a bountiful meal of roast pork, bean soup, oat bread, cabbage salad, salmon cakes and the first strawberries of the season.

"Zee queen tells me that you have questions about our faith," said Liudhard as we paused after the third sending. "I will be glad to provide answers."

"Why, thank you," I responded. "That would be most kind. 'Vespers,' for example: what is that?"

"Men of the church must pray eight times a day at set hours. Vespers falls at dusk, usually just after dinner."

"Eight times a day?" I marveled. "Does Queen Bertha do that?"

"No, she usually prays at Prime and Compline — early and late, you would say."

As I was digesting this information, I noticed a servant approach the king's chair and speak into his ear. When Æthelbert gave a nod, the thrall hurried away. The king rose. Immediately all the clatter and clamor in the dining hall subsided.

"Friends, we will now welcome Abbot Augustine and his party of monks from Rome," declared Æthelbert, gesturing toward the double doors at the main entrance.

Before we saw the men, we heard their singing: high, sonorous chanting that made the skin on my arms prickle.

"Ah, zee Deprecamur Domine," murmured Liudhard. "It's an antiphon from Gaul — I'll translate later."

As the doors were pulled back, a stream of men in dark robes filed in. Like Liudhard, the top of each man's head was shaved. Each man also wore a cord from which hung a cross, shaped like the great silver cross embedded with colored stones carried before them by the first man in the procession.

"Zee cross is a defense against demons," hissed Liudhard in my ear, but I hardly heard him, overtaken by a sudden realization: 'dark-robed men bearing talismans . . .'

Gripped with dread, I began to shake. I felt as if I were drowning in icy seas, being swallowed up by waves of sound. Clamping my eyes shut, I clapped my palms over my ears, but could not shut out the overwhelming sense of menace. A hand on my shoulder made me open my eyes. It was Radegund, staring at me in alarm.

"What is it? You're white as milk!"

"Wiswicca's vision!" I gasped. "The great evil! It has come!"

"Control yourself!" rasped Radegund. "You will offend our hosts!"

Her grip on my arm tightened; she put a smile on her face and nodded across the table, where Bertha eyed us suspiciously. I straightened and reached for my goblet with a trembling hand. The wine tasted like blood.

Leaning across me, Radegund asked Liudhard, "What are they singing?"

He cleared his throat. "We beseech zee, O Lord, in zy great mercy zat zy wrath and anger may be turned away from zis city . . ."

"This city? Do you mean Canterbury?" asked Radegund, frowning.

"Yes," said Liudhard simply. "All have sinned. But zee Christ" — he gestured to the face on a painted board being carried in — "will save us."

It was a sorrowful face, a haunting face, with great dark eyes. Blood dripped down its forehead from a cruel crown of thorns. I shuddered.

"We wear zee tonsure as a reminder of Christ's suffering," said Liudhard, indicating his shaved crown.

I did not know how much longer I could remain at the table, for my stomach was heaving, its contents ready to spill forth.

"Please excuse me," I said to the table at large, rising.

"I'll go with you," said Radegund. "Please excuse us, lords and ladies."

By now all forty monks had entered, filling the space before the empty throne chairs. They smelled of damp wool and incense. Their leader had stepped forward to face the king's table. Before I left, I noted that he was a rather small man with a weathered face and kind eyes. Then I bolted.

Outside the hall, which I managed to reach before spewing my meal on the ground, Radegund helped me clean my face and held my elbow as we walked slowly back and forth, breathing in the evening air.

"Do you feel better now?" she asked at length.

"Yes, thank you."

"Then tell me again what you said inside — something about Wiswicca and evil?"

For the first time I confided to Radegund all that Wiswicca had imparted to me: her visions, her fears, her exhortation to uphold and defend the goddess against all attackers. Radegund listened wide-eyed as I poured out the story, especially aghast when I described women bound to a cross being burned alive. She did not speak until I had finished.

"Rædwald must hear of this," she said soberly. "But we should wait until we leave Canterbury. Æthelbert is bretwalda; if he supports these men from Rome, Rædwald may be asked to follow his example."

"Bretwalda? Forgive me, but I don't know the meaning of that word either," I said weakly.

"It means 'high king.' Æthelbert is high king of all the tribes south of the Humber."

"And the Humber is ... ?"

"A river to the north, a sort of boundary line. Now, do you wish to return to the hall? Or shall we go to the women's quarters?"

"The latter, thank you. I have my own ritual to perform before bedtime," I said, very grateful for Radegund's support.

Next morning I braced myself for comments and questions about my behavior at the great hall. To my relief I was received with polite indifference — until Marguerite stopped at my table.

"I heard zat last night zee sight of zee cross drove you out of zee hall. Is zat true?" She smirked.

"No," I said quietly. "Something in the meal did not agree with me."

"Are you bothering Lady Freawicca?" Gwyneth's loud voice made us both jump.

"Of course not!" Marguerite made a face at Gwyneth and flounced away.

"She's young," said Gwyneth dismissively, "and somewhat lacking in manners. Now, Lady Freawicca, how would you like to spend your last day in Canterbury?"

Riding outside the walls of Canterbury in the company of Gwyneth, Radegund and Lise, I learned more of Gwyneth's Celtic background.

"Christianity is not new to this country," she informed us. "The Romans introduced it many, many years ago. Why, one of my own uncles was a priest of the Celtic Christian faith. He travelled far to the north, to an island in the ocean, to take instruction from the revered monk Columba. And there are still such priests scattered across the country."

"But you . . . ?" I hinted.

"The women of my family continue to worship the goddess," she said calmly.

Radegund shot me a penetrating look, as if to ask 'should we tell her?' I shook my head. We might have an ally in Gwyneth, but it was best to be cautious.

"Why do you serve Queen Bertha?" asked Lise abruptly.

"Not all who attend her share her faith," answered Gwyneth. "Several noblewomen of the court perform their own ceremonies, in private. Instead of wearing a cross, we carry . . . this."

Gwyneth lifted the hem of her gown to reveal a strange object suspended from the belt of her underdress: a ball of crystal about the size of a walnut, encased in a silver sling.

"What is that?" asked Lise, gaping.

"A medium for divination and prophecy, sometimes healing. I will say no more."

"Lady Gwyneth," said Radegund earnestly, "do you think the queen will succeed in converting her husband to Christianity?"

Gwyneth did not hesitate. "I am sure of it."

On the journey back to Rendlesham we had ample time to share our observations and reactions to the stay in Canterbury. The men expressed admiration for Augustine's sincerity and air of authority, but worried about the content of his message.

"Why, the man as much as said that our ancestors were all condemned to hell!" snorted Grima.

"Hel?" I echoed. "Loki's daughter — the goddess of the underworld? Only those who die of sickness or old age go to her kingdom."

"Nay, nay," interjected Rægenhere, "this Christian hell is different. From what I understood, it is a place of fire, a place of torture and punishment."

We stared at each other in consternation.

"On the other hand, this Augustine promises eternal life to all who accept baptism," observed Haugen. He smiled. "I liked that story about the pope and the slave boys."

"What story is that?" I asked. "I... missed it."

"Supposedly," began Haugen, launching into the story with gusto, "this Pope Gregory saw some handsome, fair-skinned slave boys in the Roman market and asked if they were pagan or Christian. He was told that they were called 'Angles.' 'Good,' he said, 'they have the faces of angels; such men should be fellow-heirs of the angels in heaven'."

Angels? Heaven? More strange new words.

Rægenhere saw my puzzled look. "I think heaven is in the sky, and angels take you there after death."

"Like Valhalla — and the Valkyries?" I ventured.

"Yes, something like that," nodded Rægenhere.

Now Edvard added his thoughts to the discussion.

"Canterbury is clearly benefitting from its association with the Continent. Such riches! Have you seen what they import? Gold, amber, garnet, ivory, rock crystal, amethyst — in return for slaves and raw materials. Trade opportunities could be expanded through these Christians! All it takes to be accepted, apparently, is a little water."

"Water...?" I began, but Rægenhere anticipated my question.

"Baptism: a ceremony using water to signify your acceptance of this new faith."

"Nay, it is more than that," said Rædwald heavily, speaking at last. "It is like an oath sworn to one's lord, offering allegiance only to him — against all others."

"What of the gods and goddesses we have worshipped all our lives?" I cried in dismay. "Are they to be forsaken?"

"So the Christians say," answered Rædwald. He shook his head. "We must wait to see how Augustine fares in Kent. His efforts may well come to naught."

Shortly before we reached Rendlesham, Radegund and I spoke privately with Rædwald, laying out for him Wiswicca's vision and its correspondence to the arrival of Augustine and his monks. Rædwald listened gravely, nodding frequently. When we had finished speaking, he lifted his head.

"It may all come down to Æthelbert. If he converts, I may have to follow. He is bretwalda and I have vowed to serve him."

My heart sank at these words, but I vowed to be faithful as well: to Wiswicca, to the goddess, to Earth Mother.

When Lise and I stepped off the boat in Helmingham a day later, I looked around me with new appreciation for my adopted homeland. Now, at the height of summer, every tree and plant seemed to breathe with life, exhaling a fragrance that filled my senses.

I was not expecting anyone to greet us at the landing, given our delayed return, but both Lempi and Gerda were waiting there — Gerda waving wildly as our boat approached. She rushed into my arms as I stepped ashore, almost knocking me off balance.

"Yes, I missed you too," I murmured, pressing her to my heart. When we finally disengaged, I took her sweaty face in my hands. "Now tell me: has Sunbeorht foaled?"

"Yes!" shouted Gerda, freeing herself to dance about joyously. "It's a mare — and I want to name her!"

"Of course you may," I assured her.

As we walked up the path, with Lise and Lempi chattering behind us, Gerda gave me all the details of the mare's birth — attended by Olaf, Roald and Gerda herself.

"... and it shivered and it got to its feet, and then Sunbeorht licked it all over," recounted Gerda breathlessly. "She's beautiful: golden-colored like her mother. I want to name her 'Sunbeem.'"

"That's perfect!" I exclaimed, stopping to hug Gerda again. "Oh, it is so good to be home and to know that all is well!"

On the way to our hut, we stopped briefly at Runa's house to see her, baby Sverre, and the new foal — all healthy and thriving.

"Your Lempi has been such a help to me!" declared Runa after greeting me warmly. "And Gerda has practically lived in that stable!"

"I'm glad to hear it," I replied. "New life must be celebrated and nurtured."

"You look... weary," commented Runa. "Did your trip not go well?"

"It was very... revealing." I sighed. "I will tell you more later, dear friend. Right now I just want to get back to my own bed."

"I understand. Welcome home, my lady."

That night as I was undressing for bed, I heard Lise and Lempi talking in their chamber — over Gerda's snores. I supposed Lise was regaling Lempi with details about dress in Queen Bertha's court — until I heard the name 'Liudhard' and paused to listen. Lise was giggling.

"Eleanor and I slipped into his room after he went to pray. She wanted to show me the special thing kept there: a water-clock. It tells the hours of the day — it measures water that drips from one container to another."

"What do you mean by 'hours of the day'?" inquired Lempi, yawning loudly.

"Well!" said Lise importantly, "Eleanor told me that there are twelve hour-times every day, and prayers must be said at certain hours — like dawn, mid-day and eventide — so they use the water-clock to tell the hours!"

"Why should it matter?" protested Lempi. "I don't understand at all."

"It's how they do things at a civilized court; that's what Eleanor said. I told her about our own marvels — Wiswicca's staff and the spring — but she said those were just pagan nonsense. I don't think she really believed me..." said Lise, her voice trailing off.

For a moment there was silence except for Gerda's loud breathing. Then Lempi burst out.

"I don't think I like this Eleanor. I don't want to hear any more about her! But... I'm glad you're back, Lise. I missed you."

"I missed you too, sister."

Smiling, I lay down on my bed and closed my eyes.

Cloak of Ashes

Although I had gone to bed without a coverlet, sometime during the night I woke overheated and burdened by heavy robes, smelling a strong odor of wet wool and incense. Twisting, I struggled to free myself and opened my eyes. A raging fire blazed before me, silhouetting a figure in full body armor. Beowulf — wielding his sword against the three huge fire-breathing heads of a single dragon!

He severed first one head, then another, and another. The sword fell from his grasp and he collapsed, just as a new head began to form at the end of the first neck. Horrified, I cried out, "Take heed! There is another!" but Beowulf lay unmoving. Rushing to him, I begged the goddess for strength. To my surprise I was able to pick up Beowulf's heavy sword.

Raising it high, I struck off the newly formed head, fire and blood gushing forth. But a second head was already reforming... and a third... Drained of strength, I stood petrified, filled with horror. With a shudder I woke, trembling and covered with sweat.

In the months that followed, both baby Sverre and little Sunbeem were a source of delight. I received almost daily reports on each.

"Sunbeem's starting to eat grass now, Lady, and her coat is changing. She's shedding her soft, fluffy hair — 'milk hair' Olaf calls it."

"You should have seen Sverre yesterday, my lady. He grabbed my fingers and let me pull him up to a sitting position. That boy is a strong one!"

Such simple joys were a welcome comfort as I waited for news: news from Denmark, news from Canterbury. Waiting, waiting... Every night I repeated the binding spell and every day I prayed that Æthelbert would not be swayed by the Christians. Each month I led the women in goddess worship at Wiswica's well. Occasionally I was called upon to deliver a baby or minister to the sick. One morning Editha appeared at my door, clearly pregnant.

"It worked, my lady. The moon blood worked. Thank you, thank you."

At harvest time I helped Gudrun organize a celebration for the whole community in the great hall, with toasts to all the gods and goddesses. During these toasts I thought of Rædwald, who had told me that Woden was the founder of his family's royal line. Olaf — as steward — supervised the harvest, ensuring that the last sheaf was left in the field for Odin's horse, or if the crops were cut and loaded into carts for winter storage in underground pits, that a green stalk was placed on top — for fertility in the coming seasons. All this was done under a waning moon.

Shortly before Yule, old Tyttla died and was duly honored on a funeral pyre. Now Rædwald was truly the king! No news had come from Denmark, but a messenger from Canterbury announced that Queen Bertha had given birth to a girl — to be named Æthelburga — and King Æthelbert was to be baptized on Christmas day. I was invited to attend the ceremony as part of Rædeald and Radegund's company. What would this mean for all of us?

When we arrived in Canterbury I was glad to see Æthelbert's hall decorated with evergreens, an ancient custom, though Gwyneth informed me that the usual fire wheel would not be lighted this year.

"Christ-mass celebrates the birth of the Christ, the most holy event in the Christian calendar," she explained. "That is why Augustine has chosen it for the baptism of the king. He will be re-born into the Christian faith."

Calendar? Is there no end to these new words?

"Is Æthelbert to be the only one baptized?" I asked anxiously.

"Oh, no! Augustine and his monks have been most persuasive! They are expecting hundreds, even thousands, to gather at the riverside."

"The river? Surely the king will not be dipped in the river!"

Gwyneth chuckled.

"I believe a special font has been prepared for the king. He will be completely disrobed and sprinkled with 'holy water' as the monks call it. After that ceremony the common people will be baptized. It should be quite a spectacle!"

She shook her head in apparent amusement.

"So . . ." I mused, "it would seem that Augustine's efforts have been . . . quite successful."

Gwyneth smiled. "Not on all fronts. His meetings with the Celtic bishops have not gone well. They find him too arrogant, too focused on discipline and organization. The Celtic Christians value personal humility and a life of service." She shrugged. "Here in Canterbury, however, Augustine has the king's full support. He is even building a new church inside the walls and a monastery just outside."

"Oh, I noticed the great piles of stone heaped outside. Are those for the . . . monastery? What does that word mean, by the way?"

"It's a house for those who serve the church. Augustine and his monks will live there, as well as the young men they take in to train as priests."

"And what of young women? Will they be welcome too?"

Gwyneth gazed at me steadily. "I cannot say. We shall see."

The day of the king's baptism dawned clear and crisp. I shivered at the thought of anyone disrobing outdoors on such a day — or worse, being immersed in the cold waters of the Stoor. Early in the morning crowds of people began to gather near the river, more and more as the day progressed. I saw old people and young, men and women, freeborn and slaves among the expectant throng, the largest assemblage I had ever witnessed. The last group puzzled me.

"Does Augustine preach to thralls?" I asked Gwyneth as we sat lingering in the great hall after porridge.

"He preaches to everyone. 'All are welcome in the kingdom of heaven,' he says."

"Strange," I pondered. "Surely no highborn lord would wish to see his thrall set on an equal footing with himself."

"I have heard," said Gwyneth, "that Christians found in slave markets are sometimes bought and freed by other Christians."

"So . . . they form bonds, new loyalties . . . but what outward sign would identify one as a Christian?" I wondered aloud.

"Have you not noticed the new necklaces worn by Marguerite and Eleanor? A pendant cross has been added to their strings of beads."

"The cross, yes. I have noticed that it's become a popular amulet."

"Come," said Gwyneth, rising. "It is time to join the others at church."

Inside St. Martin's I stood pressed between Radegund and Gwyneth, trying to keep my teeth from chattering in the clammy cold. A large, octagonal, metal tank about a foot deep and four feet wide now stood beside the altar.

"Is that the font?" I whispered to Gwyneth.

"Yes," she whispered back. "Listen: they are coming!"

The sound of chanting voices filled the small space as Augustine and his monks entered. This time one of them swung a brazier of burning incense. We guests and courtiers parted to make way for the procession to the altar. There, each man bowed before the cross, then took a place to the right or left of the font.

Æthelbert entered last, clad only in a rich fur robe. When he reached the altar, he knelt and placed his forehead on the cold paved floor. When the chanting ceased, he rose.

"Æthelbert of Kent," intoned Augustine, raising his arms above the king, "do you swear to forsake Thunor and Wothin and all those devils who are their companions?"

"I do so swear," came Æthelbert's emphatic response.

"Then cast aside your old life and be cleansed of sin!"

Two monks adroitly caught his robe as Æthelbert removed it; they held it like a screen as he stepped into the font. Augustine lifted a silver pitcher from the altar and mounted a small platform behind the font. Raising the pitcher, he began to pour a stream of water over the king's head and shoulders.

"Æthelbert, in the name of the Father, the Son, and the Holy Ghost, I baptize thee. May you ever serve the one true faith."

Three gods? Or one? The three-headed dragon flashed into my mind.

There was some delay while Æthelbert was given a towel to dry himself; then another monk handed him a long, white tunic of undyed wool, which he slipped over his head.

"Behold our brother, Æthelbert, newly born in Christ," announced Augustine.

This time Æthelbert led the procession out of the church, followed by Augustine and all the monks.

"Is th-th-that all?" I chattered. "Is it over?"

"Yes. Now there will be warming fires and feasting in the great hall," declared Gwyneth. "King Æthelbert may have given up the old gods, but he has not renounced good food and drink!"

I did not join the curious crowd who walked to the river to view the other baptisms, but I later heard Augustine himself say that ten thousand had been converted. Ten thousand! I could not comprehend such a number! Beside me, Gwyneth sniffed.

"That's the number he'll give the Pope when he writes his report. Augustine is always writing letters to the Pope."

"Letters? Do you mean ... runes?"

"No. He uses the Latin alphabet of the Romans. That's what they'll teach those young lads who train as priests. Why, Queen Bertha herself knows a little of it."

"Speaking of the queen, is she willing to receive ... visitors? I have not yet congratulated her on the birth of her daughter."

"Wait a day or two — until all this baptism frenzy dies down."

Accordingly, two days later Radegund and I visited the queen's quarters, where we found her propped up in bed, flanked by two attendants, her babe in her arms. She looked extremely pale and drawn, her cheeks mere pools of shadow.

"Did she lose a lot of blood giving birth?" I whispered to Gwyneth.

"Yes, and she has been sickly ever since." Gwyneth raised her voice. "Queen Bertha, here are Lady Radegund and Lady Freawicca to wish you well and view the princess."

"Zey are welcome," murmured the queen, smiling weakly as we approached.

Radegund had brought a clear glass flagon of mulberry wine, knowing the queen's fondness for it. I had brought a mixture of honey and butter boiled with sweet flag as a cough remedy. Both were received graciously as we handed them to her attendants.

"Queen Bertha," said Radegund after we had admired the baby's dark hair and fine features, "we must take our leave of you today. Thank you for inviting us to witness the king's ... baptism."

A little color suddenly came into the queen's cheeks.

"I did not want you to miss it," she said, her gaze full on me.

After we left the chamber, Gwyneth took us aside.

"I have something to show you — both of you."

Curious, we followed her into an adjacent chamber, which contained a small table, a straight-backed chair and an open chest filled with rolls of animal skin.

"This is what Liudhard calls his 'scriptorium,'" said Gwyneth, picking up one of the rolls. "When the queen wishes to communicate with the Pope in Rome, she dictates her message to Liudhard, who writes it in ink on these goatskins. But the queen herself signs her name — look!"

Proudly she unrolled the parchment, covered with rows of strange lines, and pointed to the bottom. There we saw B E R T A.

"Lady Gwyneth, can you read the other marks? Can you tell us what she has written to the Pope?" asked Radegund.

Gwyneth shook her head regretfully.

"Only Liudhard or Augustine himself could tell you that."

On the journey back to Rendlesham, we once again compared our experiences. Rædwald reported that King Æthelbert had urged him to consider conversion to the Christian faith, but had not absolutely commanded it. Radegund and I told him of our visit to the queen and to the scriptorium. Rædwald sighed.

"You both saw the masses of people flocking to be baptized. I fear this is one wave from a sea that will swallow us all." He paused, pondering long, then spoke. "We must learn how to swim in it without being drowned. We must find our own way in this new world."

That winter was brightened by an announcement from Gerda. She appeared beside my bed one morning to say, "I'm bleeding."

Groggily I sat up, rubbing sleep from my eyes.

"What do you mean? Are you hurt? Have you started your moon blood?

"Moon blood," she said glumly.

"Oh, Gerda!" Now I was wide awake; slipping out of bed, I folded her in my arms. "Congratulations! You are becoming a woman!"

Gerda scowled. "Lark says it's a nuisance. She says it prevents you from doing what you want to do, when you want to do it!"

"Not always," I soothed, sympathetic to her complaint. "We must celebrate! This is an important stage in your life, my sparrow."

Gerda's face cleared somewhat. "May I invite Lark to our celebration?"

"Of course. We will invite all our friends — our women friends. They will best understand the significance of this event."

I thought back to my own girlhood in Heorot. First blood had necessitated a ritual, a calling of the goddess. I vividly remembered entering a trance, and later, falling... falling... No, Gerda need not be put through anything like that.

"Come. Let's tell Lise and Lempi and begin making plans for the celebration."

At the first blood feast in our hut, eight of us crowded around the table: Gerda and I, Lise and Lempi, Gudrun and Lark, Runa and Ginnlaug. I had not told Gerda that gifts would be given, so she was surprised and delighted when we presented them one by one.

Lise and Lempi gave her a comb of antler bone and a brush with boar bristles. Gudrun and Lark had woven a small tapestry depicting birds flying above a winding river. Runa presented her with a necklace of glass beads in all the colors of the rainbow. Ginnlaug shyly handed Gerda a length of patterned braid, enough to trim a new kirtle. I gave Gerda a set of personal implements suspended from a ring: the usual pin tools for cleaning nails and picking teeth, and a spoon tool for ear cleaning.

"Thank you, thank you, thank you!" cried Gerda, dancing around the table to hug each person in turn. "I love you all!"

"Remember," said Gudrun, "if you cut your nails — or your hair — during the waxing of the moon, it will grow back more quickly."

"I'll never cut my hair!" vowed Gerda. "It is long enough to braid now."

Indeed, Gerda had blossomed into a young woman before my very eyes. As if divining my thoughts, she came up behind my chair, put her arms around my neck, and whispered impishly in my ear.

"If I am a woman now, I am old enough to marry Hans!"

That spring Olaf tried his hand at sowing seed, under Roald's watchful instruction. Not only was it a matter of pride to scatter the seed evenly, but the villagers also believed that a "missed bit" — as revealed when the first green shoots appeared — foretold a possible death in the village! As steward, Olaf was also careful to ensure that all planting took place under a waxing moon.

The waxing and waning of the moon reflected my own moods: hope alternating with despair over what might lie ahead. One morning hope was rewarded. Harig's ship docked at Helmingham, with Hans aboard... and Vögg. I could scare believe my eyes when the three of them appeared at my door.

"Lady Freawicca!" announced Vögg, his eyes shining. "We have triumphed! Skuld is dead!"

"Come in, come in, all of you, and tell me everything!" I exclaimed, tugging Vögg inside. Over my shoulder I called, "Gerda — we have visitors."

When Gerda saw Hans standing in the doorway, she gave a whoop, rushed to him and grabbed him around the waist. Hans grinned and awkwardly returned her embrace.

"I have so much to show you!" prattled Gerda. "My dog, Elki, and my horse, Sunbeem, and a magic tree — oh, I can't show you that, but..."

"Slow down, Gerda," I laughed. "Let our guests come in and take some refreshment. They have travelled far to reach us."

"Sorry," nodded Gerda, releasing Hans — whom I noticed was now a head taller than she.

As Hans gazed at Gerda, a flush crept up his cheeks. Seeing her through his eyes, I recognized the budding breasts of womanhood. Lise and Lempi rushed in from the garden to greet our guests and we were soon seated at table with mugs of cider — "pressed from our own apples," as Lempi said proudly — all save Gerda and Hans, who'd gone off to the stable with Elki barking at their heels.

"Now," I said to Vögg. "Tell us everything."

"Well," began Vögg, clearing his throat importantly, "when we first reached Denmark we visited outlying settlements to see how Skuld was being received by those who had formerly paid tribute to King Hrolf."

At the name 'Hrolf' his voice caught and he blinked several times before he could continue.

"Everywhere we found her hated and feared, for she ruled harshly, taking without giving in return. Underkings were with-holding their tribute, and biding their time. We heard that Skuld had not dared to prevent the proper burial of King Hrolf and his men: he in a ship drawn up on a headland, his sword Skofnung beside him. Nearby lay the ashes of his champions — Bodvar, Svipdag and the rest — all richly honored with weapons and treasure. After a time of mourning, a barrow was raised over them as a landmark, tall as a hill."

Like Beowulf's mound, I thought to myself, visible from far at sea.

"We also bided our time over the winter, receiving news from abroad: from Uppsala, where Hrolf's mother, Queen Yrsa, was gathering troops, and from the Gauts, where Hrolf's brother, Thori Hound's-Foot, is king. In early spring these two armies took ship, crossing the Sound to Zealand, where many free-born Danes joined them."

Vögg paused to take a long draught of cider.

"The attack on Heorot was led by Hrolf's other brother, Elk-Frodi, a huge and terrifying figure, half wild-man, half beast. Even Skuld's trolls and krakens fled before him! Together, he and Thori Hound's-Foot crashed into Skuld's hall, caught her in their huge hands, clapped a sealskin bag over her head and pulled the strings tight."

There were gasps around the table.

"Did they kill the witch then?" asked Lise, round-eyed.

"No," said Vögg grimly. "There were tortures to follow — after she was securely bound. Her eyes were gouged out, her tongue cut off. Finally, she was beheaded and dismembered, her head and bones buried in separate places, far apart."

We sat in silence, absorbing these grisly details. Then I roused myself, shaking off the horror that had seized me.

"What of Drifa and Skur?"

"They were well-received by those loyal to their father," said Vögg, "but your brother Hrethric may well be chosen king by the council. He impressed them with an amazing display of his magic."

"Magic? What do you mean?" I said, suggesting I knew the answer.

Vögg chuckled.

"Hrethric demonstrated a mastery of horses unknown in all of Denmark. He can tame a wild horse with a single gesture, and control any horse without words. He must have used some sort of magic."

A smile spread across my face. "It's a family trait of the Skoldungs," I murmured modestly.

Our visitors stayed only a few days in Helmingham, much to Gerda's chagrin. She and Hans spent most of each day together, sometimes riding double astride Sunbeorht as they roamed the countryside. When Harig's ship departed for Heorot — and other ports on his trade route — Hans and Vögg were onboard. Hans loved his life at sea, and Vögg felt called to end his days in the place where he had served his former king. He assured me that our eleven young men from Helmingham had acquitted themselves nobly in the attack on Skuld's forces, and were likely to become champions of the next king.

When Midsummer arrived, I declined the invitation from Rædwald and Radegund to visit Canterbury again, content to celebrate the solstice with my growing family. Ginnlaug was now pregnant, and Runa's boy had learned how to walk — and climb — and tumble down without tears. Besides, my knee joints ached and the knuckles of one hand were swollen and sore. I soothed them with herbal remedies as best I could, and kept the pain to myself. Travel no longer tempted me. Thus, it was with some reluctance that I responded to Radegund's summons, later that summer.

Barely ten days after the solstice, a messenger arrived from Rendlesham requesting my presence at court.

"Lady Radegund says it is of the utmost importance," insisted Per, a young man I remembered from earlier trips up and down the river.

"Very well," I sighed, "but I'll need time to prepare. I am moving more slowly these days."

This time it was Lempi who accompanied me down river, her quiet presence a comfort on the journey. She confided that Johan had not made any further overtures, but she was content to wait for whatever Wyrd would bring. I reminded myself to speak with Johan upon our return, in case it was a matter of Lempi's dowry.

The river was lovely, drenched in summer light, and abuzz with dragonflies that lighted on our heads and shoulders, then sped away on delicate wings. We had experienced heavy rains that spring, with swollen waters along the River Doep, resulting in shifting sand bars that kept our oarsmen ever vigilant. I, however, closed my eyes and basked in the warmth, letting myself be carried, free of care.

Radegund herself met us at the dock. After a warm embrace, she took my hands and looked me full in the face.

"Lady Freawicca, it's happened," she declared, her face filled with foreboding. "Rædwald has converted. He was baptized at Canterbury!"

Chapter Twenty-Three
Bretwalda

Bronze stag from top of standard in ship-grave at Sutton Hoo, England.

Shocked, I exclaimed, "How can this be?"

Radegund took my arm to lead me up the path.

"The combined example of Æthelbert and Augustine finally convinced him," she said ruefully. "Rædwald knows I do not agree with his decision, and he did make one concession: no priest would return with us to Rendlesham — despite their repeated urgings." She gave a grim smile.

"What happens now?" I asked, trying to absorb this dreaded news.

"Rædwald has promised to build an altar to the Christ — as a place for offerings and devotion — but there was no specific command to destroy our old altar. I want you to help me convince Rædwald to keep it!"

I stopped, turning to face her. "I'll do all I can."

In the great hall that evening I spoke cautiously with several of Rædwald's councilors, sounding them out on their reaction to Rædwald's conversion. Grima and Haugen were uncomfortable to be at odds with their king, but vowed to support him as their liege. Edvard was jubilant, focusing on the practical advantages to be gained from ties with the Christian Continent.

The king's sons were less enthusiastic. Eorpwald declared tersely that his father must have been bewitched at Æthelbert's court. Rægenhere was very quiet, betraying little emotion, but I noticed him watching his father with an expression of melancholy.

On display in the hall were Rædwald's baptismal gifts: a pair of silver spoons from Æthelbert marked 'Paulus' and 'Saulus,' and ten exquisite silver bowls with crosses incised on the bottoms.

"From the Pope himself," boasted Rædwald, picking up a bowl to show me. "See the fine workmanship?"

"No finer than those produced in your own workshops, my lord," I said tartly.

Rædwald stared at me, his brow wrinkling, then said quietly, "I had reasons, my lady. Walk with me tomorrow and I will open them to you."

On the morrow, after a dreamless night, I joined Rædwald for a visit to his workshops. We stopped first at the hut of Anders, the goldsmith. He was decorating a belt buckle, hammering fine silver wires onto a metal surface already cut with striations, creating a twisting beast, its tail in its mouth. Anders also showed me a pair of brooches he had recently finished: inlaid with blue and green glass, white shell, and garnets backed with gold foil. The effect was very colorful and quite lively.

Next we stopped at the bone-carvers where a group of thralls were busily producing a number of items: pins, needles, pendants, combs, knife handles, gaming pieces, spoons, weaving battens and tablets, spindle-whorls, pottery stamps, even bracelets and flutes.

"I don't want to hurry you," said Rædwald as I stood watching, "but I must visit the wood shop and put a carpenter to work constructing the cross for our new altar."

"My lord Rædwald," I said, choosing my words carefully, "You have everything you need right here. What does Christianity have to offer?"

Rædwald regarded me earnestly.

"Æthelbert is a man of honor who has always dealt justly with me. He believes that this new religion will benefit his people. Augustine's monks are even now establishing a school in Canterbury where young men will learn how to read and write in the Latin tongue. Under Augustine's influence, Aethelbert himself has drawn up a code of laws — set down in Latin by his priest — designed to prevent blood feuds and revenge killings. He sees Christianity as a civilizing force, and so do I."

"Yet, Wiswicca said..." I began, but Rædwald held up his hand.

"I know it is a grave risk to break with the old ways, and I will force no one to follow me. I recognize that my own family is... divided on the matter," he said soberly.

"Will you then continue to allow worship at the old altar? You could set up your new cross at the opposite end of the temple," I suggested.

Rædwald's face brightened. "A possible solution," he nodded. "I will think on it."

Later, in conversation with Radegund, I learned that Augustine was moving rapidly to extend his influence, establishing seats at Rochester and London, installing monks newly arrived from Rome to oversee them.

"They've dismantled St. Martin's to build a new church called 'Christ Church,' and Augustine is now called 'bishop,' apparently a higher rank than 'abbot,'" concluded Ragedund glumly. "The man is ambitious and tireless!"

Into the silence that followed I dropped a word of encouragement.

"I did speak to the king, and he is considering two altars — both old and new — in the same temple."

"Oh, Freaw!" beamed Radegund. "I knew you could sway him! He has great respect for you."

"And you did well to block the adoption of a priest for Rendlesham. How was that accomplished?"

Radegund smiled sweetly. "I told Rædwald I would abandon his bed!"

When the Christian cross was set up in Rædwald's temple — opposite the original altar — little was said aloud, but grumblings could be heard throughout the settlement. One unexpected reaction came from Beornwyn, the old crone who had assisted me in my vision trance on a previous visit. She appeared one evening at the door of Radegund's chamber, where we were talking quietly before bedtime.

"I have sumat to drive out that new god!" she croaked, waving a leather bag in one gnarled hand.

"What have you there?" asked Radegund, rising to lead Beornwyn to a table near the brazier lighted for my benefit.

"Magic!" grinned Beornwyn. "I'll show ye."

One by one she lifted out the objects in her bag: a cowrie shell, a falcon's claw, the skull of a viper, part of an amber bead, a red stone, two boar's teeth, and three small discs — one of bone, one of lead and one of iron.

"How are they used?" I asked respectfully.

"Depends... on what's needed," she rasped. "Driving away or drawing near. To drive away, you circle the target with all these things. Do it during the dark of the moon. Then chant a banishing spell over it. Thereafter, each night, remove one item at a time until all are gone." She giggled. "The victim will be gone too — or dead, depending."

Radegund and I gazed at each other over the top of the old woman's head. In unison we slowly shook our heads.

"Thank you, Beornwyn, but this... target... is not likely to respond to charms and spells," said Radegund in a kindly voice.

"You won't know 'til you try!" urged Beornwyn, awkwardly returning the objects to her bag with knuckles far more swollen than mine. "Some of these treasures were handed down from my grandam, they were, and I've never known 'em to fail," she quavered.

"Taking action to destroy the cross — either secretly or openly — would show disrespect for the king," I said slowly, "and that is not our aim."

Beornwyn sniffed and rose to go.

"Heed my words: that cross means trouble!"

When Beornwyn had left the chamber, Radegund looked at me quizzically.

"Lady Freawicca, your binding spell against the witch-queen in Denmark apparently worked, since she was overcome by her enemies. Yet...?"

"I will not go behind the king's back to undermine his authority," I said firmly. "I will not betray his trust in me."

"I see." Radegund nodded in understanding, then — her eyes lighting — she asked, "Have you visited Rædwald's new altar?"

"No. Why do you ask?"

"I think we should visit it tonight — together — now. We won't be seen if we use the outside entrance." She grinned like a mischievous child hatching a naughty plan.

"Agreed. I would like a closer look at that cross; I only saw it from a distance when the carvers carried it in to the temple."

Giggling like conspirators, we left her chamber, walking silently through the empty hall and slipping out a side door to reach the temple. The sliver of moon gave little light, and when we pushed open the heavy temple door, the interior was hidden in darkness.

"We should have brought..." I started to say, but Radegund silenced me.

"Hush! I hear something... someone is already here," she whispered.

I felt for the bag at my waist that contained my fire-starter.

"If we can find a wall torch, we'll have some light," I offered, keeping my voice low.

"Yes. Alright. Near the door — on your right — above you," she directed.

When light suddenly flared, it made us both blink, but I was sure I saw a slight movement near the old altar.

"There ..." I pointed. "Is that ... someone?" I asked, touching the knife at my waist.

"Who is here?" called Radegund in a loud voice. "Who hides in Rædwald's temple?"

A figure slowly emerged from behind the stone altar, shielding its eyes from the torch light. The figure seemed familiar.

"Lady Radegund, is that you?"

Radegund startled and took a step forward.

"Edwin? Edwin of Deira? What do you do here?"

The figure emerging from the darkness was a handsome young man with long, fair hair, his body wrapped in a dark, rumpled cloak.

"Fleeing my enemies," he said darkly. "I've been driven out of Mercia, hunted by Æthelfrith, who seeks to take my life as well as my kingdom! You are my last hope!"

"You are safe here, but why did you not come directly to Rædwald for a proper welcome? We have always received you with kindness," said Radegund.

"I don't know who to trust anymore! Those whom I thought were friends betrayed me. Here I've been praying to the gods that Rædwald will prove true to me, that he will shield me from my enemies!"

Edwin sank to his knees before Radegund and lifted the hem of her gown to his lips.

"Will you speak for me, my lady?" he implored, looking up at Radegund.

"Oh, get up! Of course I'll speak for you — but there is no need. Rædwald will welcome you as he has always done — even if you are not a Christian," she added, half-mockingly.

"A Christian? Why should I be a Christian?" asked Edwin, rising.

"Because Rædwald is now a Christian. Behold his god!" She gestured across the room at the newly-erected cross.

Lifting the lighted wall torch from its holder, I used it to ignite the others, filling the temple with light. Together the three of us gazed at the cross which loomed above us. Clearly Rædwald's best carvers were assigned the task, for the cross bore the detailed image of a warrior in full armor, arms outstretched, sword and spear at his side.

"Does it represent Tyre, the god of war?" asked Edwin.

"No. It is the Christ," said Radegund. "Come to save us all."

"I don't understand," said Edwin.

"Nor do I," sighed Radegund, "but come — you must not sleep on the floor like a beaten thrall. I will take you to Rædwald. He will know what to do."

I saw no more of Radegund or Edwin that night, but next morning I was summoned to the king's council chamber, where Edwin, Radegund and all the king's councilors were present. As we waited for Rædwald to open the proceedings, I asked Grima, "Who is this Æthelfrith that Edwin so fears?"

"A doughty warrior, known for ravaging the Britons to the north and west of his kingdom," replied Grima, nodding approvingly.

"And his kingdom is . . . ?"

"Bernicia, although he has now taken over Deira as well, which — by rights of inheritance — should have gone to Edwin after Ælla died. Æthelfrith took to wife Edwin's sister Acha, and asserts his claim through her, but it's his success in battle that counts most."

"I see," I said, though I did not fully understand.

"Edwin was being protected by King Cearl of Mercia," continued Grima, "who gave Edwin his own daughter in marriage. Something must have gone very wrong if Edwin was forced to leave Mercia. We'll soon know more."

Rædwald had raised his hand for silence and now addressed the group.

"You all know Edwin of Deira, an exile from his kingdom and a sometime visitor to our court. He now seeks sanctuary here and protection from his enemies."

The men around me nodded sagely but said nothing—until Grima called out.

"What caused you to leave Mercia, my lord Edwin?"

Edwin scowled mightily.

"Treachery! My own father-in-law betrayed me! He would have handed me over to Æthelfrith in exchange for gold and weapons!"

"How did you escape?" called a voice I recognized as Haugen's.

Edwin first hung his head, then lifted it defiantly.

"My wife clothed me like one of her women and sent me on a journey with them to a sacred spring. Under the cover of darkness we parted company and I rode day and night to reach the borders of East Anglia. Once I passed the Great Fen I threw off my woman's dress and continued on to Rendlesham. My horse almost died beneath me."

There were a few smirks at Edwin's story, but most seemed to approve of what he had done. I remembered my own little brothers once laughing at the tale of Thor dressed as a woman—unthinkable! I also wondered: what happened to Edwin's wife when the deception was discovered? Did she forfeit her own life to save her husband's?

"So . . ." Edvard was saying, "you are now being hunted by both King Cearl and King Æthelfrith?"

"They will not know where to find me," answered Edwin pointedly, "if each man here keeps his own counsel."

Have a care, young man, I thought to myself. You are the suppliant here and not in a position to dictate terms.

"My lords," said Rædwald, "We were ever at peace with Edwin's father, King Ælla, and this usurper Æthelfrith could well pose a danger to other kingdoms, including our own. I am of a mind to give shelter and protection to Edwin of Deira." He paused, looking about the room. "What is your will?"

One by one the men signaled their approval. Seeing this, the king turned to Edwin.

"Welcome to Rendlesham, my boy. You will be safe among the Wuffings."

Edwin was soon an accepted fixture at the king's court. He and Rægenhere seemed to form a special bond, frequently hunting and hawking together. I learned of this only by report, for I spent the rest of that summer at Helmingham, immersed in the daily affairs of my own household.

To thank me for my role in swaying the king, Radegund had given me a parting gift: a silver filigree needle box, shaped like a tiny barrel, and a ball of gold thread. When I showed these things to Lise upon my return home, she gave Lempi and me a sly look and began to beam.

"Have you something to tell us?" I queried.

"Yes!" cried Lise. "A marriage proposal — from Heinrich!"

"What? While we were gone?" I exclaimed

"How did it happen? Tell us!" cried Lempi.

Rejoicing, we threw our arms around Lise, although I cast a troubled glance at Lempi's face. Was she to be denied a similar good fortune?

"... and I thought we could embroider a new border on my grey kirtle," said Lise as we disengaged, "and I'll need to spend more time at the loom making blankets and linens — but Heinrich says we can wait until harvest time — and he'll be coming to see you, my lady, now that you're home again, to arrange... everything," she concluded, almost breathless.

"Well! News indeed! I shall welcome Heinrich's visit," I said, mentally adding 'and then I will pay a visit to Johan!'

It was a happy summer for all of us. Johan's proposal to Lempi came shortly after my visit to him. He confided to me that he had thought himself too old to be a suitable mate, but if Lempi were willing, he was willing. I made him promise never to mention my visit to anyone — least of all Lempi — and rejoiced in her quiet pleasure when the proposal came.

Baby Sverre was soon walking, then running, shrieking with laughter as he sought to elude the arms of his doting 'aunties.' Sunbeem joined Sunbeorth in the communal pasture during each day, but they returned to the stable at night for a bucketful of grain and an apple from Gerda.

Cloak of Ashes

Olaf was proud that his fields showed no "missed bits," and Roald saw to it that their livestock thrived. I continued to receive occasional ailing villagers at my hut, and to lead the local women in celebrations of the goddess. As the long days of summer gradually waned, I floated on a current of contentment, thankful for home and hearth, and looking forward to the double wedding of Lise and Lempi.

About a month before harvest, this comfortable cocoon was breached by news from Rendlesham. Eni, the king's brother, had been killed in a fall from his horse. A grand ship burial was to take place at Snape. All of Rædwald's subjects who could do so were invited to attend. Wilhelm, Gudrun and Lark brought the message to my household, declaring their intention to honor the king with their attendance, and urging me to join them.

"Oh, could we?" begged Gerda, clasping her hands. "I've never seen a whole ship buried before!"

"Neither have I," I admitted, though my thoughts flew back to Heorot and the flaming burial at sea of my father's death-ship. "I'll . . . I'll think on it."

"That usually means 'yes'!" cried Gerda, seizing Lark's hands to dance her around the hearth. "We could see it together!"

Gudrun laughed out loud. "That child knows you too well! But, my lady, we would be honored to include you in our party. I have not left Helmingham for many a year, and I'm looking forward to a bit of an outing."

"As an official representative," harrumphed Wilhelm, but he too looked pleased to be invited and eager to attend.

"Alright," I relented. "Thank you, friends, for the invitation. It will be our pleasure to join you."

A small fleet of three ships carried the mourners to Snape for Eni's funeral. After following the River Doep to its mouth, we sailed north along the coastline. When we reached the River Alde, we went west to Snape. Unlike King Rædwald's party, our group planned to eat and sleep on our ship, only going ashore for the funeral ceremonies.

Lark was excited to be at sea, and curious about everything. As an experienced sailor, Gerda was happy to share her knowledge with her friend, and began filling Lark's head with tales of sea serpents, mermaids, and drowned men who rose from the depths.

"Stop!" I protested. "You'll be giving Lark nightmares!"

"Oh, no," said Gudrun, who had listened avidly herself, "I have a hag stone with me that keeps away bad dreams."

"A hag stone? What is that?" I asked

"It's flint with a natural hole in it. You hang it in your sleeping space; it's like an eye to ward off evil," she explained.

"We have one of those in the stable!" said Gerda. "Roald put it there so evil spirits can't ride our horses at night!"

"Well!" I marveled. "It seems we are well protected both on land and at sea!"

Late in the day, when we reached the landing at Snape, I was somewhat surprised to find the settlement so modest in size—at least in comparison to Rendlesham. We were welcomed by a somber delegation of villagers who led us up to the great hall. There we were greeted by Eni's widow, Eadburh, and their son, Sigeberht; both were tall and thin with dark hair and eyes, which made me wonder if they were Franks.

The feast that night was adequate but not up to the standards at Rendlesham. Of course Eni had been a younger brother and thus an under-king to Rædwald himself. I wondered what their relationship had been, never having heard Rædwald speak directly of his brother. I was to get an answer to this question the next day.

After a less-than-restful night aboard ship and a cold, early morning meal, our group joined Rædwald's party for a full day of formal rites onshore. Eni's pyre was lighted by Rædwald himself, who wept aloud as the flames began to consume his only brother's body. Eni's horse and two dogs were added at midday—acts which caused Gerda great distress—but I saw none of the weapons and treasures usually given as offerings at a royal funeral. The reason lay in the village cemetery, to which we all trudged near the end of the day.

A great trench had been dug in the sandy soil at one end of the burial ground. Remarkably, in it lay a complete long boat, open to the sky.

"How did they get it here—all the way from the river?" marveled Wilhelm, "and up this incline?"

A local man overheard Wilhelm's query and answered proudly.

"On timber rollers—with horses and oxen and every man in the village, sweating at the task. We also dug the trench. We wanted to honor our king as best we could."

"By the gods," said Wilhelm, "this is honor indeed!"

"An impressive achievement," I added, awed at the scale of the undertaking.

A gangplank had been laid from the edge of the trench to the ship itself. Over this plank paced Eadburh, carrying her husband's ashes in a beautifully modeled urn. She placed it amidships, then slowly returned to the crowd of mourners, her face a stony mask. Next Sigeberht carried over his father's sword and spear, which he laid reverently on a large fur robe next to the urn.

"What are they doing?" whispered Gerda at my side.

"Provisioning Eni's ship for his voyage to the after-life," I whispered back.

"Did we bring something to give him?" she asked anxiously.

"Yes. A bucket of apples from Wiswicca's tree. Wilhelm will present it."

But first there were offerings from others in Eni's household: practical provisions such as bread and cheese and haunches of meat, and luxurious items, including a set of green glass claw beakers, identical to those used at Rendlesham.

When all had respectfully placed their gifts in the burial ship, Rædwald stepped forward and walked slowly across the gangplank. He carried nothing, and I wondered what he had to give. He stopped beside the urn and raised his right hand high above his head, so that the fading light caught the flash of gold on his finger.

"To my brother Eni," he called in a loud voice, "I give this ring: an ancient heirloom and my most prized possession."

Slipping the great Roman ring from his finger, he laid it carefully atop the urn, then with bowed head walked heavily back to join us. We all stood quietly, focused on Eni's ship as the sun sank low in the west and the trench became a vast, dark pit.

On the weary walk back to the settlement, Gerda was full of questions.

"What happens next? When do we eat? Why...?"

"There will be a funeral feast in the great hall tonight," I assured her. "Tomorrow they will begin the work of filling the trench and, later, building a mound over it — a task which could take all winter," I said, remembering the months it had taken to erect Beowulf's mound.

The feast that night was more lavish than that of the previous evening, and ale flowed freely. When toasts to all the gods were offered, I wondered if Rædwald would join in — he, a newly-baptized Christian. I saw him lift his glass and drink, but his lips did not move during the 'Wes Heil's. Was he trying to serve both religions? There was no opportunity to ask him that night. Perhaps, later, back in Rendlesham.

When our group returned to Helmingham, we found Lise and Lempi only slightly interested in our experiences at Snape, focused as they were on their upcoming weddings. Even Runa was so absorbed in her role as a mother that she gave only half an ear to my account of the journey. It made me realize that the person who had become my most intimate confidante was ... Radegund. This realization made the distance between Helmingham and Rendlesham seem shorter, and increased my own willingness to make the trip. Thus when I was invited to spend Yule at the court, I accepted without hesitation, taking only Gerda with me.

To my dismay I found that Augustine had sent over one of his priests to Rendlesham, declaring that mass must be celebrated on Christmas day in Rædwald's temple. The monk's name was Paulinus; he was a short, squat man with thick lips and a bulbous nose. We arrived on the same day and he engaged me in conversation — or tried to — as we made our way up to the settlement, followed by Per with our belongings.

"Are you a believer?" he asked pleasantly.

"In the goddess!" I said stiffly, then turned to admonish Gerda who was lagging behind with Per.

"Why do you wear those odd clothes?" asked Gerda, looking Paulinus up and down.

"Because I choose to," said Paulinus looking down at her. "They are a sign of my service to the Lord. I have taken a vow of poverty."

"Oh," said Gerda with a yawn. "Lady, how long before we get there?"

"Not long. And you'll have your own proper bed to sleep on."

"Ooh! Lise told me as much, but I didn't believe her!"

"Belief is a strange thing," broke in Paulinus. "Sometimes we find that what we once believed is not ... true."

Putting my arm around Gerda's shoulder, I glared at the intrusive priest.

"We have no need of your ... preaching," I said firmly.

Unruffled, he replied, "I am only here to save souls. Surely that is a worthy undertaking?"

Thinking of what awaited him in Rædwald's temple, I smiled.

"That may be a difficult undertaking!"

Radegund greeted Gerda and me warmly and drew us into her chamber. When the door was closed, she asked me directly, "What do you think of the priest? Will he make trouble for us?"

"The quickest way to find out is to show him the temple," I advised.

"Will he be ... outraged?" asked Radegund apprehensively.

"I'm sure he will be!" I replied.

As it happened, Paulinus was so outraged that he left Rendlesham on the next tide, fuming and vowing to "report this to the Pope!" Other than a few pangs of regret that this might create an awkward situation between Rædwald and Æthelbert, we were glad to see Paulinus go. Now Yule could be celebrated whole-heartedly, as in days of old, without the dampening presence of a priest. What we had not anticipated was a threat from another quarter.

One evening a small party of men on horseback rode into Rendlesham from the north. This in itself was reason for alarm, as most visitors arrived by boat at the riverside. Despite the winter's cold, no ice had yet formed on the Doep and it was open all the way up to Helmingham. We were sitting in the great hall at our evening meal, a Yule log roaring on the hearth nearby, being delightfully entertained by a juggler and a fellow with a harp. Suddenly Oswald, the king's steward, rushed to our table.

"My lord, an envoy from Æthelfrith has just arrived, seeking Edwin of Deira."

"What?" Edwin, who was also seated at our table, sprang to his feet. He looked about wildly, as if seeking the nearest means of escape.

"Sit down, Edwin," said Rædwald quietly. "I will deal with this. Oswald, offer these men our hospitality for the night, and tell them I will speak with them in the morning."

"Yes, my lord." Oswald bowed and took his leave.

Around the table there were looks of surprise and consternation and Edwin's face had gone pale.

"How could this have happened?" exclaimed Radegund. "We have been so careful to keep Edwin's presence here ... private."

"I hope to discover that in the morning," said Rædwald calmly. "For tonight, let us not allow our enjoyment of the season to be marred with conjectures and foreboding. Edwin, be not afraid. You are safe in my court. We will keep careful watch on our guests tonight."

The following day we waited anxiously to learn the result of Rædwald's conference with the visitors. By mid-day there was still no news from the council chamber, where Rædwald and his advisors had received the envoy. When the door finally opened, a trio of angry-faced men emerged, walked grimly through the hall, and disappeared toward the stables. When they were out of sight, Rædwald himself emerged, followed by equally grim-faced councilors. I noted that Edwin was not among them.

"What happened?" entreated Radegund, hurrying to Rædwald's side. "What can you tell us?"

"I can tell you that the honor of our court remains intact!" declared Rædwald. "Æthelfrith sought to bribe us with gold — as if we did not have wealth in our own coffers! He demanded that I put Edwin to death — a demand I flatly refused. No one dictates to Rædwald!"

Radegund sank to her knees and lifted Rædwald's callused, now-ringless hand to her lips.

"Husband, I am honored to be your wife! By the gods, you have done well!"

"By the gods?" echoed Rædwald as he gently lifted Radegund to her feet. "Time will tell."

For the rest of our stay, King Rædwald's rejection of Æthelfrith's demands was the talk of the court.

"So noble," sniffed Gertrude, wiping her eyes. "Just like his father."

"It is good that his treasury is so full," observed Hannah. "From what I've seen of the two courts, our king is even richer than Æthelbert of Kent! He can afford to be generous!"

"Surely the king's honor and a man's life are more important than wealth!" I said warmly to the circle of women around me.

Cloak of Ashes

We were seated in Radegund's chamber doing embroidery, while she was out walking with Gerda.

The two entered suddenly, along with a rush of cold air.

"It's snowing, Lady, it's snowing!" Gerda rushed up to me with cold hands and framed my face, her eyes sparkling.

"Thank you, Lady Freawicca, for loaning me your Gerda," said Radegund, shaking white crystals from her hair. "I'd forgotten the pleasure of catching snowflakes on the tongue!"

"Lady, the queen says she has a horse I can ride the next time we come. Will that be soon?" Gerda's cheeks were glowing.

"You are welcome here at any time," declared Radegund, laughing. "Any time."

We did return to Rendlesham in the spring, and Gerda did get to join Radegund on horseback for a ride along the river trail. I chose not to join them, content to know they were having a good time. Unexpected news arrived from Canterbury: Queen Bertha had died during the winter, and it was rumored that King Æthelbert was considering marriage to one of Bertha's women: Eleanor.

"Can you imagine?" sniffed Radegund, biting off a thread. "I suppose he needs someone to raise Æthelburga. Still . . ." She shook her head and held up her needle to be re-threaded. "Poor Bertha."

"Perhaps the death of her bishop, Augustine, hastened Bertha's own death," I suggested. "At least they had finished constructing the monastery church. Now Bertha and Augustine can be buried in adjoining chapels."

"How strange, these Christian burial customs," said Radegund, shaking her head. "To be closed up in a box and buried without grave goods — it's an insult to the dead!" she declared vehemently. "I hope that never happens to me!"

"If I am alive, I will ensure that it does not," I promised, then changed the subject. "Has Augustine's replacement arrived?"

"Yes, a man called 'Laurentius.' Apparently the pope himself died the same month as Augustine, but a new one has already taken his place. There is no end to these people!"

There was also no end to Æthelfrith's audacity, for a second envoy arrived at Rendlesham that spring, offering even more gold and demanding that Edwin be put to death. Rædwald refused their bribe and rejected their demand. Again, Edwin was assured of his safety. Æthelfrith's persistence, however, was a cause of concern among Rædwald's councilors.

"Æthelfrith is stubborn," muttered Grima. "He won't give up until he gets what he wants."

"Rædwald is equally stubborn," growled Haugen. "He won't give in."

As a precaution, Rædwald ordered his storehouses and stockpiles to be opened, and set his blacksmiths to work making more armor and weapons: swords, shields, spears and battle axes. The ongoing training of young warriors was intensified.

An uneasy sense of impending danger hung over the court, not dispelled by the beauties of spring. Gerda delighted in the birds arriving almost daily, greeting her favorites like old friends: larks, swallows, wrens, finches and nightingales. She was now a head taller than the previous spring, and had blossomed into an attractive young woman. Yet she still ran as heedless as a child in the out-of-doors, and gloried in her freedom.

After their marriages, Lempi had moved into Johan's house and Lise had departed to live with Heinrich in the village, so Gerda and I were left alone in our hut, save for our thrall Berit. Her sister Mari was still living with Runa and Olaf, to help with the extra work a baby entailed.

That summer Gerda introduced Sunbeem to the saddle, and was soon riding her filly every day. One afternoon she returned wearing only her under shift and bearing an unexpected treasure: carefully wrapped in her kirtle fluttered a fledgling hawk.

"It must have been pushed out by its nest-mate," Gerda declared, "for I found it in the underbrush below a very tall tree. It called to me and I couldn't leave it there to die!"

"You're hurt!" I exclaimed, noting flecks of blood on Gerda's hands and arms.

Gerda shrugged. "She resisted my rescue –but Lady, I know I can raise her, and I could train her to hunt — like Rægenhere's hawk."

"What? Hawking like a man?"

"Why not?" Gerda set her lips in a line I knew well. "I've watched what Rægenhere does with his hawk. I can do the same."

"Well . . ." I considered. "Rægenhere's bird is a peregrine falcon, not an ordinary hawk."

"But he doesn't know how to talk to his bird, and I do!" said Gerda triumphantly.

"I guess that settles it!" I said with a laugh. "We'd best start at once constructing some sort of enclosure for it."

Gerda's hawk, which she named 'Flicker,' was a voracious eater. Gerda soon tired of trying to catch mice and snakes to feed it, but found that the bird would also take bites of raw meat, including our fingers! It grew rapidly, seeming to feather out more every day, in beautiful colors ranging from brown to white on its speckled breast. One leg had been injured in its fall, which gave it a slight waddle, but it was graceful in short flights — tethered to Gerda's wrist with a length of my own silk thread!

She began coaxing it to fly from its perch to her forearm — wrapped with a towel — by rewarding it with food. After the bird became accustomed to this, she increased the distance. Taking one of the spindle whorls we used at the loom, she wound a long length of line around it and fastened the free end to Flicker's good leg. Thus she could let out line as the bird flew, and reel it back if it refused to return.

When Lark and Walthar heard about Gerda's hawk, they came to see it — or rather to see Gerda trying to train it.

"You need a hood for your bird, and a proper glove for your hand, "said Walthar. "I can make them for you, if you like."

"Oh, would you? I'm not good at sewing," admitted Gerda. "My fingers are too clumsy."

"Your fingers are ... beautiful!" blurted Walthar. Then he reddened. "I'll see what I can do."

Walthar left hastily, leaving Lark and Gerda to titter, but nothing was said about Walthar's inadvertent revelation. When I asked Gerda later that day if she were ... interested ... in Walthar, she shook her head.

"If I ever marry, it will be to Hans."

That winter King Æthelbert died in his sleep in Canterbury, to be succeeded by his son, Eadbald. Despite the installation of a bishop at Rochester, Eadbald had resisted the incursion of Christianity, staunchly clinging to traditional beliefs. He did, however, allow his much younger sister Æthelburga to retain her personal priest at Canterbury, his father's seat. And he married Æthelbert's widow, his own stepmother.

"I hear that Bishop Laurentius is outraged at this marriage," said Radegund on what had become my annual spring visit to Rendlesham. "Apparently he doesn't realize that it is customary to keep such unions within the ruling family. I see nothing wrong in it!"

I had no opinion on the matter, so kept my peace except to ask, "Will Æthelbert be buried in the monastery church?"

"Yes, near Bertha in an adjoining chapel. Rædwald will attend the funeral ceremony, but I . . . I am staying home this time. Such journeys have begun to tire me."

Something in her tone sounded an alarm in my head, and I scrutinized her closely.

"Are you not . . . well?" I asked sympathetically.

She sighed and put down the garment she'd been sewing.

"I seem to have no appetite of late, that's all."

Indeed her face did seem thinner, her cheekbones more prominent.

"I'll prepare a spring tonic for you," I offered. "That should help."

Our conversation was interrupted by Gertrude, who hurried into the chamber looking stricken.

"My lady," she gasped, "Those men — Aethelfrith's men — they're back!"

Radegund turned pale and put a hand to her chest.

"Thank the gods Rædwald is still here! But . . . three times!" She turned to me. "What does it mean, Lady Freawicca?"

"I fear it means a final ultimatum . . . and a crisis."

"May the gods be with us," muttered Gertrude.

This time Æthelfrith's delegation offered more than gold and a demand for Edwin's death; they threatened war.

After a full day shut up in Rædwald's council chamber, no decision had yet been reached. That night the king dined privately with Radegund and me.

"How can I justify shedding the blood of my subjects to save one man?" agonized the king. "I am tempted to meet their demands, to take their gold and put Edwin to death in exchange for peace in my kingdom."

Cloak of Ashes

"Husband!' cried Radegund. "You can't mean that! You have given Edwin your word that you will protect him! You must not sacrifice your honor!'

"King Rædwald," I said in the silence that followed. "With the death of Æthelbert of Kent, who is now high king of Angle-land?"

Rædwald lifted his head and stared at me, then smiled.

"Ah, I see what you are thinking. Mayhap Æthelfrith seeks to tempt me into battle that he may destroy my power and reign supreme."

"Husband," said Radegund earnestly, "if there were to be war, it would be a war of honor — better than peace with dishonor."

Rædwald rose to his feet, an unreadable expression on his face.

"Ladies, you have given me good counsel. I will consider it this night, and give the envoy my answer in the morning."

It was a sleepless night for many in the court, including me. Thankfully my wakefulness did not disturb Gerda, who snored lightly in the adjoining bed, one arm flung over her breast.

What will happen to all of us if war comes? Where would it take place? What if Rædwald is killed — or Edwin? Would a battle be worth such an outcome? Might Aethelfrith back down if Rædwald accepted his challenge? I turned and twisted, unable to rid my mind of these and other questions. Would morning never come?

I was dozing lightly when there came a knock at the chamber door.

"Lady Freawicca?" Another knock.

"Yes, I'm awake. Come in."

Gertrude appeared in the doorway, her face apprehensive.

"King Rædwald summons everyone to his council chamber — for an announcement."

She bowed and closed the door.

Quickly I slid out of bed and scrambled into my clothes. Gerda still lay sleeping, and I did not disturb her. I slipped out the door, pulling it shut behind me, and hurried down the passageway. *What will Rædwald say?*

Inside the council chamber, packed with councilors and courtiers, Rædwald sat immobile in his high seat, staring straight ahead. Beside him stood Edwin, pale but resolute. When the chamber could hold no more, Oswald shut the heavy doors with a resounding boom. I jumped, then shivered as silence descended on the expectant throng.

Unexpectedly, Edwin stepped forward. He cleared his throat but still spoke hoarsely, his voice strained.

"I would have it be known that if I am to die, it is better to receive death from the hand of this noble lord than from the hand of a lesser man. Ever has Rædwald kept faith with me, showing me no evil or disdain. I count it an honor to have had the friendship of so great a king."

Murmurs of approval rippled through the crowd, and I heard Gertrude sniffling somewhere behind me. Now Rædwald rose, his jaw set, slowly scanning the faces before him ere he spoke.

"People of Rendlesham! A grave decision has been forced upon me: to sacrifice the honor of this court and appease Æthelfrith, or to hazard the court itself in a battle we have not sought. To submit to Aethelfrith's demands would be to put our necks under his yoke. That I will not do. I have told Aethelfrith's envoy that Edwin of Deira remains my true friend and comrade — and have sent them on their way. We go to war!"

All around me shouts of jubilation mingled with groans of despair and disbelief. I was not sure in that moment what I felt. Looking about the throng, I sought Radegund's face and found it. Pride shone in her eyes as tears streamed down her cheeks. War. Rædwald was going to war.

In the days that followed, time seemed to pass more quickly. Overnight Rædwald's court was transformed from a royal house anticipating a leisurely summer to an armed camp preparing for war. Extra watches were set to alert the king of any surprise attack. Every man who could be spared from spring planting began to ready his weapons and practice their use. Fighters had been recruited from all over East Anglia and even from Kent, for Eadbald pledged his support to Rædwald and Edwin. Among the men from Helmingham were Gudrun and Wilhelm's son, Walthar, and Lise's husband, Heinrich. Now, as men flocked into Rendlesham, we women were kept busy supplying food for so many mouths.

Gerda found it all exciting.

"It's as if everyone had been drowsing and suddenly woke up!" she observed to me as we were preparing herbal packets that stopped blood flow.

"What do you mean?" I asked, busy sorting the herbs.

"Everyone is so full of... purpose. Is it always like that in a war?"

I thought back to the frequent battles between Geats and Swedes.

"In the beginning, yes. Later ... there will be bitterness and grief ... for the survivors."

Gerda stopped folding the square of linen in her hands.

"You've never told me about that part of your life before we met," she said softly. "Was there much ... grief and bitterness?"

"Yes. Yes. Now, let us resume our work."

The possibility of someone she knew dying in battle was brought home to Gerda when Rægenhere showed her his sword and sheath.

"They belonged to my grandfather Tyttla," he said proudly, proffering the blade for her inspection. "Careful — it's sharp!"

Gingerly she touched the two-edged sword, long as half her height, and asked, "Does it have a name?"

"Yes. 'Skull-biter'," grinned Rægenhere.

I shivered, envisioning the sword in action.

"And look at my scabbard," continued Rægenhere, next holding up his sword sheath. "It's lined with fleece so the sword won't rust."

"Do you have a mail shirt to protect your body?" I asked.

Rægenhere frowned. "No, but I have a helmet and shield. That should be enough."

"You mustn't get hurt, Rægenhere," said Gerda, suddenly somber. "I haven't yet had a chance to show you my hawk. I've been training her so that we can join you in a hunt."

Rægenhere's eyes widened, but he nodded courteously.

"I will look forward to that — when I return from battle."

For a time Rædwald and his councilors debated the merits of taking a land or a sea route to Æthelfrith's kingdom, finally choosing the sea when Eadbald of Kent offered to supply more longboats. A march inland would still be necessary, but the sea route would take less time and perhaps provide some element of surprise. Rædwald wished to strike a decisive blow as soon as possible.

On the morning Rædwald's forces set sail, all those being left behind were at the docks to bid them farewell.

Fervent cries of "Safe journey!" "May the gods be with you!" and "Come back to us!" rang in our ears.

Rædwald had privately asked me to consult my runes concerning the outcome of his attack. Three times I turned up Teiwaz, rune of the warrior, the same rune Eorpwald had painted on his battle shield. Tyr, god of war, gave victory in battle and protection from harm. Rædwald was reassured by this rune-casting, but he also prayed to the one god of his Christian altar, while others made offerings to Thor and Odin at the other end of the temple.

Time slowed after the army's departure. Gerda and I stayed on at Rendlesham for most of the summer, sharing concerns and doing our best to alleviate the gloom that had settled over the court. Radegund was especially fearful and distressed, wondering aloud if she had erred in urging Rædwald to battle. The three of us — Radegund, Gerda and I — frequently rode out by the river in the long afternoons. Midsummer came and went. A whole month passed with no messages, no news from the north.

I was sitting at porridge with Radegund and her women when Gerda came rushing breathlessly into the hall.

"A ship! A ship from the sea!" she panted. "It must be the king!"

"May the gods make it so," I breathed, rising so quickly I bumped my bad knee on the table's edge and gave a gasp of pain.

"Go ahead — I'll be along," I insisted as Radegund hesitated for an instant. "I'll come with Gerda."

Everyone was racing for the harbor as I hobbled down on Gerda's arm, feeling every year of my long life weighing upon me. To my intense relief, a line of ships was approaching our landing. Rædwald's army.

Rædwald himself stood at the helm of the first ship, Eorpwald at the second. And Rægenhere? I scanned the faces lining the decks, but saw him not.

Rædwald stepped to the ship's rail and held aloft his standard: a tall iron staff topped with sea eagle feathers. Beside him a young man I recognized as Per lifted a large, curved horn and sounded one long, resounding note. A hush fell over the crowd as all eyes focused on the ship where Rædwald stood, fixed as a figurehead.

"People of Rendlesham!" he shouted. "The victory is ours! Æthelfrith is dead and his sons have fled! Edwin has regained his rightful throne! And I, Rædwald, am now *Bretwalda*: high king of all Angle-land!"

Deafening shouts and cheers erupted around me; the crowd surged forward, carrying Gerda and me with it. As if in a dream I saw Rædwald step ashore; I saw Radegund reach the landing and fling herself into his arms. They were surrounded by women and men weeping for joy. Then I saw Rædwald lean down and speak into his wife's ear. Suddenly Radegund collapsed, barely caught by Eorpwald, who had leapt off his ship to join his father. I knew in an instant the unspoken truth: Rægenhere has not returned: Rægenhere is dead.

Alas for young Rægenhere.

Chapter Twenty-Four
Yeavering

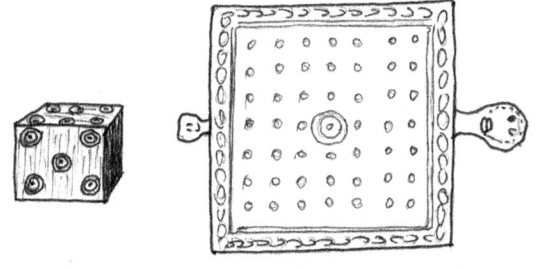

Game board found in Ballinderry, Ireland, and Viking Age dice found at Tåsen in Oslo, Norway.

We did not hear an account of the battle for many days. First, urns containing the cremated remains of those killed in battle were reverently unloaded from the ships. Those from Rendlesham were carried to the cemetery at Hoo Hill, where Rædwald led the mourners in a ceremony honoring the dead. One urn was designated for Helmingham: Wilhelm's son Walthar had been killed in the initial onslaught.

Gerda's face was awash with tears when she heard this, coming so soon after the news of Rægenhere's death.

"How can you bear it, Lady?" she sobbed, clinging to me.

It was long since I could take her on my lap and soothe her by stroking her unruly hair. She was a young woman now, with hair that hung in a thick braid down her back. Still, I could hold her as her hot tears wet my face and offer what words I could.

"As you know, loss is the way of Wyrd, my child. Men go to war and die, while women wait and weep for them."

Gerda jerked away and wiped her eyes with one hand.

"'It's not... it's not... fair!" she choked. "I'd rather die myself!"

"Oh, Gerda, sparrow, never say that! I could not bear to lose you!"

Once again we held each other close, our hearts breaking for the young men who had died and for those who loved them.

After the cemetery service, Radegund immediately shut herself in her chamber and took to her bed. She forbade anyone to enter, even her husband, and refused all food.

"Give her time," I advised Rædwald. "Her grief must have scope."

Inwardly I feared Radegund's possible descent into darkness.

Rædwald carried himself nobly, but new lines were etched in his face, and a look of hooded sadness shadowed his every move. Rægenhere's death cast a pall over the entire court. After three days of pervasive gloom, I sought out Eorpwald, the only one who still seemed capable of action.

"This can't go on!" I admonished. "You must act to break this terrible paralysis!"

"What can I do?" he implored.

"Order a banquet to honor our warriors. There tell everyone the story of what happened in Northumbria. Surely there is much to celebrate as well as to mourn? And," I added, "go to your mother. She still has one son, and she needs to be reminded of that."

Eorpwald's face darkened, but he nodded. "I will go to her," he whispered.

"And tell her," I said evenly, "that if she does not soon rejoin the court, I will send for Paulinus!"

A half-smile crossed his face as Eorpwald bowed and left the storeroom, where I had found him cleaning his war gear. As I looked around at the stacks of spears and damaged shields on the floor—loot taken from the enemy—I wondered: how many men have been sacrificed to Æthelfrith's ambition?

Radegund did emerge, pale and somehow shrunken, in time for the 'victory feast'. She had dressed in a simple blue linen gown over a white under shift. She wore no jewelry save for the silver clasps at her wrists.

Earlier, I had gone to the kitchen and talked to the cooks, instructing them to prepare the favorite dishes of both king and queen. I supervised a group of thralls in giving the hall a thorough cleaning, then had them strew fresh rushes and sweet-smelling herbs on the floor. Oil lamps were refilled, cushions plumped, tabletops scrubbed. A fresh start was needed at the court of Rendlesham.

The evening began quietly, with Rædwald and Radegund taking their places at the head of the hall, Eorpwald standing between them. To one side their scop, Gunter, softly plucked his lyre, each note falling like a balm on our bruised and aching hearts. Most of Rendlesham had crowded into the great hall in a communal outpouring of respect and support, but also with a need for consolation and reassurance.

Rædwald rose to address the assembly, simply attired yet kingly in a tunic of blue linen edged with gold.

"People of Rendlesham! I welcome you this night. We have gathered here to honor our dead and to celebrate the deeds of the living. Our enemy has been vanquished. Our kingdom is now safe to enjoy a time of peace. We will forever remember those who gave their lives that we might have this gift."

He paused, looking down at Radegund, whose face was set in a mask of stone.

"Following the feast," he continued, "my son Eorpwald will relate the whole story of our campaign, telling you in detail the sequence of events in our most decisive battle: the battle of the River Idle!"

Murmurs of anticipation swept through the hall. Beside me, at our table with Radegund's women, Gerda whispered, "Must we hear this?"

"Yes," I whispered back. "Better to hear the truth than to imagine greater horrors."

During the course of the banquet the mood in the hall gradually lightened. I heard occasional laughter, and voices raised in jest or argument — everyday sounds, comforting sounds. I watched Radegund take a few mouthfuls and turn to nod at something her husband was saying. Rædwald himself and the councilors around him ate with their usual gusto. Thus far the evening was progressing well.

When the last crumb had been cleared away and goblets refilled, Eorpwald rose to address the company. He made a manly figure in his red tunic edged with gold, his hair pulled back in a single braid.

"My friends," he boomed, "thanks to the support of men throughout this kingdom, our numbers greatly exceeded those of our enemy. Even so, we did not underestimate the threat posed by Æthelfrith and his forces. Some of you may have heard that, earlier this year, Æthelfrith put to death over a thousand Britons during his campaign in Cheshire — including hundreds of monks. Yes," he nodded at the exclamations which broke out below him, "Æthelfrith was ferocious, a grim and merciless adversary."

Even I was shocked at this disclosure, knowing that monks bore no arms and thus could not easily defend themselves.

"We landed on the coast of Lincolnshire — or 'Lindsey' as it is called there," said Eorpwald with a broad gesture, "then marched north and east along the old Roman road. We crossed the River Trent at the ford, still meeting no opposition despite a small fortification on its west bank. We continued on to the ford over the River Idle. It was there, on the east bank, that we met Æthelfrith's men."

Eorpwald paused to drain a glass of ale, then continued.

"Here we formed three columns: one led by the king, one by Rægenhere, and one by me. We advanced with standards flying and weapons at the ready. Æthelfrith rushed on us boldly with a small body of veteran soldiers, swooping down on Rægenhere's column. Swiftly he put to the sword my brother Rægenhere and many of those he had commanded."

Howls of rage and dismay erupted throughout the hall. Radegund clapped her hands to her ears as if unwilling to hear more. Eorpwald held up his hand for silence.

"Despite this sudden and appalling loss, Rædwald and I stood firm, our columns repelling all efforts to penetrate our ranks. In his repeated charges, Æthelfrith became separated from his own men and was quickly surrounded. There, on a heap of bodies he himself had slain, Æthlfrith fell."

"Who killed him?" shouted a voice from the back of the hall.

"Edwin stripped him of his shield, my spear ran through his gut, and Rædwald's sword finished him off, cleaving his head from his body."

Utter silence greeted these grisly details; then whoops and savage cries rang through the hall. Eorpwald wisely let his listeners vent their bloodlust and joy. When it subsided, he spoke again.

"Æthelfrith's army dropped their arms and fled when they saw their commander fall. We cut off Æthelfrith's hands and left them posted on the battlefield as a symbol of his defeat. We jammed Æthelfrith's head on a spear and carried it into Lincoln, one of his former seats; there we forced his subjects to erect funeral pyres for our dead."

Eorpwald momentarily bowed his head.

"After a few days of mourning we journeyed on, north to Yeavering, Æthelfrith's principal seat. The news of his defeat had preceded us and his sons had already fled. Only Edwin's sister, Æthelfrith's wife, was there to welcome her brother to his rightful throne."

My mind reeled imagining the scene. What must Acha have felt — her husband dead at her own brother's hand? What a cruel conflict of loyalties! The faces of the other women at my table reflected similar troubling thoughts. Now Eorpwald's voice rose to a shout, filling the hall.

" . . . and so we have returned, no longer fearing attack from the north. Now Rædwald controls both north and south. Rædwald is now *Bretwalda*: high king of all Angle-land!"

Amid cheers and calls for toasts, Eorpwald resumed his seat. Well done, Eorpwald! I murmured silently.

Again and again we raised our glasses: "To Rædwald! To Eorpwald! To Rægenhere! To Edwin!"

It was late in the evening when we finally left the great hall and straggled off to our beds. As I withdrew, I noticed Gunter still sitting crosslegged on the floor, lightly fingering his lyre as his lips moved furiously.

"What are you doing?" I asked, stopping to place a hand on his shoulder.

"Composing a new lay," he grinned up at me, "to be called 'Battle of the River Idle.'"

Before we fell asleep that night, Gerda had a question for me.

"What were you thinking when Eorpwald mentioned Edwin's sister? You squeezed my hand really hard!"

"Did I? I'm sorry," I said, raising up in my bed. "Her loss of Æthelfrith reminded me of how I lost my husband, Ingeld."

"What happened?" Gerda instantly sat up in her bed.

"He was blinded by my mother and stabbed by my father's sword."

Gerda gasped. "How horrible! Did it happen ... right in front of you?"

"No, I was far away in my husband's hall. Ingeld attacked my father's hall back home to settle an old feud between our families."

Gerda was quiet for so long that this time I asked her the question.

"What are you thinking, my sparrow?"

"About how strange and confusing it all is ... why people do what they do. The good and the bad seem to get all mixed up ... and you never know what's coming next!"

"You are right, dear one. All we can do is face the unknown with courage."

Gerda and I spent a few more days at Rendlesham to be sure that Radegund was getting better. After promising her that we would return at Yule, we departed with Heinrich to bear Walthar's remains back to Helmingham. It was a somber homecoming. Lise was nearly beside herself with joy to see her husband safely home, but the loss of Walthar was a terrible blow for Lark, Gudrun and Wilhelm. The entire settlement gathered to honor him as his urn was buried in the village cemetery, and I personally oversaw the funeral feast.

Harvest time gave everyone work to do, which eased the pain somewhat, but Walthar's loss reminded everyone of the brevity and fragility of life. Heinrich told Walthar's family that he and Walthar had found themselves under Rægenhere's command, and he assured them that Walthar had fought bravely and died nobly.

"At least we know he is in Valhalla," gulped Lark. "Though I never pictured my gentle brother as a warrior."

Gerda tried to comfort her friend as best she could, but I feared it would be a dark winter ahead for everyone.

Our visit to Rendlesham at Yule was a lengthy one. Radegund's health had again declined and Rædwald was clearly worried.

Cloak of Ashes 423

"She won't eat!" he confided to me. "If you could get her to eat something — anything!"

"I may be able to help," I said, "for I brought with me a cask of water from Wiswicca's well and a bucket of apples from her tree. And — with your permission — I will gather her women to perform a healing ritual."

"Lady Freawicca, thank you! You have never failed me!"

Rædwald lifted my hands to his lips, and I flushed at this unexpected gesture.

I started in the kitchen, a separate structure near the great hall.

"Have you any almonds in your store of nuts?" I asked the head cook, a burly fellow with fleshy jowls. When he answered "Yes," I instructed him to crush a handful and steep them in boiled water from the cask I provided. "It's for the queen," I explained, "her stomach."

He nodded and set to work, while I next directed one of his helpers in preparing a sauce of apples sweetened with honey. I myself brewed a tea, using water from Wiswicca's well poured over rosemary and mint leaves. Finally, I recruited Gerda to help me serve all this to Radegund.

She received us from her bed, reclining on pillows of goose down. At first she showed no interest in our offerings, simply listening as Gerda chattered on about her hawk Flicker, her horse Sunbeem, and the latest escapades of Runa's boy, little Sverre. When I handed Radegund the mug of almond milk, she accepted it absent-mindedly and took a small sip.

"What is this?" she asked, sitting up in surprise. "It tastes ... different ... but good."

"It will taste even better with this," I said encouragingly, offering a small bowl of apple sauce. "Try it."

Obediently Radegund opened her mouth as I gave her a spoonful.

"Ummm, much better than porridge and barley water," smiled Radegund. "That's what my women have been urging on me."

"I'm glad you like it, my lady," I smiled back.

Gerda could contain our "secret" no longer.

"It all comes from Wiswicca, Lady Radegund, from her tree and her spring! That water makes everyone feel better!"

"No wonder, then," said Radegund. "Now let me try some of that tea."

After this experiment, Radegund took a little more nourishment each day, and I was cautiously optimistic. Gerda and I sat beside her bed and talked to her almost every afternoon — a time when the darkness outside seemed to weigh most heavily on Radegund's spirits.

On one of those afternoons I brought Radegund's women to her chamber for a simple ritual of healing. While the women arranged themselves in a semi-circle, standing around Radegund's bed, I sprinkled pieces of cinnamon bark in one of the braziers that warmed the room. Its sweet aroma soon filled the chamber.

Gerda carried in a pitcher of spring water from Wiswicca's well and a platter of tiny honey cakes made especially for this occasion. These she placed on a chest at the foot of Radegund's bed, where an array of goblets had already been set out. Then Gerda took a place to the left of the head of the bed and I stood on the right to begin the ceremony.

"Ladies of the court, we gather here to further the healing of your queen, Lady Radegund. Together we call upon the goddess, upon Mother Earth, to spread her mantle over us as we lie fallow in the depths of winter, resting until she calls us forth again, full of new life. I will now anoint each of you with water from Wiswicca's well — itself a gift from the goddess."

Taking a small silver bowl I had previously procured from Radegund's stores, I poured into it a measure of water from the pitcher. Dipping my fingers into the bowl, I first touched Radegund's forehead lightly, then walked slowly around the ring touching each woman's forehead. I finished with Gerda, then anointed my own forehead.

"Even as the first drops of spring rain awaken the seed sleeping in the earth, so let this sacred water revitalize each of us, though spring be far away."

Next I picked up the tray of honey cakes.

"Bees are both the offspring and the messengers of the goddess. They suck the sweetness of flowers and carry pollen from plant to plant, ensuring that life may continue and wax abundant. Let us now partake of this bounty, savoring life's sweetness on our tongues."

I proffered the tray of cakes first to Radegund, then to each woman and to Gerda, taking the last cake myself.

"Now select a cushion and be seated as we eat and drink together, taking our ease. This ritual now is ended."

But it was not yet over. As we settled down companionably, beginning to nibble our cakes and sip spring water, an unexpected sound caught our ears.

"Hark!" exclaimed Radegund. "What do I hear? Bird song?"

After scanning the rafters, I looked into the dark corners of the room. In one stood Gerda, her eyes closed, her mouth open, music pouring from her lips. First came the melodious song of a nightingale, then the cheerful chirping of a sparrow, and finally she lifted our hearts with the trilling of a lark at early morning. When her song ended, we sat transfixed.

"The goddess has indeed been with us," whispered Radegund in awe. "She spoke to us through Gerda's songs."

When Gerda and I finally departed for home, we promised to return with the spring—and return we did, relieved to find Radegund on her feet and acting almost like her old self.

"Edwin has invited Rædwald and me to visit his seat at Yeavering," she confided as soon as we were alone together. "But I don't think I'll have the strength to do it... unless... you and Gerda come with us?"

"When would this be?" I asked cautiously.

"At Midsummer. It is a voyage of several days to Bamburgh, then at least a day's journey on horseback to reach Yeavering. Rædwald thinks the sea air will do me good, and I have neglected my horse Sandyfoot of late, but..."

"But what? It sounds like a marvelous excursion," I exclaimed, willing to do anything to restore Radegund to full health.

"Wonderful! Gerda could bring her Sunbeem and you Sunbeorht," said Radegund, her face growing animated. "We'll take a cargo ship to hold all the horses."

"Well!" I laughed. "It sounds as if you have already laid plans!"

She laughed too. "Let's find Rædwald and tell him the good news."

Summer came early that year, with hot dry weather day after day, causing people, animals and crops to wilt in the heat. Then a series of heavy rains left us with muddy fields, muggy weather, and swarms of insects.

"I declare!" puffed Gudrun, wiping sweat from her brow as we sorted herbs together, "We've not had a scourge like this since my grandam's time. She used to grow plantain for insect bites and stings: mashed the leaves and applied them directly to the skin."

"Wiswicca often used a poultice of comfrey for the same purpose," I offered. "And the bark of a witch hazel tree steeped in hot water to relieve swelling and itching."

Gerda and Lark entered the herb room unexpectedly, slapping at their arms and faces.

"How can you bear to work in here?" asked Gerda. "Outside there's a bit of a breeze to keep the bugs off." She grimaced. "A pretty pair we'll look, Lady, when we join the royal party!" She gestured to the bites on her arms and legs.

"Oh, when do you leave?" asked Lark, reaching for a sprig of peppermint to chew.

"Tomorrow," I answered. "That's why your mother is helping me with these herbs: I want to have a good supply to take with me on the trip north."

"North," echoed Lark. "I've never been further north than Snape. It must be ... cooler there," she said wistfully.

"For Lady Radegund's sake, I hope so," I said. "This weather must be very hard on her — oh, that reminds me Gudrun: wrap up some leaves of valerian. That's always good for anxiety and sleeplessness."

Our first day at sea brought welcome relief from the stifling heaviness along the River Doep.

"I can finally breathe again," declared Radegund as she stood beside me at the ship's rail. We had both removed our head clothes to let our hair stream in the wind, and I noticed that hers was now uniformly gray. "It is good to leave behind the ... reminders of painful memories ... at least for a while," she added.

Radegund had brought with her only one woman: Gertrude. I had brought only Gerda, so we were a small party. Two of Rædwald's councilors had joined us, Grima and Haugen, but the crew was made up of young men who expertly rowed us out to sea and hoisted sail.

We had good wind on the journey north, staying always within sight of the coast — a fact Radegund found reassuring. At night we sheltered in protected bays, but seldom left the ship except to set up cooking tripods, build fires, and exercise the horses in our hold — a task Gerda loved. The air grew colder each day and we soon donned woolen cloaks as we sped ever closer to our destination.

"Look!" called Gerda one morning. "What is that? It's covered in white, but it can't be snow."

Peering through the light mist, we gazed in wonder at a rocky island on our starboard side. Gradually, as the ship drew nearer, we began to distinguish shapes.

"Birds!" crowed Gerda, "an endless number!"

She ran to the bow to ask Rædwald if he knew what they were called, and came back to report.

"They're puffins! Aren't they wonderful? I'd like to take one home with me," shouted Gerda above the cries and screams of the birds massed along the rocky ledges.

Indeed they were unusual, even comical birds, with squat bodies and colorful bills, but I was not sorry when we left their clamor behind. As we passed another island, Gerda was entranced by a large gathering of gray seals, sunning themselves on the rocks.

"Ooh, look at their big eyes!" she crooned. "They look so appealing, so... sad."

I remembered having a similar reaction as a girl at Heorot when I saw complete sealskins stacked in the market on trading days. As we scudded through the waves, I felt almost like that girl again. A glance at Radegund's glowing face told me that she too was feeling the bracing effects of wind and water.

After these exhilarating days at sea, I was almost sorry to see the rugged cliffs that held the great fortress of Bamburgh. How many years have passed since my own ship first landed in Angle-land? It seems a lifetime ago. Our men sailed this ship right up onto the broad, sandy beach, where we disembarked to set our feet on not-so-solid ground.

"What are these nasty-looking black things?" grunted Gertrude as she hiked up her skirt to step over a series of dark blobs on the sand.

"Sea coal," chuckled Grima. "There must be a vein of coal somewhere nearby."

Despite the cold, Gerda took off her leather slippers to run ahead; she clambered up a sand dune, then ran back down again, laughing like a child.

"We will set up camp here tonight," called Rædwald, "and leave for Yeavering in the morning."

"Here?" questioned Radegund. "Why not in Bamburgh?"

"The fort is hewn out of granite; it's very cold and dark inside. I think you'll be more comfortable here, my dear," said Rædwald, giving her a quick embrace.

That night we killed and plucked the last of our chickens to prepare a stew, and ate ravenously seated around the fire.

"They raise a lot of sheep in Northumberland," observed Rædwald as we ate. "We can expect some fine lamb dishes to be served at Edwin's table."

"How big is this Northumberland?" I asked Rædwald, for it seemed to me that we had traversed an immense amount of coastline.

"Edwin's kingdom reaches from the Firth of Forth in the north, to the River Humber in the south. It combines the former kingdoms of Bernicia and Deira."

"I see," I said, though I had only a vague idea.

"Will we sleep on real beds there?" asked Gerda suddenly.

Rædwald laughed. "I am sure we will."

The next morning we mounted our horses for the trip inland. Earlier Gerda had climbed up to the fort and reported that she could see a complex of buildings in the far distance that must be Yeavering. She was keen for the ride; Radegund and I less so, though we both had fine leather saddles to cushion our bones. Rædwald rode a magnificent white stallion named 'Starfaxi' — a horse which reminded me of the sacred horses I'd once seen at Uppsala.

We left our ships in the care of a small party of men who would stay at Bamburgh until our return. Our roadway to Yeavering lacked the broad paved surface of a Roman road, but was a wide, well-worn path nonetheless. Clearly it had been used for many years; the surface of protruding rocks had been worn smooth by countless feet, hooves and cart wheels.

As we rode west we left behind the low, flat coastline, first encountering high moorlands, then a series of heavily wooded ridges and valleys. From time to time Rædwald called out with commentary.

"We're passing through the Cheviot Hills; there is good game here — roe deer and boar."

Cloak of Ashes

He glanced back at the string of wagons where, in addition to our sea chests, a pack of hunting dogs was being transported — some as gifts for Edwin. Their baying resounded in the valleys, often drowning out Rædwald's words.

I was more interested in people than in dogs or deer.

"Has Edwin been able to re-unite with his Mercian wife?" I asked as we ambled along.

"No, in fact it's been reported that she is dead — by whose hand we know not," replied Rædwald.

"Oh, poor Edwin!" lamented Radegund. "I hope our visit will cheer him."

"You needn't be too sorry for him," said Rædwald dryly. "Edwin is already looking for a replacement. A king needs his lady beside him to rule wisely." He glanced at Radegund, who smiled serenely.

As the land grew ever steeper I was glad for Sunbeorht's sure-footedness, and glanced back to see how Gerda was faring. She looked completely confident on her Sunbeem, and Rædwald was saying something about Æthelfrith to Radegund, so I returned my attention to them.

"Lucky for Edwin that Æthelfrith drove out the Britons who once occupied Yeavering. It was called 'hill of the goats' in their language, apparently an ancient cult center and place of burial. It enjoys a fine defensive position, located on a whaleback."

"A whaleback? What is that?" I asked, riding closer to the royal couple to better hear.

"This one is a long, flat ridge or terrace with ring ditches at the eastern and western ends. You'll soon see; we should reach Yeavering well before nightfall," said Rædwald cheerfully.

Sunbeorht's warmth beneath me was a welcome contrast to the increasingly chill air as we rode on, now heading north. By late afternoon we had entered the shadow of a river valley lined with marshes and fertile plains. Great birds, disturbed by our passing, rose up and flapped slowly away.

"Cranes," called Rædwald, pointing, "and that's a greylag goose."

"Can we expect to find those served at Edwin's table?" I teased, but Rædwald made no response.

At the end of the valley a twin-peaked hill rose above us.

"Yeavering Bell," called Rædwald. "We're almost there."

Indeed, we soon saw a number of substantial timber structures ranged along the whaleback, including not one but two great halls, a strange tiered structure beyond them, and a high double palisade around what appeared to be a large enclosure for horses and cattle.

"Much more grand than I expected," uttered Radegund, as a guard rode out to greet us.

We were escorted to the farther, slightly smaller hall, where we found everything in readiness for our arrival... including real beds! The attendants there spoke with a strange, lilting accent, making me wonder if they were related to the Britons I'd heard so much about. One girl, who bore the strange name 'Ceridwen,' told me that her family had served at Yeavering for generations.

We brought good appetites to the welcoming banquet that night, but I almost lost mine when we encountered a familiar figure dressed in a dark robe, his semi-bald head shining in the lamp light: Paulinus!

"What are you doing here?" I blurted as he came forward to greet me.

"Private matters," he purred, "between Northumberland and Kent. Welcome to Yeavering."

"Here, now, priest, that is my office!" called Edwin, glancing over from the group where he stood with Radegund and Rædwald. "Come friends," he said expansively, "let us take our places and feast together this night, shortest of all nights. The bounty of my kingdom is at your disposal."

Certainly the fruits of the sea were well represented at Edwin's table: oysters, mussels, cockles, winkles and whelks. I sampled only a few of the briny treats, almost too tired to eat. Gerda, however, tried every dish, smacking her lips and licking her fingers with relish.

"I'm glad to see that your girl enjoys our food!" smiled Edwin from across the table.

Gerda grinned and I nodded, the hubbub in the hall making it difficult to be heard. To my chagrin, the priest Paulinus was seated beside me, so I could not totally ignore him. I found his smell — damp wool soaked with sweat — especially rank tonight.

"How fare our friends in Helmingham?" he inquired blandly during a lull between servings.

"I know not of whom you speak," I said stiffly.

Cloak of Ashes

Paulinus turned to gaze at me with his great round eyes.

"Rædwald has given permission for my fellow monks to visit all the settlements along the River Doep, and I am praying for a great harvest of souls there."

I turned to him in disbelief.

"First, we are not cabbages to be ... harvested! We are people who worship the goddess, people who honor the Earth Mother, people ..."

My voice had risen and heads were turning in my direction.

"Softly, softly," murmured Paulinus. "The weak must give way to the strong; ancient ignorance and error must inevitably be dispelled by knowledge of the one true god."

"Is that why you're here?" I hissed. "to poison Edwin's mind with such ... preachings?!"

"No," said Paulinus calmly, "I am here at his invitation, to negotiate a contract of marriage between him and King Eadbald's sister, Æthelburga of Kent."

My jaw dropped at this, but I snapped it shut and did not speak to Paulinus again for the rest of the evening. When the feasting finally ended, I took my leave ahead of the rest, leaving Gerda to return with Radegund and Gertrude. Back in my chamber, I sought my bed and lay down on it to examine my thoughts.

Bertha first brought these Christian monks to Kent and then persuaded her husband to be baptized and adopt their beliefs. I have no doubt that Bertha's daughter will do the same: she will marry Edwin and convert him to her beliefs. These Christians will swallow up the whole world if they can! Oh, Mother, how can I stop them?

In anguish of spirit I fell into a fitful sleep; I did not even hear Gerda and the others come in.

The next morning I woke before the rest, dressed quietly and slipped outside to talk alone in the cold, gray mist. Lost in thought, I unexpectedly felt a hand on my shoulder.

"You'll need this, my lady. Even at midsummer it is damp and chill at Yeavering."

It was Ceridwen, the young woman I had spoken with the night before.

"Thank you," I said, accepting the cloak she held out. "You are most observant, and most thoughtful. Will you ... will you walk with me?"

"Gladly," she smiled.

For a time we strolled side by side in silence.

"Tell me," I said, stopping abruptly, "When Æthelfrith was king here, did you serve Queen Acha?"

Ceridwen stopped also and stood quietly. "I did."

"Where is she now?" I asked bluntly.

"I'm not sure," said the girl slowly. "After Edwin slew the king, Queen Acha fled with her younger children — perhaps to Mercia, perhaps all the way to Wales. She feared for their lives."

"Tell me one more thing," I persisted. "When Acha was queen, whom did she worship?"

Ceridwen stared at me in perplexity for a moment, then her face cleared.

"Why, the goddess, of course!"

My heart leaping, I asked, "Did she have a special place of worship — and can you show me where it is?"

Ceridwen nodded, twice.

The place to which she led me was located at some distance from the great halls and outbuildings. After walking through a grove of trees, we came upon a large clearing centered by a stone altar. Around it the grass had grown knee high; clearly this place had not been used recently.

"Our sacred space," murmured Ceridwen at the edge of the clearing. "We dare not enter without a priestess to lead us."

"I am such a priestess," I assured her, "but you need not enter with me. Wait here."

Before she could protest, I strode boldly through the grass. When I reached the altar, I took out the knife at my waist and severed a lock of my hair. Placing it on the altar, I reached for my fire-starter and struck a spark. When the acrid smell of burning hair met my nostrils, I knelt, placing both hands on the ground.

"Goddess! Earth Mother! I implore you! Accept my sacrifice, hear my plea! Do not forget your people even if they stray, chasing after new gods. We need your life-giving powers. We need your blessing. It is Freawicca who calls you, Freawicca who has been ever faithful to serve and honor you. Hear me ... hear me!"

Shuddering, I fell forward and began to weep in sudden despair. Again I felt a gentle hand on my shoulder. Again, Ceridwen.

"Rise, my lady. The goddess has heard you. Look up!" She gestured to the sky, where the mist had cleared.

I felt the welcome warmth of sun on my hair and rose to embrace it.

By the time we had walked back to the hall, our morning meal was already being served and I smelled a wonderful but unfamiliar aroma. Ceridwen saw me sniffing the air and explained.

"It's bacon! King Edwin is treating you royally!" At my questioning look she added, "Side meat from a hog's belly — one of Edwin's favorite cuts."

Once I'd tasted it, it became my favorite too. Gerda told me that she had already consumed several strips of the lean, tasty meat.

"And Lady, there's to be hawking and hunting later today. May I join the men? Please?"

"You'd best ask Rædwald how he feels about that," I replied. "You didn't bring Flicker..."

"But I want to watch and learn," she said earnestly. "There's been no one willing to teach me since... since Rægenhere died."

"I see. Well, you have my permission — if Rædwald consents."

Joyfully, Gerda gave me a quick embrace and hurried off to the great hall where the men were dining. We would not see each other again until evening, when a great banquet was to be held in celebration of midsummer — after the usual balefires.

During the day most of Edwin's court and guests swarmed to the edge of the whaleback to bask in the blazing bonfires positioned at regular intervals along the ridge. I did not see Paulinus among the crowd and wondered if Christians even celebrated Midsummer. I soon tired of the merry-making and excused myself from Radegund and Gertrude to seek a more restful place.

I found it at the quarter circle of wooden seats, arranged in tiers and facing a platform with a tall post at its center. Someone stood beside the post, lifting a head to place upon it. For a moment of horror I thought it might be Æthelfrith's! No, it was an animal head, a pig's head.

"What are you doing?" I asked the young woman who turned toward me, her task accomplished. It was Ceridwen again!

"There's been no recent sacrifice of oxen," she said calmly, "so we are substituting a pig's head." She nodded toward a wooden structure nearby. "That shed holds all the skulls of oxen sacrificed over the years — countless skulls. I shiver and bow when I pass it."

Sinking down gratefully on one of the long wooden benches, I asked, "What is the purpose of *this* place?"

"The king uses it to address large assemblies," she began. "I think it was built to resemble a Roman theater. Did you notice the plastered walls inside the great hall? That's Roman too. Our former kings wanted to imitate the mighty Romans," she concluded, amusement in her voice.

"I was too weary last night to notice such details," I admitted. "Tonight I will take note."

Indeed I did, awed by the dimensions of the huge timbered hall, with a ceiling that soared so far above me I could barely see the smoke holes. Its walls were made of planks as thick as my hand was wide, set upright in the ground and covered with white plaster that gave needed light to the shadowy interior. In size and splendor it vied with Heorot and Hrolf's hall at Roskilde, a sumptuous hall indeed.

Roast lamb was served at the feast that night, along with an array of tempting and delicious dishes: sage eggs, rye bread with apple butter, salmon, lettuce salad with cucumbers and radishes, vegetable soup, beets, and a sour cream custard.

The banquet ended with an exchange of gifts. First King Edwin presented Rædwald with a great stone scepter, a savage-looking thing. The stag-crowned whetstone was as long as a sword and as heavy, for Edwin carried it outstretched on his two hands. When I examined it later, I admired the four finely carved faces at the upper end of the whetstone, and the proud bronze stag atop the ring above the stone — a fitting image for the ruler of all Angle-land.

"By the gods," shouted Grima, "a whetstone made by giants! Does anyone here remember that story about Thor battling the giant Hrungnir? King Edwin, where is your scop? Let's have a tale!"

The baying of hounds interrupted this request, and all eyes turned to the main entrance. Straining at their leashes, two huge dogs charged into the hall, almost pulling the men who held them off their feet.

"My gift to you, King Edwin," said Rædwald, rising to shout above the din. "The finest dogs in my kennel."

Cloak of Ashes

One dog was gray with a heavy, thick coat, small pointed ears and a high-set tail that curled over its back. The other dog had a similar tail but was black with a smooth, sleek coat.

"I got them in trade from Norway," declared Rædwald. "Excellent trackers, both of them."

"By the gods, a handsome and most welcome gift!" Edwin shouted back. "We will take them out tomorrow to hunt for boar and deer!"

After the gifts, riddling and story-telling entertained us. To the amusement of the court, Gerda guessed the first riddle, recited by one of Edwin's young men:

I am a strange creature shaped amidst combat.
When my master bends me, releases my limbs,
A venomous dart flies from my bosom.
What flies from my belly can kill a man
If deadly venom I previously swallowed.
When I am unstrung I obey no one.
When I am skillfully tied, I am quite ready.
Say what I am.

"I know the answer," called Gerda from our women's table, rising to speak confidently. "It's a bow and arrow!"

I nodded with pleasure at her success. Back home Gerda had her own bow made of yew, and arrows of hazel wood, their tips hardened in the fire. She seldom used it, however.

"Well done! Now you may tell a riddle!" shouted Edwin from the head table.

Suddenly and unaccountably shy, Gerda sat down abruptly, but she was rescued by another man who rose to take her place: Paulinus, seated at the king's table.

"I have no riddle, but I have a parable to set before you, a story about the brevity of mortal life," he proclaimed loudly, surveying the hall.

"King Rædwald, King Edwin, and all you folk here assembled," he intoned, "I say to you that the life of man is like the brief flight of a little sparrow which flies through the hall in winter. It comes in one door and goes out another, warmed for a moment by the hearth fires within. But before and after it must face the winter's blast. Even so is the life of man; we do not know what comes before nor what follows after — unless we embrace the one true god, who guarantees eternal life."

Paulinus sat down slowly, nodding his head for emphasis. Around me there was muttering and confusion.

"What does he say?"

"There's some truth in that."

"What god did he mean?"

The somber mood produced by Paulinus' parable soon passed as more riddles were proposed, songs sung and tales told. The evening ended with Edwin's scop telling the tale requested earlier about Thor and the giant's whetstone. The scop was a man of middle age with a scraggly beard and a strong voice; he recited the old story while staring at the smoke drifting up to the ceiling.

> A duel of strength   they fought that day
> A contest of weapons   Mjollnir to whetstone
> Strongest of gods   Thor with his hammer
> Strongest of giants   Hrungnir and stone
> With mighty heaves   each threw his weapon
> Missiles in mid-air   met with loud clashing
> Hammer hit stone   stone flew in fragments
> One shard lodged fast   in Thor's wide forehead
> Thor struck down Hrungnir   then called for Goa
> Goa the sorceress   mighty in magic
> 'Dislodge this fragment   stuck in my skull!'
> Spells she sang softly   soon the shard loosened
> Pleased with her progress   Thor thought to reward her
> Though deed not yet done   Thor called to the woman
> 'Goa, your husband   returns soon from war!'
> Up jumped the woman   broke off the spell
> Could not remember   words aptly spoken
> Could not continue   spell too soon broken
> The shard stayed lodged   in Thor's forehead.

Hoots of laughter and delighted cries greeted this telling.

"By the gods," shouted one man, "It's what my wife often tells me: never disturb her in the middle of her work or I'll be the worse for it!"

I had listened with half an ear, as I already knew the story well. What held my attention was the young boy who sat at the scop's feet, his lips moving soundlessly with every word spoken above him. Curious, I waited until others had left the hall to approach the pair, now sharing a shank of lamb in a quiet corner.

"Good even, master storyteller," I began, addressing the scop. "Is this your son beside you?"

The man nodded, hastily rising and reaching out a greasy hand to bid the lad rise.

"This is my boy, Thomas. He is learning the old stories so as to take my place one day."

"May the gods be with you, Thomas," I said cordially. Then an idea struck me. "Tell me, Thomas, do you know the story of Beowulf and the Grendel monster, or Beowulf and the dragon?"

The lad's eyes widened and he smiled eagerly as he pushed back a shock of unruly black hair.

"No, Lady, but I'd be glad to learn!"

"Good!" I studied the pair intently as the idea grew in my mind. "You would have to do the shaping," I said, nodding at father and son, "but I could give you a full account of those great battles. Beowulf's exploits deserve to live through the ages — and you would be the source."

To my delight both father and son nodded enthusiastically.

"Shall we begin tomorrow morning?" I asked, immensely pleased to have such a worthy task before me. Again, they nodded.

One afternoon at Radegund's insistence I joined a party leaving on horseback to view a Roman wall reportedly built by a past emperor.

"What is so special about an old wall?" queried Gerda as we rode north, giving voice to my own thought.

"You'll see," answered the man who was leading us. "It's a monumental defensive wall built to keep out the warring tribes — Picts and Scots — who used to swarm down from the north. It is a fine piece of work."

Despite my doubts, I was truly awed by the massive structure we drew up to. Built of stone and turf, it loomed above us higher than a mead hall, and extended to the right and left as far as I could see. In thickness it appeared to be as wide as my horse was long.

"It reaches to the sea on both sides of the island," said our guide, "and there were once forts located at regular intervals; some of them still stand."

He gestured toward a tower at some distance to the west, and we turned in that direction. Finally we stopped and dismounted, allowing our horses to munch on the rich grass while we nibbled on bread and cheese — and bacon — washed down with a fine ale. Full and content, I leaned my back against the ancient, sun-warmed stone and closed my eyes, trying to imagine the lives of the soldiers who had manned this defense long years ago.

"Lady Freawicca? It's time to leave." Radegund's voice woke me from a pleasant slumber. "Were you dreaming? You were smiling."

"Yes." I yawned and stretched, letting Radegund help me to my feet. "I dreamed of Beowulf."

Before we left Yeavering I sought out Ceridwen, who had taken such good care of me during my stay. One night, for instance, she had brought a thick, brown fleece to cover me, keeping out the chill that penetrated my bones.

"It comes from a wether. Their fleece grows heavier because they've been castrated," she had informed me cheerfully. "My grandfather's father once raised brown sheep; the white ones you see came from the Romans."

On the day before my departure I gave her a gift of medicinal herbs.

"Ceridwen, you know much about the old times, the old ways. If Edwin takes a Christian wife, would the women here still worship the goddess?"

Ceridwen paused. "Some of us would. I can't speak for all," she said judiciously. For a moment she looked down shyly. "I have a gift for you too — to keep you safe on your journey home."

Looking up, she opened her left fist to reveal a large animal tooth.

"It's from an ox — the same ox sacrificed when this hall was built," she said, glancing about the guest quarters. "My own grandfather is buried under the door sill."

"What?!" I exclaimed in shock and surprise. "Was he too . . . sacrificed?"

"Yes," she nodded, matter-of-factly. "It was an honor. He supervised the construction and he now guards the hall."

"Still . . ." I shivered in revulsion, then collected myself enough to receive the gift she offered. Clutching the worn tooth in one hand, I seized her hand with my other. "Thank you. I shall treasure this always, as... as a sacred gift."

To the two Thomases, father and son, I gave a handful of hack silver. We had met each morning during my stay at Yeavering so that I could recount the details of Beowulf's major battles. I did not include personal information, such as his marriage to Hygd or his relationship with me. Better, I thought, to leave in listeners' minds the image of a great leader and warrior, beloved by his people, an example to others of what a good king should be.

Thomas the younger was filled with pride as he recited for me a part of the lay his father had already composed.

"That's very good," I said approvingly, then hesitated. "I now realize that I've forgotten to tell you about many things: Beowulf's grandfather, Hrethel, and details about the Swedes..."

"That's alright, my lady," assured Thomas the elder. "I can still include them. My boy will help me listen and remember. Tell us as much as you can in the time remaining."

Chapter Twenty-Five
Sutton Hoo

Gravestone cross of the 800's from Middleton, Yorkshire, showing a Viking warrior laid out in his grave with his weapons.

The improvement in Radegund's health lasted only a short time. She lingered through the rest of that summer, but died peacefully in her sleep one night during harvest. A messenger, Per, was sent to Helmingham to bring the sorrowful news and invite us to the funeral.

I could scarce believe his words, my heart rebelling at this painful loss. Radegund had become a sister to me, a dearly beloved sister. As usual in times of sorrow, I turned to Gerda for comfort.

"Do you remember," I asked her after Per had left our dwelling, "that story Paulinus told about the sparrow in the mead hall?"

"Yes," she said gently, "but why do you ask?"

"I've been thinking about what comes after death. I've always believed that we women go to the house of Freyja. Surely I will see Radegund again, there?"

"Of course you will," exclaimed Gerda. "That is . . . if Rædwald allows her body to be burned."

"What?" My head jerked up as I shook off my lethargy. "Why do you say that?"

Gerda shrugged. "It's just that these Christians are now insisting on full body burial in the ground . . . with no grave goods. As king, and a Christian, Rædwald may feel that he must set an example."

"No! He can't! He mustn't!" I cried. "I promised Radegund that I would never let that happen! We must go to Rendlesham immediately!"

I need not have worried. Apparently Radegund had made her wishes quite clear to her husband, for we found a huge funeral pyre under construction when our party from Helmingham arrived at Rædwald's seat. After we were welcomed, Rædwald took my hands and spoke somberly.

"I rule all of Angle-land, but I could not save her. Your herbs did not save her, nor did the prayers of the monks sent over from Kent. All I can do now is honor her final wish: to let her sleep in the fire."

I nodded, returning his long embrace as silent tears ran down my face.

Later, I helped Radegund's women select the items to place on her pyre: headdress pins, necklaces, gold pendants, silver slip-rings, workboxes and weaving tools, a comb, a girdle-hanger, silver drinking cups, wrist-clasps, a large cauldron, and a wooden bucket. I added the silver needle case she had once given me.

It was a crisp autumn morning when we all gathered near the river to say farewell to our queen, our sister, our friend. I stood between Gudrun and Gerda and raised the dirge as Radegund's body was encircled in smoke, to be gradually consumed by fire and reduced to ashes. All day Rædwald stood beside the pyre, his face a mask of silent sorrow. Beside him stood Eorpwald, his face etched with grief. When twilight finally fell, I keenly felt that yet again something precious, something irreplaceable, had gone out of my life, out of this world.

At Yule that year King Rædwald made a surprising announcement. He was taking a new wife: Eadburh, his brother's widow. She would be coming to Rendlesham in the spring, along with her son Sigeberht — Rædwald's nephew, now soon to become his stepson.

"Well!" exclaimed Gertrude to me at my annual visit, "I know such unions are customary in royal families, but I can't help thinking..."

"You don't have to say it," I said grimly. "I know just what you're feeling. No one could ever replace Radegund!"

Gertrude gave me an aggrieved look.

"We both know that to be true, my lady. No, I was thinking more of the stepson, this Sigeberht. When we visited Snape for King Eni's ship-burial, I overheard Sigeberht arguing with Eorpwald about who should do what. I don't think they're going to get along!"

"Really!" I was troubled but intrigued by this information. "Tell me, Gertrude, are Sigeberht and his mother... Franks?"

"Yes, and Christians too. Mark my words: there will be changes made when that woman and her son come to Rendlesham!"

Gertrude's dire warning was not immediately borne out. Eadburh and Sigeberht did come to Rendlesham, but Rædwald did not remove what they termed the "pagan" altar in his temple, and for many months all seemed to go well.

Overall, Rædwald's reign was a time of such peace and stability that it was often said a lone woman with her new-born child could walk safely from coast to coast anywhere on the island. This ignored, however, the fact that warfare with the Britons was ongoing, though sporadic, and there were occasional forays into neighboring kingdoms by Penda of Mercia.

The smoldering hostility between Sigeberht and Eorpwald flared into the open when Eorpwald discovered that Sigeberht had desecrated one of the images in Rædwald's temple: he had cut off the prominent penis on Frey's statue. To keep peace in the court, Rædwald dispatched Sigeberht to his mother's relatives in Francia. After his departure, calm returned.

During this time I kept to my home and household, seldom leaving to visit Rendlesham, getting frequent reports from Per, who came to see Gerda. For her part, Gerda paid attention only to her hawks and her horses — for she now had several of each. Every day I gave thanks to the goddess for Gerda, for life and for health, despite the aches that increasingly plagued me.

Year after year passed in a kind of dream, though I noted many changes around me. Monks were now visiting every village, preaching and baptizing converts in the local rivers. Even Gudrun and Lark had been drawn to such events, and Lark spoke approvingly of the training schools being built. Wilhelm, however, balked at the taxes levied to build churches and monasteries. "These Christians always have their hand out," he growled.

Paulinus had become bishop of York, one of Edwin's seats in Northumbria, and wielded extensive influence. It was said that he had baptized a thousand converts in the River Glen near Yeavering, but I discounted that number, remembering the extravagant claims of Augustine on an earlier occasion. I had to admit, however, that Christianity was spreading over Angle-land like a rash, and I knew not how to stop it.

To be honest with myself, I had seen little evidence to justify my mother's emphatic warnings. Women seemed to be treated as fairly as men by the monks, who even welcomed female slaves into the church. This disregard for differences of class and status did disturb me, but I could not see that it was harmful to females in particular. In fact new opportunities for women seemed to be opening up as monasteries were established all over Angle-land. These places of learning primarily trained young boys to become priests, but women were also welcomed and often assumed positions of leadership and authority.

It pained me deeply, however, to see the gods I had worshipped my whole life being discredited, belittled and abandoned. What disasters might we be calling down upon ourselves? Would crops fail and animals cease to breed?

To guard against the dangers inherent in abandoning old ways for new, many folks wore a cross dangling at their neck, but also carried a tiny Thor's hammer or spear of Odin as an amulet at their waist. I had also heard Wilhelm speak wryly of traders who accepted baptism more than once in order to make a sale or gain access to Christian markets.

One night I woke in a sweat from a disturbing dream. I had witnessed a sea eagle flying high above me, proud and confident lord of the skies. Its breast suddenly pierced by an arrow, the bird fell to earth.

When I approached the body and turned it over with one foot, the face of King Rædwald stared up at me.

Shaken, I consulted my runes, asking what this dream might portend. Raido greeted me, the journey rune. I pondered: was the king in danger from some unexpected quarter? Should he fear an ambush? I had not visited Rendlesham for several months, but news from the court had contained no hints of opposition or danger. I decided to wait for possible additional revelations or visions. They came almost immediately.

The next day I was sitting in my herb garden, sorting herbs for drying, when a sudden gust of wind shook Wiswicca'w apple tree. One of the apples fell with a soft thud and rolled to my feet. Idly I picked it up and used my knife to slice it in half. A face peered up at me... Rædwald's face. I gasped, dropped the apple, got to my feet and hurried inside the hut.

"What's wrong?" exclaimed Gerda, looking up from the table where she was braiding a new rope for her horse. "You look as if you've seen a ghost!"

"Perhaps I have," I replied, trembling all over. "Something may be very wrong at Rendlesham."

When I told her what I had seen, Gerda calmly went outside to retrieve the apple halves. As she laid them on the table between us, I could clearly see that it was just an apple. Rædwald's face was not displayed there.

"But I did see his face!" I declared. Then I told Gerda about the earlier eagle dream.

"A warning? An omen?" suggested Gerda, now serious. "What are you going to do?"

"Nothing yet. I need to know more."

Gerda jumped to her feet.

"Not a vision quest! You almost died the last time you attempted such a journey! Don't do it!" she pleaded.

"Calm yourself," I soothed. "There are other methods of gaining information. Tell me: what do we have in the house that Rædwald would have touched?"

Gerda considered.

"There's the bridle he gave me for Sunbeem... and that hood for my new falcon..."

"The hood will do. Please bring it."

Gerda went to the back room where she kept her birds on perches and soon returned with the hood.

"Thank you, dear one. Now I need to be alone."

Obligingly Gerda went off to the stables to visit her horses, and I settled in to clear my mind. Holding the leather hood in both hands, I sat quietly at the table, summoning up a vision of Rædwald's face: his ruddy cheeks, the bushy eyebrows and piercing grey eyes. Strangely I seemed to be looking down at him from a height. Gradually a sort of framework began to take shape, something dark and rectangular. Holding my breath, I let the image come into focus... It was a coffin. Rædwald was lying in a coffin.

I dug my fingernails into the leather, gripping it hard to keep from fainting. There could be no mistake. This was a death warning.

As Midsummer was near at hand, I decided to use the opportunity to report my visions to the king. Thus, after Gerda and I arrived at Rendlesham on a brilliant summer morning and were conducted to the women's quarters, I asked Gertrude, "Where might the king be found?"

"I think he's in the mews," she said, "attending to one of his new falcons."

"Oh, good!" exclaimed Gerda. "I'd love to see his new birds! I know the way, Lady."

Before I could speak, she set off confidently in the direction of the stables. Shrugging and smiling at Gertrude, I followed Gerda.

Rædwald was pleased to see us.

"Lady Freawicca, it is good to have you back at Rendlesham, but what is amiss? Your face betrays you. What news do you bring?"

"I am sorry to say I bring dire omens and portents of death, my lord," I said grimly.

"Death?" He placed the falcon he was holding back on its perch and carefully hooded it. "Whose death?"

"I fear it may be yours, my lord," I answered steadily.

Rædwald fixed me with a piercing stare. "I see that you have much to tell me. Is this a matter to set before the council or is it for my ears alone?"

"Your ears," I nodded, "and this is a suitably private place in which to talk. Gerda," I added, "already knows of what I will speak."

Rædwald looked dubious, but directed me to a pair of chests opposite the cages and brushed chaff from the lids so we could be seated. He called to Gerda, who was walking down the row of cages examining each bird.

"I was just about to feed them. There are pieces of pigeon meat in that bucket if you'd like to take over for me."

"Gladly!" enthused Gerda. She took up the bucket and started down the row.

"Now, tell me everything," said Rædwald.

I began by pointing out that he had always valued my insights in the past; not to report my visions now would be to break faith with him. When I had finished my account of the falling eagle, the apple and the face in the coffin, Rædwald stroked his beard thoughtfully

"I have no doubt that you have seen what you tell me, but I question the circumstances. Outside forces? Yet I know of no current threats to the kingdom. My own health? I am strong and hearty, in the prime of life..."

"Ah, my lord," I interjected. "Beware of pride! Any man can be laid low when he least expects it!"

From the distant past I heard an echo of my father's voice, counseling Beowulf, and I murmured aloud.

"For a brief time is your strength in bloom; it quickly fades. Then soon will follow sword or illness, fire or water, or age itself. Your eyes will dim and death will arrive to sweep you away."

Rædwald bowed his head, reflecting.

"You speak wisely, my lady, and I will heed you. What do you advise?"

"My lord, no doubt you have considered the legacy you wish to leave behind you, but have you given thought to how you wish to be laid to rest?"

"What do you mean?" he said frowning.

"As there are two altars in your temple, there will be conflicting ideas about what is appropriate for a king of your stature — and a Christian," I said.

Rædwald smiled faintly. "I see what you mean."

We sat in silence for a time. In the background I could hear Gerda clucking to the falcons as she offered bits of raw meat to each bird. Finally Rædwald spoke.

"A ship burial would be my choice — like my brother Eni's burial."

I nodded in agreement.

"As you know, my lord, such a burial requires a great deal of advance preparation: selecting the ship, finding a suitable site, getting the ship to the site . . . Or," I paused, remembering my father Hrothgar's final send off, "you could be buried at sea in a ship set aflame — but then no marker would be left, no mound to identify the place."

Rædwald lifted his heavy eyebrows in surprise.

"Lady Freawicca, you clearly have given this a great deal of thought!"

Wearily I nodded.

"Yes, my lord, I have thought of little else since the warning came. I also think that the gods have favored you by sending these omens. You are being given the chance to determine how you will be remembered. You are a great king, a noble man. Your reputation, your fame, the legacy you leave to your son and to the kingdom, will all be influenced by the funeral you receive."

Rædwald had listened silently, frequently nodding in agreement.

"Lady Freawicca, I thank you for your words. I will not now speak of this to my wife, but I will begin preparations for a ship burial — somewhere near Rendlesham. I do not fear death, which comes to us all, but it is important to my people that I be remembered as a worthy king of the Wuffing line."

During the rest of that summer I heard frequent reports from Rendlesham. The king and the court were well; nothing was amiss. Per told me privately that a crew of young men had been set to work digging a long, rectangular trench atop a ridge above the River Doep, and another crew were using timber rollers to haul a ninety-foot longboat up to the ridge — all this at some distance from Rendlesham. I smiled to hear it.

Harvest time came and went. I led the women of Helmingham in a celebration of the goddess, though it was difficult to move without pain and I could no longer join in the dancing. Rædwald had invited me to visit once again before winter closed in, and I had reluctantly agreed. Thus it was that I found myself in Rædwald's hall when he was struck down.

It was blood-month and we were standing near the throne chairs — Rædwald, Eadburh and I — discussing menus for the upcoming feast. Eadburh had just said that roast pork would be a nice change after a summer of eating fish and game. Rædwald had opened his mouth to speak, when a strange look came into his face. His mouth twitched and he shook with a kind of spasm. As I watched in horror he dropped slowly to his knees, then — without saying a word — pitched forward.

For an instant time stopped. Eadburh reacted first, flinging herself on her husband's body, shrieking. Slowly I sank to my knees beside her and took his hand. I felt nothing; the life force had gone. Two of Rædwald's men appeared suddenly, knelt and carefully turned him over. His face was grey, his eyes staring. The king was dead. Rædwald was dead.

"Call Eorpwald," I said tersely, jerking my head at one of the men. "Rædwald's son must take charge immediately."

Rising slowly and painfully I helped the queen to her feet and guided her to her throne chair.

"Cover the king's body," I commanded the second fellow, "and bring wine. The queen is in shock."

Carefully the man spread Rædwald's cloak over his body, then ran from the hall. I took Eadburh's hand and stroked it gently, crooning to her as if she were a babe.

"Wyrd has been cruel to you, Queen Eadburh, taking two husbands before their time. Now it is our duty, our privilege, to honor Rædwald as he deserves — royally."

"A Christian burial," sobbed Eadburh, clutching my hand. "No burning! He must be given a Christian burial."

Eorpwald rushed into the hall stony-faced. He seized me by the shoulders and swung me around to face him.

"How did this happen?" he demanded. "Was my father poisoned?" He glared at the still weeping Eadburh. "Did *she* kill him?"

"No, no, Eorpwald, calm yourself," I said gently. "His heart gave out, for he died in an instant — too fast for any poison."

Eorpwald's hands fell to his sides.

"Forgive me, my lady. You were ever my father's friend, and I trust your words." His head sank. "What must I do?" He choked, staring down at the still form on the floor.

"First, lift your father's body and place it on his table, so that the queen and I may bathe it properly," I instructed. "Then alert the council of his death."

For a moment Eorpwald stood stricken.

"I thought we had years for funeral preparations. I thought it was premature to be digging a place for a burial ship. Now, suddenly, his life is over: not killed in battle, like Rægenhere, but struck down — apparently struck down by the gods."

"So it seems," I murmured. "The ways of Wyrd cannot be known."

Eadburh and I stripped Rædwald and gently bathed his body with an herbal wash — the same mixture I had used to bathe Beowulf's body: rosemary, lavender and lemon thyme. She did not speak, her face pinched and white. For the first time I pitied her, seeing her not as Radegund's replacement, but as a woman who had just lost her husband.

After a time of working together silently, I ventured a suggestion, not sure how much Rædwald might have told her about his advance preparations.

"Like his brother, Eni, King Rædwald would expect a royal burial — even a ship burial. Don't you agree?"

Eadburh paused and looked up, her eyes red-rimmed. She nodded, but again did not speak. I stared at the still, pale body of this man once so vital, so powerful. It bore the scars of many battles, and I noticed for the first time that he had lost part of a finger on his left hand. His hair had gone completely white over the years, and now his full lips lost their color as the pallor of death crept over his body. Noticing this, we hastened to finish our work, so that we might dress him while his limbs could still be moved.

Eadburh brought out a full set of clean clothing from Rædwald's chamber: fine linen trousers, a long-sleeved shirt dyed a golden hue, a richly-textured red tunic with gold embroidery on the cuffs and hem, and a woolen cloak yellow as honey. On his feet we slipped soft leather boots and tied his leggings with cross garters.

"He is every inch a king, even in death," I observed to Eadburh as we finished laying him out.

Rædwald's councilors had respectfully waited outside as we worked, but now came in quietly to pay their respects to their former king and his widow. I slipped out, leaving Eadburh to greet them alone. As I made my way to Rædwald's temple I saw Radegund's women — or rather, Eadburh's women — wandering in a daze outside the hall, weeping openly, and even men such as Grima and Haugen looking stricken and confused as they filed in to take a last look at their leader.

In the temple I found Eorpwald just placing a sacrifice on the altar to Odin: a freshly killed piglet.

"Hear my plea," he called out, raising bloody hands to the silent image. "Great god, receive Rædwald into Valhalla. My father was a mighty warrior who deserved to be one of your companions."

I stood silent for moment, then cleared my throat to alert him to my presence. Drawing near, I laid a hand on his shoulder.

"Fear not, Eorpwald. As I washed your father's body, I marked him for the gods with my knife. I traced the warrior rune on his right shoulder blade. He will most certainly join the champions in Valhalla."

Eorpwald turned to stare at me, then seized my hand and raised it to his lips.

"Thank you, my lady, thank you! I should have done it myself, but my mind was blank."

I nodded in understanding. The shock of Rædwald's death had staggered all in the court. Rædwald had been the heart that animated Rendlesham. With his death it was once again in danger of paralysis. This must not happen!

"Eorpwald, your stepmother is willing to allow a ship burial for your father. It is your duty to see that this happens. Speak to the council immediately — now, before the priests learn of his death. Rædwald should be honored with the most splendid funeral ever seen in Angleland, not buried in a box like a slave!"

Wordlessly Eorpwald nodded.

"It shall be done."

As he left the temple, I reflected: perhaps even now Rædwald is being welcomed to Valhalla by my beloved, Beowulf.

Next I sought out Oswald, Rædwald's old steward, to ascertain the readiness of the burial site. I found him outside one of the storehouses, directing thralls in hanging hams to cure. Oswald was bent with age and could scarcely lift his head, but his eyes were bright and his greeting indicated that I would likely find in him an ally for my plans.

"Lady Freawicca! May the gods be with you!" He spoke with gusto, seizing my hand in a grip that was surprisingly strong. "I know we have you to thank for the advance funeral preparations. Yes," he continued, bobbing his head, "Rædwald told me about your fateful premonition, some time ago. He also charged me with the task of overseeing the preparations — without unduly alarming the court."

I smiled sympathetically.

"From what I've heard and observed, you were successful. But tell me: just where is the site and how soon will we be able to make use of it?"

Oswald released my hand and pointed toward the Doep.

"It's a short distance down river, located on a prominent ridge. The ship is already in place, ready to receive... our king."

As his voice cracked, I too paused, sharing his moment of grief.

"Tell me please, if you know, whether news of Rædwald's death has been sent to the bishop?"

"Not by me!" snorted Oswald. "I have no use for that man and what he represents!"

Now I smiled broadly.

"We agree on that, friend Oswald," I said emphatically. "In fact I am hoping that Rædwald's funeral can be conducted without... interference..."

"From the church!" Oswald nodded vigorously and seized my hand again. "I'll get to work immediately."

As we women began to assemble the grave goods that would accompany Rædwald on his final voyage, I told Eadburh that her demand for a Christian burial would be satisfied by a ship burial, but that Rædwald's status as a high king — as bretwalda — must also be signaled by a rich assemblage of goods. I did not say anything about its value to Eorpwald, as Rædwald's son and heir, since Eadburh's own son had been banished.

We were fortunate in the time of year, for the cold nights — along with herbs — would preserve Rædwald's body while we made the necessary funeral preparations.

In thinking back over the years I had known Rædwald, I saw him as performing many roles. He was the warrior who defeated Æthelfrith at the Battle of the River Idle. He was the great king who placed others on their thrones and accepted their tribute. He was the gracious host who delighted in providing fine food and drink and entertainment for his guests. He was a man who kept his beard meticulously trimmed and loved a good game of dice. Oh, — and yes — he was also a baptized Christian, who had sought to benefit his people by cautiously adopting new ways. All these roles, I believed, should be represented by the items chosen for his burial ship.

On this trip to Rendlesham I had brought only Berit, as Gerda had been busy training one of her horses to the saddle. Now I sent for Gerda, wanting her beside me during this momentous undertaking. Radegund was gone, Rædwald was gone, and I felt in my bones that my own time was near.

Rædwald's body was removed to the temple, where he could lie in state for viewing by the court and the inhabitants of surrounding settlements. A table had been brought in from the great hall, covered with a pallet and draped in blood-red silk. On this platform in the center of the room — between the Christian and pagan altars — rested Rædwald's still form. Even in death his face wore a commanding look and his brows still bristled above eyes now forever closed.

From among his father's weapons and armor Eorpwald chose a finely decorated sword, an axe hammer and nine spears. He folded Rædwald's mail coat between a piece of woven fabric, then reverently brought out his father's helmet and shield, carrying each separately. These were items of such magnificence they moved me to tears.

The great circular shield was made of linden wood, the same wood used in Beowulf's shield, I remembered. It was covered in leather dyed a deep rich red. Its iron boss was elaborately decorated, the central stud embellished with garnet. The shield board itself was decorated with gilded metal forms: a flying dragon facing a fierce bird of prey. Around the rim twelve dragon heads alternated with pairs of gilt-bronze horses. All in all, a beautiful display of fiercesome images.

Eorpwald held up Rædwald's helmet to show me that it had been made from a single sheet of iron, hammered into shape, then decorated with silver bronze plates. The ear flaps and neck guard were likewise solid iron. It included a complete face mask, with heavy eyebrows, nose guard and mustache. A dragon figure extended form the ridge of the helmet down to the nose guard, and boar images decorated the cheek-plates.

"Did Anders make this?" I asked in awe.

"No, he works primarily in gold," answered Eorpwald. "This was made by a metalsmith father brought over from Uppsala, a man named 'Holger', a master smith."

"He was indeed a master," I declared, marveling at the intricately detailed scenes on the helmet plates. One showed warriors with horned helmets dancing and carrying spears; another depicted a battle scene with a fallen warrior being trampled by a horse.

"Did Rædwald actually wear this helmet?" I asked.

"A few times, and then only with an otter fur cap beneath it to cushion the weight," said Eorpwald.

As further emblems of Rædwald's royal position, Eorpwald selected one of the feather-crowned iron standards carried before the king when he was on the march, then added the heavy whetstone scepter which had been given to Rædwald by Edwin.

Will Edwin now become bretwalda? That seems most likely, especially now that he is allying himself with Kent through his marriage to Æthelburga.

Eadburh insisted that the two silver spoons given to Rædwald at his baptism be included, along with the ten silver bowls that came from the Pope. Eorpwald readily assented to this, despite his disapproval of his father's shift in belief.

Gertrude, Hannah and I assembled the domestic items to accompany Rædwald: cauldrons, wooden tubs, bowls and wooden bottles. The pair of drinking horns Gertrude selected were truly magnificent: huge auroch horns with silver gilt mounts at the mouth and bird-headed terminals. Equally grand was a set of maple wood bottles with heavily gilded silver panels.

I personally selected a large hanging bowl which I knew to be one of Rædwald's favorites, for at its bottom stood a tinned bronze fish, its silvery body inlaid with red enamel.

"But it's patched!" objected Gertrude, pointing to three obvious repairs.

"Yes, but patched by a master," I countered. "Look at the workmanship on that large oval patch with bird heads. Rædwald loved this bowl, and it's going with him!"

Meekly Gertrude nodded as I added it to the stack.

The man who had patched the bowl, Anders the goldsmith, also suggested items to be buried with his king: Rædwald's great gold belt buckle and a pair of ornate gold shoulder clasps with garnet and enamel inlay—splendid pieces that reflected Rædwald's love of elaborate jewelry.

"I was also working on a gold and garnet purse for Rædwald," declared Anders, "and it's almost finished. In one more day I could have it ready."

"Very good'," nodded Eorpwald. "I've seen that piece; the birds of prey you're using would accord well with the bird on Rædwald's shield."

"And we can fill the purse with coins from the Continent," added Eadburh, who had quietly joined us in the temple where the grave goods were being assembled.

"To pay his passage to the next world?" queried Eorpwald, eyeing his stepmother suspiciously. "I thought you did not believe in such ... requirements."

Eadburh flushed and shook her head.

"I do not, but ... others do."

Eorpwald stared at her a moment, then said simply, "Thank you."

There seemed no end to the goods brought through the wide doors of Rædwald's temple: a huge silver dish reportedly acquired in trade from a place called Alexandria; a set of fourteen bone gaming pieces with a die made of antler; a six-string lyre made of maple wood — this from Rædwald's current scop, Pieter — and more cloaks, all of them golden in color. I wondered: did Eadburh fear that her husband might be cold in the coming winter? She was clearly concerned for his welfare in the afterlife, for she also brought his favorite goose down pillow to place beneath his head.

On a chill autumn mid-morning we gathered in the temple. Rædwald's coffin had previously been brought inside on a cart, which was placed beside the platform. Other carts to carry the grave goods stood on either side of the two altars. Respectfully, Rædwald's body was placed in its coffin by Eorpwald, Edvard, Grima and Haugen. At his feet were heaped little piles of goods: a leather tunic, cups and bowls, his mail coat, the axe hammer, several knives and combs, bottles of ointment, a silver ladle wrapped in silk and his otter fur cap. On either side of his pillow Eadburh carefully placed a pair of indoor shoes, then gently spread a golden cloak over his body.

During all these preparations I had been surprised by Queen Eadburh's easy acceptance of what were clearly non-Christian practices. Her compliance proved deceptive, however. Just before Rædwald's coffin was to be removed for transport to the burial site, a host of black-robed priests burst into the temple and moved quickly to block the outside exit.

"Finally!" cried Eadburh, rushing forward. "Bishop Mellitus, I feared you would be too late to stop this unholy burial!"

The man she addressed had a long, pinched face with a sour expression which grew even sourer when he saw the carts being loaded with grade goods.

"This is evil! This is wicked!" he shouted. "Where is the king's son? I must speak with Eorpwald!"

Eorpwald stepped forward from beside the coffin to face Mellitus.

"I am here. What do you want with me?" He planted himself before the angry priest.

"My son, your father was a baptized Christian!" asserted Mellitus. "All this wealth should not be buried in the ground, lost to God and man alike!" he declared with increasing vehemence. "As King Æthelbert honored the church at Canterbury, you could honor your father by building a church for him here. Then he could rest in consecrated earth in God's own house, not lie buried and forgotten on some windy bluff!"

Eorpwald's face had grown darker and darker during the priest's fulminations. Finally he held up his hand as if to ward off further words and declaimed loudly.

"First, I am not your son; I am the son of King Rædwald! I honor my father as befits a son of the house of Wuffing! I honor my father as befits his position as bretwalda! Rædwald's name, his deeds, his lineage shall not be forgotten! This wealth is his by right, not booty to be claimed by you or your church!"

Eorpwald glared at the priest and took a step forward, but the man did not back down. Now Eadburh came up behind Eorpwald and laid a hand on his shoulder. He whirled to face her.

"You! So you sent for this priest! Did you also send for Sigeberht in exile? Do you think to have me replaced on my father's throne by your own son?"

Eadburh blanched but stood her ground. She did not answer Eorpwald, speaking instead to the priest.

"Bishop, you should know that this young man has been influenced, misled, by a pagan priestess among us: that woman!"

She pointed directly at me where I stood near the coffin. The priest turned to stare at me, his eyes like a hawk.

"So, you are the abomination I've been hearing about! Stand forth, woman!"

So, the moment of confrontation has come. Mother, I shall not fail you.

"Priest, you have no power to command me! I am a guest at this court, a friend and advisor to King Rædwald himself."

"The former king, I believe," sneered Mellitus. "Now you think to lead his son into wicked ways."

"It is not wicked to honor the dead as they deserve," I replied coldly. "King Rædwald deserved and would expect no less."

During this exchange I was dimly aware that others were crowding into the temple, surrounding the small island of priests. Then I heard a familiar voice: young Per.

"She's right! Lady Freawicca speaks truth!"

"Frea-wicca?" repeated Mellitus, drawing out my name. "So you are an avowed witch!"

"I am chosen by the gods to be healer, helper and seeress. I am a servant of the goddess."

"Heresy!" shrieked Mellitus. Grasping the heavy cross that hung about his neck, he held it out and lunged toward me, crying "Maledicat Dominus! Maledicat Dominus!"

Eorpwald grabbed the man before he could reach me. At the same time Gerda's voice rang through the temple.

"Touch my mother and I'll have this bird tear your eyes out!"

Confusion and alarm gave way to admiration as Gerda strode into the temple from the great hall, bearing a falcon on her wrist. Her russet hair stood out like a halo and her dark eyes flashed. She was breathing hard, her cheeks flushed, but she spoke with authority.

Mellitus gaped at Gerda, looking back and forth between us.

"Witch's spawn?" he muttered, then backed away, shielding his eyes as Gerda took off the falcon's hood, exposing its sharp, cruel beak.

"Thank you, Gerda, but no more," I said quietly. "This man cannot harm us."

She dutifully replaced the hood, grinning like a child.

"Don't they teach you any manners in church?" she said reproachfully to the cringing priest. "Ladies are to be greeted with respect and courtesy — and my mother is a great lady!"

Mellitus swallowed hard but said nothing. As he looked around apprehensively, it became apparent that he was isolated, ringed by courtiers with angry faces. He cleared his throat.

"My apologies. My judgment may have been... hasty."

Now Eadburh stepped forward and assumed her role as hostess and advisor.

"Friends, this has been a difficult time for us all. I suggest that we take more time to consider what we do. Let us break bread together before making any final decisions. I will order a banquet in Rædwald's honor. Tomorrow morning is soon enough to act on whatever we decide."

Amid a few disgruntled murmurs, Bishop Mellitus hastened to accept her proposal.

"Wisely spoken, Queen Eadburh, wisely spoken. We accept your hospitality."

Eorpwald and Rædwald's councilors spent the rest of the day in argument with the priests, wrangling over what was and was not proper for the burial of a great Christian king. At Eorpwald's invitation, I had joined the group in Rædwald's chamber, but did not speak.

Mellitus began by declaring that prayers must be said by himself and dirges sung by his companions at the grave site. This was met with polite indifference by the council, who had already made it clear that the ship burial itself would go forward just as planned. They were also adamant that the grave goods already assembled would accompany Rædwald on his journey.

"But no human sacrifices!" cried Mellitus. "I absolutely forbid it! In fact, no sacrifices of any living creature: man, woman, ox, horse, cat or dog!"

This drew disapproving looks from the council. I knew that Rædwald's horse would usually be sacrificed and added to the burial, along with his favorite hunting dogs. To my surprise, Eorpwald agreed to this condition.

"We can always add them later, when the priests are gone," he murmured to me beside him. I nodded, hiding a smile.

Mellitus had avoided looking at me all through the afternoon, but when the meeting broke up, he stopped to address me.

"Lady Freawicca," he began, emphasizing the word 'lady,' "I trust you are satisfied with these arrangements? Rædwald must and will receive a Christian burial," he said triumphantly.

"It will be as Wyrd decrees," I answered calmly. "Now please excuse me. I must rest before the evening banquet."

Cloak of Ashes

In the chamber I was sharing with Gerda, I found her looking through my bag of herbs, sniffing each packet.

"What do you need?" I asked, yawning wearily.

"Something to loosen tight bowels," she answered without looking at me.

"Oh? I did not know you had a problem. Here, let me do that."

I sorted through the packets until I found the leaves I'd recently acquired from a foreign trader.

"This is senna — a potent purgative. A few leaves crushed and mixed with food will be effective."

Gerda smiled broadly as I handed her the packet.

"Good. Very good."

"Don't use too much," I cautioned, "or it will cause cramping."

Still grinning, Gerda nodded and left the chamber, leaving me to my rest.

That evening two young thralls struggled into the hall carrying a huge pig roasted whole on a spit. It was then carved by a burly cook and distributed to the tables by a host of serving girls. Boiled carrots and onions accompanied the meat, along with oat bread, cabbage salad and bean soup — some of Rædwald's favorite foods.

"You dine well at Rendlesham," observed a tall, gaunt priest at the next table when I happened to look his way. I nodded.

"King Rædwald prided himself on his hospitality," I called out and turned back to my food, but only for a moment, cut short by a sudden sharp pang of grief.

The great giver of great gifts is gone. From a full heart, thank you Rædwald. Your life was a great gift to us all.

Blinking back tears, I paused for a moment more before I could resume eating. Beside me Gerda seemed to have little appetite, picking at her food and glancing frequently around the hall.

"What's the matter?" I inquired. "You seem ... distracted."

"I'm just waiting for the last course: honey apples made from those buckets of apples I brought with me — from Wiswicca's tree."

"I hope you did not give all of them to the kitchen," I protested in alarm. "I wanted to add a tub of them to Rædwald's grave goods."

"Don't worry. I saved the best for that very purpose. Oh — excuse me."

Gerda rose abruptly from the table and made her way to the entrance door where a group of serving girls had appeared with the final sending. She pulled aside two of them and pointed at the table where Mellitus and his priests were seated. When Gerda returned to our table, her face bore a curious expression.

"What were you doing?" I asked.

"Oh, just seeing that everyone gets what they deserve," she answered cheerfully.

The next morning we rose early to join the throng at the harbor. It seemed that all of Rendlesham was there, though only Rædwald's family and courtiers would be going to the burial site today. The only ones missing were Mellitus and his priests. Eorpwald paced and fumed at the water's edge.

"If they don't come soon, we'll lose the tide!" he huffed, looking back up the hill. "Per, you have strong legs; run back and see what's keeping them. We can't wait much longer."

Per was off in a flash, sprinting up the path we had recently descended. While we waited, Eorpwald reexamined the carts being loaded onto the boat, to be sure that nothing had been overlooked. No, nothing had been left behind, including my tub of golden apples. Per soon returned, panting heavily but laughing, tears streaming down his face.

"What's wrong?" cried Eorpwald. "What's happened to them?"

Per bent over to catch his breath, then straightened, still shaking with laughter.

"They are shitting themselves as they rush for the latrines! A flux seems to have seized the whole lot of 'em!" he gasped.

Eorpwald stared at Per in perplexity, then gave a great laugh himself.

"So, the gods have spoken! Then let's take ship. No ... wait. In their absence we can now include Rædwald's stallion. Per, run back again and get the horse! You there, Sven, go help him! Hurry!"

As we waited I turned to find Gerda, but she had somehow disappeared. Per and Sven shortly returned empty-handed.

"Starfaxi is gone — he's not in the enclosure," panted Sven.

"We'll have to go without the horse, then," snapped Eorpwald. He turned. "Queen Eadburh and Lady Freawicca. You and the other women take the first ship with the coffin. I'll follow next." Now he turned to the waiting councilors. "Time to get on board, my lords."

Cloak of Ashes

As we hurried onto the boats, I reached for a steadying arm, and found Per.

"Have you seen Gerda?" I asked anxiously. "'She's missing too."

"I'll look for her," he promised, "as soon as you are safely on board."

Relieved, I let him assist me across the gangplank and find me a place to sit. Rædwald's coffin had been place amidships, and despite a prevailing breeze from the south, no detectable odor emanated from it. Not knowing how long the funeral preparations might take, I had daily sprinkled crushed sage and rosemary on and around the body, counting on their piney scent to mask any odors.

Queen Eadburh was visibly distressed at the absence of Mellitus and his monks, moaning over and over, "What could have happened?"

I had an idea of what might have happened, but could not confirm it until I found Gerda.

Our rowers leaned into their task, and soon we were plowing through the water, rushing with the tide toward Rædwald's final resting place. We sat in silence, thinking our separate thoughts. Finally we pulled up at the base of a bluff that towered above the river.

"Surely this cannot be the place," exclaimed Gertrude shading her eyes as she looked up. "It's so high! How could any ship be pulled up such a height?"

"If you'll remember, they did it at Snape for Eni's burial," I reminded her. "There, I was told, they used timber rollers and an army of men!"

Eorpwald's ship was now run up on shore next to ours, and men began jumping out in the shallow water to assist us. A third ship arrived, then a fourth, and soon a string lined the shore. From one of them emerged Gerda, followed by Per.

Eorpwald took charge immediately, first selecting eight stalwart men to carry Rædwald's coffin. Its lid had been secured with ten wooden cleats, hammered down on each side before the coffin was loaded on ship. Now it has hefted aloft for the climb to the top of the ridge — along a gradually ascending path which wound back and forth.

Queen Eadburh and Eorpwald followed behind the coffin, Eadburh leaning on Eorpwald's arm. I walked with Eadburh's women and the council members, joined partway up by Gerda, who flashed a grin but said nothing. Behind us the zigzag line of mourners stretched down the hill.

As we pressed ahead, I saw occasional evidence of the more direct path taken by those who had pulled up the burial ship. There the earth was scarred, the gorse and heather trampled and broken. Even if every man in Rendlesham had lent a hand, I still marveled at the strength and determination it had taken to reach and prepare Rædwald's grave site — evidence of their love and respect for their now former king.

When we finally reached the top of the ridge, it was midday under low, dark clouds. I caught my breath at the scene before me: a sturdy, ninety-foot longship lay before us, resting in a long rectangular trench. Beyond and below it, the River Doep wound like a snake, glistening in the occasional streak of sunlight.

A large wooden chamber with gabled ends had been build amidships to house Rædwald and his belongings, its roof left open to receive them. The whole ship was so neatly nestled in its shallow trough that one could easily step down into it from the ground above. A short distance away great heaps of dirt and bracken were piled, later to form the mound which would be erected over the burial ship.

In the center of the chamber, directly above the keel, the men positioned Rædwald's coffin, then respectfully withdrew. By now the carts of grave goods had also reached the site, pulled by willing volunteers. Everyone seemed eager to take part in this most momentous event.

Queen Eadburh removed several gold-colored cloaks and spread them over the coffin, openly weeping as she did so. Next she set out the two silver baptismal spoons and the nest of silver bowls at the foot of the coffin, muttering something that could have been a prayer.

At the head of the coffin Eorpwald placed his father's great iron helmet, his mail coat, his baldric with Anders' recently completed purse containing the thirty-seven gold coins attached, Rædwald's sword and scabbard, and the set of gaming pieces. On either side of the coffin he wedged a spear to guard Rædwald's parade gear.

Now each member of the court selected an item to add to the coffin or to the chamber itself. Gertrude placed his two huge drinking horns and the maple wood bottles squarely on the center of the coffin, both wrapped in cloth. Hannah set the great silver dish at the east end of the lid, filled with food for Rædwald's journey: a haunch of venison, a generous chunk of roast pork, three trout and a stack of oat cakes. Next to it she placed a little pottery bottle of honey.

"He always had a sweet tooth," she sniffed as she returned to stand beside me.

At the east end of the chamber Berta set the cooking cauldron, then used Per to help her hang a series of bowls on the wooden pegs located there. Below them she placed an iron lamp with a cake of beeswax fuel.

At the west end of the chamber Grima positioned Rædwald's great shield, propping it upright against the wall. Next to it he placed Pieter's lyre, encased in a beaver-skin bag. Haugen secured the whetstone scepter in an upright position next to the shield, and Edvard wedged Rædwald's iron standard into the floor of the chamber. Others added bronze bowls and more spears. When all were finished, I placed my bucket of golden apples from Wiswicca's tree to one side of the coffin.

Now it was time for speeches. As Rædwald's son and heir, Eorpwald spoke first, recounting his father's successes in battle, his championing of Edwin, his long and peaceful reign thereafter. He said nothing about his brother Rægenhere or Rædwald's conversion to Christianity or the loss of his mother Radegund. It was rightful that he did not, but these losses lay heavy on my own heart.

Rædwald's councilors spoke next, praising Rædwald as a king, a warrior, as a leader and friend. When they had finished it was time for us, the women, to raise the dirge, the death song for Rædwald. Keening and wailing, our voices rose into the sky. Swept up in a great wave of grief, some fell to the ground sobbing and moaning, while others lifted their hands and faces in silent lamentation.

Near me, Eadburh covered her ears as if horrified or overcome by this outburst of raw emotion, but it seemed to me that our song of woe was far more fitting than the chant of her priests would have been. Slowly, slowly, we circled the ship, saying a last farewell to the man who had been our great king.

After the sun had set, torches were lighted and placed around the perimeter of the burial ship. Stepping back and gazing at this embrace of fire, I grieved that Rædwald's body had been denied the flames, but exulted in the glorious spectacle before me.

Surely no one present will ever forget such magnificence! Like Beowulf's passing, King Rædwald's funeral will be carried down to future generations, celebrated in song and story.

"Come," said Gerda softly at my side. "Come. The tide has turned. It is time to go."

"A moment more," I murmured.

Indeed the tide of our lives has also turned. Oh, Mother, I have done what I could to keep our world from being lost. Now it is in the hands of the goddess.

"Gerda," I said, wiping my eyes and straightening my shoulders, "is there a name for this place?"

"Yes," she nodded, "Sutton Hoo."

"Sutton Hoo," I repeated to fix it in my mind. "I am ready to go now."

As we began our descent, I looked back at the ridge, all ablaze.

"Gerda, when my times comes, let me sleep in the fire."

"Never fear," she said softly, taking my hand, "you will have your cloak of ashes."

FINIS

Epilogue

Bronze cloak pin with gilt and silver decorations, Gotland, Sweden

My lady mother, Freawicca, has grown much weaker and more fragile. Although we all do our best to care for and comfort her, I fear she may not survive the winter. She urges me to look to my own future and hints that I could do worse than to marry Per. My heart lies in another direction, however. Come spring, if my lady mother has passed from this earth, I will leave Angle-land and travel north.

My old friend Hans now commands his father's ship. Together we will sail for Norway, the land of my birth. He tells me that the Christians have not yet penetrated that country, that one may still live free there in the old ways.

Lark speaks of going north too, up the coast, but she wants to join a monastery under the leadership of a woman named 'Hilda.' I could never survive such a life, bound and circumscribed by hours, prayers, and proscriptions. I am a sparrow, not a falcon, but even a sparrow must have room to spread its wings.

Author's Note

Silver hammer of Thor amulet, Skåne, Sweden

Although the person buried at Sutton Hoo has not been definitely identified, scholars conjecture that it might well have been King Rædwald of East Anglia, who died in c. 624 A.D. The burial was not discovered until 1939, shortly before the outbreak of World War II. The major artifacts unearthed at Sutton Hoo in the 1940s are on display at the British Museum in London, along with the Roman ring from Snape.

A recreation of the original burial site with replicas of the artifacts may be seen at the Sutton Hoo Museum near Woodbridge, England — a World Heritage site — including what remains of the royal burial grounds.

In Norway the Oseberg ship burial, a rich female and possibly royal burial of a later date, may be seen at the Viking Ship Museum in Oslo.

The epic poem *Beowulf* was written down in Old English, in England, sometime between the middle of the seventh and the end of the tenth century, but the characters and events it describes came from Scandinavia in the sixth century. The only surviving manuscript of the poem is housed in the British Library in London. It is conjectured that this epic poem was handed down orally for generations before being recorded, perhaps by a literate monk in the court of a regional king, such as Edwin's court in Northumberland.

Christianity was re-introduced to England in 597 A.D. with the arrival of Augustine, sent from Rome by Pope Gregory to convert the Angles. Despite setbacks, it soon spread throughout the island. The Christianization of Scandinavia was a more difficult undertaking, begun in the eighth century and not consolidated until the twelfth century.

The *Saga of King Hrolf Kraki* was written by an anonymous author in fourteenth century Iceland. Built on almost a thousand years of oral traditions, it shares with *Beowulf* many of the same characters and settings.

Rogers

$12.30

1428341

Moisture Damage 6/2024